Ann McIntosh was born in the Tropics, lived in the frozen north for a number of years, and now resides in sunny central Florida with her husband. She's a proud mama to three grown children, loves tea, crafting, animals (except reptiles!), bacon and the ocean. She believes in the power of romance to heal, inspire and provide hope in our complex world.

Traci Douglass is a *USA TODAY* bestselling author of contemporary and paranormal romance. Her stories feature sizzling heroes full of dark humour, quick wit and major attitude, and heroines who are smart, tenacious and always give as good as they get. She holds an MFA in Writing Popular Fiction from Seton Hill University, and she loves animals, chocolate, coffee, hot British actors and sarcasm—not necessarily in that order.

Also by Ann McIntosh

The Nurse's Pregnancy Miracle
The Surgeon's One Night to Forever
Surgeon Prince, Cinderella Bride

Also by Traci Douglass

One Night with the Army Doc
Finding Her Forever Family

Discover more at millsandboon.co.uk.

THE NURSE'S CHRISTMAS TEMPTATION

ANN McINTOSH

A MISTLETOE KISS FOR THE SINGLE DAD

TRACI DOUGLASS

MILLS & BOON

First Published in Great Britain 2019
by Mills & Boon, an imprint of HarperCollins*Publishers*
1 London Bridge Street, London, SE1 9GF

The Nurse's Christmas Temptation © 2019 by Ann McIntosh

A Mistletoe Kiss for the Single Dad © 2019 by Traci Douglass

ISBN: 978-0-263-26992-5

MIX
Paper from
responsible sources
FSC® C007454

This book is produced from independently certified FSC™ paper
to ensure responsible forest management.
For more information visit www.harpercollins.co.uk/green.

Printed and bound in Spain
by CPI, Barcelona

THE NURSE'S CHRISTMAS TEMPTATION

ANN McINTOSH

MILLS & BOON

For Tom, Vanessa and Patrick,
who've improved my life immeasurably.
You helped me grow up more than I helped you!

CHAPTER ONE

AT HER FIRST sight of Eilean Rurie, or Rurie Island, rising like a granite fist from an angry, frothing sea, Harmony Kinkaid gave a satisfied nod.

Rugged black cliffs fronted dismal light green hills wreathed in mist, and the overcast sky was giving everything a sad gray tone. Mizzly rain pattering down on the ferry deck in fits and starts elevated the entire scene to the epitome of dreary.

After the year she'd had, it was the perfect place for her.

Set in the sheltered curve of a sea loch, Eilean Rurie was just far enough from the west coast of Scotland to give Harmony the sense of leaving everything behind. Of course, she had no idea what she was facing once she got there. Being on a somewhat remote island and not knowing anyone would be out of her comfort zone, but she was determined to be up to the task.

The job had come up suddenly, but at just the right time. And when Caitlin, a friend from nursing school, had called out of the blue, Harmony hadn't been able to help thinking it was a sign.

"Hey, I'm in the hospital in Fort William, and I won't be able to go back to work on Eilean Rurie. Can you take over for me until Dr. MacRurie finds a permanent replacement?"

"What's wrong?"

"Preeclampsia. They've put me on bedrest for the duration, and the island's too remote to make it feasible for us to stay there. I know you're in between jobs, and I hoped you'd be willing to fill in for me."

Caitlin was expecting her first child, and Harmony had heard the stress in her usually placid friend's voice. But before she'd been able to reply, Caitlin had continued.

"It's very different from working in London but Cam—Dr. MacRurie—is easy to work for, and there are only about two hundred and fifty people to tend to overall. It would mean being away for Christmas, though…"

Harmony's fingers had tightened on the phone, and she'd hastily swallowed the lump in her throat and replied, "That's all right. Of course I'll do it. I could definitely use the money."

And, even more importantly, it would mean not having to spend the holidays alone in a bare house that had used to be Christmas central.

Before Gran had died, and Mum had decided to take off to Yorkshire with her new man, Fred.

Oh, she wasn't angry about Fred. He was a nice man, and Mum deserved to have a life after devoting hers to looking after Harmony and then Gran too. It had just felt horribly like a betrayal when Mum revealed her holiday plans.

"Fred's got some time off over Christmas, and he wants to spend it with his children and grandchildren. It would be a good time for me to meet everyone, so I've agreed to go."

Harmony had been so shocked and hurt she hadn't even been able to reply.

Mum must have seen her reaction on her face, because she'd quickly added, "You're welcome to come too."

The worry in Mum's tone had brought Harmony back to her senses. "No, Mum. You go and have a great time. I have a few applications out there, and I'm going to want to be on hand if anyone calls me to come in for an interview."

Yet inside it had felt like the last straw in an awful year. First her two-year relationship with Logan had ended, and only a couple of months later Gran had passed away unexpectedly, leaving Mum and Harmony heartbroken. Her mother's mother had lived with them since her dad had died, when Harmony was only six, and had been an integral part of their little family.

Then, as if those things weren't enough, Harmony's boss of six years had decided to retire. Although the staff had been assured their jobs were secure, one of the first things the new GP had done was let them all go.

When Mum had dropped her bombshell Harmony had been totally set adrift. She didn't like change. Life had been fine the way it was, and now suddenly it was all upside down. The loss of their traditional mother/daughter Christmas in particular had left her in a tailspin.

She felt as though everyone and everything she cherished about the season was gone, and all she could anticipate was loneliness. Just thinking about it made her eyes watery.

But maybe saying to heck with Christmas and having the enforced alone time that was ahead was exactly what she needed. Getting away from the familiar to really think about where she wanted to go in life.

From all she'd heard and read about small communities like this one, she wouldn't be surprised if it took a lot longer than she would be around for people even to warm to her. That suited her just fine. Peace and quiet were what she was looking for. Although it would be lonely living by herself for the first time, and in a new environment to boot, it would also be the best opportunity to contemplate her next move.

"Your first trip to Eilean Rurie?"

The deckhand's voice pulled her out of her sour thoughts, and she blinked to chase away the silly tears before they fell.

"Yes," she said, as the ferry rounded the end of the island and headed to what she assumed was the port.

"Bit drab looking right now, but it'll be better in a few days."

"What happens in a few days?" she asked. But he had already hurried off—no doubt to prepare for docking.

Other than a magical transportation of the island to a tropical location, Harmony couldn't think of anything that would make it look better. The town and dock area continued the gray-on-gray theme, although she had to admit that had more to do with the overcast day than anything else. Most buildings were either whitewashed or cream-colored stone, and the overall effect was of a somewhat quaint, old-fashioned village.

The cry of sea birds and the sound of the wind along with the brisk, damp air was strangely invigorating, and Harmony felt a little surge of excitement. This peaceful place, far from the rush and noise of London, would surely be perfect for the quiet contemplation she needed to figure out her future.

The serene effect was shattered by a *whoosh* that was easily heard over the ferry engines, and the sight of a man rocketing up from the water. It took Harmony a couple of confused seconds to realize he was wearing a water jetpack, which had propelled him high into the air. As she watched he swooped down, then started twisting and turning close to the surface of the loch, doing stunts.

She couldn't decide whether or not riding the contraption was crazier than going into the no doubt freezing water but, however she cut it, he was clearly out of his gourd. Horrified and fascinated all at once, she stood watching his performance as the ferry moved closer to shore.

He shot high into the air again and then, in an instant, plummeted toward the water. Harmony wanted to close her eyes, so she wouldn't see him die, but couldn't look away, covering her mouth to curtail the shriek of fear rising in her throat. Somehow, seemingly inches from the water, he got the spluttering jetpack back under control and rose again.

She turned away, her hands shaking, pretending to fuss with her luggage so no one would realize how scared she'd been.

Why did people do these daredevil things? Didn't they realize how dangerous it was? That they could lose their lives doing that kind of nonsense?

Anger superseded her fear, and she mentally cursed the man who'd upset her just before she was supposed to meet her new boss. Her heart was pounding, her shoulders were up around her ears, and her stomach roiled. Taking a deep breath, she forced herself to relax as best she could.

Taking out her compact, she slicked on a little lipstick

and, noticing the stress lines between her brows, forced herself to release as much tension as possible.

A little calmer as the ferry approached the dock, she glanced down at the shore, trying to see if she could pick out Dr. MacRurie. There was one elderly man there, but Harmony was sure he wasn't the doctor, who Caitlin had said was in his thirties. Hopefully he hadn't forgotten she was arriving today, although no doubt she could find her own way to the surgery and the apartment above it where she was staying. The village wasn't that big, after all.

Glancing at her watch, she realized the ferry was actually a few minutes early. The doctor was probably on his way—unless there'd been a medical emergency somewhere.

Without thought she let her gaze track back to where the man with the jetpack had been, and found him wading out onto the shingles alongside the loch. Even from a distance she could see he was in amazing shape, with the wetsuit clinging to muscular thighs, bum, and torso.

Suddenly, as though sensing her interest, he turned and looked back at the ferry. It would be impossible for him to make her out from that distance, but still she ducked away, embarrassed for no good reason. Nothing wrong or illegal about admiring a man's backside—especially when he couldn't see you doing it. And she did love a good backside…

Hopefully he was just a visitor to the island and she wouldn't have to interact with him. That way she wouldn't be tempted to tell him how crazy she thought he was, doing what he'd been doing. Besides, even if she hadn't been turned off by his daredevil stunt, good looking men were on her no-no list right now.

Her experience with Logan had been lesson enough.

She'd thought him the perfect fit for her: a handsome yet staid and sensible Certified Public Accountant with a solid head on his shoulders. At least that was what she'd thought until he'd told her he was in love with an intern at his office and was giving up his job to move to Australia with her and start an Outback tour company.

She'd been totally gobsmacked, in equal parts desperately hurt and angry.

Her mum had seemed sympathetic, but unsurprised, while her gran had said, "He's too boring anyway."

But Logan's lack of excitement was one of the things she'd liked best about him. The last thing she wanted in her life was someone like Dad, whose recklessness and need for adventure had gotten him killed on a mountain that, because of his health concerns, he should never have been climbing. She wanted someone safe, reliable, who wouldn't break her heart or leave her to struggle on her own to raise their child the way her mum had had to.

Maybe she was better off on her own long term, anyway. Loving others just brought pain as far as she could tell.

As the ferry docked, Harmony put her baleful thoughts aside to heft her tote bag onto her shoulder, then pull up the handle of her wheeled suitcase. Taking another deep breath, she set off for the gangplank, ignoring the flutters of anxiety in her stomach.

Somewhere along the line she'd come to the conclusion that life went on, and that what happened was out of her hands. All she could control was how she faced it, and this new job, in this strange place, was to be met head-on, and with a certain amount of panache, to make up for her fear of the unknown.

Pausing to let an older lady go ahead of her, Harmony ran her hand over the faux fur collar of her favorite tweed trench coat, letting the softness of the fabric soothe her jangling nerves. She'd thought about wearing more casual clothes, but dismissed the impulse. Just because her new job was on an island it didn't mean she wanted to arrive looking as though she didn't take it seriously. Besides, she liked nice clothes; she felt more confident when she was well dressed.

With her head determinedly high, Harmony went down the gangplank to the dock. When no one stepped forward to meet her, she kept walking toward the building marked "Dock Master's Office" for all the world as though she knew where she was going.

Suddenly four older ladies, whom she'd thought were there to meet the woman she'd let go down the gangplank ahead of her, surrounded her, bringing her progress to a screeching halt.

"Nurse Kinkaid?" one of them asked with a smile. "You *are* Nurse Kinkaid, aren't you?"

"Yes."

"Oh, wonderful! Isn't it wonderful, girls?"

Unsure about what was so wonderful, Harmony made no comment, simply plastered a smile on her face as all the women seemed to be speaking at once.

"So lovely to have you!"

"Are you Scottish?"

"What a looker you are!"

"Do you craft?"

"How old are you?"

"I adore your coat!"

Stunned by the barrage, Harmony let go her suitcase and held up her hands, one of which had her umbrella in it. Three of the ladies fell silent and stepped back in unison. The fourth stood her ground, the smile on her face never faltering.

"Don't mind those chatterboxes, Nurse Kinkaid. A bunch of magpies, they are."

She held out her hand and Harmony instinctively took it, receiving a hearty handshake.

"I'm Eudora Moxley, but call me Dora. And these old bags are Ingrid, Sela and Kat."

"Katherine," the tallest of the others growled.

"Kat's a little touchy about her name, but don't let it worry you. It's the English coming out in her."

"For goodness' sake, Eudora." The other woman huffed. "I've lived here for nigh on thirty years. Don't I merit being Scottish by now?"

"You got here thirty years too late for that, Kat," one of the other women interjected, although whether it was Ingrid or Sela, Harmony had no idea. All the women except for Katherine tittered.

"That's enough of that," Katherine retorted. "The nurse is going to think we're loopy."

"Oh, but we are—and best she knows it from day one," Dora retorted, giving Harmony's fingers one last squeeze before finally releasing them. "We're the Crafty Islanders, in charge of—well…almost everything here on Eilean Rurie. We wanted to be on hand to greet you and welcome you to the island."

"Thank you," Harmony replied weakly, still somewhat shell-shocked by what they called a greeting but felt more like a mugging. "Do you have any idea where I might find Dr. MacRurie?"

"Oh, he'll be along any minute now. The Laird is always on time, and the ferry was early."

"Laird?" Wasn't that Scottish for some kind of a peer? Caitlin hadn't mentioned anything about him being a peer.

"That's just a nickname, dear," Katherine said. "Although he does own most of the island, Cam's not one to stand on ceremony. It's not like he's a duke or anything like that."

"There you go. That's why you're not Scottish yet, Kat." Dora smirked. "Laird is far better than Duke any day."

"Tosh" was the testy reply. "You've no idea what you're talking about."

And they started in on each other again, leaving Harmony's head swimming as insults and ripostes flew back and forth.

If these ladies really did run the place, how did they get anything done? Whether they would impact her ability to do her job was another question she really wanted answered too. As assisting nurse and office manager, she'd brook no interference in her work.

"Ladies," she said, loudly enough to cut through the arguing, and was relieved when they all stopped and looked at her. "It was lovely meeting you, but if you would just point me in the right direction…?"

"No need," Dora said, beaming at something behind her. "Here comes the Laird now."

Instinctively Harmony turned, looked, but all she saw was the guy in the wetsuit coming up along the sea wall. No one else.

Then it struck her—hard.

Her new boss was the handsome jetpack daredevil with the nice bum.

Oh, no.

CHAPTER TWO

CAM WAS STILL buzzing with adrenaline from the jet-pack as he made his way up from the beach along the path on the seawall. It had been such a rush he'd ridden it for longer than he'd planned, and had missed his chance to change before meeting the ferry. Hopefully his new nurse would be the easygoing type, and wouldn't be fazed by meeting her new boss when he was wearing a wetsuit.

It was a shame he hadn't been able to give Sanjit permission to offer water jetpack rides to visitors, but he'd had to nix the idea even though Sanjit had put up a good argument.

"It could be a new draw for visitors in summer, when we have our slump. Another activity to add to the website, making a trip here more attractive at times other than Christmas."

"True, but the liability issue is one we can't get away from." He'd slapped the younger man on the shoulder, then reached for his towel. "It's a lot of fun, but one major accident and the entire island would suffer the consequences."

It was true. Because the MacRurie Trust owned most of Eilean Rurie, no matter what insurance Sanjit might purchase to cover operating a water jetpack rental, the trust—and Cam as its director—would still be considered liable should anything go wrong. One major lawsuit might break the bank, or at least severely deplete it. He considered the island to be entrusted to him for posterity, so protecting it and its inhabitants was his first order of business.

But, wow, it had been tempting to give Sanjit the go-ahead—if for no other reason than being able to ride the jetpack himself.

Approaching the dock, he saw the Crafty Islanders had beat him there, and had a well-dressed woman he assumed was his new nurse and administrator surrounded. She seemed to be fending them off with her umbrella—a sight which made Cam snort, as he tried to hold back laughter.

Not that he blamed Nurse Kinkaid in the slightest. The CIs *en masse* were a force to be reckoned with. There was no doubt in his mind they were peppering her with intrusive questions and firing off comments before she could even decide whether to answer or not. That was their usual *modus operandi*, and they could frighten the stoutest of souls.

"Please don't scare off my lifesaver," he muttered, picking up his pace, hoping to break up the interrogation before it got too bad.

Then the young woman looked over her shoulder, her thick, curly hair swinging away from her face as she did so. Her gaze tracked past Cam, then snapped back to him, and her eyes widened.

Cam, midstride, had to catch himself so he didn't falter under what he could only describe as the glare she sent him.

But even with lines between her eyebrows and her lips pursed into a disapproving rosette, she was gorgeous. He had only a moment to register her high cheekboned face and skin like golden syrup mixed with cinnamon before she turned back around, but the effect lingered.

Something about the curve of her cheek and chin, the long line of her throat, gave him a jolt of adrenaline on top of the residue already keeping his nerves jangling. It had been a very long time since the sight of a woman had brought him to total awareness, filling him with curiosity and inciting the kind of physical interest he least expected, or wanted.

Since leaving his job with a refugee agency four years before, and taking over the management of Eilean Rurie, he had made the island his base. The transition to being in one place after travelling the world had been difficult, but in a strange way it had afforded him the chance to do more of the adventurous activities he enjoyed.

He had time to travel now, to climb, cave, to do whatever else he wanted, and he was having the time of his life. There was no room in his life for the kind of visceral fascination he felt with just one glimpse of this young woman.

It would be okay, he reassured himself as he finally neared the group. She wouldn't be around for very long. He just had to get through the Christmas rush, and then he could find a permanent replacement. Ignoring this strange attraction wouldn't be too hard.

"There you are—finally," Dora said.

"You'll be late for your own funeral," Sela added.

"The later the better. But I'll have you know I'm exactly on time," Cam retorted, giving his watch a pointed glance before turning to the silent young woman and holding out his hand. "Nurse Kinkaid, I presume?"

"You presume correctly," she replied, seeming to

hesitate for a moment before taking his outstretched hand and giving it a brief, firm shake. "And I understand you're Dr. MacRurie?"

Her eyes were gorgeous. Hazel, fringed with dark, tightly curled lashes, they matched her skin tone and gave her the look of a haughty lioness. Her watchful gaze, coupled with the low, husky voice made his toes curl.

Taken aback, especially by his reaction to her, all he could manage to say was "In the flesh."

"You mean in the wetsuit, don't you?" Ingrid asked, making all the CIs snicker.

Suddenly aware of his state of undress—which hadn't bothered him in the slightest before—Cam frowned, making them all giggle harder. Nurse Kinkaid didn't join in, but the little lines between her brows quickly came and went.

"Yes, well… If you'll come with me to the Dock Master's Office, Nurse Kinkaid, I'll change and take you over to the surgery."

"So, did you give Sanjit the approval to run his new business?" Katherine interjected, before he could make his escape.

"Unfortunately, no."

"Liability?" asked Ingrid, who was a retired barrister, and Cam nodded.

"Got it in one." Before any of them could get going again, he quickly added, "Let me take your suitcase, Nurse Kinkaid, and we'll be on our way."

As he matched actions to words the CIs chorused their goodbyes, peppered with lovely-to-meet-yous and we'll-catch-up-soons, all aimed at the new nurse—who, wisely, exited their orbit with just a friendly wave and the slight upturning of her lips.

"Will we see you at the planning meeting this evening, Cam?" called Dora.

"Of course," he called back, making sure not to break stride in case they took it as an invitation.

"Wow," the nurse said, as soon as they were out of earshot. "They're something, aren't they?"

"That they are," Cam said, but was suddenly protective of the women who often drove him bonkers. "But, despite being a pain in my rear most of the time, they're invaluable to the island. With such a small population it's good to have people willing to get involved and organize things."

"I'm sure. However, I hope that doesn't apply to your practice? I find I work best with only one boss. Causes far less confusion."

"Good Lord, no." Cam actually laughed at the thought of the CIs butting into his real work.

He opened the door to the Dock Master's Office, and stood back for her to enter ahead of him.

"They're involved with practically all other aspects of life on the island, though, just so you know."

"I can see that being the case."

She'd stepped through the door ahead of him and Cam found himself admiring her figure, which was full and curvy. Lush hips swayed with a siren's rhythm as she walked, mesmerizing him until he caught himself and resolutely tore his gaze away.

Even more aware of the wetsuit, and feeling silly in the face of his new, rather formal nurse, Cam said, "If you'll wait here, Nurse Kinkaid, I'll get changed as quickly as possible and take you to your apartment."

"Please, call me Harmony," she said, while looking around the office. Seemingly without conscious thought, she straightened a pile of magazines on the table beside the door. "When I hear 'Nurse Kinkaid' like that, I instinctively look around for my mother."

"Sure," he said, seeing an opening to get to know her better but unable to take advantage of it. She completely unsettled him, making him want to get away and catch his breath, not to mention get out of his wetsuit. "I'll remember that. Be right back."

But as he shimmied out of the wetsuit he found himself wondering what she'd look like if she truly smiled. Something told him that rather prim mouth would turn sumptuous and appealing.

Become eminently kissable.

Cam cursed to himself.

She's definitely going to be a problem.

He just had to make sure that, no matter what happened, the problem didn't involve him.

The interest she stirred in him wasn't something he'd ever consider acting on. Even if getting involved with an employee wasn't tacky—which it was—he liked his relationships short and with no strings attached. No matter how quickly her tenure on the island would be over he'd have to work with her, and the chances of it all going sideways were large.

Finally dressed in his street clothes, he grabbed his jacket and went back out into the main part of the office. Danny Smith, the Dock Master, wasn't there, so Harmony was still alone, standing in front of one of the myriad pictures on the wall. It was a painting of one of the rescue boats that used to be launched from the island in rough seas back in the early part of the twentieth century.

"That's my great-grandfather in the prow of that boat," he said, going to stand beside her. "They were probably going out to help with a sea rescue after a

wreck—or at least that was what the artist was por-
traying."

She sent him a brief glance, and once more he felt
a zing of electricity when he realized her eyes were
more green than gold. Getting used to them was going
to take some doing.

"Do you still have a lifeboat station here?" she asked.

"I wish," he said.

How many times had he stood staring at this painting, imagining himself on that boat, fighting the seas,
on his way to save lives?

"Now the Coast Guard handles all the rescues. In
the old days almost all the islands had manned boats,
because it took the authorities much longer to get to
the site of a wreck. Now, once someone radios the he-
licopters can be in the air in a matter of minutes. The
private rescue units aren't needed anymore. I think the
last one was disbanded here in the nineteen-seventies."

"Hmm."

It was a noncommittal sound, and he figured the conversation was over. "Shall we head over to the surgery?"

"Sure," she said, but she stared at the painting a little
longer before turning away.

He led her out through the other side of the building, which took them onto the main street through the
village. This time of the afternoon, there weren't many
people around, but he knew many of the residents were
peeping out from behind their curtains. Everyone knew
the nurse was arriving today. Everyone was curious.

As they walked he pointed out the Post Office, the
grocery store, the pub, and Sanjit's restaurant, thinking
them the most important.

"The Ladies from Hades?" she said, obviously catching sight of the pub sign, with a kilted and armed Highlander painted on it.

"It's a play on the nickname for a famous Scottish regiment."

"The Black Watch," she said, surprising him. "Must have been opened by an ex-military man. And you have a curry shop here too?"

He wanted to ask how she knew about the Black Watch and their World War I nickname, but left it for another time.

"We're actually very lucky," he explained, speaking a little louder than usual because of the sound of her suitcase bumping along behind him over the cobbles. He'd left the sliver of sidewalk to her and her high heels, since the last thing he needed was for her to twist her ankle before she even started working. "Eilean Rurie has attracted a variety of artists, farmers, and business people over the years, making our population rather more eclectic than some of the other islands."

"Like the owner of the curry shop?"

"Exactly. Sanjit Gopaul came here on vacation with his parents and, for whatever reason, fell in love with the island. He came back and asked if I'd be willing to let him open a restaurant, and I said sure. That was five years ago. He's been an amazing addition to the island and shows no signs of wanting to leave. In fact, he also runs a canoe rental and tour operation during the summer, and he's always looking for new businesses to start."

"Including that jet thing?"

There was no mistaking the disapproval in her voice, and his look at her profile found it echoed there in her pursed lips. It made Cam's hackles rise a bit.

"Yes, like the water jetpack. I was sad to have to

tell him no. It was a lot of fun. Wouldn't you like to have a go?"

She gave him a bland look, all censure erased from her expression. "I should say not. I'm not into that kind of thing."

Striving for a light tone, he teased, "What kind of thing? Having fun?"

Looking into the window of the shop they were passing, she replied, "More like stuff that'll get you killed or maimed."

"Ha! It's safe as houses if you're careful and know what you're doing."

The skeptical look she gave him scorched him to his toes.

"No wonder you didn't give him permission to offer it to visitors." Then, as if tired of the discussion, she changed the subject completely. "Your village is beautiful —although I'll admit when I first saw the island from the ferry I thought it looked like something out of a very scary story."

That made Cam chuckle, even though he still felt the sting of her retort about the jetpack. He knew the exact vista she was talking about.

"Eigg Point, no doubt—before you round the headland and see the village. That sheer black cliff with the sea foaming around its base does look like it belongs in a horror movie on a misty, overcast day like today. On a sunny day, though, when the hills are so startlingly green they look like they were drawn with crayon and the water is smooth and clear, it's very different. There's the surgery," he added, pointing across the grassy village green to the three-story building beyond.

"That's your surgery? It looks more like a fancy hotel!"

Cam chuckled. "My great-grandfather built it to try

and attract a decent doctor to take up residence. I used to tease my grandfather that he only took up medicine so he'd be able to work in the second nicest building on the island. He didn't deny it."

"I don't blame him," she said.

The appreciation in her voice was pleasing.

"Normally I'd cut across the green to get to the surgery, but it's pretty wet right now and your heels would sink in."

"Thank you."

She had a prim way of speaking he rather liked, and an intriguing way of pronouncing some words that gave unusual flavor to an otherwise very North London voice. Caitlin had mentioned that Harmony's mother's family had originally come from Jamaica, and he thought he could hear an echo of that migration in the nurse's voice. It was so nice, especially with its husky tone, he was tempted to keep her talking so he could go on hearing it.

"Patients come in through either the front door or the one closest to the car park on the north side," he told her as they approached the surgery. "But you have your own entrance on the other side."

Cam led her around the building, and as they got to the door heard her give a little gasp.

"Oh! What's that back there?"

She was looking up the hill through the trees, along the track he used every day.

"That's the nicest building on the island—Rurie Manor."

Big hazel eyes stared at him. "You live there?"

"Yeah," he said, opening the outer door and holding it for her, once more pleased at her awestruck reaction to his home. "But only in a small part of it. Most of the Manor is a hotel now."

Harmony turned back to stare at the Manor a moment more, before stepping through the door and into the entryway.

Cam glanced at his watch. Time to test his glucose levels.

Handing her the keys, he said, "There's another door at the top of the stairs, and the door behind me leads into the surgery, so I sometimes come in this way, but otherwise you'll be the only person using it. Go on up and check out your apartment, and I'll bring up your suitcase in a moment."

"Thank you."

Her slightly stiff reply made him want to break the ice a little more. He was used to a relaxed atmosphere in his practice and hoped to establish that type of working relationship with her too. Even with his niggling suspicion he should actually keep her as distant as he could. Just standing in the small entryway she seemed too close, with her citrusy perfume warming the air between them and those golden eyes surveying him with solemn intensity.

"Hopefully life on the island won't seem too tame and boring for you after living and working in London. At least Christmas should be exciting."

His words stumbled to a halt, arrested by the flash of pain crossing her face.

"I'm looking forward to the quiet," she said, turning toward the steps and hitching her tote bag higher. "And Christmas can pass me by and I won't complain."

Had he somehow put his foot in his mouth? He couldn't see how. Everyone loved Christmas, didn't they?

But even as he was trying to figure out what he'd

said wrong he found himself staring once more at her delectable rear end, until it sashayed around the corner of the landing and disappeared.

CHAPTER THREE

HARMONY STOOD IN the middle of the apartment, not even taking in the space around her, annoyed at herself for being so curt with her new employer. Not to mention for the sarcastic comment she'd made to him earlier about the water jetpack.

It wasn't really like her to be that way, but hearing him make light of her innate dislike of risky behavior had irked her—so, like her mother always said, she'd run her mouth, speaking before thinking.

But there was something about him that had put her on edge from the first time she'd looked him in the eyes. He was, she had to admit, a fine specimen. Handsome, in a rugged, outdoorsy kind of way, with brown hair just shy of ginger and blue-gray eyes, his looks alone made him a standout. Couple his face with a body that looked amazing even in a wetsuit, and Harmony knew he must make women's heads turn faster than wheels on ice.

But it wasn't his looks that were making her snarky. There was an air about him—an aura of confidence and ease that, conversely, made her tense and jumpy. And when he'd mentioned Christmas, just as she'd promised herself a hiatus from the entire season, it had brought all her pain flooding back.

For almost as long as she could remember Christmas

had been a special time for Mum, Gran and Harmony. There was always a flurry of baking, both English treats and Jamaican. And a night specially planned to trim the tree while listening to a variety of holiday music or old movies.

They'd also watch *Greetings from Yaad*, an hour-long special filmed in Jamaica, in which people could wish their loved ones in England a Merry Christmas. Harmony had used to dislike the amateurishly filmed show, until Gran had said, "We may not know any of these people, but it makes me happy to hear the accents of my youth."

That had always led to conversations about old times in Jamaica, and even how things had been for Gran when she'd first moved to England. She'd been part of the Windrush generation, coming from the colonies to help with the rebuilding efforts in the UK after World War II. She'd had to leave all her family behind, including Mum, but once she'd gotten herself a job and somewhere to live she'd started saving so she could send for her husband and daughter.

Grandpa had decided he didn't want to live in England, so eventually Mum had travelled to the UK with her Uncle Shorty, Gran's brother. Uncle Shorty, a perennial bachelor, had settled in Birmingham, but had come to visit every Christmas until he died, adding to the family fun. Harmony could still remember his plaid driving cap, his booming laugh and the way the scent of smoke and cologne clung to his clothes.

On Christmas Eve they'd have neighbors and friends in and out of the house, each one of them bringing a little gift, receiving goodies in return.

Until they'd passed away her other grandparents had come too, on Christmas morning, even after Dad hadn't been there anymore, and all Harmony remembered was the joy and closeness. The laughter and sometimes a few shared tears too.

All that was gone now—and darn Dr. MacRurie for reminding her of what she'd lost this year.

But it wouldn't do to start their working relationship off on a bad footing, and she wondered if it would be politic to apologize to him for her behavior.

Harmony considered that option, then dismissed it. Unless he brought it up, she wouldn't either. Less said, soonest mended, right?

Suddenly realizing she was in danger of having the doctor come up and find her still standing there like a ninny, Harmony quickly took off her coat and shoes, stowing them in the entryway closet. Then she took a really good look around.

The apartment was a lot larger than she'd expected, with an L-shaped living and dining room and a kitchen almost as big as her mum's. There were also not two but three good-sized bedrooms, all tastefully decorated with a combination of new and more traditional furniture. And the bathroom, with its deep soaker tub and a separate shower, made her coo.

The entire space had obviously been modernized, but whoever had done it had been careful to keep a lot of the original Victorian elements. The living room fireplace, which was lit, had the most amazing carved mantel and pillars, along with a tile surround and hearth. There were medallions on the ceiling, and intricately carved jambs around the doors. Even the door knobs were decorative, and Harmony found herself smiling as she palmed one of the floral patterned porcelain ovoids.

She staked out the bedroom she wanted, which had a sleigh bed and large windows that were letting in the last of the afternoon light. Outside was a tiny balcony, just big enough for a miniscule wrought-iron table and matching chair, and in the distance was Rurie Manor, sitting in solitary splendor on the top of a gently sloping hill.

It looked gorgeous, and she wondered if she'd get a chance to see the inside. Although if it had been turned into a hotel, she might be disappointed.

Hearing Dr. MacRurie coming up the stairs, she went back into the living area just as he came through the front door.

"Here you go," he said, putting down her suitcase, seemingly not at all put out by her ill-mannered behavior. "Have you decided which room you want? I'll put your case on the luggage stand for you."

"Thank you. That one," she said, pointing to the still open door, determined to put her best foot forward.

He wheeled the suitcase across the living area, speaking as he went. "I hope you'll be comfortable here. Caitlin and her husband had a dog, so I gave them a cottage instead—for convenience. Knowing you'd have to be here over the holidays, I figured this place is big enough that if you have someone come for Christmas they can stay with you."

There he went with the whole Christmas thing again!

"I won't." It came instinctively, pain pushing the brusque words out. Drawing herself up, and not wanting to sound as churlish as she felt, she added, "But thank you."

"Oh." He'd put her bag in the room and was standing in the doorway, his gaze sharp. But all he said was "Well, if that changes you'll be all set. But if not at least you won't be bored. This time of year is nice and busy."

"This time of year? What's so special about it?"

Giving her a surprised glance, he said, "Caitlin didn't tell you?" Then he answered his own question. "Of course, she had other things on her mind. Eilean Rurie is famous for its Winter Festival. Well, it used to be called the Christmas Festival until the eighties, when my grandfather changed the name. We're called the North Pole of Scotland, and we attract hundreds of people every year."

Oh, come on.

"You're kidding, right?"

"Nope."

He gave her one of his killer smiles, and Harmony's stomach fluttered, making her look away in case her reaction showed.

"Did you know that celebrating Christmas—well, really it was Yule back then—was banned in Scotland in the sixteenth century? Christmas Day wasn't made a public holiday until 1958, and Boxing Day was only recognized in the seventies. My great-grandfather decided he wanted to make the holidays a big splash, and encouraged all the islanders to do it too, once the ban was officially lifted. It evolved into the Christmas Festival, and then the Winter Festival, and it's grown with each year."

Plunking herself down onto the squishy sofa, Harmony only just stopped herself from putting her head in her hands in disbelief. Hundreds of people, running around singing carols and doing who knew what else?

Just shoot me now!

Yet the smile on the doctor's face told her there was only one of them in the room who viewed the upcoming festivities with horror. The happy anticipation on his face spoke volumes, and it made Harmony pull herself together once more, even while wondering how many other times this man was going to throw her off-kilter.

"How on earth do you accommodate hundreds of people here? The village doesn't look big enough."

"Well, the manor has a lot of rooms, and most of the villagers offer bed and breakfast services, using their spare rooms, or even small apartments attached to their houses. Most of the temporary staff are island kids coming back for winter break, but the others who don't have a place to stay have dormitories behind the church. A couple of really entrepreneurial souls have even put up a few tiny houses on their properties, and rent those out to visitors. We also get quite a few daytrippers, and the ferry runs more frequently to accommodate them. Most of the residents benefit in some way from the festival. If they didn't we wouldn't bother. It's a lot of work."

Harmony shook her head in disbelief, still not sure he was telling the truth. "But there's nothing going on. No one's putting up lights or decorating."

"It's too early," he said, somewhat cryptically, then added, "Poke around downstairs tomorrow, if you like, or just rest up from your trip. The surgery is closed on Saturday afternoon, and Sunday, although everyone on the island has my number and will call if they need me. I've made a list of numbers and left it on the hall table for you, in case you need anything, and the CIs have stocked the fridge—although, who knows what they put in there? Ingrid's a vegan, and Katherine's always on some kind of diet, Dora has a sweet tooth that won't quit, and Sela is crazy for cheese."

By the time he'd finished his recitation Harmony found herself chuckling. "I'm sure I'll be able to make a meal of whatever they've left, and I'll bless Dora forever if there's a chocolate something in amongst the rest."

Cam was grinning too. "I have no doubt there is, but if you feel up to it nip over to the pub too. They do a really great Scotch pie on Saturdays."

"Maybe I will," she said.

"Right, well… I have to go. Final planning meeting tonight, and it will no doubt be a fractious one. When we get to this time of year they usually are, because everyone is so frazzled and behind on everything. If you need anything give me a shout. I always have my phone on me."

He paused halfway out through the door.

"Oh, and there's an Armistice Day ceremony at the cenotaph on Monday, starting at ten. Come along, if you'd like."

Then he was gone, clattering down the stairs, leaving her to wonder why, when she had been so determined to stay away from Christmas, she'd landed in the North Pole of Scotland. And why, having decided to ignore men, she found her boss so damned handsome.

Cam had been right about the meeting being contentious, but he couldn't seem to keep his mind on the grumbles and arguments going on around him. Instead he found himself thinking about his new nurse. Her sometimes curt way of speaking, juxtaposed with her delightful throaty giggle as he listed the CIs eating habits, made her a fascinating enigma. And, yes, her delicious looks.

Even though he wasn't interested in relationships he was still all-male—able and willing to appreciate a beautiful face and a lovely curvy figure. As long as he remembered he could look but not touch, it was all good.

"Melanie, the theme was decided back in February. It's not our fault if you've not gotten on board with it."

At the sound of Dora's firm rebuttal Cam pulled his thoughts away from Harmony Kinkaid and back to the battle of wills going on in front of him.

"But it's silly. We did Love as a theme before. Why do it again?"

Melanie was as stubborn as ever, and as one of Scotland's best-known living potters always felt her word should be law. But Dora never fell in line with that concept.

"That was nigh on twenty years ago. And what better theme could we have for the Winter Festival than that? No matter the religion, or the holiday, love is at the center of them all, isn't it?"

Cam intervened, before things got too heated.

"Melanie, you know full well it's too late to change the theme, so either you've gone with it or not. The choice was yours."

Then Hugh Jacobson had a complaint about the decision to extend the festival hours to ten at night. "The strain on the electricity grid will increase, along with the costs. I don't subscribe to this."

Cam doubted that was his real reason for complaining. Hugh was probably worried that the extra noise and lights would disturb his mother, but didn't want to come right out and say so.

"Hugh, the new wind turbine provides more than enough power to cover the additional load, and the generators were serviced last month. The increased revenue for us all will more than offset any additional costs, so I'm sure we'll be fine."

"But the noise…the lights on until so late. It's untenable."

"I'll buy you some blackout curtains when I go to the mainland next Wednesday," Sela interjected, and although Hugh still looked unhappy the meeting moved on.

Afterwards Cam realized he wasn't the only one thinking about Nurse Kinkaid—although, perhaps not in the same way.

"I thought your new nurse might have come to the meeting. She looks as though she'd be a good addition to the planning team" was Dora's opening sally.

The last thing Cam wanted was to spend more time with Harmony Kinkaid than necessary. His unsettling reaction to her made keeping her at arm's length a good thing. Besides, every time he'd mentioned Christmas she had withdrawn at the talk of the season.

But there was no way he was letting Dora and the rest of the nosy CIs know that. His nurse would get no peace until they'd ferreted out the reason for her aversion.

So, trying to protect her as best he could, he said, "First off, let her settle in a bit before you expect her to get into the middle of island life. And, secondly, she's only going to be here for a short time. Why would you think she'd be interested?"

"Oh, I don't know that she will be, but it's always nice to have a fresh face and a new viewpoint in the proceedings. I'm hoping she'll lend a hand once she finds her feet."

Thankfully, before he had to think up another round of excuses as to why Harmony probably wouldn't, Dora and the other ladies were departing with hugs and waves, according to their personal preference.

As he strode down Main Street Cam considered the unlikely friends, each so different and yet all completely devoted to the others. They were the soul and the back-bone of the Winter Festival—a point Cam had to concede, despite being almost always annoyed with their attempts to interfere in his life too.

Their organizational skills alone were worth their collective weight in gold, but along with that they also contributed in so many other ways. Designing and sewing costumes, painting backdrops, deciding on the lighting for the public areas and the decoration of the green, making sure everyone who needed help got it… The list went on and on.

If they'd just accept the fact that Cam wasn't the type to be controlled or tied down, and nor would he be guilt-tripped into things, they'd all get along much better. He'd had enough of that growing up—from his mother. The last thing he needed now was to have four more women fussing over him, trying to get him to do what they thought was best.

When he'd been diagnosed as a type 1 diabetic at the age of four, his mother's reaction had been to coddle him, fearful of what might happen if he did any of the normal childhood activities. If it hadn't been for his grandfather, taking him in hand at the age of eleven and teaching Cam how to control his disease, encouraging him to be more adventurous, Cam had no idea how he might have turned out.

Nearing the cemetery, Cam instinctively turned in, walking the familiar path to the spot under a gnarled and now bare oak where a number of his ancestors were interred.

"Evening, Grand-Da," he said, reaching down to brush a couple of late-fallen leaves off his grandfather's headstone. "Just left the planning meeting. All the usual nonsense for this time of year. I wonder if there'll ever be a time where things run smoothly."

The bench was cold, yet dry, and the evening breeze

brisk, but Cam settled in for a little visit. Stuffing his hands into the pockets of his jacket, he looked up at the sickle moon.

"Got a new temporary nurse in today and I'm hoping she'll work out okay."

He was hoping more than anything else that Harmony Kinkaid wouldn't turn the relatively stable island world upside down.

Wouldn't turn *his* world upside down.

As long as she did her job, he shouldn't care about anything else. He just needed to get through the winter rush with someone he could count on to keep the surgery going and his patients taken care of, along with aiding with any injuries. After that he'd have the time and head space to find a permanent employee.

All he could hope for was a certain level of professionalism and competence from Harmony Kinkaid. If she could produce that, all would be well.

CHAPTER FOUR

DAY THREE OF her island experience and Harmony looked at the clock again, giving a huff. Thank goodness this was a temporary position, because otherwise this place would drive her to drink. She'd been waiting for Dr. MacRurie's next patient to arrive for almost ten minutes and there was no sign of him. No call either.

She'd spent Sunday exploring the surgery, making lists of things she needed to get done. The lower floor held the waiting room, an X-ray room, the records room, two examination rooms and Dr. MacRurie's office, along with a reception/office area for Harmony and, in the back, a kitchenette.

Climbing the steps to the second floor, she'd found a larger office, now clearly used for old records and abandoned furniture, and five bedrooms, which seemed set up to house patients. This had been confirmed when she'd located a relatively modern elevator at the back of the building—big enough to accommodate a stretcher. Having not noticed any corresponding doors downstairs, she'd ridden it down and realized it came out into what she'd assumed to be a maintenance closet behind the kitchenette.

When she'd asked the doctor about the second floor the next morning he'd explained that occasionally they'd have a patient who needed overnight observation. Or, if the weather was forecast to be terrible and he was worried about outlying elderly folks, he'd bring them in and house them there.

While Caitlin had written her up a list of duties, with notations on where to find things, in just that first go-through Harmony had been able to see areas in need of improvement. Caitlin was a fine nurse, as Harmony knew, but her administrative skills left something to be desired. At least in Harmony's opinion.

She'd spent the first part of Monday morning trying to put the records into some semblance of order. The files weren't stored to her preferred specifications, and she had broken a sweat moving armfuls of records back and forth. Then, and only then, had she started on a pile of notes that hadn't been dealt with—probably from the time between when her friend had left and the present.

Luckily she was an expert in interpreting "doctor write," because Cameron MacRurie's penmanship was something to behold. She'd often thought that doctors wrote so poorly because their brains were going faster than their hands could follow. If that were the case, her new employer must be a genius!

They'd opened early, because of the Armistice Day ceremony, and she was down in her office before seven. But her frustration levels had risen as their eight o'clock patient had been a no-show, and the eight thirty had sauntered in almost fifteen minutes late. To add insult to injury, the woman had insisted there was no need for Harmony to do any kind of pre-examination tests.

Not that Harmony hadn't tried to get her job done.

"Dr. MacRurie will expect me to have weighed you, taken your blood pressure and temperature, plus asked you about the reason you're here so I can make notes."

"Och, no," Mrs. Campbell had rebutted, in the strongest Scottish accent Harmony had heard since arriving on Eilean Rurie. And from her steely glare Harmony had been able to tell she meant business too. "The Laird'll do all that himself. I'll show myself in."

And before Harmony had been able to react the elderly lady had marched right past her and into Dr. MacRurie's office without even a knock on the door.

Rushing after her, file in hand, Harmony had expected a reprimand from the doctor, but all he'd said was "Ah, here's your file, Amelia. Thank you, Harmony."

Taking it as a dismissal, and thankful not to have got a flea in her ear from him, she'd scuttled back to her desk. Yet, it had still burned when Mrs. Campbell had marched past her at five past nine without even a fare-thee-well.

She wasn't used to patients totally dismissing her that way, and now, with their nine o'clock also a no-show, she was decidedly out of sorts.

She decided it would be best to ask how she was supposed to handle this type of situation, so she walked down to the doctor's office and knocked.

"Come in," he called, and Harmony pushed open the door, just in time to see him pulling up his shirt. "Is Mr. Gibson here?"

"Um…no," she replied, surprised to realize he was injecting himself with an insulin pen. Taken off guard, she forgot why she was there and asked, "You're a diabetic?"

"Yes. Have been since I was four."

He said it casually, but Harmony was still taken aback. Caitlin hadn't mentioned this, and all around the room there were pictures of him doing all kinds of dangerous stuff: mountain-climbing, caving, hang gliding, hiking through remote-looking terrain… Not that having diabetes should preclude him from doing any of those things, just as her father's heart condition hadn't stopped him from indulging his own daredevil spirit.

But look how that had ended.

Already in a bit of a snit because of the patients, now she found her mental comparison of Cam to her father was making her cross her arms, trying to hold in the spate of words hovering on her tongue.

Instead of letting them loose, she took a deep breath, then asked, "Did you plan to tell me?"

Cam glanced up, his eyebrows lifted. "Why would I tell you something so mundane when you'd no doubt find out about it sooner or later?"

Although his tone was even, there was an unusually cool expression in his eyes.

"Well, I'm your nurse. The only other medical practitioner on the island that I know of. What would happen if you went hypo or hyperglycemic and I wasn't aware of your condition?"

"I'm very well versed in the monitoring and treatment of my diabetes, and I haven't had an incident in ages. Don't fuss, Nurse Kinkaid."

She wanted to ask what he meant when he said, "ages," but there was no mistaking the steel in his voice. Not to mention his reversion from calling her Harmony to Nurse Kinkaid, so she kept her mouth shut, for a change.

"Was there something you wanted?"

He was putting away his diabetes kit, and although the chill might have gone from his voice, Harmony still felt the flick of his disapproval keenly.

She adopted a formal tone in return. "What is your official policy on missed appointments?"

"Reschedule the patient."

Really annoyed now, Harmony said, "No, I mean how do I charge them for not showing up nor even calling to say they wouldn't be coming? Do I do it through the mail?"

Cam's eyebrows rose again, and he stared at her for a moment, before chuckling. "Ha! Only do that if you want to have a stream of highly upset people coming in to see you. Don't worry about it."

"But it's a waste of my time, and yours. Don't you charge them at *all*?"

Cam got up and stretched. "Most of the time everyone keeps their appointments, but this time of year things get a little crazy."

Distracted by the sight of his muscles rippling beneath his shirt, Harmony tried to look away, but she had a hard time forcing herself to meet his gaze.

"Since Mr. Gibson hasn't shown up I'm going to run back up to the Manor before the ceremony. After it's over I have a quick house call to make, and then I thought I'd take you around the island and show you where the patients you'll need to visit live. Interested?"

"Sure, that'll be really helpful." She'd been worried about losing her way on her rounds, so that was a relief.

"Actually, you can come with me to see Mrs. Jacobson too. She's just a few steps away from the surgery, and I'll be asking you to start looking in on her, as well. She's in the final stages of liver failure—cirrhosis caused by hemochromatosis, poor soul. She moved here to be close to her son, Hugh, once she'd decided not to undergo any further treatment. I've had her on a bi-weekly visit, but I think it's time to increase the frequency."

"Do you need me to pull her file?"

"No, I have it here," he replied, tapping the folder on his desk.

He spoke a little more about Mrs. Jacobson's prior treatment, and what he'd prescribed to battle the ascites and hepatic encephalopathy. It was, in effect, palliative care, and Harmony wasn't surprised he wanted to up the number of times she was seen.

"I told Hugh I'd be by at one, so maybe grab something to eat after the ceremony, and if you could be ready at a quarter to, that would be great. Oh, and do you have a pair of wellies?"

She'd been wondering why they needed fifteen minutes to go a few doors down when he asked the question and it distracted her. "I haven't worn Wellington boots since my days in the Guides. Do I need them?"

"Some of the farmyards will be a quagmire after the rain we've had, so they'd be a good idea for when you go to do your rounds."

Unimpressed with the thought of messing up her trainers, which were pretty new and had been a splurge buy, she asked, "Is there somewhere I can buy some?"

Cam shook his head. "You'd have to go to the mainland—or order online and have them delivered, which would take longer. We have a bunch of them up at the Manor. What size do you wear?"

"Seven and a half."

"Okay." He sent her one of his heart-stopping smiles. "I'll hunt out a pair for you."

Cam was already heading for the door and Harmony watched him go, still stinging from his earlier set-down, and annoyed at the way her heart leapt and fluttered whenever he grinned that way.

The thought of spending time with him as he showed her around the island flustered her. Hopefully it was just because he was her boss and she wasn't used to him yet, she mused, knowing it was more. She was attracted to him—which was another wrinkle in what was already a situation so far outside her comfort zone as to be in a different universe.

It would be a lot easier not to have a physical reaction to him if he were a little less handsome and didn't have a gazillion-kilowatt smile. Not even the knowledge that he was a risk-taking daredevil could stop those butterflies from invading her insides whenever he entered the room or smiled her way.

But it should, she reminded herself. The very last thing she needed was to be attracted to a man like her father. The type of man who put his need for adventure before everything else—even his health, or the people who loved him.

Cam made his escape, wondering how he was going to get through the next month and half.

Harmony Kinkaid, his fussy, big-city nurse administrator, was already making him crazy.

She'd rearranged all his files, so he couldn't find anything. She wanted to come down hard on patients who didn't turn up for their appointments. She'd silently showed her displeasure when he'd mentioned he'd be leaving on a hiking and rock-climbing trip to Peru just after Hogmanay, even when he'd said there'd be a locum to fill in for him.

But it had been her expression when she'd realized he had type 1 diabetes that had really aggravated him. She, of all people, should know it was no reason for him not to live fully.

Thank goodness for Grand-Da, who'd shown Cam

that the disease wasn't an impediment to having a good, exciting life.

"It's something to be managed," Grand-Da had told him in his habitual no-nonsense way, that first summer he'd come to stay. "Once you learn how to do that anything is doable. You just have to accept you have it and be smart about it."

Learning how to control the effects of his diabetes had given him a freedom beyond his wildest imagining. Gone had been the days when he'd only watched other boys enjoying themselves, never being allowed to join in. And at the age of thirteen Cam had embraced his new-found independence with gusto. Pitting himself against nature, or against his own limitations or fears, had brought him fully alive.

He'd seen Harmony glance at the pictures on his wall, had almost been able to hear her internal dialog regarding the pastimes he chose. As she was a nurse he was surprised at her reaction. Hell, there were type 1 diabetics playing rough professional sports. It all came down to how you took care of yourself and managed the disease.

Maybe he wouldn't be so testy if it wasn't so close to the opening of the Winter Festival and everyone wasn't going bonkers. He'd had one or other of the CIs on the phone almost constantly, complaining about something or needing help with different situations. They kept trying to get him to recruit Harmony too, but so far he'd been able to still keep them at bay.

Settling into his vehicle, Cam ran his fingers through his hair and sighed.

The truth of it was, for all her annoying qualities, his attraction to Harmony hadn't abated one little bit. All morning, whenever they'd been in the same room,

Cam had found himself watching her—not as a boss assessing a new hire's abilities, but as a man admiring a beautiful woman. He'd found himself liking the way she moved, liking the scent—something floral and sweet today—that wafted around her, and her expressions with those flashes of emotion she tried so hard to hide.

And those amazing eyes were golden again today. They had him constantly checking to see whether they'd changed to green again...

Despite her trying to boss him around and compulsively rearranging things, he couldn't get his mind off her.

"Don't be ridiculous," he muttered to himself, as he got True Blue started and, after her usual complaints, into gear. "You only just met her. It's just the draw of the unknown..."

But his words rang hollow in his own ears, and he was still obsessing over Harmony Kinkaid as he drove home, looking forward to spending the rest of the day with her.

And mentally kicking himself because he was.

CHAPTER FIVE

CAM STOOD WITH his head bowed as John Harris read out the list of islanders who'd served in World War I and World War II. The Armistice Day ceremony was being held at the cenotaph at the north end of the village green, and Cam was aware of Harmony standing next to him, all her attention on the elderly wheelchair-bound gentleman.

He was one of the patients she'd be checking on when she was on her rounds, and Cam had promised at least to point out those who were attending, even if he didn't get a chance to introduce her to them all.

As the "Last Post" was played by a cadet, Cam watched in his peripheral vision as Harmony fished a tissue out of her pocket and dabbed at her eyes. He was always moved by the "Last Post" too—the long first call, and the trill of the bugle running and then coming back to the mournful last notes.

John Harris, ninety-eight years old and a veteran of World War II, had tears streaming down his cheeks too, and Cam knew he was probably remembering his old friend Dougal, who'd died the year before. The two men had enlisted together, served together, and had been friends all through their lives.

After two minutes of silence the National Anthem

was sung, then the crowd began to disperse and Cam took Harmony over to meet John Harris and his son Martin.

From then on it was a round of introductions, which seemed to last forever, before they could break away and head back to the office.

"Oh, my..." Harmony said, almost as though she were apologizing. "Those ceremonies get to me. My father's family are almost all military, so they always strike home, but I think Grandie would have approved of this one. He liked a nice simple observance rather than a lot of pomp and circumstance."

"I'm glad to hear you think he'd have approved," Cam replied. "Was your father in the military too?"

Her lips pursed as she shook her head. "No. He had a congenital heart defect which made him ineligible. He tried to sign up, to follow in his father's, uncles' and cousins' footsteps, but the army turned him away."

"That must have been hard on him."

Cam wondered why the subject of her father had made those lines come and go between her brows. But they were at the side door of the surgery now, and he opened it so she could step through.

"I guess so," she replied, with a touch of frost in her voice. "But he made up for his disappointment."

Before he could figure out what to say to that, she turned toward the staircase leading to her apartment.

"I'll see you at a quarter to one," she continued. "I promised the CIs I'd meet up with them for lunch and I want to change before you and I go on our tour."

"Don't let them talk you into doing anything you don't want to. The Winter Festival gets crazy, and they've already been trying to get me to recruit you to help. I've been valiantly staving them off."

She paused, her hand on the railing, one foot on the lower step, and looked back at him over her shoulder. "Why?"

Self-conscious under her golden perusal, he shrugged. "You just didn't seem too keen whenever I mentioned the festival or Christmas."

Her lips twisted briefly to the side, then softened into a rueful little frown. "Sorry," she muttered, and then cleared her throat. "It's not that I don't want to help, it's just... I'm a little low on Christmas spirit this year."

It shouldn't matter to him why. In fact, he should be glad of it, as it meant she'd be disinclined to get too involved, giving him time to get over this unwanted attraction. Yet his curiosity was stronger than any sense of self-preservation. Harmony didn't seem the type to open up very often, so her showing him even a little chink in that practical armor was enticing.

"How come? Just too far from home?"

"That doesn't bother me," she said, but he heard uncertainty in the stout declaration.

Then she sighed, and turned back to face him.

"The truth is my gran died earlier this year, and Christmas was always a special time for us to celebrate together. It just won't be the same without her and Mum."

"Well, you have space here. You could ask your mum to come up and spend the holidays with you."

The cheerful note he'd tried to infuse into his voice seemed to have the opposite effect to what he'd intended as she slowly shook her head.

"Mum's finally getting a life of her own. Her new gentleman friend has invited her to Yorkshire to meet his family, so that's a non-starter." Drawing herself up to her full height and tipping up her chin, she continued, "But it's fine."

That should have been the end of it, but he knew all too well what she was going through—the loneliness that cloaked the soul after the loss of someone pivotal in your life. The feeling that nothing would ever be the same without them, and the unsure sensation of the world being off-kilter, perhaps never to right itself.

"I get it. Really I do," he found himself saying. "Those firsts are always the hardest. When my grand-da died I didn't feel like facing the holidays either."

Harmony's lips came together in what he'd previously thought of as her disapproving expression. But now he was left wondering what it really meant, considering the pain lingering in her eyes.

"You were close to your grandfather?" she asked.

"Oh, yes. Closer to him than to my parents. I lived with him for a couple of years, and I used to come here every holiday I could to be with him. Even when I got older, if it was reading week at university, you name it, I'd be on Eilean Rurie. It was only after I started working with the aid agency that I didn't get back as often as I'd have liked."

"My gran had lived with us since my dad died, when I was six," she replied. Then, as though suddenly aware of what she was saying, she added, "I'm sorry. I don't usually have a pity party in front of my boss. I think the ceremony this morning has made me a little emotional."

"Don't apologize, please. I don't mind."

Those big golden eyes, slightly misty with tears, drew him in…had him fighting not to step forward. She was all he could see. The world had shrunk to just the woman in front of him, so valiantly battling for complete composure.

Normally he shied away from too much emotion, never trusting it to be genuine. His mother had been a master of using feigned sadness or disappointment to manipulate—until she'd realized it no longer worked on him and had turned it off like a tap.

Harmony Kinkaid was just his temporary employee—a woman he'd known for a couple of days. Why, then, was the urge to comfort her so overwhelming?

His heart was suddenly hammering, and alarm bells were going off in his head, but he paid the warning no mind. Instead he stepped closer and rested his hand on her shoulder, rather than on her cheek the way he wanted to. Her lips were soft now, full and inviting.

Begging to be kissed.

Cam exerted a Herculean effort and dragged his gaze away from her mouth to focus once more on her face.

"I'm sorry you won't be with your family this year, and that you've lost someone so important to you that it doesn't even feel worthwhile celebrating, but it'll be okay. You just wait and see."

And his chest grew suddenly tight as tears gathered at the corners of her eyes again. When the first one slipped free, before he could give in to the urge to wipe it away, she turned and started up the stairs, leaving him staring after her, confusion his only companion.

Cam had been right about the CIs trying to corral Harmony into helping with the festival, but she'd told them she'd only just got to Eilean Rurie and really needed more time to find her feet. While they'd grumbled about it, by the time they'd left the pub Harmony thought they'd given up on the idea.

Crossing the green to the surgery, Harmony thought again about her earlier encounter with Cam. She'd been obsessively going over it, alternately ashamed of telling him anything and grateful for his sympathy. But what totally floored her was her visceral reaction to having him so close.

When he'd touched her shoulder she'd wanted to make the tiny movement that would have been necessary to get close enough to hug him. The simmering attraction she'd felt from the first moment she'd seen him had threatened to boil over. For an instant she'd thought he was going to make the first move...kiss her. She was almost sure his gaze had dropped to her mouth. The anticipation that had fired through her had been like an electric jolt, and just remembering it brought another shock of desire.

"Get a grip, Harmony," she admonished herself out loud, letting herself into the building, her cheeks hot, her insides fluttering as if a wild bird had invaded her stomach. "He was just being kind."

Besides, she hardly knew him. *And* he was her boss. *And* she was off men, to boot.

It was imperative that she got herself together and got real. She was here to do a job and that was all. Not to play Santa Claus, nor to make a fool of herself because she was feeling like Scrooge. And certainly, *definitely*, not to lust after her gorgeous daredevil boss, who had "heartbreaker" written all over him.

The CIs had been quick to tell her that Cam was single, and she'd been thoroughly grilled on her own status. She'd had no problem telling them about her break-up earlier in the year, although not in detail, since it had got them off the subject of Christmas.

She determinedly pushed all thoughts of her conversation with Cam aside, focusing on work instead. A quick look at the time told her she had just a few minutes to run upstairs and comb her hair before he arrived—if he was on time.

His rather *laissez-faire* attitude toward the way his practice was run would have made her think him a little scatterbrained if he hadn't been so clearly intelligent. But he'd frowned when she'd rearranged the filing system, and given her a blank look when she'd asked why there were over four hundred records when there were less than two hundred and fifty people on the island.

And she was still wondering why they needed fifteen minutes to go just down the road.

He did turn up at the appointed time, and Harmony's heart-rate picked up as she watched him from her bedroom window. He got out of his vehicle to open the gate before driving around to the front of the building. She made herself walk slowly down to join him, neither giving in to nor showing any of the silly eagerness bubbling inside her.

Outside, she found him leaning on the hood of his car, as handsome and relaxed as a magazine model. Clearly he wasn't suffering from the same reaction she had, and she was determined to meet his cool with all the calm in the world.

Cam explained the extra fifteen minutes while they were walking over to the Jacobsons' cottage.

"Hugh is in denial about the terminal aspect of his mother's disease, and he has a tendency to want to speak for her, saying how well she's doing rather than letting her tell me the truth. He's also a bit of a fusspot when it comes to time. If I get there a little early he doesn't have the tea ready yet, so I get a few minutes to talk to Delores alone and find out exactly how she is, and if there are any new developments. I keep the more clinical aspects, like taking her temperature and blood pressure, for when he's in the room, so he feels as though he's in the thick of it."

It made sense, and she made a note of it for future reference. Hearing his logic also made her contemplate how different this job was going to be from her last. There everything had been regulated, and although they'd got the chance to get to know some of their patients quite well, the little personal touches like those Dr. MacRurie had just described had often been missed.

The visit went as predicted, with Hugh Jacobson greeting them at the door, rushing to the kitchen to make tea, and apologizing for it not being ready when they got there. The doctor winked conspiratorially at Harmony, making her silly stomach flutter, and he pushed open the door to the front room where his patient was.

Mrs. Jacobson was a quiet lady, who smiled when she saw Dr. MacRurie and Harmony and seemed to know the drill. Wasting no time on small-talk, she answered the doctor's questions while her son was out of the room. But then, with a quick glance toward the open door, she grasped Cam's wrist, stopping him mid-sentence.

"It won't be long now, Cameron," she said, in her soft brogue. "But I just want to make it through Hogmanay. I don't want Hugh to be sad every Christmas because I died around the holiday."

Tears stung the back of Harmony's eyes, but Dr. MacRurie just patted Mrs. Jacobson's shoulder and said, "We'll do our best to see you through till then, Delores."

"Good," she replied, seeming to relax slightly in her chair. "I want to see the lights this year, even if I can't get out to enjoy the festival."

Harmony couldn't tell this sweet lady that it wouldn't

matter to her son whether she made it through to the New Year or not. Her passing would hurt him whenever it happened, and he'd miss her every holiday thereafter.

Later, after they'd drunk tea with mother and son and were walking back to the vehicle, Cam said, "She didn't know she had hemochromatosis until after the menopause, and it had already caused extensive liver damage. She's not the complaining type, as you could see, and attributed the symptoms to simply aging. Hopefully we can keep her going the way she wants."

No matter how unprofessional it was, Harmony didn't feel able to discuss it just then. Not when seeing Mrs. Jacobson had brought all the pain of losing her gran rushing to the fore.

She made an noncommittal sound. Then quickly said, "I guess you weren't putting me on when you said there's a Winter Festival, although it's hard to picture." All she saw was a tiny village—nicer today, with the sun out, than it had been the last couple of days, but nothing special.

Cam opened the passenger door of his aged utility vehicle and Harmony tried not to wince at the metallic creak.

As she climbed in, he replied, "Wait and see. I think you'll be pleasantly surprised."

But she was still skeptical. After all, how fancy a show could the inhabitants of a tiny place like this put on?

CHAPTER SIX

CAM WALKED AROUND the front of the vehicle, glancing in at Harmony through the windshield. She was fussing with the seatbelt which, like most things in True Blue didn't work as it should, and just a glimpse of her furrowed brow and pursed lips made him smile.

Cranking open the driver's door, he levered himself into the seat just as she got the belt wrestled into submission. She was casually dressed, but the jeans, white shirt and red anorak did nothing to camouflage her lovely figure. Cam rather wished it did, so he wouldn't find himself admiring it so much.

Firing up the engine, trying to ignore how good Harmony smelled, he dragged his thoughts back to business. "I forgot to ask, can you drive a manual?"

"Yes," she said.

But just as he was coaxing the vehicle into gear and, and it ground its way into first, he glanced across and saw her concerned expression.

"My grandfather taught me, but although he always said if I could drive a stick shift in Jamaica I could drive anywhere, I don't know if I can manage *this* beast."

Cam chuckled. "No, I have an estate car for you to use. I'm the only one who drives True Blue. She's very persnickety."

"True Blue?"

There was no mistaking the laughter in her voice, and it made Cam's grin widen. "She's held together with baling wire and tape, but she's never let me down anywhere I couldn't walk home."

The sound of her amusement filled the rattling, groaning vehicle and made Cam unaccountably happy. He realized he'd never heard her laugh that way before; not a giggle but full-on belly laughter.

What started as a quick glance at her had him staring, his gaze riveted on her face. Amusement had taken her from beautiful to stunningly gorgeous, and it was only the need to watch where he was driving that tore his attention away.

"You live on a very small island. I'm guessing you'd be able to walk home from just about anywhere—am I right?"

He cleared his throat, being careful not to look at her again. "Yes, but don't tempt fate. We're in this together now."

That exchange seemed to set a good tone for the rest of the time they spent together. Harmony even relaxed slightly, so Cam asked about her grandfather, and heard the story of her grandmother travelling to England alone.

"She explained it by saying that Granddad had 'small pond' syndrome. He wasn't happy with the thought of leaving a place where he was known and had a certain status to start over in a much larger pond, where he'd have to begin again at the bottom."

Cam couldn't really relate. As a child he'd lived in more countries than he had fingers, and before moving back to Eilean Rurie he had seen even more working for the aid agency, which had sent doctors to refugee camps and disaster zones all over the world.

Despite his desire for a stable home when he was young, if given the chance to start over somewhere new and exciting now, he'd probably take it. With his past experience, being tied to the island sometimes chafed.

Still trying to get a handle on her family, he said, "Oh, I thought at first perhaps it was your father's father who taught you to drive?"

"No," she said. "My dad was half English, half Scottish. No Jamaican roots."

Something in her voice stopped him from asking anything more about her father, so he just said, "How often do you get to go to Jamaica to see your family?"

"I went most summers before I started nursing school. I haven't been back in a while, though, and I should go soon. Granddad isn't getting any younger, and now he's my last grandparent left."

"I hardly knew my mother's parents, and my father's mother died before I was born. I think it made the bond between Grand-Da and me all the stronger."

"Did your mother's parents live far away?"

Cam eased True Blue into neutral and brought her to a stop at a T-junction before he replied. "No. It was my parents who moved around all the time. My dad is an archeologist, my mother's his archivist, and he loves working in the field—the more obscure and distant the dig, the better. The Middle East and Southeast Asia are his specialties."

The peripatetic nature of his childhood was something he rarely, if ever, talked about, and he was glad to be able to divert Harmony.

"Okay, now, it might seem logical to think this road goes all the way around the island, but it doesn't. If you

continue along here you get to the Harris farm, and then
to a dead end where we have a wind turbine installed.
So you need to remember to take the turn here, rather
than go straight."

Fighting the wretched gearbox, he made it back into
first and turned the corner to continue circling the island. Since he'd introduced her to most of the people
she'd be seeing on her rounds, he decided to simply give
her the tour and then take her back home.

The less time they spent together, the better.

They crested a slight rise in the rolling terrain and
the sea came into sight in the distance.

"Oh! How lovely!" Harmony said suddenly. "Can we
stop for a second? I promised Mum I'd take pictures,
and I'd forgotten up until now."

It was a glorious day, although chilly, with a cloud-
less sky, and he found her reaction to the vista charm-
ing. For all his wanderlust, to Cam, Eilean Rurie was
the most beautiful place in the world, and he loved to
see others appreciate it, as well.

As he brought the vehicle to a halt she fished her
phone from her bag and then hopped out. Cam followed,
noticing the way the breeze caught her curls and made
them bounce.

She started snapping pictures. "I told Mum about
the ferry ride, and she asked then if I'd remembered to
take any pictures. I felt pretty silly telling her I hadn't."

"Your mum's okay with you being so far away?"

Harmony shrugged lightly. "I don't think she was
happy with the idea, but she knew I needed a job, so
now she's taking it in her stride, I think. I've been keeping her updated all along the way, and I got a chance
to talk to her this morning before her shift. She's sent

my other suitcase already, or I'd have asked her to put in a pair of wellies."

"I have a pair for you. At the Manor."

Her lips twitched. They didn't purse, just twitched. "Did you forget them?"

"No," he said, stuffing his hands in his pockets, not sure whether to be annoyed at her implication. "I washed them off and left them out to dry. We're going to drive right past the front entrance to the Manor anyway, so we'll stop and you can get them."

Her eyes were shining when she turned toward him, and heat radiated up his spine as she smiled.

"Oh! Can I take a look inside? I'm so curious about what it's like."

"Sure," he said, then had to clear his tight throat and get a grip on himself. What was it about her smile that made his entire system go into overdrive? "But we don't start opening up most of the bedrooms until later this week."

Harmony blinked at him, her eyebrows dipping briefly before she turned back to take another picture. He played back his words in his head, trying to figure out her reaction, and then suppressed a groan.

Had he really just mentioned bedrooms, as though they were what she should see? And now that he'd realized the connotations he could picture her in bed—all smooth golden-syrup-and-cinnamon skin and luscious curves, those wild curls spread across his pillow. Somehow, though he didn't know how or why, he knew her eyes would be greener then, inviting him close, and closer yet...

His reaction to the image was visceral: a shock of heat along his spine, lust turning his blood to lava.

She still had her back to him, had made no reply, and

he dragged himself from his fantasy to rush into speech, trying to salvage the conversation and his sanity.

"We only keep part of the hotel open for most of the year, since we just get dribs and drabs of visitors. But next week the entire place will be opened up and aired, and the decorating started, so you'll get a chance to see all of it."

"Okay."

That was all she said, leaving him wondering if he'd gotten himself out of the suggestive hole he'd unthinkingly dug.

Harmony took a deep, silent breath, pretending total concentration on her phone, all the while trying to shake her imagined visual of Cam in bed.

Naked.

Aroused.

Making love to her.

Those chiseled lips on hers…his large, capable hands all over her body.

She was blushing. The heat caused by an intense rush of arousal had traveled from her chest into her face. So she kept her back turned to him, trying to get herself under control.

What on earth was wrong with her? She'd met handsome men before, even dated a couple, but none had affected her the way Dr. Cam MacRurie did.

Finally she got herself centered, and although her cheeks still felt warm, she thought she'd dare to turn around.

"I've got enough pictures," she said, trying not to look at him. "Shall we…?"

They got back into the vehicle and he ground it into first.

"True Blue sounds like her gearbox and clutch need some help," she commented, just to break the silence, which was weighing on her and giving her too much time to think.

"We only have a few cars on the island, since a lot of people use bicycles or scooters, so our mechanic went off to look for greener pastures. I'd have to take her over to the mainland on the car ferry to get her looked at. She's sounded like this forever, so I'm not too worried."

They drove through a cut in the low hills—a twisty road, with rough autumn-colored moorland punctuated by the occasional gnarled tree or low copse on each side. In the distance the hills rose, dark stone stark against the heather and grass. It was, Harmony thought, beautiful in a stern, unflinching way.

"Do you get much snow here?"

"Not really—the occasional heavy fall but usually just a light coating. Our location is pretty sheltered, and because the hills aren't very high storms tend to pass over us quickly."

Just then they crested a hill and there below was a small settlement and the sea again beyond. The afternoon light was wonderful, and the sun, which would set about four o'clock, hung low in the sky, casting a golden glow over the whitewashed buildings.

"Our fishing village," Cam said as Harmony leaned forward to see better. "My great-grandfather moved it here after a storm destroyed the old fishing village a little way down the coast. The entire spit of land gave way, and over the years the sea has eaten most of it up. You can still see the old buildings and what remains of the rescue station when the tide is low."

She risked a glance at him, but when heat threatened to overtake her again, looked away.

"How long has your family lived here?" she asked.

"Almost two hundred years," he said, and she couldn't help smiling at his obvious pride. "In 1853 my three-times great-grandfather won the island in a game of whist."

"A game of what?"

"Whist. It's a card game. The story is that the island's owner at the time was a bit of a wastrel. He lost a lot of money to my ancestor, and paid with the land. Charles MacRurie took the island, which was sparsely populated at the time because it was only used as a summer retreat and hunting lodge, and turned it into his private fiefdom."

"Clearly he wasn't the humble type, since he named it after himself."

Cam chuckled. "From all accounts he was not. At all."

They continued around the coast, with Cam pausing every now and then for her to take pictures, and Harmony keeping the conversation away from the personal and on the island and work.

She was amazed to hear there was an alpaca farm, which produced hand-spun wool, an artists' collective, and a pottery with a world-famous potter. Somehow it had never occurred to her that so small a place would have such an interesting and diverse set of artisans.

When Cam pointed out her patients' homes, and the side roads she'd need to take to get to them, she was able to ask informed questions, since she'd already read all their files. Cam slanted her a raised-eyebrow glance, but didn't comment beyond answering her.

As the gates of Rurie Manor came into sight he said, "The road continues on past Eigg Point, and then goes back to town, but we'll take the back road when you're finished looking around the Manor."

Call it cowardice, or the effect of the heat she could already feel building in her belly and snaking out to fill her chest, but Harmony had changed her mind.

"Why don't I wait until everything is decorated?" she asked. "I'm due to check on Hillary Carstairs tomorrow, aren't I? So I'll take the car and drive myself back to the surgery. It'll give me a chance to read her file more thoroughly and do any research I need to."

"Sure, if you'd like," Cam replied, giving her a look which she avoided, quite sure her cheeks were red again. "But it wouldn't be a problem for you to come in now."

She firmly refused, even though close up the Manor was so beautiful she itched to get inside and see it for herself.

Instead she put deeds to words, collecting her borrowed Wellingtons and then hightailing it out of Cameron Mac-Rurie's vicinity as fast as possible.

CHAPTER SEVEN

HARMONY WOKE UP to an almighty roar and clatter, which got louder and then seemed to be coming into the surgery itself. They were back to their usual nine o'clock opening schedule, and normally she would have been awake long before seven, but she'd hardly slept and had hit the snooze button a few times.

"What on earth...?"

The noise was coming around the corner of the building, and she could swear that everything in the place, including her teeth, was rattling.

Kneeling on the bed, she pulled back the curtain and saw, in the gray morning light, two large lorries and a caravan going past. As she watched someone jumped out of the first truck to open the gate leading to the Manor and the cavalcade drove through. It was only when the trucks were going up the path that she realized there were a couple of SUVs following behind, as well.

She watched until the last vehicle was through, and the gate was closed behind them, before letting the curtains swing shut again. Reaching over and turning on the bedside lamp, now wide awake, she wondered what was going on. More vehicles than she'd seen on the entire island had just passed her window.

Sliding out of bed, she reached for her bathrobe,

resigned to getting an early start on the day, although she'd planned to spend another half an hour in bed. Mum was working afternoons, starting yesterday, so there was no early-morning prework call to look forward to, and no good reason to be up earlier than necessary.

Not that she could talk to her mother about the main thing on her mind—Dr. Cam MacRurie, who'd cost her sleep and had her mind and body in a tailspin. While her mother was no prude, Harmony knew the fact that her daughter seemed to be going ga-ga over a man she'd literally just met wouldn't sit well with Delilah Kinkaid.

Heck, it didn't sit well with Harmony either, but she couldn't get the darn man out of her head.

Tossing and turning half the night, thinking about Cam, had left her frustrated and testy, wishing she could stay in the apartment all day and not have to face him. However, there were tasks that needed to be done in the surgery, and despite Cam telling her there was no rush she preferred to be ahead of the game, rather than stressing when a deadline loomed and she was unprepared.

Having showered and had some oatmeal, she went downstairs to the surgery and was surprised to see, through the front window, a crowd of people on the village green.

Going closer, to look out through the glass, she realized there was more than just people. There were a couple of pieces of what appeared to be farm equipment, some open-back vans, and lots of ladders, loaded pallets, coils of rope and large wooden boxes.

Harmony blinked a few times, trying to figure out if she was seeing things. There were only two hundred and fifty people on the island, give or take, and it appeared that all of them, probably plus a few more, were milling about on the green.

"What are they...?"

She almost had her nose pressed to the glass, trying to see what was happening. In the midst of it all was a figure in a Santa hat she was almost sure was Dora, who was gesticulating this way and that like a conductor on a podium.

Another figure broke from the group and came toward the surgery, and Harmony hurriedly scooted back to her desk.

She'd met the man in the pub—Broderick Thompson—and wasn't sure she liked him very much. He was a smooth talker, a little too full of himself for her liking, and his light gray eyes had seemed to be undressing her rather than holding her gaze.

Hopefully he wasn't on his way to the surgery, but if he was she'd rather present an air of professionalism rather than be caught gawking out of the window.

Sure enough, the door to the entryway opened a few seconds later, and the man who was the gallery owner came in, sleek smile in place, sandy blond hair ruffled by the wind, exposing his scalp.

"Harmony, beautiful lady! I saw the lights come on and came over to ask if you'd be joining us."

"I'm afraid not, Mr. Thompson," she replied, not returning his smile. "I have work to do."

His eyes took a break away from crawling all over her chest to glance around the empty waiting room. When he looked back at her his eyebrows were raised in exaggerated surprise.

"I can see how busy you are. *So* busy that I guess you wouldn't have time for a coffee with me? But I know the surgery doesn't officially open until nine, and Lalli's has opened early for the workers, so I'm sure you can spare a few minutes."

"No, I actually don't have the time."

She made no effort to soften the refusal, and she thought his eyes hardened, although his smile stayed in place. Unfortunately, instead of leaving, as she'd hoped, he actually had the temerity to come over and plunk his skinny bum on the corner of her desk.

"Come on, now. All work and no play makes for a less than *harmonious* life."

Harmony just barely stopped herself from rolling her eyes at his heavy-handed banter. "I really have to get on with my job, Mr. Thompson. Was there anything else you wanted?"

He leaned forward, almost in her space, but Harmony held her ground, clenching her teeth as his gaze dropped to the front of her shirt again.

"Well…"

He let the word trail off suggestively, and Harmony narrowed her eyes. If this twit thought she was going to put up with any of his nonsense let him try her! She was ready.

"Broderick. Not lending a hand outside?"

Cam had come in through the back so quietly neither of them heard him. Harmony jumped with surprise, and when a wave of embarrassed heat rose in her chest she berated herself for it.

She wasn't doing anything wrong.

Broderick Thompson got up and stretched. "Just came in for the First Aid kit. Dora sent me."

Lying creep, Harmony thought, furious enough to want to smack him over the head with the kit once she'd fetched it from the store room. Instead she placed it on the desk, doing her best not to glare.

He picked it up, and gave her another of his smarmy smiles.

"So, what time for coffee later?"

Behind her she heard Cam's office door open, but his footsteps stopped. She knew he was listening, and the thought of him believing she'd go out with Broderick Thompson made her more curt than perhaps she should be.

"I already told you no, Mr. Thompson, and I tried to be polite about it too. If you'd prefer I be rude, ask again."

Broderick's cheeks reddened, but to his credit he just shook his head as he picked up the kit and said, "Can't blame a chap for trying. See you both later."

She restrained the urge to make a rude noise as the door closed behind her, but it was hard not to kiss her teeth. Very aware of Cam, still standing by his door, she reached for the supply list on her desk, intent getting on with the audit she'd put at the top of her day's to-do list. He'd explained that he usually put in a big order for a number of medical necessities just before the festival, in case they were needed, but much of it lasted the rest of the year.

"Whoa," he said, and the amusement in his voice made her want to blush all over again. "Remind me not to rile you up."

With her nose in the air she swept past him, on her way to the medical stores.

"I think it's be almost inevitable that you will at some point," she retorted, before she could stop herself.

The sound of his laughter smoothed the last of her ruffled feathers and she found herself smiling too as she set to work.

* * *

Cam was still chuckling to himself as he sat at his desk to switch on his computer.

Originally he'd come down to see if the noise of the arriving equipment had woken Harmony, and to tell her to take part of the afternoon off since she'd started so early. He truly loved this time of year, despite the stress of putting on the festival, but his excitement had shriveled on finding Broderick Thompson leaning close to Harmony, as though about to kiss her.

Her guilty start when he'd spoken had made the rest of his good humor flee, but hearing her give the other man that set-down had restored it. Clearly she had the good sense to see through that Lothario.

Even though Broderick ran a profitable business at the gallery, somehow acquiring really good artwork and having successful yearly exhibitions, he was a bit of a menace otherwise. The women on the island who had known him longest had learned of his wandering eyes over time, but to him every new arrival was fair game.

Cam wasn't surprised he'd tried it on with Harmony, but her clear and cutting refusal had been a thing of beauty.

Would she do the same to him, should he try to kiss her?

He realized he wanted to—badly. Every movement of her lips, whether they were smiling, pursed, or speaking, made him want to taste them.

And he wanted to know what she'd feel like in his arms. Those amazing curves snuggled against him, her arms around his neck, his mouth on that long, lovely throat.

Or anywhere else on her body she'd let him get at.

Arousal hit him, heating his blood. Shifting in his seat,

he tried to banish the vision of a naked Harmony from his mind, so as to not cause himself any more discomfort. For goodness' sakes—what was he? Fifteen? Getting turned on just daydreaming over a woman he hardly knew?

Mind you, Harmony would make any red-blooded man think dirty thoughts.

And she made him completely forget what he was supposed to be doing—like actually turning on his computer instead of starting blindly at the still blank screen.

Hitting the switch, he waited for the machine to boot up.

The physical attraction would be so much easier to quell if he didn't actually like her so much. Yes, she was fussy, and bossy, and on a couple of occasions she had reminded him of why he preferred a single life by giving him one of those "oh, really?" glances that activated his stubborn independent streak. But none of that negated his very real desire to get to know her better.

Much better.

Intimately, even.

She was his employee, though. Temporary, but on his payroll nonetheless. Professionalism dictated that he not get involved with her, no matter how short a time she was supposed to be on the island. Besides, there was an innate danger in getting too close to a woman like Harmony, even for a little while. She had the kind of forever vibe he assiduously avoided.

He might be an adrenaline junkie, but forever was one heart-stopping trip he didn't want to go on. Not when it would mean changing the life he enjoyed so much, and having someone else to consider every time he wanted to make a decision.

His childhood, stunted by his mother's fear over his diabetes and his own need to allay her panic, had made him recognize his need to be free of those types of entanglements. Even now, when he was speaking to his mother on the phone, he omitted telling her too much, knowing she'd be frightened to hear about his adventures. That was about enough of an emotional burden as he could manage.

The computer beeped, the cursor flashed, waiting for him to put in his password. Doing so absently, Cam found himself remembering Harmony's sadness when she'd spoken about how much she missed her grandmother.

He understood, completely. The first Christmas after Grand-Da died had been the hardest of Cam's life. Only the fellowship of the islanders, who missed the old man as much as Cam did, had eased the pain. It was a shame Harmony and her mother wouldn't be together to remember the old lady and all the good times the three had shared.

Then he frowned as the first notification to pop up on his screen was an email from Dora entitled To-Do List.

"Really?" he muttered to himself. "Don't you think that after four years I know what needs to be done?"

Yet still he opened it, and sat running through the various points until the phone rang.

Since Harmony was in the back, he called out, "I've got it!" and picked up the receiver.

"Cam MacRurie speaking."

"Cam? Are you coming by today?"

"Hello, Hillary," he said, noting the strain in the woman's voice. "Is everything all right?"

"Oh, yes, of course. I just wondered…"

"My new nurse, Harmony, is scheduled to come out and see you, Hill," he said gently. "Will that be okay with you?"

"Oh, yes, of course," she replied, and the automatic answer told him more than her words. "It's just that I don't *know* her. How will I know it's her? And I haven't had a chance to tidy up…"

"Don't worry about it, Hill. I'll come out with her and introduce her properly. That way next time you'll know who it is. Will that suit?"

"I… I…"

She faltered, and Cam waited, guessing she was trying to gather her thoughts.

"So you'll come, then?"

"Yes, Hill. I will." He infused as much of a soothing tone into his voice as he could. "I'll see you in a little while."

"Thank you." The relief in her voice was patent. "Thank you, Cam."

After he'd hung up the phone, Harmony, who'd come to the door, asked, "Her anxiety getting the best of her?"

Cam nodded, pleased that she'd picked up on that from the file. Hillary Carstairs had been born with spina bifida, yet had lived life to the fullest, getting around with leg braces and a cane until her later years. She had two children, one of whom still lived at home and helped his father on the farm.

Now confined to a wheelchair, Hill had developed agoraphobia and an anxiety disorder, which made her increasingly isolated. He'd prescribed antianxiety medication, which she'd refused to take, and offered to refer her to a specialist, but again she'd refused— perhaps because of having to go to the mainland for appointments.

It was at times like this when Cam felt the restrictive nature of the island keenly, and chafed at not being able to provide what was necessary.

"I'll ride out with you," he said to Harmony. "It'll allay some of her stress, and hopefully she'll be okay with you coming alone the next time."

"Okay, but it seems a shame to interrupt your day that way. No doubt you have scads of stuff to do."

Cam happily closed the email from Dora and grinned. "It's not an issue. Hill's health is the most important."

Besides, Hillary and Gavin's farm was in one of his favorite parts of the island, and showing it to Harmony suddenly seemed like a great idea. In fact, there was nothing he'd like more—although why that was wasn't something he wanted to think about too deeply.

CHAPTER EIGHT

THE CARSTAIRS' FARMHOUSE was filled with the evidence of Hillary's weaving business, although Harmony had seen no sign of the alpacas when they drove up, which was disappointing.

Hillary Carstairs was stressed and apologetic, but Harmony was adept at handling patients with anxiety disorders, and had her calmed down in a fairly short time. Hillary even agreed to allow Harmony to do her examination and change her catheter.

"Everything looks good," Harmony told the older lady as she helped her back into her wheelchair. "But I see from your chart that you've refused treatment for your anxiety disorder and agoraphobia. May I ask why?"

Hillary's eyes shifted away and she knotted her fingers together. For a moment Harmony thought she didn't intend to answer. When she finally spoke there was an air of surrender in the words.

"I've been poked and prodded and I've taken medication my entire life. Why would I add even more? Besides, going anywhere in this contraption takes so much effort. It's not fair to Gav."

Harmony tweaked the ends of Hillary's skirt so it lay

flat, thinking through her answer before saying, "You realize what an anomaly you are, right?"

Hillary frowned slightly. "What do you mean?"

"Well, you've lived to be in your sixties with spina bifida. Had two children and a full life. It's only in the last few decades that spina bifida has been considered something other than a childhood disorder, since people diagnosed with it weren't expected to live very long. Why give up now?"

Hillary shrugged, but she was obviously listening, her gaze steady on Harmony's face, so she continued speaking.

"You already have some limitations placed on you by your disorder. Why not deal with what you can, so you can continue enjoying your life to its fullest?"

There was no reply, but as Harmony packed up her kit she left it at that, hoping she'd given her patient some food for thought.

They left the bedroom and found Cam and Gavin, Hillary's husband, in the large farmhouse kitchen, leaning on the counter, sipping from teacups.

Gavin was a short, stocky redhead with an infectious grin, who asked, "All right, then, love?"

"Yes," Hillary said, smiling back at him. "Everything is fine."

But Harmony found herself the recipient of a piercing interrogatory glance from Gavin, who only visibly relaxed when Harmony nodded her agreement.

"Good, good… Want a cup of tea, ladies?"

At their affirmative responses he set about pouring cups for them from the pot, while a black-and-white collie came over to say hello to Harmony. She bent to pet it, getting a lovely cold nose in her neck and a couple of licks before the dog slunk off in typical collie style to flop down on a cushion in front of the fireplace.

Gavin said, "I was just telling Cam that I've moved the flock up to the old croft, which is why they weren't hanging over the fence watching to see who was arriving."

"They're a nosy lot," Hillary said. "I miss seeing them when I look out the window."

"I was hoping to get a glimpse of them when we arrived," Harmony said, adding a murmur of thanks as she took the cup from Gavin.

"Cam can take you up to get a look," he replied, turning to Cam as he continued. "Take the four-wheeler."

"I will," said Cam.

"Oh, that's not necessary," Harmony said, at the same time.

Cam laughed. "I think it's a grand idea. And, if you don't mind, I'd like to show her Ada Tor."

"Go right ahead," Gavin replied, resting his hand on his wife's shoulder as he passed. "I don't need the UTV again until later this evening."

Everyone else looked pleased as punch at this idea, and Harmony realized she'd look churlish and ungrateful by refusing, so she plastered a smile on her face. But she wondered what kind of vehicle it was they'd be taking, what kind of terrain they'd be traversing, and if any of this was safe.

She got her answer after they'd finished their tea. While she stowed her bag in True Blue, Cam and Gavin went into the barn. After a short time there was the clatter of an engine, which sounded like a large lawn mower, and a small four-wheeled vehicle came stuttering out. It had two seats, a flatbed in the back, no doors, and it bumped across the farmyard as though it had a complete lack of shocks.

Filled with trepidation, she cautiously approached as Cam brought it to a halt nearby.

At least it probably couldn't go very fast, she thought as she got in.

But with the way Cam drove it over the rutted tracks it might as well have been a race car. Even terrified half out of her wits, and hanging on for dear life, Harmony had to admit he handled the little vehicle well, with the kind of casual capability she couldn't help but admire.

When they got to a gate she got out rather shakily to open it, and then closed it behind the UTV once he'd driven it through.

"All right, there?" he asked with a grin as she got back in, before setting off again after her curt nod.

The land undulated, but Harmony got the sense they were going more uphill than down—a supposition that was proved as they went around a rise and she looked back to see the farmhouse below them. Ahead in the distance was a stone building, and even farther away what looked like a jumble of boulders all piled up together.

At the sound of the UTV, the alpacas came moseying out, and Harmony couldn't stop her little squeak of pleasure on seeing their cute, curious faces. Cam brought the vehicle to a halt and Harmony got out for a closer look.

The alpacas kept their distance, with the one in the front eyeing her suspiciously. As she got closer to the fence it huffed, and she stopped.

Cam came up beside her and pointed. "That's Sandro— the male. He's pretty protective of his flock. Not much of a spitter, according to Gav, but I wouldn't chance going much closer when his ears are flat like that."

"I was hoping to pet one," Harmony replied. "They look so soft…"

"Got their winter coats on," he replied, and she saw him looking at her out of the corner of her eye. "You really like animals, don't you?"

"I do. Gran had a little scruffy dog for years, and he and I were best buds. She didn't want to get another after Hobo died, and I was so busy I didn't think I'd have enough time to care for an animal myself, but recently I've really been thinking about getting a pet soon." It was her turn to look at him, now, wanting to see what his expression told her as she asked, "Don't you like animals?"

"Love them," he said, which came as no surprise to her, really. He seemed the type.

"So how come you don't have a dog or three?"

Cam shook his head. "Maybe one day I will, but right now a pet would tie me down too much. Every time I want to go away I'd have to find someone to look after it."

Unable to decide whether that was a smart or a self-ish way to be, Harmony made no comment. Instead she made soft, hopefully enticing sounds to the alpacas, trying to coax them closer, but they weren't interested and, after a short time, they turned and started back toward the building.

"That was where Gavin's parents lived," Cam said. "He and his four siblings were born and grew up in that crofter's cottage. Gav built the farmhouse for himself and Hillary when they married, and after his parents had passed away, and none of the children wanted to come back here to live, he converted it into a supplementary barn."

"Wow. Seven people in that little building? Must have been cramped," he said as they were heading back to the vehicle.

"I think they were used to it," he said, as they got back in. "And they spent enough time outdoors to make it doable. They all had to help on the farm when they weren't at school, and with sheep—which is all Gav's father had back then—there's always something needs doing."

Further conversation was curtailed by the racket of the motor starting up. Then they were off again, heading for the up-thrust of boulders, which she discovered was far larger and higher than she'd first thought.

Cam left the path and bumped across the field, straight for it. Harmony was hanging on, wanting to tell him to slow down but finding the words caught in her throat. He finally slowed, then stopped within a couple of yards of the rocks. When he turned off the vehicle the sudden silence rang in her ears.

There was a wild, stark beauty to the landscape: gray rocks interspersed with autumn-colored ground cover and a few bare-limbed trees. In the sky a raptor of some type circled, and the whisper of the wind was the only sound. When Cam spoke it was in a low tone, as though he didn't want to break the spell of quietude.

"Come on. Let me show you the best view in all Eilean Rurie."

They got out, and Harmony followed Cam to the boulders. But when he started to climb she hung back, shaking her head.

"I'm not going up there," she said, trying not to show her instinctive fear. "I don't know how to climb."

Looking back at her, he said, "This isn't climbing, really. Just a little scramble. It's perfectly safe, and if you're not feeling confident go ahead of me and I'll guide you."

Oh, how she regretted not wearing the Wellington boots, which would have given her a solid reason not even to attempt the climb. But she'd worn her trainers instead, and with Cam's eager expression and outstretched hand she was completely torn.

Anything to do with climbing—even what he called a scramble up some boulders—filled her with terror.

"Scared?" he asked, his eyebrows going up. "Are you afraid of heights?"

Was there a condescending note in his question? Whether there was or wasn't, it got Harmony's dander up and she lifted her chin.

"No, I'm not," she said, gathering her courage and stepping up on the first rock. "Lead the way."

Cam climbed with the ease of familiarity, but made sure to look back often and make sure Harmony wasn't having any difficulties.

They didn't talk, except when he warned her of a longer step, or a spot where there was a crack to watch out for. She was obviously inexperienced, hesitating in places, searching for a good hand or foothold in areas where, to him, it was obvious. But he had to admit she was game, and she grew even higher in his estimation.

He'd been sure she'd refuse to go to the top of Ada Tor. In fact, he would swear she'd been petrified when he'd suggested it. Yet here she was, more than halfway to the top, soldiering on. Hard not to admire her grit.

When he got to the top he reached back to help her up the last little bit, but she ignored his hand and scrambled up by herself. As she stood beside him, dusting her hands off on her jeans, he watched her look around, and he saw the dawning pleasure on her face at the vista laid out before her.

The land fell away in dips and swirls, the contours and colors reminding him of a Van Gogh painting, and in the distance lay the sea, a smooth blue expanse so far away. Just visible to the southeast were the roofs of the town, and to the west the little crescent of buildings making up the fishing village. Sheep and a few horses dotted the fields, but it was the quality of the air and the perfect height of the sun that really brought out the island's splendor.

"How lovely…" she breathed, turning to look back toward where the mainland was just a smudge on the horizon above the trees along the northern coast.

"I told you it was the best view," he said, and found himself taking in the familiar sight and appreciating it even more than usual. Something in her awestruck expression made him see it through fresh eyes.

"Is this rock formation natural?" she asked, still turning slowly to see everything all over again.

"I think it is," he replied. "Although there isn't another like it on the island. Legend has it that there's a Celtic princess buried under it, but I don't think it's true."

"Hence the name Ada Tor?"

"Yes."

He sat down on a handy rock, still gazing out. After a moment she joined him, and he shuffled over to give her more room. Her fresh, sweet scent wafted over him and stirred something deep inside.

In the distance a truck rumbled along the road, and she pointed to it briefly. "I can't get used to seeing so many vehicles here all of a sudden. It's surprising after hardly seeing any at all."

"They're probably delivering Christmas trees to Angus's farm. He always gets his early because he has so much work to do. The rest will come later in the week."

Harmony sighed quietly, and he somehow knew she was thinking of her family and all she'd miss this year.

"Will you tell me what you used to do with your gran and your mum for Christmas? I'm curious to know about some of your customs."

She gave him a sideways glance, before staring out at where the truck had disappeared into a dip in the land.

"It wasn't much different from other English families, I guess," she said, but then proceeded to prove herself wrong.

It was as if a dam had broken, and Cam could only listen as she listed all the things she'd be missing this year. There were things he'd never heard of—what on earth was a gizzada, or jonkanoo?—but other things he completely understood. Lots of poinsettias, since they were such a popular tradition in the Caribbean. Watching favorite movies, listening to beloved songs. Decorating the tree together and inviting everyone they knew to come by to exchange gifts and have drinks.

It wasn't so different from what happened here, he thought as she fell silent. Some different cultural traditions, of course, but the picture she painted of family and friends, of a community sharing laughter and joy, labor and company, was the same.

Without thought he looped his arm around her shoulders and gave her a quick squeeze. When she stiffened he almost let his arm drop, but then she turned her face to look at him and he froze, captivated and enticed by her solemn eyes, her soft lips.

The wind had died, and their faces were so close together her breath rushed warm across his mouth. Cam inhaled, wanting to take it into his lungs, hold on to it just for a moment.

Want spiked through his veins, so strong it wrapped around his chest, making it tight. It was there in her eyes too, he thought, the same anticipation and curiosity that was heating him through.

Then she blinked, color flooding her cheeks with a rose-toned blush, and Cam finally heeded the danger signs flashing in his head as they pulled away simultaneously.

The sensation of having her warm, soft body against his side lingered, though, reminding him of what was so close and yet should be ignored.

He cleared his throat, searching for a memory of what they'd been talking about so as to bring them back from the sensual ledge they'd stepped out on. "Christmas at your house sounds wonderful. I'm sorry you won't have that this year."

She turned her face away from his, but not before he saw that her eyes were misty.

"I just have to accept it'll never be that way again," she said quietly, a little quaver in her voice. Abruptly she rose and turned back toward where they'd climbed up. "Let's get down now. I have work to do."

He followed her lead without comment, but inside he was wondering what, if anything he could do to make the season ahead better for her.

Despite knowing it was ridiculous, his heart had ached on hearing her pour out her pain. And he certainly shouldn't want to hold her, comfort her, kiss her the way he was drawn to do.

Yet that was exactly how he felt.

CHAPTER NINE

I'VE HAD ENOUGH of this...

"This" was the Christmas music playing through the office, and Cameron MacRurie's occasional attempts to sing along.

He might be Laird of Eilean Rurie, and a good, well-respected doctor, but his singing left a lot to be desired!

Yet even as she had the sour thought Harmony found herself smiling and shaking her head. The song playing was an old one, sung by a crooner her grandmother had loved.

Harmony could almost hear Gran saying, *Lawd, tell the man to stop caterwauling.* But it would have been said through laughter, and the old lady would have gone and sung with him, trying desperately to get him in tune.

Not that it would have helped Cam, who was clearly tone deaf.

As the days had gone by she'd found herself shaking her head at Cam's behavior a lot—when she wasn't ready to murder him, that was.

On the day after they'd climbed Ada Tor, while still reeling from their near-kiss, she had been horrified to see him up on the half-built scaffolding being put up around one of the oaks on the green. Then, the next day, she'd come into the surgery to find not only that Cam had beaten her to work for a change, but that the reception area was packed to the rafters with boxes, as well.

"What on earth is all this?"

It had taken everything inside her to keep her voice below a shriek—especially when she'd spied the cobwebs liberally festooning the cartons.

"Decorations," he'd said, with just a hint of smugness in his voice. "I checked the calendar and, since we don't have any patients today, I figured it was the perfect time to bring them down. Don't look so annoyed."

Annoyed? She'd been livid.

But then he'd added, "It's a part of being Laird. I have to set a good example. And I hope, as my employee, you'll see fit to help me."

So she'd been stuck. How could she have refused without looking as truculent as she'd felt?

The kicker was she'd enjoyed it—once she'd gotten over her snit. Even being hyperaware of his movements, of every accidental touch of their fingers or his body brushing past hers, she'd found herself relaxing into the joy of bringing Christmas to the surgery.

The decorations were a mixed bag: some obviously old, some new, some elegant, others as chintzy as they came. But Cam had a story for almost all of them.

It had taken them most of the day to get most of them set up, with a break for lunch at Sanjit's restaurant. Cam's grandmother's porcelain Christmas village, dating from the fifties, delicately beautiful, had been placed on a shelf where it could be admired out of reach of little hands. His grand-da's collection of Christmas greetings cards from around the world had been strung on lengths of tinsel along one wall. An impressive nutcracker collection had ended up liberally covering almost every surface possible in the surgery, and paper festoons were hung all over the ceiling, with old-fashioned lanterns in between.

They'd argued over the placement of those, with Cam wanting to put them up willy-nilly and Harmony insisting on a more regulated design. She'd won, of course, and he'd been forced to admit that it looked better than he'd have ever imagined.

"The Christmas trees are coming in a couple of days by ferry," he'd told her, when she'd asked what he wanted to do with the tree ornaments. "We'll get that done up once I pick one out."

Spending that time with him had been so much fun, but in a strange way seeing him like that, being in close proximity with him again for an entire day, had also felt dangerous. Both the trip to the Carstairs' farm and their working together to decorate had taken him out of the "hunky doctor fantasy material" zone into something more intimate.

She kept replaying that moment she'd thought he would kiss her in her mind, telling herself she wouldn't have let it happen, but knowing she would have given in to her own desire. To her own chagrin she wanted to experience his kisses—and more.

That evening, curled up in front of the fireplace, Harmony had realized just how much she was starting to *like* Cam on top of being physically attracted to him. She liked his enthusiasm. The way he wasn't afraid to go head to head with her, but how he also backed down once he realized she just might be right. His tenderness as he'd brought out his grandparents' favorite decorations and told her their stories had touched something deep inside her.

Her ex, Logan, was the ultimate pragmatist. The

kind of serious man who thought everything through and then announced the way things would go. He wasn't sentimental in the slightest, and he'd shied away from anything that even remotely resembled emotion even when they were alone. She'd thought him safe and steady, only to have him prove otherwise.

Somehow she was sure everything would be different with a man like Cameron MacRurie. It was there in his eyes. In the way he listened so intently when she was talking. In his smile...in his speech...even in the way he moved. The kind of man he was called out to the secret self she alone knew: the romantic, sensual side of her she rarely acknowledged.

And that secret part of herself wanted Cam—badly.

But, she reminded herself, Cam was a daredevil, a risk taker and, like her father, he appeared to turn a blind eye to a medical condition that could cause serious damage if not managed properly. Worse, it could be deadly.

As a nurse she knew she was being unreasonable about Cam's diabetes. With all the new ways of treating and managing type 1, people with the disease were living fuller lives than ever before.

However, as a woman, and one who knew what it was like to lose someone because they refused to accept their limitations, Cam was the last kind of man she needed in her life. Getting close to people just led to heartbreak, in her opinion.

Meeting him had had her thinking of her father more often than she usually does, drawing comparisons that made her both angry and sad. And no doubt having just lost Gran contributed to her general train of thought.

As the December first opening of the Winter Festival fast approached, the entire island was like a beehive, with everyone buzzing to get everything in place. Vendors were starting to arrive, and Harmony had been surprised at the number of people suddenly on the island, all pitching in.

Not even the rain, which came hard and fast one afternoon, deterred the workers for long.

"Come on, come on!"

The CIs took refuge in the surgery as the thunderstorm rolled overhead, and Dora was not pleased at the delay.

"Telling the storm to hurry won't make it pass any faster," Katherine commented helpfully, and then took a sip of her tea. "Besides, for once we're ahead of schedule. Relax for a moment."

"Hush!" Ingrid interjected, as herself, Dora, and Sela all gave the other woman dirty looks. "You'll jinx us."

Just then Cam came in, his hair soaked, his shirt damp enough to cling to his chest and arms. Harmony hurriedly looked away, his delectability quotient making her mouth water. Rising, she to the back and got him a towel, just as one of the CIs asked what on earth he'd been doing to get so wet.

"Got caught with just my windbreaker on," he said, taking the towel and giving Harmony a smile that almost melted her on the spot. "Gave my hooded anorak to one of the lads from the mainland who didn't have one. I have another at home."

Another reason to like him—although there were so many others screaming at her to keep her distance.

"I'm glad you're here, ladies. There's something I want to discuss with you."

Harmony wasn't sure whether he was including her or not, but Cam didn't tell her to come with the others when they trooped into his office, so she stayed where she was, feeling ridiculously put out.

It wasn't as though she was *involved* in the preparations for the festival. In fact, other than the surgery decor she'd done her level best to stay out of it. Although watching it all happen around her had made her realize what a Scrooge she was being. Everyone else, from the oldest to the youngest, was lending a hand, and excited about it too.

Even her shut-ins wanted to hear every detail of what was happening in the village. Mr. Harris, in particular, had been talking her ear off about how things had been done "in the old Laird's time."

"All this hullabaloo about scaffolding around the trees to hang the lights? Not in our day! We'd shinny up those trees like squirrels and string the lights that way."

"Now, Da," his son Martin had said, sending Harmony a wry smile. "You have to admit the trees were smaller back then."

"Och, not so much smaller. And there was that big old oak that came down in the storm of seventy-two. She was a grand old tree—taller than any of them left there now!"

"Will you come to see all the lights, Mr. Harris?"

Harmony had just finished doing the older man's wellness check, noting that his oxygen saturation levels were fairly good and the edema in his feet was reduced. He'd been diagnosed with level two congestive heart failure just over a year ago, but had continued to work on the family farm until he'd fallen one day while out looking for lambs. After that, his son had put his foot down—although, he admitted, keeping his father in was like herding cats.

Cam had told her that Martin had gotten a gaggle of geese and put his father in charge of those, to make sure he had something to do that was close to the house.

"Of course." He'd sounded outraged that she'd suggested otherwise. "Wouldn't be Christmas without seeing the fair and all the lights and the gewgaws people put up, would it?"

Harmony was brought back to the present when she heard Dora clearly through the closed office door.

"It's not possible, Cam. Not at this late stage."

Then came a babble of voices, and a few shushing sounds, all of which left Harmony eaten up with curiosity. So much so that she was tempted to put her ear to the door—an impulse she was ashamed of immediately thereafter.

"'Eavesdroppers hear no good of themselves,'" she muttered, once more quoting her Gran, who'd been full of annoying sayings.

Oh, great, this place is turning me into my grandmother.

Thankfully, just then the door opened, giving her something else to concentrate on.

"Hello, miss," said a Christmas tree with legs, coming into the surgery. "Just dropping this off for the Laird. I'll leave it here, by the door, if that's okay with you?"

"Yes, that should be fine," she said, eyeing the huge fir as the man carrying it finally extricated himself from its grasp.

The ceilings in the surgery were high, but she wondered if it would fit or if, like in a Christmas comedy, they'd have to cut a hole up to the second floor to accommodate it. Trust Cam to choose the biggest tree of them all!

The CIs came out of Cam's office like a tornado, with Dora in the center. She was scowling, but Harmony thought the twinkle in her eyes looked rather danger-ously amused.

"Good—the rain's stopped. Back at it, ladies. Espe-cially since the Laird has added to our plate. Harmony, I'll see you over at the Manor this evening, right?"

Surprised, Harmony was about to say she didn't know what Dora was talking about when Cam quickly replied, "Yes, she'll be there."

Then the CIs were off, already bickering again.

"What's going on at the Manor tonight?"

"Progress meeting and the Manor's tree-decorating and lighting. I like for everyone to have a hand in it and see all the decorations before the craziness starts in earnest," he said, heading for the surgery Christ-mas tree. He whistled. "She's a beauty, isn't she? Not as magnificent as the Manor tree, of course, but per-fect for in here."

"Don't you think it's a bit big? And when did you plan to tell me about tonight?"

Cam was rummaging in a box and emerged, trium-phant, with the tree stand before he replied, "It's the perfect size—and I thought the CIs would have told you, so I didn't bother."

He shrugged apologetically.

Did he have to look so adorable doing that? she won-dered, inexplicably annoyed.

They spent the rest of the afternoon putting up the tree—which was only just short enough for the star to fit at the top. It took both of them to wrestle the tree into the stand, and then Harmony went to get water to fill the receptacle while Cam cut away the netting holding the boughs against the trunk.

"Don't put the water in yet," he said, pulling the tree a little farther from the wall. "We're going to have to decorate the side that'll be seen through the window and then push it over. The water will make it heavier and harder to move."

They argued over the lights.

"If you wrap some close to the trunk, and then more at the edges, you'll get better depth of light," she said.

"*Depth of light?* What on earth does that mean?" he asked, his lips quirking.

"I can't believe you're the Laird of the North Pole of Scotland and don't understand that most basic of concepts."

He rolled his eyes, but gave in eventually. Of course then they argued about whether the white lights or the colored should go near the trunk, but she gave in on that one and they put the colored ones inside and white outside.

As they took out ornaments and placed them on the tree they looked specifically for those related to the Winter Festival theme of "love."

Finding a tattered but beautiful little heart made of felt, with an intricate design embroidered in the center, Harmony held it up. "This is perfect. A little stained, but right in line with the theme."

"Wow," Cam said, holding out his hand for her to give it to him. "I haven't seen this in years. The design is like a luckenbooth—a traditional Scottish betrothal gift. My grandmother made it, and Grand-Da used to put it on the tree in the Manor. I wonder how it got in with these?"

Instead of putting it on the tree, Cam slipped it into his pocket and Harmony's chest ached, just a little, when she noticed him touching the spot where he'd secreted it every now and again.

Later, after they'd finished decorating the tree and

tidying up, he said he was going back to the Manor. When, a few minutes later, she saw him crossing the green, she knew he was going to the churchyard, as he so often did, to visit with his grandfather.

Why that should make her like him even more—*want* him even more—she didn't dare consider.

CHAPTER TEN

"WELL, GRAND-DA, EVERYTHING seems to be going smoothly, for a change. The trees are strung, the shops and roadways are decorated, and the firs all came in without incident. Remember that one year when they didn't get loaded onto the ferry?"

Cam had the churchyard to himself, as he usually did, but he was stooping at his grandfather's headstone since he'd forgotten to bring anything to wipe off the bench. It wasn't unusual for him to come by and give Grand-Da updates on his life, but today was different. He'd started with the mundane because the specific felt too hard.

"Tonight is Manor night. The place looks beautiful, as always. Got a really nice tree this year. I think you'd be pleased."

Despite his inviting her a few more times since his *faux pas*, Harmony still hadn't been up to the Manor. In a way he was glad, since she'd be seeing it at its best tonight. On the other hand he was nervous. He wanted her to like it, even love it, the way he always had.

Running his finger over his grandfather's name, Cam forced himself to get to the point.

Grand-Da had always hated prevarication.

Get to the point, son.

Cam could hear his grand-da's voice in his head, the tone a mixture of annoyance and amusement. He'd always been able to talk to the old man about anything, although sometimes it had taken a while for it to come out, since Cam had been used to keeping his own counsel about a lot of things.

"I..." He cleared his throat and tried again. "Harmony found the heart. The one Gran made for you the first Christmas you were together. I don't know how it got into the boxes in the surgery, or why I never noticed it was missing."

It made him remember the story Grand-Da had told, about meeting Gran in London, knowing right away that he wanted to marry her. Gran hadn't been interested. She'd had other plans.

She was a city girl, your Gran. Had no interest in a Scottish country lad—doctor or no. Oh, she gave me a merry chase, and I had to seduce her around to my way of thinking, but I knew there would never be another like her in my life. If she hadn't eventually had me I'd be a lonely old man now. Instead I always have her love to keep me company.

It was as though he was sitting in front of the fire again with Grand-Da, chuckling to himself over the story. He'd been too young then to appreciate the strength and depths of true love. Yet the tale had always touched him, deep inside, and now to suddenly have it come back...

"Are you trying to tell me something, Grand-Da?" he asked aloud.

Cam was a man of science, but there were times like this when he had to wonder about greater forces and how they could manifest in life.

He didn't *want* to want Harmony. Didn't believe real

love could blossom in the space of less than three weeks. Yet the draw she exerted, the mix of comfort and excitement he felt in her presence, was unprecedented in his experience. And when he'd seen that heart in her hand, that gorgeous, beaming smile, her eyes alight with pleasure, something had shifted inside him. A sea change of the soul.

"She's my employee, Grand-Da, and she's bossy. Plus, she's not at all into adventuring. I think it scares her."

The first was a sticking point, but the second he really didn't mind. In fact, he rather liked arguing with Harmony. She was logical, and forthright, and didn't hesitate to give as good as she got—which made it all fun.

The third point, however, was a bad one.

His friend Josh had sent him a video of a group BASE jumping with wingsuits. One of the men had been wearing a helmet cam and the footage as they arrowed along the side of the mountain was amazing. Josh had suggested they learn, and make it a part of their next adventure trip, and Cam had been researching equipment and locations when Harmony had come in to ask him a question.

She'd taken one look at the video playing on his computer and had frozen, her lips tightening, those lines between her brows suddenly appearing.

"Looks like fun, doesn't it?" he'd asked.

"No."

It had come out so forcefully, it had taken him aback.

"It looks like craziness. The type of stupidity that can get people killed."

Then she'd turned and walked out, apparently forgetting what it was she'd come for, or so disturbed she hadn't been able to bear to stay in the room.

"She's not for me, Grand-Da. I won't be hemmed in by anyone again. I need someone who'll want to go on adventures with me—not nag me to take care of myself, or get bent out of shape every time I want to do something fun."

It was just the wind rustling through the branches, but it sounded suspiciously like Grand-Da's laugh.

"Right—enough of this," Cam said, levering to his feet. "I'll just put it all out of my mind, get through the festival and send her on her way again."

It felt good to have made the decision, but he found he'd taken the heart out of his pocket, was holding it in the palm of his hand.

For a moment he thought about leaving the heart on Grand-Da's headstone, but instead he put it gently back into the pocket of his coat. He'd never known his grandmother, who'd died the year he was born, but suddenly he felt closer to her, handling something she'd made. A piece of her heart in the form of a heart.

Touching Grand-Da's stone one more time, he went over to Grandma's and touched it too.

And when he left the churchyard he felt both at peace and more confused than when he got there.

"First time at the Manor?" Dora asked Harmony as they stood to one side in the Manor's ballroom, each juggling a little plate of hors d'oeuvres and a drink.

"That obvious? I'm gawping, aren't I?"

And who could blame her? Everything about the house made her want to gasp. It might have been converted to a hotel, but it had lost none of its charm or its grandeur. For goodness' sakes, it had a real, live ballroom, complete with intricate parquet flooring, plaster swags on the walls and ceilings, and massive gold mirrors, which reflected the bank of windows on the other side of the room.

"I think we all did the first time we got a chance to see inside the manor," Katherine replied. "It's a thing of beauty."

Harmony couldn't argue with that assessment. She'd had an Elizabeth-Bennett-sees-Pemberley moment the first time she'd glimpsed Rurie Manor, but she'd have never imagined how truly glorious the inside of the old house would be.

"When Cam told me most of it was a hotel I pictured them having gutted the place to modernize it and make it usable, but they've really kept all the lovely old features and atmosphere, haven't they?"

"Oh, yes," Sela agreed. "The Manor has been lucky in her custodians. The MacRurie family has kept it wonderfully. And in this day and age that's no small feat."

"The family has always been smart about it," Ingrid said, gesturing with a piece of celery for emphasis. "I think it was Cam's great-grandfather who turned it into a corporation and a trust, so they could avoid a lot of death duties and keep the place running. Not that they were lacking in funds. They all have that entrepreneurial and inventive streak in them, so they weren't dependent on inheritances alone."

"Really?" This was another facet of Cam's family coming to light for Harmony, and she couldn't hide her curiosity.

Dora nodded, swallowing a bite of cake before elaborating. "Cam's however many times great-grandfather—the first one to come here—was a train baron, who had a number of patents for various parts and equipment the railroads used. And the old Laird—Cam's grand-father—invented some kind of... What was it, girls?"

"A valve," Katherine supplied.

"Yes—a valve for a nebulizer machine to make it work better. And Cam's got a few patents himself...for safety equipment, I believe."

"He needs it," Harmony said, hearing the snap in her own voice and regretting it the moment she'd spoken.

Dora gave her a bump with her hip—Harmony assumed because she didn't have a hand free to swat her with.

"He's adventurous—but that's a good thing in a man, isn't it? Who wants an old fuddy-duddy?"

Harmony would have argued the point, except the topic of their conversation chose that moment to come over to where they were standing.

"Everyone having a good time?" he asked, with one of those smiles that never failed to make Harmony's knees weak. "Had enough to eat? Put an ornament or three on the tree?"

"I don't think that poor tree can take even one more bit of decorating, Cam. Especially the spot where the children were standing."

His smile turned to a grin. "Yeah, that side's looking a little heavy low down, but they had a grand time doing it."

"Have you taken Harmony on the tour yet?" Dora asked—a little too innocently to Harmony's ears.

"No, I thought I'd wait until things calm down a bit. I have to make my rounds and keep things flowing."

"You don't have to—"

What should have been a polite declining of the tour earned her another hip-bump from Dora and a poke in the back from Katherine to boot.

ANN McINTOSH   103

"What?" she asked, since what they'd done was obvious. "Cam's been running around like a chicken with its head cut off. He doesn't need to give me a tour if he doesn't want to."

Cam rolled his eyes. "Just keep her here until things quiet down and I'll be back to get her," he said to the CIs, adding, "Don't let her slip away. You know she'll probably try."

"Back at you," Sela muttered behind Harmony's back.

And before Harmony could ask the other woman what, exactly, she meant by that, the CIs started arguing about the configuration of the vendors' caravans parked in the field behind the green and the moment was lost.

Every time she tried to give the CIs the slip and get out of there before the end of the party she was foiled. She didn't know why she was so resistant to getting a tour of the house from Cam. Okay, that was a lie. She didn't want to be alone with him right now. Not after seeing him so carefully putting that felt heart into his pocket, with a hint of deeply held emotion that had just melted her heart.

Gorgeous Cam in a wetsuit could be used as fantasy fodder. Dr. Cam could be treated strictly as an employer. Daredevil Cam could be firmly held at bay. But tender Cam? Sentimental Cam, who had immediately gone off to speak to his grand-da after she'd found that little ornament?

That Cam might well be irresistible, and Harmony knew her limitations.

But he wouldn't take no for an answer. As the staff were cleaning up, and the CIs were saying their goodbyes, he firmly guided her back into the hotel and took her through it completely. Even the kitchens, and upstairs to see the guest bedrooms.

Everywhere was beautifully decorated for the holidays, and lit in such a way as to enhance the best features of the house and its ornamentation.

"Rurie Manor is beautiful, Cam. Even the kitchens."

He laughed softly, taking her elbow to lead her back to the staircase. Just that small touch had heat pooling low in her belly. His obvious love of the house his ancestors had lived in and cared for all those years was patent, and she liked him even more for it. There was no hint of him taking it for granted, or being in any way anything but appreciative of being able to live there and oversee its upkeep.

"My ancestors loved Victorian splendor—even the later ones—so whenever there were renovations or updates to be done they naturally leaned in that direction. I'm not complaining, though. They really tried their hardest to keep the best features of the house."

"They did a wonderful job—and I can see you're carrying on the tradition."

At the foot of the grand staircase he hesitated. From farther down the hall she could hear staff talking softly, the clink of crockery and glassware, and the sound of a trolley being wheeled across the floor. There was the front door, just a matter of feet away, and Harmony knew she should make her departure. But she didn't.

The warmth of his hand on her arm, the fresh, warm scent of him, the way his gaze traced her face, all conspired to keep her there.

"Would you like to see my little corner of the Manor?"

No smile on his face. His voice low and serious.

Harmony's world tilted, leaving her unsteady, frightened, and she knew that a decision lay before her like the drop off a cliff.

Walk away and stay safe or step over?

Would she fly or plummet?

"I don't know that I should," she said, being honest, hearing the anxiety she was fighting echoing in her voice. Or was it the rush of desire through her veins making it quiver that way?

Cam's fingers shifted on her arm and he stepped a little closer. Without thought she moved to meet him, so they were only a hand span apart.

"It probably wouldn't be wise," he agreed, even as his head dipped toward her and her lips rose in invitation.

The kiss was light at first, an exploration, but it went to Harmony's head like a shot of one hundred percent proof rum. Firm lips searched hers, drawing her closer, setting her alight with a wild surge of arousal. Her arms went around his neck instinctively, and his encircled her waist, pulling her flush against his chest. The sound he made low in his throat washed through her—a benediction and a promise, all wrapped into one.

Deepening the kiss felt inevitable. Right and true to what was growing inside her. But the force of it almost knocked her off her feet. Clinging to him, she surrendered to the fire, taking his scent into her lungs with each rushed inhalation, her body tightening and softening all at once.

When he broke the kiss, lifted his head, she kept her eyes closed a little longer, savoring the untamable zing of passion discovered as it thrummed beneath her skin.

Finally forcing open lids that felt weighed down with need, she found herself trapped in his gaze, and the gleam of his desire, the rapt, stark lines of his face, let her know she wasn't alone in the wanting.

Then common sense crashed the party. And although she wished with all her heart she could just show it to the door, she knew she wouldn't.

Cam must have seen it on her face, because he sighed gently and brushed a finger over her cheek.

"Did you drive?" he asked.

"No," she replied, regretfully sliding her arms down from around his neck. Although her hands didn't seem to want to let him go, coming to rest on his broad chest. The feel of his racing heart beneath her fingertips almost made her change her mind about going.

"I'll walk you down," he said.

"Okay."

She couldn't help hoping he might kiss her goodnight. And he did better than that, kissing her silly in the apartment foyer, just inside the door.

Harmony lost herself in his arms. Every sipping kiss, each deeper exploration of her mouth, each brush of his hands, which had somehow found their way under her coat, dragging her under.

"You're delicious," he said into her neck, his voice muffled by the fur collar of her coat. "I should go before I can't."

"Yes, you should," she agreed, dragging his mouth back to hers, aware of the dichotomy of her words and actions.

She didn't want him to go. That much was obvious. But how much further was she willing to take this?

Letting him go, taking a step back, was the hardest thing she'd ever done, but somehow she achieved it.

"This is *so* not a good idea." She swallowed, trying to sound normal when every nerve in her body was tingling, her libido gone haywire. "You're my boss."

Cam's eyes were dark, his pupils so dilated they

looked black, and when he scrubbed his fingers through his hair she saw his frustration.

Then one corner of his mouth kicked up. "Your temporary boss."

A huff of amusement escaped her throat, although there was nothing laughable about the situation. "True, but…"

She wanted to say she wasn't into casual sex, and that he wasn't the kind of man she'd ever get involved with otherwise. Wanted to list the complications their sleeping together might cause to a working relationship. Probably point out that there was no way they could sneak around without the entire island knowing what was happening.

Yet none of it crossed her lips. Mainly because it didn't seem terribly important just then.

"Look," he said, holding up both hands as though in surrender. "I know neither of us planned on this happening, but I'm not averse to us…*enjoying* each other while you're here."

Harmony thought about what he'd said. The temporary nature of it should be a turn-off, but strangely it wasn't.

Cam MacRurie wasn't the kind of man she'd ever get seriously involved with. He was too much like her father—a reckless adventure-seeker, who didn't take his medical condition seriously enough. She might have been young when her father died, but she remembered the turmoil, the pain both her mum and herself had gone through. It had shattered their world, left them devastated and emotionally scarred.

No, she realized. If she was going to be able to enjoy whatever this was sparking electricity between them, it would have to be with the inner understanding of the relationship's transient nature. Once she embraced that she'd be okay, because then she wouldn't get emotionally involved.

And, man, did she want to enjoy Cam. He was a temptation she hadn't expected and didn't want to resist. Her entire body reacted to the thought, and in that instant her mind was made up.

Slipping past him, she started up the stairs, and when he didn't follow she turned her head to look at him over her shoulder.

"Aren't you coming up?"

CHAPTER ELEVEN

HE KNEW HE shouldn't go up to her apartment. Despite what he'd said to her, Cam knew he was probably already in over his head. Making love to Harmony might just drown him. But in the back of his mind his grand-da's words rang.

Being afraid is never a good reason not to do something, son. It's a reason to consider whatever you're about to do carefully, but not a good reason to avoid trying.

Harmony frightened him badly. The way he felt when he was with her, worse when he held her in his arms, was beyond any sensation he'd ever known. It made him want to run, to avoid going deeper, and yet she was irresistible.

So he followed her gently swaying hips up the stairs, his arousal climbing with each step he took, anticipation sparking along his spine as he watched her slip off her coat.

Earlier that evening he'd noticed how her red sweater gave her skin a beautiful glow, had thought it was the perfect color for her. Now all he wanted was to get rid of it, so as to get to the golden skin beneath.

The lure of the unknown was heady.

What kind of lover would she be?

The need to know was like a fire in his soul, a kind of insanity he couldn't wait to embrace.

She was fitting the key into the door when he came up behind her on the landing. He couldn't keep his hands off her, and encircled her waist from the back, nuzzling her hair aside to set his lips on her neck.

Harmony shivered, a little moan breaking in her throat. Encouraged, he kissed and licked, scraping his teeth gently over the frantic pulse. When her head fell back against his shoulder, giving him better access, Cam took full advantage.

Then she had the door open and they shuffled into the hallway, his arms still around her, his mouth still on her skin.

"Cam…"

God, the breathiness in her voice almost undid him. He turned her in his arms, ravenous for her mouth again. The urgency he was fighting seemed matched by her own. Tugging and pulling, breaking away from each other's mouths only long enough to get her sweater off over her head, they were soon stripped to the waist.

He picked her up, and she wrapped her legs around his hips as he carried her through the darkness to her bed. They tumbled onto it, locked together, as though fused by passion.

Now—now he could explore that luscious body the way he'd wanted to the very first time he set eyes on her.

He took his time, despite his driving need, slowly removing the rest of her clothes, touching, kissing, caressing each inch of her body as he did so. She did the same to him, rolling him onto his back and straddling his thighs to get at his fly.

There was a moment of shared laughter as they realized he still had his boots on and, now they were trapped in his trousers, he couldn't reach them. She levered them off, then removed his socks. Tugging off his trousers, she began a slow rise up along his legs, teasing him the way he'd teased her.

After a very short time Cam sat up to yank her against his chest.

"Why'd you stop me?" she asked.

But he knew she knew why, because she was making him crazy, and he told her so, receiving another long, passionate kiss in response.

Lying side by side, they discovered each other's weak spots, the places and touches that made the breath catch, the body tremble, that had moans and soft cries of pleasure filling the room.

Their passion built, but Cam wouldn't be rushed, and when she tried to hurry him along he captured her roving, unrelenting hands and held them above her head.

"Behave."

It was a hoarse rumble, and the sound she made in response made his body tighten even more.

"I don't think that's really what you want, is it?" she replied, twisting her wrists between his fingers and arching her back so her breasts rubbed back and forth against his chest.

"No," he admitted. "But I want to take my time, to make it good for you, Harmony."

She froze, and in the dim light filtering through the curtain he saw her eyes close for a moment.

When they opened she'd quieted, and she said, "Kiss me again, Cam."

He'd never been happier to comply with a request in his life.

Sinking into the sensation of mouth on mouth, the sweet tangle of her tongue with his, was as natural as inhaling. When he released her wrists and her hands found his body again—gentler now, not as insistent—the sweep of them across his skin set his nerve endings afire.

Coming up for breath, he didn't know whether minutes or hours had passed—knew only that the desire he'd thought so intense before had grown exponentially, become impossible to contain.

Rolling to the side of the bed, he searched along the ground with his hands. Harmony snuggled up to his back, wrapping a leg over his, her lips weaving magic spells along his nape and across his shoulders.

She paused long enough to ask, "What are you doing?"

"Trying to find my trousers. I have a condom in my wallet."

"Mmm…" She was back at her sorcery, shifting behind him, her mouth following the line of his spine, her hand fluttering over his stomach and heading south.

With a harsh sound of triumph he found his clothes, dragged them toward him. Fumbling for his wallet, he had to pause to grab her hand, lest she make him lose control.

She giggled and he rolled over, trapping her beneath his body. "You're a bad, bad girl."

Harmony blinked up at him. "And you like it, don't you?"

No need to answer. She knew he more than liked it.

Keeping her still as best he could, he fished out the condom.

"Want me to put it on?" she asked.

"Oh, hell, no. That would finish me off."

She laughed softly again, and replied, "No finishing without me."

He couldn't help laughing with her as he rolled away

to put on the condom—and she was waiting, arms outstretched, when he rolled back.

"Are you sure you're ready?" he asked. The need to make it perfect for her was paramount in his mind.

"Come here" was her only reply, and she suited actions to words, drawing him close, welcoming him into her body.

And of course he obeyed, finally where he'd dreamt of being since the day Harmony Kinkaid had landed on Eilean Rurie.

In her bed and in her arms.

Harmony awoke the morning after the Manor party alone. Cam had left before daylight, and although she hadn't wanted him to go, she knew her time on the island would be far more complicated if he didn't. People tended to look askance at women who slept with their bosses.

Not that it worried her overly much. December was a stone's throw away, the festival set to begin. By the end of January she'd be gone, and whatever gossip and ill feelings they might inspire with their affair would die down quickly once she left. She was more than willing to deal with the fallout for a couple of months if she could keep seeing Cam.

The night had been amazing. Magical, in a way. At least for her. Who knew that laughter could add such a new dimension to sex? Logan had been as businesslike in bed as he was in every other facet of life.

Funny to know that she'd felt closer to Cam, more connected, than she ever had with a man she'd spent two years with. It came from knowing Cam MacRurie cared—actually cared about her experience rather than just his own.

When Logan had dropped his bombshell she'd been more angry than hurt, which had made her question her motives for being with him to begin with. It had become comfortable, and his staid demeanor had seemed to make him the perfect partner. Yet, in the end his defection hadn't broken her heart as much as dented her pride.

Being with Cam seemed risky—way outside her comfort zone in a million ways—but since it was preordained to last only for a short time, she could simply enjoy his company without too much angst.

Checking the time, she hopped out of bed and into the shower, smiling to herself at a few unusually achy muscles, all an indication of how thoroughly loved she'd been the night before.

Her phone rang right on time, and Harmony hurried to pick it up.

"Hi, Mum. Everything all right?"

"Yes, yes," her mum replied, as she always did.

Sometimes Harmony wondered what her mother wasn't sharing, perhaps in an effort not to distress her daughter.

"You sound bright and cheerful this morning."

Harmony stifled the chuckle rising in her throat. "It's a beautiful day here, and last night there was a party up at the Manor. I had a good time."

"Hmm…" Her mother didn't sound convinced. "Are things still crazy there with the festival? No chance of you coming to Yorkshire over the holidays? Even for a couple of days?"

"No, Mum." Why did her mother keep trying to rope her into her Yorkshire trip? "I'll have to be here for the duration. There's supposed to be hundreds of people coming through, and although Cam says there'll be additional medical help on hand, he and I will still be the first line of defense."

"Okay, okay. It's just…"

There was a wistful tone to her mum's voice…a sorrow Harmony felt down to her toes.

"It's just what, Mum?"

"Oh, nothing important. Tell me more about what's going on there."

Lowering herself to the edge of the bed, Harmony said, "No, Mum. Tell me what's making you sad. I'm not a baby anymore, who needs to be protected. I want to know."

There was a long silence, and when her mum spoke next Harmony knew she was near tears, if not already crying.

"It's just that I miss you…and the closer it gets to Christmas, the harder it gets."

"Oh, Mum. I miss you too. But you have your trip to look forward to, and Fred to keep you company…"

"But it's not the same. I was dreading Christmas, and I didn't feel up to any of the things we used to do, but now…"

How could she have been so blinded by her own grief and hurt as not to realize that her mum probably didn't know how to face the holidays without Gran? After all, she'd felt the same way when her mum had said she wouldn't be at home for Christmas, but she hadn't had the brains to make the connection then.

Harmony's heart hurt, and tears were filling her eyes to slip down her face. But she knew she had to be strong for her mother—just as her mum had been strong for her all these years.

"Listen, Mum. I know you miss Gran, but she wouldn't want you be wallowing in grief. I can almost hear her saying, *Lawks, who turned on de tap?* if she knew you were crying over her."

It made her mum laugh through her tears, the way Harmony had known it would, to hear Harmony impersonate her grandmother.

"I know nothing is the same this year," she continued gently. "But maybe it's time for you to think about *you*, to figure out what's best for you rather than anyone else. Start a new tradition...teach Fred how to bake a Christmas cake. I don't have the answers, and I'm so sorry I'm not there for you when you need me, but I love you and I want you to be okay."

"Thank you, love," her mum said, after a little pause and what sounded like a blowing of her nose. "You're right, you know. Even if you'd been here it still wouldn't have been the same, and we might have ended up moping around instead of enjoying any of it. And haven't I always been the one telling you to go off and live your own life? But here I am...crying because you've done just that."

"This job is only temporary, Mum." Why did this reminder to her mother make her suddenly feel even more depressed? "I'll be back before you can convert my room into whatever you've been planning all these years."

That earned her a heartier chuckle than her mum had been able to manage before, and they finished their conversation on a lighter note than when it had started.

But Harmony's heart was still heavy as she finished getting ready and headed off downstairs to open up the clinic. Although, the secretive intimate smile Cam gave her when he came in a few minutes later did a lot to lift her mood.

Though the smile on his face faded, concern darkening his eyes. "What's wrong?" he asked, his gaze searching hers.

She didn't know why, but it made her smile. "Don't worry, it's not remorse over a wild night."

He visibly relaxed, coming over to perch on the edge of her desk, lifting a gentle finger to touch her cheek. "Wild, huh? Not sure how to take that. But don't change the subject. You've been crying."

How on earth did he know that, when she'd been careful to use an extra touch of concealer under her eyes to camouflage the signs?

"I was talking to my mum and I realized what an insensitive beast I've been."

He was so easy to talk to, with his eyes never leaving hers, all his concentration on what she was saying as it all poured out of her.

"How could I not realize how much harder it would be for *her*, this first Christmas without Gran?" she concluded, trying her best not to let the tears start up again.

"You're dealing with your own grief," he said, his hand on her shoulder providing more comfort than a simple touch should. "It's made it hard to see that her grief is what made her agree to go to Yorkshire with Fred. All you saw was her abandoning you, and the loss of all the things that meant Christmas to you."

"You're right," she agreed, miserable again.

"Harmony, come into my office and away from the windows. I think you need a hug, and if I give you one here then I may as well have slept all night in that wonderful bed of yours."

She chuckled, but got up, wanting that hug in the worst way.

"Wonderful, was it?" she teased, as she followed

him into the office and watched him close the door behind them.

"Or wild, if you prefer," he retorted, enveloping her in his arms, taking her weight as she leaned against him.

At once she was more relaxed, and muscles she hadn't even realized were tight unraveled in the warmth of his embrace.

"Either one works for me," she mumbled, wishing they could go upstairs and do a hands-on assessment of which adjective worked better.

If she wasn't careful, she warned herself, Cam would turn her into a sex addict, and the withdrawal symptoms when she left would be horrendous.

CHAPTER TWELVE

"HARMONY, YOU HAVE to help me!"

Hearing Dora's near shout on the other end of the line made Harmony's heart-rate go into overdrive.

"What's wrong? Are you hurt? Where are you?"

"I'm at home. Come quickly."

"Do you need Cam?"

He was out, checking on a visitor who'd fallen off his scooter earlier in the afternoon, leaving Harmony to close up the clinic. She hoped she could deal with whatever it was happening to Dora.

"No, no. Just you. Hurry!"

Grabbing her jacket and a medical kit from the back, Harmony swiftly locked up the surgery. Normally in an emergency she'd drive, although Dora's house was only a short way away, but with the number of people on the roads, and walking all over the place, it would be a lot quicker to walk.

Or in this case trot—which was what she did, weaving her way through the throngs of visitors.

Hard to believe it was already midway through December, with the Winter Festival in full swing. Harder yet for Harmony to reconcile the sleepy little village she'd first seen on arrival with the wonderland it had become.

The lights, banners, decorations, and Christmas trees

in every window gave the village a truly festive air. And it wasn't just the village. A night drive around the island revealed light-encrusted fences, trees, and houses, a variety of seasonal lawn decor, and even a forest of firs in a field, all lit up and open to the public to walk through.

"Angus Stewart does that every year," Cam had told her. "He tried growing a grove of firs, but the soil was wrong, so instead he buys the trees and sets them up like a miniature forest. And right in the center he has baskets of rowan and a stack of Cailleach logs for anyone who wants burn them in his nightly bonfire."

"Cailleach logs?" she'd asked, bewildered. "What are those? And why burn the rowan?"

"Cailleach is also known as the Hag of Winter. It's an old tradition to carve her face on a log and then burn it to banish the cold, the darkness, and any coming hardship. The rowan is supposed to burn away any hard feelings between friends or family members."

Every day she learned something new. When she'd first heard about the festival she'd pictured something far less elaborate—although, to be fair, Cam *had* tried to warn her from the beginning.

On the other side of the green the fair grounds were a mass of people all day, and up until it closed at ten at night. She'd been twice already—once with the CIs and again with Cam—and she'd likened it to a cross between a Renaissance fair and a long, ongoing party. While she'd politely passed on the haggis, she'd enjoyed the Yule bread and the clootie pudding.

"It similar to a Jamaican Christmas pudding," she'd told the CIs. "But blander. Ours has rum, and a lot more fruit. My gran kept her fruit soaking in rum and wine all year long, so as to have it ready for Christmas."

The CIs had exchanged strange looks over that tidbit,

but Harmony hadn't been able to get them to say why. Maybe it sounded alien to them—just as things like the Cailleach and neeps and nips did to her. It was a whole different world, but she was loving it.

Especially since Cam, as the Laird, had lately taken to wearing a kilt.

It was easy now to see why women went bonkers over men in kilts. With his calves on full display, and the green, red and gold tartan swinging when he walked, he looked delicious!

Finally getting to Dora's cottage, she raced up the path to knock on the door. It was flung open, and a frazzled-looking Dora dragged her inside.

"Thank goodness you're here."

She hadn't released Harmony's arm, just continued to pull her through the living area toward the kitchen, her cat meowing and weaving between their legs. Meanwhile, Harmony was trying to assess whether Dora had an injury anywhere. With her strange behavior, maybe she'd fallen and hit her head?

"I need help."

"With what? Are you hurt?"

They got to the kitchen and Dora pointed inside, the picture of tragedy personified.

"Mince pies!"

"Can you imagine?" Harmony said later that night to Cam, when he arrived at her apartment. "There I am, thinking she's hurt, running like an idiot down the street to her place, only to find out she's baking mince pies and has fallen behind on production! I could have strangled her."

Her expression of outrage had Cam too busy laughing to reply, and Harmony flung a cushion at him in response, even though she was laughing too.

"She had me there until nine o'clock, cranking out twenty dozen pies. Thank goodness that's one of the things Mum makes, so I wasn't completely clueless. It could have been clootie pudding."

Cam didn't mention that twenty dozen was the number of pies Dora usually made every evening by herself during the festival.

"Did you have a good time, despite being used as unpaid labor?" he asked.

"Oh, I got paid," she replied, with a groan, flopping back onto the couch.

The royal blue terrycloth robe she was wearing gaped slightly at the throat, giving him a tantalizing glimpse of cleavage.

"I ate enough mince pies to give myself colic, but, yes, I enjoyed it thoroughly. Dora makes me laugh."

Her eyes glowed, amber tonight, and her smiling face warmed him quicker than the roaring fire. He went over and poked the logs, suddenly wishing she was up at the Manor with him.

They'd agreed for discretion's sake that he'd come down to see her at night when he could, since she'd either have to drive up to the Manor or he'd have to walk her home. Both of those scenarios would make it clear to anyone seeing them what was going on.

Each night since that first one he'd told himself it would be good to take a break, to sleep in his own bed and not get too used to having her in his arms. And each evening after dinner, when he was sure the island was settling down for the night, he'd found himself at the surgery side door, letting himself in.

She'd become his new obsession—and he was beginning to think she was far more dangerous than skydiving, caving and free-diving all rolled into one.

"I think the cat's out of the bag for us," he said, not wanting to spook her, but being honest. He didn't want anyone to make a comment she wasn't prepared for.

"I thought it might be," she replied, a cautious note in her voice. "You coming out of the surgery the other night instead of driving down from the Manor was probably more than enough to set tongues wagging."

Most visitors to the island came fully prepared to enjoy the sights and were a good-humored lot. There had only been one skirmish so far, when a pair of friends, having had too much beer, had got into a wrestling match outside the pub. It had been swiftly broken up, and the two friends had been sheepish after their nonsense, and apologetic.

But when the call had gone out for Cam to come and examine the patient, who was sitting on the curb outside The Ladies from Hades, he'd been with Harmony, and had had to leave from there right away to investigate.

He had to ask. "Do you mind? That people know we're seeing each other?"

What was he going to do if she said yes and decided they should stop?

"Do you?"

He still had his back to her, facing the fireplace, but he stuck the poker back into its stand and turned around.

"No." Not only didn't he mind, but he didn't care either. "It's really no one's business but ours."

"Okay."

"What does that mean, Harmony? That you do mind but you're okay with it?"

Her smile was beatific, a balm to his racing heart.

"No, I don't mind. We're adults having a good time

with each other. Sure, the employer/employee aspect might make people a little upset, but I don't think they'll tar and feather me."

The muscles in Cam's neck relaxed.

But then she added, "Besides, I won't be here that much longer. It'll all blow over after I'm gone."

The words struck him like a claymore to the gut. It was the one thing he didn't want to think about—had assiduously avoided contemplating.

"Have you started looking at applicants yet?"

She sounded so cool, as though discussing the weather, while his insides rebelled at the notion of her leaving. Somehow, though, he had to match her calm. He, who more than everyone knew her leaving was both inevitable and right, wouldn't be the one to quibble.

"It'll have to be when things wind down, I'm afraid. There's just no time for it now."

"Fair enough," she said, rolling her shoulders against the arm of the couch, dropping her gaze for a second before meeting his again.

Her eyes had changed—gone from amber to green.

"Do you know your eyes change color?"

She tilted her head as though unsurprised. "I've been told that."

Cam stalked closer to the sofa, those amazing eyes following his every step. "Sometimes they're gold, sometimes hazel, and now they're green."

"It's the genetics wheel of fortune," she replied. "My dad's family mostly have green eyes, and my mum's father came from near a place called Seaford Town, where there's a settlement founded by Germans who immigrated to Jamaica. His eyes are light too, so I got the recessive genes."

Beside her now, Cam sank down onto the couch,

and she moved over to give him space to fit right into the inward curve of her waist. He braced one hand on the back of the couch, the other on the arm, bracketing her, hemming her in.

She didn't move, just watched him.

"Doesn't explain why they change color like that."

"Does it matter?"

She touched his face, a butterfly brush of soft fingers, soothing and arousing all at once.

It did to him. Was it an emotional barometer he could use to interpret her mood? Or just a trick of the light? A reflection of the color she was wearing?

"You're beautiful," he heard himself say, the spur-of-the-moment words flowing off his tongue.

Harmony smiled—a seductive curve of her lips that drew him to them—and Cam had no intention of resisting. All this talk about her leaving made him mad, ravenous for her, as though putting his mark on that glorious body, making her cry out with pleasure, would somehow make her stay.

But he held back. Once he started kissing Harmony it was hard to stop. He wanted to make her a little crazy, and watch her while she came apart.

He snaked a hand under her robe, found the soft flesh of her thigh. "What do you have on under here?"

The touch of her tongue to the middle of her lower lip sent heat up his spine, had his body tightening with need.

"Why don't you look and see?"

Using his free hand, he tugged on the tie at her waist—just as his phone rang.

Cam dropped his chin to his chest and cursed.

Harmony laughed. "Such language, Dr. MacRurie. You should be ashamed."

He moved over to pick up the phone from the hall table, still muttering invectives under his breath. "Cam MacRurie."

"Cam, it's Gillian. Those guests I was telling you about are at it again. The mother has tripped near the bonfire and got a nasty burn on her leg. Can you come take a look?"

Suppressing another curse, Cam replied, "I'm on my way," before hanging up.

"What's going on?" Harmony had sat up and tightened the belt on her robe again—damn it.

"The couple staying over at Gillian Strom's are up to their old tricks. Mother has got burned by the bonfire."

They'd already gotten drunk one night and had a nasty argument in front of all the other guests, and their kids—one eleven and the other thirteen—were menaces. Cam was just about ready to send them packing.

"Need me to go with you?"

Sighing, he pulled his coat off the rack and shook his head. "No, stay where it's warm. Depending on what I find when I get there I might have to head straight back to the Manor."

He'd have to walk up to get True Blue and, depending on how late he was, coming back down to the surgery might not be feasible.

"Just take the estate car and your emergency bag from the surgery. Then come back when you're finished." She shrugged, seeming unconcerned, but those lines came and went between her eyes. "We already agreed our secret is probably out. Would it matter terribly if we're completely out in the open about what's going on?"

"If I had time I'd come over there and kiss you for saying that." Cam was shrugging on his coat, bracing himself for the stiff breeze he knew was awaiting him outside. "Keys?"

"On the hook by the door," she replied, getting up. "And in case you were still wondering..."

When she opened her robe Cam froze, every sinew straining to go back to her. She was completely nude, her skin glowing with a natural golden-brown light that seemed to come from within. Her lush body, all soft curves and secret glorious places he loved to explore, was the epitome of everything he desired, all in plain sight.

"Just to maybe give you an incentive to come back," she said, a little smile coming and going across her face.

"I'll be as quick as I can," he choked out.

He forced himself to turn toward the door.

Wanting nothing more than to stay.

CHAPTER THIRTEEN

A STORM ROLLED through the following day, bringing a coating of snow that, to Harmony's mind, added the final touch to the Winter Festival scene. To her surprise, she was enjoying the season far more than she'd expected or even wanted to—probably because everyone seemed so determined to make her a part of things. On one hand, it was heartwarming. On the other, she sometimes viewed it as almost a betrayal of Mum and Gran, although she knew neither of them would want her feeling that way.

"Don't get attached," Katherine warned her as she stopped by the clinic in the early afternoon to drop off a package for Cam. "Snow never lasts long around here. Something to do with the sea currents and how fast the storms pass over."

Harmony was more intrigued by the package than the Eilean Rurie weather patterns.

"What's in here, Katherine? It smells divine."

The older woman shrugged and said, "I don't know. Just dropping it off for Dora. Probably something for up at the Manor."

Giving the package an appreciative sniff, Harmony got up to take it into Cam's office. "Darn it," she said.

"I hope I can get him to share. It smells a lot like one of my gran's gizzadas."

"Your gran's what?"

"Gizzada. It's a little tart with coconut filling." Harmony paused in Cam's doorway to look back at Katherine. "I've been such a slug this year. If I'd thought of it I'd have ordered the ingredients and made some for you all."

"Well, too late now, I should think," Katherine said in her brisk way. "Unless you want desiccated coconut. There's always some of that around."

"No, that wouldn't work. You need real coconut— straight from the shell and grated."

"Good luck finding that anywhere around here," Katherine called. "I have to run. Make sure Cam gets that, please."

"Yes, ma'am," Harmony muttered to the sound of the closing door.

Katherine, of all the CIs, was the hardest to get to know. Both Sela and Ingrid had asked for her help during the Winter Festival, giving her an opportunity to get better acquainted with them. Katherine, however, seemed to be a mist-shrouded island of mystery in their midst.

Going back to her desk, she looked out at the little flakes still coming down, wondering how things were going with Cam. They'd had a guest with chest pains up at the Manor, and he hadn't checked in since he'd left to examine her. The good news was that she hadn't heard a rescue helicopter flying in, and nor had he called to tell her to prepare one of the beds upstairs.

Another bit of good news was that the backup medical team was on duty that night, so she and Cam could spend some uninterrupted time together. He'd suggested

Angus Stewart's fir forest and she'd agreed, although staying in was appealing too. She was determined to spend as much quality time with Cam as possible, and they could talk freely when they were alone. Not to mention be intimate.

The burn he'd gone to look at the night before had turned out to be minor, but he'd still been annoyed when he got back.

"That family are the one problem this year," he'd complained. "We usually have at least one, but these people take the cake. I read them the riot act, as politely as I could, but if they don't shape up I'm asking them to leave. Gillian's so fed up she said she'd refund them their money just to be rid of them."

Harmony had commiserated, having seen the family in action at the fair. The two boys had relentlessly heckled one of the performers, while the parents had stood by, beers in hand, as though nothing was going on.

After that she'd taken Cam to bed, warming his chilled flesh with her own, loving him until he'd turned the tables on her, taking her to heights of pleasure she'd thought were only fantasies dreamt up by authors.

Cam MacRurie definitely knew his way around a woman's body—or at least around hers—but for her it wasn't all about the sex, and that was worrisome. Yes, it was definitely worth it—having a man who could give her intense, mind-blowing orgasms—but the flipside was the sense of closeness she felt with him, the comfort and emotional attachment that was beginning to grow. At least on her side.

In her head she knew he wasn't the man for her. In a short time the Winter Festival would be over and Cam would be going on his next adventure. Maybe even trying that insane winged suit freefall thing. Just the sight of it had made her blood run cold and then boil with anger. Knowing he endangered his life with those types of activities made her want to smack him silly.

She was totally convinced there was no place in her life for a man like that. All she had to do was keep reminding her heart of it and everything would work out fine.

Checking the time, she called her mum, who was probably about to get ready for work. Although Delilah Kinkaid had enough seniority to request one shift and stick to it, she still rotated with the rest of the nurses.

"Hello, love."

Her mother sounded bright, chipper in a way she hadn't in a while, and it made Harmony smile.

"Hi, Mum. It's snowing here."

"Ha! We've had rain, and they're saying that's probably all we'll get before Christmas."

"Yuck," Harmony replied, although up until today Eilean Rurie had been similar. "Are you looking forward to your vacation?"

"More so than ever," Mum answered.

She must be having a rough time at work to be so enthused.

"Day after tomorrow is my last shift, and then I'm off for two whole weeks."

"Good for you."

But, even understanding why her mum had chosen to go to Yorkshire, and not being in London herself, it still made Harmony sad to know they wouldn't be together at Christmas.

Snapping herself out of self-pity mode, she asked, "How's Fred?"

And then she got a good laugh, hearing about her mum making him take her to the ballet, after being given tickets by a friend who'd broken her leg and couldn't go. Her mum, like Gran before her, was a born storyteller, and the tale was all the funnier for her going back and forth between English and patois, interjecting Jamaican phrases into the conversation.

By the time they hung up Harmony was still chuckling, and over her brief lapse into the doldrums.

Cam came in just then, knocking the snow off his boots at the door, those amazing eyes trained on her the entire time.

"You were talking to your mum? How is she?"

Surprised, since he'd come in after she'd hung up, she asked, "She's fine—sounded much more cheerful. But how did you know I was talking to her?"

"You have a special glow after your calls with her." He went past her desk, his hands full with his medical bag and the portable EKG machine. "It's obvious how close the two of you are."

Harmony got up and followed Cam into the medical store room, talking as she went. "We *are* really close. It still feels weird to know we won't be together at Christmas, but I guess that's how life's supposed to go." Not wanting to fall back into depressing thoughts, she asked, "How's the patient?"

"No signs of myocardial infarction, and she's feeling a lot better, but I suggested she get her gall bladder function checked when she goes home, and in the meantime stick to foods she knows don't give her indigestion. Turns out she has a lot of food allergies."

He'd stored the EKG machine away while he spoke, and when he turned around and tugged Harmony into his arms she squeaked, surprised by the swift move. But as soon as she was in his arms she melted, her muscles going pliant, her heart-rate kicking up.

"Looking forward to tonight?" he asked, in between feathering kisses across her cheek.

"Mmm-hmm…" She sighed, tipping her head to the side so those talented lips could find her throat.

"Good," he murmured against her neck, making goosebumps fire up and down her back and arms, and her nipples tighten to ultra-sensitive peaks. "I thought we could have dinner at the Manor after, and you could stay over."

She stiffened, and he leaned back so he could see her face. When he lifted a finger to stroke between her brows she knew she'd been frowning.

His voice gentle, he said, "I thought we agreed it didn't make sense to hide our relationship? Have you changed your mind?"

She'd made a point not to go up to the Manor, and had never seen his part of it—all in an attempt to maintain at least a modicum of distance from the rest of his life. Yet she had agreed there was no need for the discretion they'd tried to maintain to this point, and refusing to go with him, to sleep in his bed for a change, seemed silly.

But she was still unsure. Did this signal a change in their relationship? A new facet that could add more complexity to the situation?

The expression on his face—so serious, almost hurt—had her pushing her reservations aside. And when she replied, "Knee-jerk reaction, I guess. Of course I'll go," his smile made her heart sing.

Cam forced himself to let Harmony go and guided her back to the main part of the office. He had a patient coming in at three o'clock, and she was due to go and do her wellness check on Delores Jacobson as soon as she'd checked that patient in.

He was tired. Run off his feet by the festival. But he was enjoying it more than ever before. Somehow having Harmony to share it with had brought back the joy of it, which had been lacking these last couple of years.

From the reception area he heard Harmony start singing along with the Christmas song playing on the audio system, and he leaned back, smiling.

How different she was from when he'd first started playing them, when her lips had pursed, her brows coming together in that frown of hers. He'd picked music she'd mentioned that her gran had liked—not because he wanted to remind her of her sorrows, but because he truly felt hearing those songs, remembering the good times, would help her heal. Maybe he'd got it right.

Suddenly noticing both the box on his desk and the mouthwatering scent coming from it, he called, "Harmony, what's this on my desk?"

The singing stopped and she came to stand in the doorway. "I don't know. Katherine dropped it off—said that Dora asked her to."

"Oh." He was itching to open it, but instead swiveled in his chair to put it on the shelf behind him. "I'll have to take it up to the Manor before we go out."

"What is it?" she asked.

"Just some baked goods for…"

Damn it. He'd been about to say they were for dinner that evening at the Manor but he'd invited her to eat there tonight, and he didn't want her to see what was in the package. Not yet.

Thinking quickly, he said, "For one of the guests. Dora promised to make something specific for him as a special commission."

"Okay." Her face fell. "I was hoping they were for you and I could share. That scent takes me back to my mum's kitchen."

"Sorry," he said. "Maybe we can ask Dora to make you some."

"What are they?"

"No clue," he answered, trying his best to look innocent, and not sure he'd achieved it when those little lines came and went between her brows.

Luckily, just then he heard the front door open, and Harmony went to greet his patient and check her in.

She left to see Delores while Carmen Henriques was still with him, and after seeing the young mother and her baby to the door he rushed back to open the box full of pastries.

The gizzadas looked just like the ones he'd seen online, but just to be sure he pulled up the page with the pictures and the recipe again.

Gizzada—also called Pinch-Me-Round, because of the way the shortcrust pastry is pinched to create the free-form tart base—is a Jamaican delicacy.

The filling of grated sweetened coconut, spiced with nutmeg, vanilla and a hint of ginger, has a soft consistency, in contrast to the firm yet flaky shell.

Okay, he'd have to see if Dora had managed to capture the taste, as well as the look.

"Oh, yes!" Cam mumbled through a mouthful of deliciousness. Even if Dora hadn't perfectly captured the Jamaican flavor, she'd definitely created something absolutely mouthwatering.

Hopefully Harmony would like the gizzadas, along with his other surprises, when Doris made them again on Christmas Eve.

Early on, he'd realized his main mission that year would be to make sure Harmony enjoyed Christmas and found again the joy the season could bring. But he'd had no idea how to go about it until inspiration had struck.

If they could incorporate some of the things she'd said she missed about the holidays into the Winter Festival, maybe it would not only soften her grief, but make her feel a part of everything.

Dora had been incensed, saying it was far too late to add anything more to the plethora of activities and tasks each of them had taken on. In the end he'd had to compromise, agreeing that they'd add some Jamaican treats and traditions into the Christmas Eve celebration, which would give them enough time to sort things out.

Since then Cam had been inundated with calls, mostly complaining about the difficulty in finding ingredients, but as always the CI's seemed to be coming through for him.

As he ate the last of the gizzadas, so as to leave no evidence for Harmony to find, he realized his obsession with Harmony was overtaking his life.

Part of him rebelled at the thought. Another wondered if it were so bad. Before long she'd be gone, and he'd be back to his happy, carefree life.

Somehow thinking that didn't make him feel any better.

CHAPTER FOURTEEN

ANGUS'S FARM WAS crowded when Cam and Harmony arrived, but with almost an acre of fields turned into a fantastical tree maze there was more than enough room for everyone. And because they'd waited, opting for a late dinner at the Manor, by the time they got there most of the families with little ones getting cranky and needing to be fed were getting ready to leave.

The temperature had fallen with the passing of the cloud cover, and snow still lay glistening on the branches, although it had been mostly trampled away underfoot. It gave the already beautiful scene a sublime sparkle, and Harmony felt her spirits soar just looking at it.

Angus waved them through the makeshift turnstile with a grin. "Good to see you, Laird and Lady. Enjoy your ramble."

Harmony blushed to hear herself described that way, but thankfully she was too bundled up for it to be noticeable. And when Cam took her gloved hand in his she was tempted to tug it away again, but restrained herself.

"Are you warm enough?" he asked.

"Yes, thank you," she replied, sounding rather prim even to her own ears.

But her stiffness evaporated under the spell of the tree maze.

It was like walking through a fairytale, and all the children seemed to feel it. Although some of them ran hither and yon, it was with the joyous abandon of puppies, and with a minimum of noise, as though they instinctively knew that too much clamor would spoil the experience. Others were content to wander with their parents, looking at the lights, trying to find their way to the center.

The scent of the firs was divine, and even with the lights she could see constellations of stars in the cold, dark sky. Some of the trees had ornaments on them, adding to their beauty.

Cam released her hand to loop his arm over her shoulder, and being tucked up against his side perfected the experience.

They didn't talk much, just the occasional, "Oops, back we go," or, "Look at that," when a particularly beautiful tree came into view, and she appreciated the lack of chatter. There were some things in life best experienced in reverent quiet.

Angus had followed the theme of Love, so most of the decorated trees had heart ornaments on them, and one in particular caught and held her attention. The ornaments on it were all rustic hearts, made from wood, or wire, in old-fashioned fabrics such as gingham, or of tin.

It brought to mind the little red felt heart Cam had slipped into his pocket and made her wonder what he'd eventually done with it. Had he hung it on the tree at the Manor, where it had had pride of place for years? She was tempted to ask him about it, but didn't.

These last few days she'd found herself weighing the intimacy of everything she did, said, or asked, holding back as best she could, not wanting to open up any more to him than she already had. Nor to have him do the same with her, knowing it wouldn't take much for her to fall completely in love with Cam.

In many respects he was perfect: thoughtful, kind, respectful of her opinions and her wishes. His lack of arrogance was refreshing, especially since Harmony felt there was much he could be arrogant about. Being nominal Laird of Eilean Rurie could have certainly gone to his head, but it hadn't. There weren't that many men she knew who'd handle the situation as calmly and democratically as Cam did.

Heck, she'd worked with doctors who'd thought because of their profession they should be worshiped. Cam was both Laird *and* doctor, but he didn't put on airs because of it.

The laughter they shared was the icing on a rich and delicious cake. Even when they were making love it felt joyous, free and right. It was a whole new experience for her, and one she knew she'd miss terribly when it was all over.

And it would be over all too soon—because in the end Cam MacRurie was too scary a proposition. His daredevil ways, his need for a stronger and stronger adrenaline rush, would one day end in disaster, and she was determined not to be around to witness it. She'd had enough tragedy and upheaval in her life that she would not put herself into that kind of situation.

So, even if Cam were inclined to want her to stay longer, she'd have to say no and go back to London—even though Eilean Rurie had sneakily, quietly, snuck its way into her heart. Much as its Laird seemed set to do.

"Here we are," he said softly, breaking her out of

her reverie as they rounded a corner to the center of the maze.

Harmony gasped, enchanted all over again. "How lovely!"

There was a gazebo entwined with greenery and thousands of fairy lights, red bows and hearts artistically placed throughout. It was a place to sit and dream, to soak in the spirit of Christmas.

Cam guided her forward to it, bringing her to a halt just beneath the first crossbeam.

"Look up," he said softly.

She did, and realized he'd stopped her under a kissing ball made of mistletoe.

"Cameron…" It was a warning, even as her heart beat a suddenly frantic tattoo against her ribs.

But he just smiled, and said, "Tradition can't be denied, Harmony. It's bad luck if you do."

"I've never heard that before—"

He stopped her protest with his lips, and she'd never been happier to be silenced, melting into his embrace, his kiss.

Yet it wasn't a passionate one. Instead there was a tenderness to it she almost couldn't bear. His closed lips moved over hers so sweetly it made her want to cry. If a kiss could be a prayer, or a benediction, this was what it would feel like.

Wanting nothing more than to sink into it and never have it end, instead she gently pulled away—just as a family came around the corner and the children's exclamations broke the mood.

A little dazed, she asked, "Where are these Cailleach logs you were telling me about?"

Anything not to think about how that chaste, glorious kiss had shaken her previously solid foundations.

"Over there." He pointed to where a lean-to had been set up to keep the wood dry.

Easing out of his arms, she went to investigate them, Cam following slowly behind. They were strangely beautiful, the faces roughly hewn, but with a haunting quality Harmony appreciated. Cailleach was portrayed on some as old, careworn—winter personified—in others as younger, yet still mature, with wisdom and promise in her knowing gaze.

"Angus and his sons carve them all through the year, but this year I wonder if they'll have enough," Cam murmured, as though also somehow under the spell of all those wooden eyes looking up at them. "Our visitor count is up tremendously."

She wasn't surprised. Everything about the Winter Festival had surpassed her expectations, and the residents of Eilean Rurie put their all into making it amazing and fun.

"Pick one," Cam said, then reached out and took the very one she'd had her eye on.

Harmony didn't tell him that, though. It was the kind of moment best left to pass unremarked, showing as it did another albeit small similarity between them. Another intersecting point.

After she'd made her choice, and Cam had picked a couple of rowan branches, they went back through the maze to the bonfire. There Harmony contemplated the reds, yellows and blues of the flames for a moment, feeling a sense of destiny mixed with melancholy taking over her spirit. Funny how before she'd come to the island she'd considered herself supremely practical—all business. But here she was discovering new depths of emotion, a strange connectivity.

She smoothed her fingers over her Cailleach's face, and then tossed the small log into the flames. The knowing gaze seemed to glow for a moment, and then it was consumed.

Perhaps it was the beauty of the night, or the sense of having undergone a kind of spiritual shaking, but Harmony was left feeling on edge. As though the Cailleach had tried to warn her that not all efforts to banish the darkness actually worked.

There was a commotion near the refreshment tent, and they both turned to look just as Angus came barreling through the crowd toward them.

"You're needed, Cam," he said, looking shaken, his eyes wide. "We have a medical emergency."

Cam rushed off with Angus, and Harmony took off at a run to the car, to fetch their medical bags, her heart hammering as she wondered what she'd find when she got back.

And ruing, just a little, the interruption of their peaceful, lovely night together.

The patient was a young boy, perhaps two or three, who was lying unresponsive in his mother's arms.

When Cam tried to take him from her she hugged him tighter, turning away and shouting, "No, don't touch him. Don't touch him!"

"I'm Dr. MacRurie—"

But the woman wasn't listening, just screaming and crying, clutching her son to her chest. Even with all that Cam could see the little boy's chest heaving as he obviously labored to get air into his lungs.

A quick look around didn't find anyone who looked as though they were with the woman, and Cam was momentarily at a loss as to how to proceed.

According to Angus, the woman had suddenly cried out, saying her son had collapsed. When Angus had looked at him it had appeared the little boy's face was exceptionally red, but he hadn't seen any sign of seizing. Angus's youngest daughter had epilepsy, so he was familiar with what seizures looked like, but until Cam had a chance to examine the little boy he couldn't rule anything out.

Turning to Angus, who was hovering behind him, Cam said, "Call out the medical team. Tell them we need the ambulance, stat. And get me some warm blankets."

"Take him into the house if you can," Angus said, before hurrying away.

Cam stooped down close to the mother, trying to get her attention. "Your son needs medical attention. I'm a doctor. Let me help him."

But it was clear she wasn't listening. All she did was moan and rock back and forth.

Suddenly Harmony was there. Putting down the medical bags, she knelt in front of the woman and took her face between her palms.

"Shh…" she said. "Hush, now. We're here to help your son."

Surprisingly, the woman quieted, although she didn't release her convulsive grip on her child.

"What's his name?" Harmony asked, holding the mother's gaze.

"C-C-Cameron," she stuttered, tears still flowing down her cheeks.

"Well, would you believe me if I told you that's Dr. MacRurie's name too? Let Cam take a look at your Cameron, okay?"

As she spoke Harmony released the woman's cheeks and slowly reached for the little boy. Cam held his breath, waiting to see if she'd succeed in getting the mother to surrender the child. In the back of his mind he knew the clock was ticking. Depending on what was going on with the little boy, time could very much be of the essence. The delay chafed.

There was a collective sigh of relief from the crowd that had gathered nearby when they saw Harmony ease the child from his mother's arms.

"Take him inside," Cam said. Then, to the mother, "Come with us."

He didn't wait to see if she complied, taking off after Harmony as she ran toward the nearby house.

Once inside, she lay the little boy on the kitchen table, swiftly beginning to unzip his little parka, undressing him so Cam could do a comprehensive examination.

"Appearance of urticaria on his face and neck," she said as she worked. "And angioedema of the lips. Some sign of urticarial spreading to the chest and arms."

Cam had out his stethoscope and was listening to the child's chest. "Dyspnea and wheezing present," he replied.

The mother had come in behind them, hoarse sobs breaking from her throat as she watched them.

"I'm going to check his tongue and throat," said Cam.

Harmony had already taken out a tongue depressor and silently handed it to him, before tilting young Cameron's head back so he could get a good view.

But there was little room in the poor little fellow's mouth. His tongue was swollen and Cam knew they had to act quickly.

"Epinephrine—point one mil," he said, and watched as Harmony found the auto-injector and dialed in the amount. When she handed it to him he quickly injected the little boy in his thigh. Then he balled up a blanket and elevated Cameron's legs.

"Do you want to give him a dose of diphenhydramine also?"

Cam shook his head. "Not yet."

He was watching little Cameron, listening once more with his stethoscope to see if the wheezing began to lessen. When it did, he took the stethoscope out of his ears and made another visual inspection, noting the rash was receding and that two bright brown eyes were now looking up at him in some dismay.

"Mum, come and reassure Cameron that everything is okay," he said, waving the mother over, hoping she wouldn't upset her son more than necessary—which no doubt would happen if she started wailing again.

He heard the sound of the ambulance coming and looked across at Harmony. She was stroking the little boy's hair, speaking to him and his mother in soft, soothing tones.

Cam touched the mother's arm lightly, and she turned tear-filled eyes his way. "Your son has suffered anaphylaxis," he explained. "A severe allergic reaction. Does he have any known allergies?"

"No. None," she said, her eyes widening.

"Do you remember him eating anything unusual just before he went down?"

She shook her head. "No… We went through the maze, and he was running around as usual. We'd just come back to the tent and I was about to buy him something to eat when he collapsed."

"I think I might have an idea," Harmony said quietly.

When Cam looked at her she was holding up a tiny piece of fir.

"I did a mouth-sweep, just in case. This is what I found."

"Oh, Cameron!" his mother said, before breaking down into tears again.

CHAPTER FIFTEEN

THE NEXT FEW days were a blur of activity. With less than a week before the Christmas Eve Gala Cam was kept hopping, while Harmony held down the fort at the clinic. The medical team from the mainland, who usually alternated with Cam for the evening shift, was now put on call all day, in case Cam was on the other side of the island when someone needed attention.

For the most part, however, there wasn't much Harmony couldn't manage. There were some headaches, a few minor lacerations and some wonky tummies—usually from an overconsumption of sweets. Nothing else, thank goodness, as heart-stopping as the emergency at Angus's farm.

The weather had held, with the storm the meteorologists had earlier predicted blowing away to the north, but another one was due the next day, with wind and snow, followed by colder temperatures. Cam and all the organizers were rushing around, trying to secure the tents many of the vendors used to ensure the wind gusts didn't cause too much havoc.

She missed having Cam around all the time in the clinic, singing off-key, being annoyed because she'd rearranged some cupboard or filing system. Mind you, he'd been a lot better about those things once he'd realized she'd actually improved efficiency. When she'd first arrived she'd seen his instinctive protective reaction, but had forged ahead anyway.

Her next suggestion would be for a really decent computer system, but she had a feeling he'd balk when faced with hiring a data entry firm to deal with all the older records. Although, in reality, there weren't that many people in residence. She could probably manage to input the information herself, in between patients.

Harmony drew herself up, shaking her head at the thought. She wasn't going to be here long enough for that and, depending on the reliability and precision of his new hire, he might not want him or her to take on the job.

The one constant in this busy time was sharing the nights with Cam. Whether he picked her up and she stayed at the Manor, or he came and crashed in her apartment, they were together. It worried her how often she awoke in the night and reached out to touch him, as though needing the reassurance of his presence before being able to go back to sleep. Or how waking up in the mornings and having his arm around her gave her a sense of comfort and joy.

Good grief, now she was even starting to think in Christmas lyrics. And, worse, realizing it had created an earworm, so "God Rest Ye Merry, Gentlemen" played in her head on repeat for the rest of the day.

She was going to meet Cam up at the Manor that evening, but he called to let her know he was running a little late and would pick her up. For an instant she thought about telling him she'd stay alone in the apartment that night instead, but she felt a sense of the clock ticking the moments she'd have with him away.

Surely she could plan and execute a slow, steady withdrawal in January, leading up to her departure instead? So she agreed. And that night, as he made slow, lingering love to her, Harmony let the thought of leaving drift away, so as not to allow it to taint the pleasure of being in his arms.

The next morning she was in the kitchen, mixing the ingredients for quick pancakes together, when Cam came out of the bedroom, his diabetes kit in hand.

"Is that bacon I smell?" he asked, coming around to kiss the side of her neck. "Yum!"

She'd been up for a while, but knowing how busy he'd been had let him sleep awhile more.

"And pancakes to go with it. Won't take me more than a few minutes," she replied, just as his phone rang.

"Sounds amazing." He was already heading for the phone, which he'd left on the coffee table, and spoke over his shoulder. Picking it up, he answered, "Yes, Angus, what can I do for you?"

Then Harmony saw his face change, grow stern and angry, and when he let out a curse she instinctively turned off the flames under the half-cooked bacon and pushed the pan off the burner.

"I'll be right there," he said, putting down his kit and heading for the utility room behind the kitchen.

"What's going on?"

"Two children apparently went out to the old fishing village last night when the tide was out."

She went to stand in the doorway, watching him pull out his wetsuit and a bunch of harnesses with ropes attached.

"They must have fallen asleep in the old rescue station

and by the time they woke up the tide was coming in. The older one made it back, but the younger is still out there. Angus says he's sure they were drinking."

"Did anyone call for the Coast Guard?" she asked, hoping to hear they had and that they were on their way. That Cam wouldn't have to do what she was sure he was planning to do.

"Yes, but it'll take them a while to get here. If the boys have been out all night they could have hypothermia, and we need to get that youngest one off there before the tide comes all the way in. It's the pair from Gillian Strom's place and the mother says the youngster's not a strong swimmer."

He was coming out, laden with gear, and she stepped back to give him room to put them down by the door. Then he took off at a run for the bedroom.

Harmony stood there, frozen for a moment, panic making her insides churn, fogging her brain. All she could think of was Cam going into the rough water which, raging with the tide and incoming storm, would suck him away. Every bit of her turned cold, as icy as the sea he was planning on fighting.

Then common sense took hold, and she hurried into the kitchen to grab a couple of protein bars and a bag of dried apricots she'd spied in the cupboard. Dropping them into her bag, she rushed back to the front hall to pull on her boots and jacket.

When Cam came out of the bedroom, she called out, "Take your levels before you go."

He didn't even look at her, just snapped, "I'm fine. Don't fuss."

"But—"

The look he gave her as he tugged on a jacket, made

her turn to ice again. "There's no time and I'm fine. I don't need you to tell me what to do, Harmony."

As soon as the words had left his mouth Cam regretted them. Not just because what she was suggesting was wise, and the right thing to do, nor because it was a reminder he actually needed. No, it was the way Harmony's face paled, and her eyes widened and gleamed green with hurt.

Before he could say anything her face tightened, and her brows drew together as she said, "Don't be an ass, Cameron. You can't save anyone if you're in distress yourself. So I'll drive. You can take your levels and at least eat something. I've got a couple of protein bars and some dried fruit ready to go."

"You can't drive True Blue," he said, trying to figure out how to do what he needed to and still get out to the fishing village as quickly as possible.

Harmony just made a rude noise and pushed past him to grab his diabetes kit. At the door she picked up his medical bag, her bag, and his car keys. Then, as she went out, she said, "You're the one who's in such a damned hurry, so let's go."

By the time he got the gear stowed in the back of the vehicle she had it running. He'd heard her cursing under her breath as she tried to adjust the seat, which hadn't been moved in God only knew how long, but when he got in she was belted in and seemed ready. The determined look on her face would have amused him at any other time—but not today, with so much on the line.

Cam watched Harmony struggle for a moment with the clutch, which was stiff, and the gear lever, which was misaligned.

"I'll drive," he said, impatience taking over.

The look she sent him should have incinerated him on the spot, and without a word she slammed the vehicle into gear.

As they took off along the Manor driveway, Harmony blew the horn to get the early risers ambling around out of her way, and Cam fought his very real inclination to ignore the snacks on the seat between them and the kit on his lap.

She was right. And he knew it.

Who would be helped by his being stubborn and stupid about his disease the way he had been as a child, when he'd hide from his mother when he knew it was time to test his blood or eat a snack? She'd used to tell people he didn't like the needles, but that hadn't been true. What he had hated was the way her over-solicitous care had made him feel—as though he had no control, wasn't able to have a normal life.

He'd gotten past all that with his grandfather's help, but now he realized the residual effect of his early years clung to him like an old, foul coat. Yet in a flash he knew Harmony wasn't like that. She'd made no mention of his diabetes since the first day she'd found out—never asked about his levels, or whether it was time to take them. Instead she'd clearly taken his word that he knew how to manage the disease.

Grabbing one of the protein bars, he tore the wrapper open and stuffed half of it into his mouth. As he chewed, he debated the necessity of taking his levels, and decided getting some food into his system was more important. He rarely suffered the "dawn phenomena," when his blood sugar spiked on waking, and didn't see why it should happen today of all days.

He finished the rest of the bar before saying, "I'll test my levels before going into the water, okay?"

Cam wanted her to know he understood what she'd said, and that he agreed, but when she only grunted in reply he felt his heart sink. Exactly when her good graces had become so important to him Cam wasn't sure. Moreover, when she'd become such an integral and necessary part of his life was an unknown too—but she was just that.

He'd fallen for her—all the way. For her charm and kindness, her spunky spirit and practical nature. Even for the fear in her eyes when she'd realized what he was about to do, which showed her concern for him. All of it.

The knowledge stole his breath, making his already racing heart skip a beat. The urge to blurt it out to her almost overtook his common sense, and he stuffed part of another bar into his mouth to stop it coming out.

This wasn't the time or the place. Besides, right now the distraction of thinking about what he was going to do, and if there was any hope for a deeper relationship, could be fatal. Pushing it all aside was one of the hardest thing he'd ever do, but he tried anyway.

By the time they got to the shore near the old fishing village he'd managed to eat both protein bars and a handful of apricots, and he made an effort to check how he felt. Sometimes he could feel the subtle signals his body sent, telling him his levels were high or low, but right then all he could feel was the surge of adrenaline.

As they pulled up behind Angus's vehicle he heard Harmony gasp—no doubt at her first sight of what they faced to rescue the boy.

Although the derelict rescue station was still above the waterline, waves were breaking high upon it, spray flying to the seaward side, water swirling and frothing in strong eddies on the landward.

Cam, from experience, knew the path to get from the

shore to where the boy lay, curled on his side on what was left of the station, wouldn't be easy. Debris and obstacles stuck up through the sand the entire way, but it was a place he'd explored many times over the years, and he felt no trepidation about the rescue.

Angus came over as soon as they'd got out of the vehicle, and followed as Cam went to the back to get his wetsuit.

"Annie Howell was going out to tend her sheep when she saw the older one crawling out of the water and heard the younger one crying for help. Lucky for them she had phone signal and called me."

Cam was already stripping down to his briefs. "Why didn't she call me right off?" he asked. Even a few minutes could make the difference between the tide engulfing the child or not.

"I'm closer—and she thought we could use the boat and get him. Once I got here and realized the tide was too low I immediately called you. I sent the older boy back to Gillian's, where I understand he's puking his guts out in between fits of shivering. From the smell of him, he got into some whisky. He's a fairly good swimmer, his mum said, but his brother isn't—which is probably why he didn't try to make for shore with the older one."

"Damn it," Cam said. It had become even more imperative to get to the younger child now, who not only could be suffering from hypothermia but alcohol poisoning, as well. "Does anyone know how long they were out there?"

Angus shook his head. "The tide turned at three thirty this morning, and wouldn't have started covering the sandbar until about five. I'm thinking they spent the night out there—or at least went out after their parents were sleeping."

Cam was in his wetsuit, reaching for his gloves, when he felt a touch on his arm.

Harmony held out a lancet to prick his finger, her expression stern, unyielding. Without comment he stuck out his hand, and she collected the sample on the test paper, turning away to where she'd placed the glucometer on the car bumper.

Cam pulled out the harnesses and Angus helped him to unwrap them, the two men discussing the best way to rescue the boy. Harmony walked away with his kit and Cam knew, with a sense of relief, that meant his blood sugar levels were good.

From then on it was all business. Angus and his son Colin secured the lines, while Cam got into a life vest and one of the harnesses, attaching another set to a ring on the vest with a carabiner.

Once he'd checked everything was in place to his satisfaction, Cam said to Angus, "Make sure the Coast Guard helicopter is coming. I'm sending this child to Skye for treatment once he's on shore."

Then, with a quick look for Harmony, who was nowhere to be seen, he went into the water, all his concentration on avoiding getting swept away or gored by debris.

CHAPTER SIXTEEN

HARMONY WAS BACK at True Blue, getting out the warming blankets and anything else she thought they might need when Cam came back with the child. She'd not been able to just stand there and watch him go into the water. She had wanted to tell him not to, to wait for the Coast Guard, but knew it would have been no use.

Cameron MacRurie was not only a doctor intent on saving a patient, but the kind of man who thrived on pitting himself against nature. It would have been impossible to stop him.

Yet even as she told herself she wouldn't look Harmony couldn't help it, constantly checking over her shoulder to follow Cam's progress as she tossed a couple of towels onto the back seat, hoping they'd be needed. That the sea wouldn't swallow Cam whole.

She'd allowed him to tempt her into an affair which had now become so much more. It was her fault that the fear she felt for him was so overpowering—a byproduct of the feelings she'd let grow inside. For all she'd told herself it would be a fun fling, she now had to accept that the emotions she felt as she watched him battle the frothing tide had little to do with sex.

No. She'd let herself fall for him, even knowing

where that would lead. There was no one to blame but herself.

Annie Howell came over and offered Harmony a steaming cup of coffee, which she took with thanks.

"Don't worry about the Laird," she said, using her chin to gesture toward the water. "He knows these waters better than almost anyone else, and he's trained in water rescue too. He wouldn't go in if he didn't think he could get to the bairn and bring him back safely."

Yes, he would, Harmony thought sourly. Even if he thought it too dangerous, he'd die trying.

She was still hurt by his reaction earlier, when she'd tried to get him to take his levels before they left the Manor. His response had been completely out of character, and over the top too. Yet her fear overrode all of that, leaving her shaken and cold.

There was a shout from the crowd around the shore, and Harmony spun toward it in time to see Cam clinging with one hand to a piece of wood sticking out of the water, clearly fighting to keep from being swept away. When he grabbed it with his other hand and seemed to get his feet back under him she realized she could breathe again.

"Almost there now," Annie said in a calm voice, but Harmony heard the undercurrent of worry.

Cam was trailing a rope, which was secured to the shore, but even so, if the tide caught him and they had to drag him back, he could get injured.

He got to the platform and heaved himself up onto it. Harmony could see him examining the boy who, after a moment, struggled into a seated position. Cam put on the child's life jacket, attaching it to his own before swinging his feet over the side and pulling the child into his lap.

This was the dangerous part. Harmony could hear the child's screams of fear, saw his legs flailing as Cam pushed back into the water.

How he found the bottom was something Harmony didn't understand. She realized she had her fist tight to her mouth, her teeth digging into her knuckles, but she couldn't help it as she watched Cam's torturous, inch-by-inch progress back to shore. Angus and Colin, and Martin Harris, who'd arrived to help, kept the rope taut, winching it in.

Cam and his burden were near shore when Harmony was snapped out of her horrid fascination by the sound of an approaching helicopter. Picking up the warming blankets, she trotted down to the shoreline, so as to be there when Cam and the boy were heaved back onto dry land.

In the background she heard a commotion, but didn't pay it any mind, too intent on watching Cam make the last few agonizing steps through the breakers, and Angus wading in to help him carry the child up onto the shore.

Feigning a calm she didn't at all feel, Harmony rushed forward with the blankets as Cam unhooked the carabiner that was keeping the boy lashed to him. Quickly wrapping the child in the blanket, she held out her arms for him, but Angus was already carrying him toward where the helicopter team was coming along the road from where they'd landed. They had a stretcher with them, and Angus surrendered the child to them as Cam sank down onto the rough grass at the edge of the loch, panting.

Harmony draped the other blanket around his shoulders and he looked up to nod, give her a little smile. But she didn't have it in her to return it, her insides still churning with the tension engendered by what she'd just witnessed. She reached out to grip his shoulder, as though needing touch to reassure herself that he was there, still alive, in front of her, and he turned his head to kiss her fingers.

"That was a workout," he said, between gasps of air.

Harmony watched the rescue team going back up the road, the child's father with them. "What condition was he in?" she asked.

"Freezing cold, but with enough fight left in him to almost drown me on the way back," Cam answered, but his humor fell flat.

Angus came back over and stooped down beside Cam. "The Coast Guard is flying him to Skye and his dad is going with him."

"I'm going to go too," Cam answered. "Just to make sure he's okay. I should make a report, too, since we had to call out the rescue copter. Do you have time to take me over, Angus? I can wait for the ferry if you can't."

"Get you home to warm up and let me know when you're ready. I'll have the boat waiting," Angus replied immediately.

That news seemed to give Cam back the energy he'd expended on the rescue, and he heaved himself to his feet to take off the harness and hand it to Martin, who was collecting up the equipment.

Harmony surreptitiously checked Cam out for injuries, dropping behind him a bit as he strode toward the car. Then she was beside him in a flash, her heart rushing as she grabbed his arm.

"You're hurt."

He sent her a sideways glance, the edge of his mouth kicking up in a slight grimace. "Yeah. Caught the edge of something when that rogue wave knocked me off my feet. Tore my wetsuit."

Harmony let go his arm, staring at him for a long moment before turning back toward the vehicle. Here she was, fretting because he'd cut open his calf, and he was worried about his damn wetsuit! She strode off, leaving him to follow.

Cam stood on the passenger side of the vehicle with Angus as Harmony got in and started True Blue, hoping that when she cranked up the heat the old girl wouldn't expire. Martin and Colin had brought the ropes and harnesses to stow in the back, and through the window Harmony saw Cam twist, as though looking at the laceration on his leg. She'd have offered to put a pad on it at least, until they got back to the Manor and she could examine it properly, but his reaction earlier made her reluctant.

He was the doctor, after all, she thought a little sourly. If he wanted a bandage on it he would do it himself.

Cam finally parted with Angus and got in, still in the wetsuit, and Harmony reached into the backseat for the towels she'd stowed there. Then she jammed the vehicle into gear and drove a little way down the road to turn around.

"Well, that went as well as could be expected," he said. "Although Angus believes the father may try to cause some problems. I'll have to see which way the wind is blowing when I get to Skye."

She was coming down off the frightening high, suddenly exhausted, hardly able to think properly. All she could do was concentrate on not crashing True Blue on the narrow island roads.

"What kind of trouble?"

"Oh, he was quick to deny that his kids had been drinking, and he said something about how dangerous the old station was."

"But it's fenced off—and clearly marked with 'No Trespassing' signs." Outrage superseded her exhaustion for a moment and her fingers tightened around the steering wheel. "And how ungrateful could he be? When you went out there after that child…got injured rescuing him."

"Don't get upset," he said quietly. "I'll deal with whatever happens. And it's just a scratch, Harmony. I've gotten worse injuries doing far less important things."

No doubt he meant all his crazy pastimes. She didn't answer, knowing that to do so would probably precipitate a fight. One she had no business picking with him, since theirs wasn't that kind of relationship. Just because she'd realized she loved him it didn't mean she had the right to question his life choices—especially since she knew there was no happy ending for them.

Cam MacRurie was far too dangerous a proposition for her, and if she'd only thought that before, now, after watching him put himself in harm's way and get hurt doing it, she knew it for a fact.

"And," he added quietly, "I need to apologize for what happened earlier, when you told me to take my levels before we left. I was out of line, the way I reacted, and I'm sorry."

"There's no need—"

"There's every need, Harmony, especially as you were right and doing nothing more than looking out for me. I guess I'm just used to going my own way, doing my own thing, without anyone questioning me. And I saw how scared you were, knowing I was going to do a sea rescue."

"That's fine," she said, knowing she was being curt, but not knowing how else to react. The pain of loving him and knowing she could never trust him to keep himself safe was too much to deal with right now. The urge to rage at him was strong, but she had her pride, and that had her saying, "I never told you not to go after that boy, did I?"

"No, you didn't, and I appreciate it." He sighed, but the air stuttered out of his lungs, and her quick glance caught him shivering. "I've always been the adventurous type, even as a kid, but my mother had a hard time with the fact of my having diabetes, and did everything she could to curb anything she thought was too dangerous. My grandfather, by teaching me how to manage my disease, set me free, and once I was old enough I let rip at whatever caught my fancy. I love the exhilaration of pitting myself against nature, or even against my own limitations. It makes me feel alive."

She pulled up at his private entrance to the Manor and engaged the handbrake before switching off the ignition and turning to him. His teeth were chattering.

"Go inside, Cam. Let's get you warmed up."

He reached out from beneath the towel he'd draped over his shoulders to grip her wrist, arresting her as she was opening her door.

"I need to know that you understand why I snapped at you earlier and forgive me."

Knowing he wouldn't move until she answered, Harmony said, "Yes, I forgive you—but I can't promise not to say anything if a similar situation arises. It's the way I am, and I can't change that."

His look of relief was immediate, and he leaned over to press his chilled lips to hers.

"I'm not asking you to change, Harmony," he said,

thankfully releasing her and reaching to let himself out of the vehicle. "I just need you to understand."

And she did understand—perhaps all too well.

After setting a lukewarm shower, and helping him out of the wetsuit so he could get in and warm up, she ruminated on his words. Everything he'd said echoed within her, bringing back conversations she'd had with her mother about her dad.

"I think he took risks to prove something to the army after they rejected him over his heart defect," her mum had said, and the sadness and anger in her voice was still fresh all these years later. "It were as though he was driven to go after that high of surviving when they told him he wasn't fit to do what they needed him to."

Her dad had driven race cars and motorcycles. Then he'd done skydiving, trying for lower and lower jumps, or longer freefalls. Eventually it had been climbing. He'd been working toward free-climbing when he'd died.

The friends her mum was still in contact with all called him by his old nickname "Risky Ricky" when they spoke about him, telling stories about his daredevil ways. Mum laughed along with them, but Harmony had seen the lingering pain in her eyes.

It wasn't hard to see the correlation between her father's need to prove himself and Cam's drive for adventure. Had his mother's overprotective behavior done the opposite of what she'd wanted? Pushed Cam to prove that, despite his diabetes, he could do whatever anyone else did, no matter how dangerous?

The whole situation was overwhelming and, coupled with the fright she'd just had, made her teary-eyed.

She couldn't go through what her mum had—didn't want to put herself in a situation where she lost the man she loved because of his recklessness and need for another adrenaline rush. It cemented her determination to distance herself from Cam as soon as possible, before leaving him became harder than it already was.

Somehow seeing that deep laceration on Cam's leg just made it worse. She wanted to dress it, to tell him compulsively to keep an eye on it, but held her tongue. He didn't want her fussing—he'd made that clear. So she just kept a weather eye on him while he took care of it himself, aching inside with the worry of infection and the slow healing so dangerous to diabetics.

Once he'd left to go to Skye, promising to let her know when he'd be back, she pulled out her laptop and started looking through job search sites, trying to find her replacement. Knowing that the sooner Cam hired someone new, the sooner she could leave.

CHAPTER SEVENTEEN

CAM STAYED ON Skye overnight, making sure the young boy was recovering from his ordeal and doing everything necessary to report the incident properly. It kept him busy, and he didn't get back to Eilean Rurie until the evening of December twenty-third.

The preparations for the Christmas Eve Gala were in high gear, with everyone rushing about trying to put the finishing touches to the church hall, where it would be held, but when Harmony had offered her help it had been refused.

"Too many people barging about in there as it is," Katherine had told her the afternoon after Cam had left for Skye, when she'd stopped by the clinic.

Although it was a Sunday, Harmony had opened up the clinic in case of emergency. After all, she hadn't had anything better to do with Cam gone.

"You're better off staying out of it."

"Whatever happened to 'many hands make light work'?" Harmony had asked, amused by the other woman's sour tone.

"That went out the window about three days ago," had been the crisp response. "If you really want to help, come by my place later and help me make clootie pudding."

Knowing the other woman's reputation for efficiency,

Harmony hadn't bought it. "You don't really need my help, do you?"

"No, I don't—but I could use the company. I hate baking, but this year I ended up on the list to make the puddings and I don't want to. At least having company will make it less painful."

So she'd spent the evening at Katherine's, discovering much more about the other woman than she'd dreamed possible, considering how closemouthed Katherine usually was. She'd spoken about her childhood in Bristol, and how her father hadn't believed in education for women.

"I left home at sixteen, and put myself through university. He didn't understand my ability with numbers and thought I was wasting time and money becoming an accountant. Apparently, I should have been married and having children instead."

It was toward the end of the evening. They'd finished cleaning up the kitchen and the puddings had been boiling. Wine had been poured and they'd settled into comfortable chairs in the living room.

"How on earth did you end up here?" Harmony had asked.

The last part of the story had been about some of the fun times the older woman had had, living in Southampton in the nineteen-seventies.

"I came here originally as bookkeeper at the Manor." She'd smiled slightly—a rueful twist of her lips. "I saw the ad in a newspaper and on a whim applied. I was adventurous back then, and I thought it would look good on my résumé too. I had an idea that one day I'd go to Australia to live, and I knew the more work experience I had, the better."

Harmony had believed she knew what had happened next. "You fell in love with the island and never left?"

Katherine had given her a sharp glance, and then looked down at her wine glass for a moment. "No," she'd replied, lifting her gaze to meet Harmony's. "I fell in love with the Laird."

Surprise had arrested Harmony's hand, so her wine glass hovered halfway to her lips.

"Not *your* Laird, of course," Katherine had continued. "The old Laird—Cameron's grandfather. He was a wonderful man, as handsome as could be, and I fell head over heels. He'd been a widower for a few years by then, and although everyone knew he was still grieving I thought eventually he'd be ready to move on."

She'd fallen silent, her gaze going to the fireplace, her eyes getting a faraway look, as though she were revisiting the past in her mind. Not knowing what to say, Harmony had waited, wondering how the story had turned out.

"He never did get there," Katherine said. "And I wasn't the type to throw myself at him—to let him know how I felt. Instead I just stayed, became his friend, did whatever I could to protect him and look after him. Sometimes… Sometimes I wonder if things would have been different if I'd told him…"

Before Harmony had been able to comment Katherine had stirred, her gaze sharpening. "Some men only have room in their hearts for one woman, and the old Laird was just that type. I still believe I would have had to leave out of embarrassment or a sense of self-preservation if he'd realized how I felt, and I'd rather have had all those years of friendship with him than not. Life is full of hard choices, and I stand by mine."

Knowing Katherine wouldn't want sympathy, Harmony had just nodded. But inside she'd ached for the other woman, who'd perhaps missed her chance at love because she'd not had the courage to say how she felt.

"I was here when Cameron came to live with his grandfather. The old Laird was so worried about him... Cameron was an angry young man, sullen and withdrawn."

"Cam?" Impossible to reconcile the man she knew with a description like that.

"Oh, yes. His grandfather asked me, 'If I don't help him what kind of life will he have?'"

"Cam said his grandfather set him free." Harmony hadn't wanted to go into what he'd said about his mother, but knew Katherine would appreciate the knowledge that Cam understood what his grand-da had done.

The other woman had smiled and nodded. "It wasn't easy for Douglas. He of all people knew how dangerous Cameron's diabetes could be, but he was determined to help his grandson accept the disease and learn how to manage it. He fretted constantly as he watched Cameron gain confidence and become the rambunctious boy he was meant to be, but he knew he had to give the boy the independence he needed."

The conversation had stuck with Harmony, still running through her head later that night, as she'd lain in bed, unable to sleep.

Cam was independent because his grandfather, who'd loved him dearly, had helped to make him that way despite his own misgivings. Harmony wished she had that same strength of character, but she didn't, and knowing her own weakness made her cry.

She wished she could talk to her mum about it, but she wasn't in a place, mentally or emotionally, to do so. No doubt her mother would have a lot to say about the situation, and Harmony wasn't at all sure she wanted to hear her mother's input.

Everything in her strained both toward Cam and away from him, and she felt trapped in an internal tug of war.

He called her when he got off the ferry the next evening.

"I'm just heading home to shower and change. Come up in a while, okay?"

She thought it strange that he wouldn't just stop by so she could walk with him to the Manor, but agreed to go up in about an hour.

As she strolled up she found herself greeting people she'd come to know in the short time she'd been on the island. Although she'd lived in the same house in Stoke Newington most of her life, and had friends of long standing there, the sensation of belonging she felt on Eilean Rurie was different. Somehow knowing you depended on your neighbors the way everyone on the island had to made fitting in a bit easier.

Funny to think how she'd worried that she'd stick out like a sore thumb and have a miserable couple of months. The stereotype of small places being unfriendly and hard to assimilate into certainly didn't apply here. She'd been welcomed with open arms, and knew she'd miss it terribly when she left.

Slipping in through Cam's private entrance, she found the most delicious scent reaching her nostrils, and she inhaled deeply as she shrugged off her coat and toed off her boots.

"What are you making?" she asked, walking through from the entranceway into the kitchen.

"Sugar cookies," he replied, giving her a broad grin.

"I promised to make some for the gala tomorrow, and I was worried I wouldn't get back in time to do it."

Harmony surveyed the unholy mess on the counter, the flour and sugar on the floor, and shook her head. "Not something you do often, I suspect."

He chuckled. "Never done it before, but I think I'm getting the hang of it. I was going to borrow cookie cutters from Dora, but ended up picking up some for myself on Skye. Are you going to just stand there, or are you going to help me?"

Harmony laughed, opening the cupboard and taking out his broom. "I'm going to sweep up that flour before one of us slips and falls—then I'll help."

He looked so adorable, with a gingham pinny tied around his waist and his hair still damp from his shower, her heart raced and her stomach fluttered. The whole concept of steeling herself against the love and attraction she felt toward him seemed laughable.

"How could anyone be this messy?" she teased as she swept up the flour and sugar.

Cam shrugged, stamping out another biscuit and dropping it on a baking sheet. "I'm a pretty decent cook, but this is my first foray into baking, so excuse me if I didn't realize the mixer would send half the ingredients flying if I cranked it up to the highest speed."

That made her giggle, and they teased back and forth as she helped him with the next batch.

"How're you planning to decorate them?" she asked, when the sheets were finally in the oven and Cam was rolling out the next block of dough.

His blank look had her laughing all over again.

"Decorate? I'm supposed to decorate them too?"

"Otherwise they'll be pretty boring," she replied, getting her amusement under control. "Do you have any food coloring? Oh, never mind—I'll just look."

"All the baking supplies are in the last cupboard," he said helpfully. "On the left-hand side."

She found some ancient food coloring and some plastic bags and, as Cam watched with interest, made some colored sugar to sprinkle on top of the biscuits.

When she'd finished it was time to take the first batch out, and she showed him how to make designs on the cookies with the sugar. Once the baking sheets had cooled they put the next batch on, and into the oven they went.

Cam picked up one of the first set of cookies and bit into it.

"Mmm…" he said, his eyebrows going up. "Not bad at all, if I might say so myself. Try it."

He moved closer to her, holding out the biscuit for her to bite, and something in his eyes made her heart leap. Obediently she took a bite, and nodded in satisfaction.

"Delicious," she said, after swallowing.

"Yes…" Cam agreed, but she knew he wasn't talking about the cookie.

His gaze was on her lips, his expression intent, and when he leaned in to kiss her Harmony melted just like the sweet confection had melted in her mouth.

"I missed you so much last night." His lips were against her cheek, his arms warm and strong around her waist. "I couldn't wait to get home to you."

She didn't reply, just cupped his cheeks and pulled his lips back to hers. She couldn't admit how much she'd missed him too. To do so would be too revealing, even as she felt the bonds tying her to him tighten.

Picking her up, he carried her to the living room and laid her down on the couch, kissing her again and again. Time slowed, became irrelevant, as kisses turned to caresses and Cam slowly stripped her of her clothes and her defenses. Saying no to his lovemaking never entered her mind. Instead she reveled in it, crying out with pleasure as he took her flying.

"You're so beautiful," he whispered, his face harsh with need.

"So are you," she said, the words coming from her soul.

And when they were ready and she straddled his body, taking him deep, the pleasure she derived wasn't just from the sensations of his body in hers, as amazing as those were. Her joy was deepened, widened, by seeing his ecstasy as she took him to the edge and they plunged over together.

They came back to earth with a bump as the smell of something burning permeated the room.

"The cookies!" Cam cried, levering her off him and setting her back down on the couch before taking off running for the kitchen.

Still on a high, Harmony found herself laughing so hard at the thumping and cursing coming from the other room she couldn't get up.

Cam stalked back into the living room and stood over her, glowering. "Funny, is it?"

"Hilarious," she replied, gasping for air, holding her aching sides.

He pounced, growling, and they wrestled back and forth, with Harmony still suffering fits of giggles and Cam trying hard not to join in but eventually succumbing.

Entwined, they let their laughter turn to gasps for air, and Harmony relaxed into his embrace, blissfully satiated. Unthinkingly happy.

When he went up on his elbows she opened sleepy eyes to look up at him. Cam's expression banished her lassitude—brought her to full and frightened awareness. "Stay here with me, Harmony. I love you."

CHAPTER EIGHTEEN

HE HADN'T MEANT to blurt it out like that, but something in the moment, in having her in his arms right then, had made him say it.

Having accepted that his love for her was deep and true, he knew the yearning for her while he was on Skye had just cemented it in his heart. It wasn't just physical intimacy with Harmony. There was something between them that both soothed and excited his soul, that made his lonely heart whole.

Her look of shock didn't surprise him. After all, he'd surprised himself with his words, although they were heartfelt. What he wasn't prepared for was the strength and ferocity with which she pushed him away.

Rolling away almost had him falling off the couch, which would have added embarrassment to what was already beginning to feel like a very bad scene. Insult on top of injury, or the other way around.

"No, no, no…" She got up, turned her back on him, covered her face with her hands for a moment. "Oh, Cam. Why did you have to say that? Spoil everything."

"Because I mean it," he said, not sure whether to be angry or sad. "I love you. I want you to be with me always. What's so wrong about that?"

"I can't!" It was almost a moan, and when she turned

to face him her face was pale, her eyes green and tragic. "It wouldn't work. I *can't*."

Wanting to take her in his arms, but knowing she wouldn't want that, he stayed where he was, flattening his hands against the cushions beneath him to stop himself from reaching for her.

"Why wouldn't it work?" He had to ask—to make sense of what she was saying. Was he the only one who felt how right they were together? Was he alone in knowing that what they shared was deeper, truer than mere passion?

She lowered herself into an armchair, pulling a throw pillow from behind her to hug it, as though shielding her body from his view. Or using it as a barrier to separate them.

"I… I never told you about my dad, did I?"

What did that have to do with anything? he wondered, but just shook his head.

"Remember I said he had a heart defect and wasn't fit for the army? Well, after that it was as though he had to prove there was nothing wrong with him. He was a daredevil, Cam—like you. His friends called him 'Risky Ricky' because of how he behaved—never cautious, always going full tilt into whatever crazy thing he was doing. He was a man who'd try any ridiculous stunt or sport as long as it gave him an adrenaline rush. Car or motorcycle racing, skydiving, mountain-climbing— you name it, he did it."

Cam wanted to argue—to say he wasn't that way, didn't do any of the things he did in an effort to prove anything to anyone but because he loved the adventure. But she was crying, and he couldn't bear the sight. It clogged his throat, making it impossible for him to respond.

"Eventually it killed him, Cam. He wanted to free-climb, and he wasn't ready for it. Or maybe his heart finally gave out on him. No one knows for sure. All we know is he lost his grip on that cliff and fell to his death."

"Harmony. I'm so sorry."

She held up her hand, tears still falling, but her face had taken on an expression of determination, and the lines between her brows were more pronounced than he'd ever seen them.

"I don't need your sympathy, Cam. I just need you to understand. I was six when he died. My mother was left to raise me alone. It took her years—*years*—to get over his loss. The entire time I was growing up she wouldn't date, struggled on her own. Because of his selfish need to prove himself he deprived me of a father and Mum of a husband. I had to listen to my mother cry at nights, when she thought I was asleep—had to see my grandparents get old before their time because of the death of their son, whom they'd loved so much."

She took a deep, shuddering breath and wiped her hand over her face, trying to erase the tears.

"I can't risk going through that again, Cam. I know why you do what you do, and I know how addictive extreme sports can be, so I would never ask you to give them up. However, I can make the choice not to watch you do them. Not to put myself into a situation where one day you might leave and never come home. I'm not strong enough to handle that."

Her words struck him like a series of knife-blows, each lacerating his heart a bit more until it felt as though there was nothing left of it.

Yet even though the pain was extreme, made him nauseous, his first impulse was to tell her that she was right. He'd never give up doing what he wanted—no matter how dangerous. And that impulse told him more about himself than he wanted to know.

"I understand," he said; they were the only words he could find in the midst of the fog clouding his brain. "I truly do."

What else could he say as he watched the woman he loved get up and start putting on her clothes?

Suddenly keenly aware of his own nakedness, he got up to tug on his trousers, realizing his hands were shaking as he did so.

Harmony dressed without saying anything else, and he trailed her to the entranceway and watched her put on her boots and then her jacket. When she turned to face him her face was expressionless, but the green of her eyes told him everything he needed to know.

"I've written up a job advertisement for my position," she said, her voice flat. "With your permission I'll start sending it out to the agencies. Perhaps put an ad in the Glasgow newspapers, as well."

He nodded, and somehow found his voice, despite the ache spreading out from his chest, choking him. "Yes, of course. Thank you."

A little smile tipped the edges of her lips, but there was little amusement in it and the sight was another heart-blow.

"Polite to the last," she said softly. "You really are an amazing man, and one day a woman with a stouter heart than mine will be very, very lucky to have you."

But I only want you.

Before he could say it, beg or plead the way everything in him told him he should, she was gone, shutting the door quietly behind her.

* * *

Around her were the sparkle of lights, the beautiful melodies of Christmas songs, the laughter of children. All the sounds of joy and happiness. But Harmony wondered if she'd ever feel either again.

Everything in her wanted to go back, to say she didn't mean it, but she couldn't—just couldn't put herself through living with and loving Cam.

Not when she knew what that entailed. What the likely outcome would be.

Who would put themselves into a situation like that knowingly, willingly, as though tempting fate to destroy them by stealing the person they loved away?

Letting herself into the surgery, she trudged upstairs. She'd never felt more alone.

The only person she could talk to, who she knew would understand, was her mother, and she was loath to disturb her on her vacation. They'd spoken a few times since she had gone to Yorkshire, and Harmony was happy to know she was enjoying herself and liked Fred's family. She'd sounded happier than she had in a long time, and Harmony didn't want to upset that.

Yet eventually she ended up calling, desperate to hear her mother's reassurance that she was doing the right thing. If anyone would agree with her stance it would be her mum.

She'd hardly said, "Hello," before her mother asked what was wrong.

Unable to hold it inside, she let the entire story go, telling her mum how she'd fallen for Cam, and how he wanted her to stay but she couldn't.

"He's just like Dad," she said, crying. "I can't bear the thought of going through what you did, Mum."

"If he's like your father, dear, you shouldn't be afraid."

Startled, considering all she'd told her mother about Cam's adventures, she asked, "What do you mean, Mum?"

"Well, the truth is that your father was a wonderful man—loving, caring, intelligent and, yes, adventurous. But it was that combination that drew me to him, and I knew what I was getting into when I married him."

Her mum took a deep breath—Harmony could hear it through the receiver.

"Your father might have felt he had something to prove, but I really think it was more a case that he knew he was on borrowed time and wanted to live his life to the fullest. However, he'd told me that climb would be his last. He wanted to be home more—for you and for me. He just never had the chance to make good on that promise."

Shocked by her mother's revelations, Harmony said, "You never told me that, Mum."

"It hurt too much to think of. I felt cheated and angry."

Sinking down onto the couch, Harmony tried to take in what her mother was saying, but she couldn't escape what was, for her, the bottom line.

"I don't think I can deal with it, Mum. The thought of him going off to do all those crazy things, perhaps never to return."

"That's something you have to decide—but don't let cowardice cheat you out of something beautiful," her mum said softly, and the sympathy in her voice was almost Harmony's undoing.

"I'm afraid, Mum. I love him so much, but I can't stand the thought of losing him because of some silly extreme sport."

"Harmony, think about this carefully. I loved your father, and I knew who and what he was when I married him. I went into it with my eyes open, although I never expected to lose him the way I did. I was young, and I thought we'd both live forever. But although it ended tragically I wouldn't change anything—not one moment of the time I spent with him. We were happy for the short time we were together, and that's what I clung to all those years when I mourned him, even through my anger. Plus, he'd given me you, and you and your Gran kept me going even on the days when I thought I couldn't put one foot in front of the other."

"Oh, Mum…" Harmony was crying again, but they weren't the wrenching, heartbroken tears she'd shed earlier. There was a softer quality to them—healing rather than hurting.

"Do what's right for you, darling. But don't let fear alone rule your life. Nothing is promised. No one knows what the next day will bring. You have to live fully, wholeheartedly, and hope and pray for the best. Don't trouble trouble, 'til trouble troubles you."

Hearing one of Gran's favorite sayings made Harmony chuckle, but coming as it did through her tears, it sounded more like a hiccup.

"I miss Gran so much," she said. "And I miss being with you right now."

"I miss her too. And you. I didn't think I could face Christmas if it wasn't for this trip with Fred to take my mind off how much we've lost this year, but without you here to celebrate with us it won't be complete."

They fell silent for a moment, with Harmony thinking how lucky she'd been to have her mum, and her gran, to raise her. Just like Cam with his grand-da, she wouldn't be the person she was today without them.

Then, ever practical, her mum said, "Do you want to leave the island? We'll be in Yorkshire for another week. You could join us and go back to London on the train when we leave."

Horrified at the thought of leaving Cam shorthanded during this busy time, she said, "No, of course not. I won't leave until I've found a replacement. I won't let my personal issues interfere with my work. Besides, God alone knows what mess the surgery would be in if I did."

Her mum laughed softly, and said, "That's my girl—full of vinegar and Scotch Bonnet peppers. Now, have a good think about what I've said. I know you're not the type to take chances, but some chances in life are worth taking."

"Okay, Mum. Love you."

After they'd hung up Harmony sat for a while thinking about everything. Talking to her mum had brought to mind her conversation with Katherine, and how she'd missed out on love perhaps out of fear of rejection and hurt. She contemplated it all until the headache pounding behind her tired eyes overtook her and she realized making any decisions was impossible.

After all, tomorrow is another day.

Another of Gran's sayings, culled from one of the old lady's favorite movies.

With the comforting words echoing in her brain, Harmony went to bed. And, although she hadn't thought it would happen, she fell into a deep and dreamless sleep.

CHAPTER NINETEEN

CAM WAS UP before first light next morning, finally giving up on his attempts to sleep. He'd tossed and turned the entire night, getting only snatches of shallow slumber, his brain refusing to shut down.

Very different from last evening, when he'd stood staring at the closed door and through a fog of pain and despair had been unable to form a coherent thought except for the hope that Harmony would come back.

Stumbling back to the living room, it had soon occurred to him to go after her. In the end it hadn't happened.

He'd been at war with himself—unable to understand how she could be so completely determined not to stay. At the same time at the back of his mind was the thought that it was better this way. If she couldn't accept him as he was, what hope was there for them to make a life together?

Those were the two thoughts in his muddled head until he'd lain down in bed. Then his brain had gone into the type of whirring overdrive that was incompatible with rest.

What she'd told him about her father made so many things he'd noticed before come into sharp focus. How scathing she'd been about the water jetpack, her reaction to the sky suit video. And it also made him appreciate how frightened she must have been watching him get into the water to rescue the boy stuck out in the old fishing village. Yet she hadn't tried to dissuade him from doing it—just done everything she could to make sure he was fit for the job, even in the face of his disagreeableness.

She was a woman worth giving up the world for and he knew it. What he *didn't* know—and this was the part that frightened him—was what kind of person he'd be if he gave up all the things he enjoyed for her. Would love turn to resentment as he watched his friends doing all the things he wished he could?

It seemed asinine to allow what were really just diversions to dictate his happiness, when true, lasting happiness was within reach. Especially as he wasn't planning to keep doing extreme sports forever. No matter how fit he kept himself, at some point he'd have to dial it back. And he'd always thought if he had children he'd definitely keep his activities to the less dangerous type.

Not that he considered what he did particularly dangerous. Walking across the street could be dangerous if you didn't pay attention to what you were doing, and he was meticulous in his preparations and research before doing anything.

But there was no getting around her fears, and he wasn't sure he could leave his adventures behind just yet.

He couldn't help wondering if it was even fair of him to ask her to see it from his point of view. In reality, they both had a point. Her fear was no less important than his drive to experience new things. To pit himself against his fears and test his abilities.

One thing was clear, however. The thought of losing her was haunting.

Would he ever get over her? He doubted it. He'd never been a big believer in love at first sight, or soul mates, but he remembered how he'd almost stumbled over his own feet the first time he saw her…how his heart had pounded. And every moment in her presence after that had just pulled him closer, made him fall harder.

If a friend had told him he'd proposed to a woman he'd only known for a few weeks Cam would have suggested slowing it down, making sure it wasn't just hormones. But here he was in love with Harmony, knowing in his heart that it was forever.

Cam sat on the edge of his bed, head in hands, wondering how to work it all out and finding no immediate answer.

He didn't want to face anyone, wished he could stay in with his thoughts, but tonight was the Christmas Eve Gala and he had so much to do. Hiding was impossible.

It was as he was leaving home to go to the church hall that a horrible thought struck him.

Suppose Harmony decided to leave today? The first ferry would be docking at eight. Did she plan to be on it when it left?

He pulled out his phone to call her, then realized it was still too early. Not that she was a late riser, but suddenly, after what had happened the day before, he wasn't comfortable calling her before office hours.

Of course, she might have taken off before office hours.

When he got down to the clinic he saw the apartment was dark and his heart sank—only for it to soar with relief when he looked back at the front of the building and realized she was already in the surgery.

So he called her, wanting to hear her voice, although he'd try to keep things businesslike.

"Hello?"

There was a cautious note to her voice and his heart ached to hear it. Even before they'd come to know each other well her confidence had shone through.

"Hey," he responded, wanting to ask if she was all right but not doing so. "I just wanted to let you know I'm over at the church hall if you need me for anything."

"Okay," she said, still stilted. "If I need you I'll call. But I know it's a busy day for you. The temporary medical team will be around, so I'll only bother you if it's an emergency."

"Right. Thanks."

He wanted to keep her on the line, and found himself standing still on the street, no longer walking, his feet itching to turn and go to her, just to see her face.

But all he could say was "Talk to you later."

Forcing himself to continue on toward the church, he braced himself for the day. Time to put on a happy face, since he couldn't stand the thought of having to explain to anyone, especially the CIs, why he wasn't his usual self.

Dora was like a whirling dervish, dashing about and making sure everything was set up to her specifications. Cam soon made himself useful, and had to smile when he saw some of the decor. The CI's had taken his request to make Harmony feel included to heart. Hopefully she'd like it.

Cam left a couple of times, to deal with matters on other parts of the island, keeping himself as busy as possible. Yet his thoughts never strayed far from Harmony.

Back at the church hall that afternoon, Dora came over, finally looking pleased. "The caterers are set up and already at work, and we're finally finished with the decorations. How does it look?"

"Wonderful," Cam said honestly. "You've outdone yourselves this year."

"You like what we've done for Harmony?" Dora looked unsure. "Do you think *she'll* like it?"

"I'm sure she will," Cam replied, suddenly struck with the thought that if he wasn't careful Harmony might not even see it. She was just the type to withdraw into herself and not come to the gala at all. And that wouldn't do. "Can I put you in charge of making sure she gets here on time? I have to go down and greet the guests at the ferry."

To his disbelief, Dora didn't even look surprised. If anything, her smile widened. "I will. It's going to be our best Christmas Eve Gala ever."

Cam smiled with her, but inside he knew it wouldn't be for him. Nothing would be the best without Harmony.

All day, while treating a variety of minor medical issues, Harmony had wrestled with the question of whether she would go to the gala or not. She knew how busy the CIs had been preparing for it, and wanted to be supportive. But she wasn't sure she was ready to face Cam, and wondered if her being there would make him uncomfortable. It was clear he loved Christmas, and he had been so excited whenever he spoke about the gala she knew he was looking forward to it immensely.

She kept busy in between patients by going over the advertisement for her replacement compulsively, and yet never quite got around to hitting Send to the various job sites. And the entire time her mother's revelations about her father kept playing through her head.

No matter what she thought of Cam's adventurous nature, or the reasons he'd gotten involved with extreme and dangerous sports, he was a very responsible person. It was obvious in everything he did. There was nothing truly selfish about him, even considering his determination to do the things she was so afraid of. To him they were just activities he enjoyed. It might have started as a way to exert his independence, but it had become important to him for other reasons. She suspected it was a way to stretch himself, maybe blow off the stress of his career and keeping the island running and profitable.

No, the real problem was with her.

There didn't seem any way to get past her fear.

Every time she thought about the video he'd been watching, with those crazy people jumping off cliffs in just a flimsy suit, not even a parachute, her blood froze. She didn't think she could bear watching him go off, knowing that was what he was planning to do.

Yet the love she felt for him was so strong she wasn't sure how she would be able to walk away. Oh, she'd no doubt that she'd do it, if only for her own self-esteem. But what would life be like after that? She had no idea—knew only that it would be bleak.

The question of whether or not she'd go to the gala was answered with a call from Dora.

"Harmony, we'll be by to collect you at seven for the gala."

"Oh, I don't—"

"Seven," Dora interrupted, in her brook-no-nonsense tone, effectively cutting off any resistance Harmony might have tried to put up. "And don't be late."

She didn't even wait for Harmony to respond, simply hung up, the conversation over as far as she was concerned.

And despite her heavy heart, and her misgivings about spoiling Cam's night by being there, Harmony did as ordered and was ready when the CIs arrived to collect her.

Without an extensive choice of wardrobe, she'd put on a red knit wrap dress she'd packed into her suitcase on a whim, and was happy that she had. Pairing it with knee-high boots that had small pointed heels—what she'd always thought of as her "witchy boots"—she knew that at least her feet and legs would be warm. It had been windy during the afternoon, as another snow squall came east off the sea, and there was the promise of snow in the air again.

She was shrugging into her coat when the ladies arrived, and even though she was used to their habit of talking over each other, Harmony sensed a special excitement in their rapid-fire chatter. Not to mention the way they surrounded her and whisked her out the door, as though they were afraid she'd change her mind.

"Wow!" she said as they walked through the small parking area in front of the church hall and she saw the usually rather prosaic building for the first time. "This looks amazing."

There was a series of arches set up along the path leading into the hall, all decorated with white and gold ornaments that twisted in the breeze, refracting the light from hundreds of tiny bulbs.

Pausing on the path, she was just admiring their handiwork as the first bits of snow started to fall, adding to the ambience, when Katherine said, "For goodness' sakes, let's go inside."

"What's the rush?" Harmony asked.

But none of them answered, just hustled her forward under the arches and into the building. In the vestibule they took off their coats, and Harmony followed the older ladies inside.

And came to a halt, her mouth falling open.

The hall looked lovely, but what immediately caught her eye was a tree covered in poinsettias, strategically placed so it was the first thing anyone entering the hall would see. Interspersed between the silk blooms were golden hearts.

The CIs were all watching for her reaction and Harmony felt her eyes sting as she looked at their hopeful faces.

"Did you do this for me?" she asked, her voice hitching.

"Well, Cam said you told him you always had poinsettias at Christmas, but we couldn't get enough plants in time, so unfortunately silk will have to do," Ingrid replied.

"It's beautiful!" she exclaimed, giving them all a round of hugs. "How sweet of you."

"Look at the tree skirt," Dora said. "Sela made it special."

Harmony went closer, then stooped down to get a better look.

"Jonkanoo!" she cried, as she recognized various figures from the traditional Jamaican Christmas bands, who dressed up and danced in the streets. "Sela, it's gorgeous."

"It certainly caught *my* eye. It's so much like the prints we have at home."

The voice came from behind her. It was one she recognized but couldn't believe she was hearing.

She looked up and had to put a hand on the ground to stop herself falling over. Then she was on her feet, rushing for a hug.

"Mum! Oh, Mum…" She pulled back, tears filling her eyes. "What are you doing here?"

"We were invited," Mum said, brushing Harmony's cheek with her hand.

"The Laird arranged it all," Dora said, with a suspicious little crackle in her throat.

Harmony suspected there wasn't a dry eye in their little group as she hugged her mother again, swinging her from side to side. Then she was hugging Fred, who was beaming from ear to ear, and she was introduced to his daughter, his son-in-law, his son and three grandchildren.

Yet, through it all, even with joy coursing through her heart, she was aware of one thing.

Cam wasn't there.

She knew because she kept looking for him—even when the CIs took her to show her the special dessert table, with gizzadas, sweet potato pone and Jamaican Christmas cake, the latter baked by her mother.

"How did you manage all this?" she kept saying, but the CIs just laughed and patted her shoulder.

Eventually the family group made their way toward the table reserved for them, but Harmony still couldn't see Cam anywhere.

"Did you meet Cam?" she asked her mother quietly.

"He met us at the ferry and took us up to the Manor. I haven't seen him since just before you came in, though."

Her mum's hand on Harmony's arm kept her in place for a moment.

"I think he's wonderful, Harmony. When he contacted me and asked if we'd come for Christmas I knew he was someone special. Selfless. The rooms he's putting us in should be making him money, not being given away, but he wanted you to be happy."

Then, with one long, meaningful look at her daughter, she let go and went to sit with Fred, leaving Harmony to chew on what she'd said.

CHAPTER TWENTY

THE SNOW WAS starting to come down harder, and the small, glittery flakes that had first fallen were replaced with bigger, fluffier ones. Cam brushed off the bench with his gloved hand, then sat facing Grand-Da's grave, looking up into the cloudy sky at the snow drifting earthward.

Every moment spent putting together the perfect Christmas Eve for Harmony had been worth it just to see the astonishment and happiness light up her face. He'd stood at the back of the room, out of the way, where he could watch her unfolding surprise and see her reaction, and his heart had soared when she'd hugged her mother, happy tears on her cheeks.

"I wish you could have seen it, Grand-Da. It was one of the most beautiful moments I've ever witnessed."

It had taken a lot of finagling and some downright deception to put it all together. When he'd first got the idea he'd been wary of calling Mrs. Kinkaid out of the blue and asking her if she would come to the island. After all, she didn't know him from a hole in the wall. Yet Harmony's mother had been gracious, and almost embarrassingly grateful for the opportunity. Cam thought she might even have been crying a little when he'd spoken with her the first time.

But he knew what it was like to go through the first Christmas after you'd lost someone seminal in your life, and both Harmony and her mother were facing that alone rather than together. The year he'd lost Grand-Da, Christmas hadn't held the same magic for him until his island family had rallied around. His parents and cousins had made the effort to come too, and having everyone together had rendered the season not just bearable, but a lovely tribute to the old man.

Shoving his hand into his pocket, he fingered the felt heart. He'd kept meaning to put it on the tree up at the Manor, but somehow had always ended up sticking it back into his coat pocket. It reminded him of Harmony—of the day he'd realized the attraction he felt was far stronger than he had ever imagined.

"That's what Christmas is supposed to be, right, Grand-Da?" he said into the cold, wintry night. "Family. Joy. Love."

"And you've done so much to make my Christmas perfect, Cam."

The snow had muffled her footsteps, so he hadn't heard her approach, and when he turned to look Harmony was standing just behind the bench.

"I thought I'd find you here," she continued, coming forward to sit beside him.

"Just a little visit with Grand-Da. Being out here helps me think."

He couldn't take his eyes off her beautiful, shining face. Her eyes sparkled brighter than any of the holiday lights, shining amber in the glow of the nearby streetlamp.

"Thank you." The words were simple, but behind them was a wealth of joy.

Cam shook his head. "I don't need your thanks, my love. Just to know you're happy is enough for me."

She reached out then, and took his hand. She wasn't wearing gloves, and instinctively he covered her fingers with his to keep them warm.

Harmony looked down at their hands, and then back up at him. "I've never been happier, Cam. But it's not complete without you."

Something shifted inside him—a deep soul-shudder that brought with it the realization that he'd do anything—*anything*—to keep this woman in his life.

He took a deep breath, the cold air filling his lungs and seeming to blow all his previous doubts away. Reaching across, he took her other hand. When she placed it in his, his pounding heart felt a little lighter.

"I'll give it all up—the mountain-climbing, skydiving, caving, hang gliding, everything—if you love me. I never want to hurt you, or make you worry. If that's what it takes to have you with me forever, I'll do it. I don't want anyone but you."

Harmony shook her head, those darling little lines coming and going between her brows, and he felt his heart break once more, thinking she was rejecting him again.

"I don't need you to do that," she said quietly, her gaze intent on his. "It's part of who you are...your adventurous spirit. It might make me feel more secure if you stopped, but it wouldn't make you happy, and letting you live your best life is important to me."

"The very best life I could live is with you," he replied, meaning it more than he'd ever meant anything in his life before. "You're all that matters—all I really care about."

Her frown faded and she smiled then—a sweet curve of her lips that made his heart race a little faster.

"I'm not willing to let my fears keep me from being with you, no matter what you decide. Go dive off one of those mountains in that wing suit and enjoy yourself. I won't promise to be there to watch you, and I can't say I won't be scared until I have you back safe, but I know you're not reckless. I know how responsible you are, and that you'll be as careful as someone doing something like that can be. But I also know that if you gave it all up for me you might eventually resent me, and I couldn't bear that. So go off to Peru, or wherever else you want to, and I'll be here, waiting for you when you come home."

He knew then there was no way he was letting her go and he told her so.

"I want to settle down with you, have children with you, make new traditions and have the happiness only you can give me. All those sports and pastimes are fun, but they're nothing when compared to the thought of having you by my side for the rest of my life."

Her gaze searched his for a long moment, then she smiled, and he somehow knew it would all be okay.

"Are we always going to argue over who's right?" she asked, the mischief in her gaze lightening his mood. "Even when we're trying to give in to each other?"

"I suspect we will, love," he replied. "But I look forward to every spat."

The wind picked up, just for an instant, and the snow swirled as though dancing a jig across the ground. Cam thought for a moment that the creak of the trees was like Grand-Da's laugh.

"I have something for you," he said, not knowing

where the thought came from, but feeling the rightness of it.

Letting go one of her hands, he reached into his pocket and pulled out the heart, holding it out to Harmony. She took it, releasing his other hand to trace the luckenbooth design. Then she pressed it over her own heart, and when she looked up there were tears in the corners of her eyes.

"Cameron MacRurie, are you giving me your heart, having already stolen mine?" Despite the quip, her voice was a little wobbly. "I promise to take good care of it."

He held out his arms and she slid into them, wrapping hers around his waist.

"You already had my heart, Nurse Kinkaid."

The wind faded slightly and Cam noticed for the first time the sounds of chatter and laughter from the hall, the holiday music borne on the breeze. It seemed to typify the happiness filling him to overflowing as he held Harmony close, felt her snuggle into his embrace.

"This is perfect, Cam." She was whispering, as though loath to speak too loudly lest the aura of peace and love surrounding them be broken. "I'll always remember this Christmas, this night, as the happiest of my life."

"To date, maybe?" he teased, thinking about all the days and nights to come, knowing the future was suddenly brighter than he'd ever imagined it could be.

She raised her head, brought her lips close to his, and said, "Definitely."

The temperature was dropping, and her mother was waiting in the hall. If he kissed her he might never want to stop. But resisting her lips was the hardest thing he'd ever done.

"We should go back inside," he muttered, sublimely

aware of her breath against his face, the sweet, lush sensation of her body resting so perfectly on his. "Everyone will wonder where we are."

"No, they won't," she said, getting a millimeter closer, so he wasn't sure how there was actually still empty space between their mouths. "They're all smarter than that. Now, shut up, Dr. Laird, and kiss me."

So he did.

* * * * *

A MISTLETOE KISS FOR THE SINGLE DAD

TRACI DOUGLASS

MILLS & BOON

To my family, and to all those lovely summers
we spent together on the beaches of Pentwater…

CHAPTER ONE

"I'm sorry. Could you repeat that, please?" Dr. Christabelle Watson blinked at the rather uncomfortable-looking lawyer sitting across the desk from her. "I don't think I heard you correctly."

Dylan Carter, the only attorney in tiny Bayside, Michigan, and therefore the person handling her aunt Marlene's estate, took a deep breath. "Um…okay. Sure. It says here your aunt left half of her practice to you and the other half to Dr. Nicholas Marlowe."

Nick, who sat next to her, shifted in his seat and straightened the dark jacket of his suit. Once he'd been a pediatric surgeon in Atlanta. Now he was back in their hometown as well, working as a GP.

Her aunt Marlene had been a general practitioner as well, a pillar of the Bayside community, liked and respected by all. Seemed everyone had turned out for her aunt's funeral earlier in the day and said their fond farewells and given condolences to Belle on her loss.

A loss that had been made even harder because she'd had no idea her aunt's cancer had progressed to stage four—terminal. Her chest ached anew with sorrow and regret. If only she'd known her aunt was so sick.

If only…

She tried to console herself with the fact that even

if she had known the severity of her beloved aunt's illness, it wasn't like she could have easily flown home to Michigan anyway. Not with a packed list of new patient consults back in California and a practice partnership on the line. Aunt Marlene wouldn't have wanted that anyway. She'd hated being fussed over, especially when she didn't feel well.

Belle sniffled and twisted a tissue in her hands. Everything was such a mess.

Life had certainly taken a strange turn in the past twenty-four hours. Yesterday her boss, Dr. Reyes, had wanted to meet with her about the partnership right before she'd received the call about her aunt. Now the world as she knew it had changed forever. She'd filled out the required bereavement paperwork with Human Resources, made her quick excuses to Dr. Reyes, then rushed to catch a red-eye flight to Lansing.

Everything after that was a bit of a hazy blur.

She cleared her constricted throat and forced herself to focus on the attorney once more. "There must be some mistake."

"Nope. No mistake." Dylan frowned at his copy of her aunt's will and pointed at a few particular lines. "Right here. See?"

He held the document toward her so she could look for herself.

She squinted down at the legalese. Yep. Right there in black and white.

All assets divided equally between Christabelle Watson and Nicholas Marlowe.

Nick too took the opportunity to lean in and Belle sat back fast, keeping as much distance between them as possible. His scent—soap and fabric softener—was the same as she remembered. His warmth penetrated the sleeve of her black blazer, sending tingles of unwanted awareness through her. Darn him. Even after everything he'd put her through, she still had the same tingling reaction whenever he was around. Not that she'd let him know.

Nope. Where Nicholas Marlowe was concerned, Belle had built her barriers high and strong.

Still, bone-deep exhaustion and grief threatened to overwhelm her, and she blinked hard against the sting of unshed tears. As a physician, she'd learned to mask her emotions behind a thick layer of professional stoicism— a necessity when personal feelings could lead to disaster with a patient. There were some who said she'd gotten too good at it, though, like with the few men she'd dated over the years. But at times like these it was the only thing that kept her going.

She clasped her hands in her lap to hide the slight tremble in her fingers and ignored the vibrating cell phone in her pocket. "Can you at least tell me how long it might take to get this all settled, Dylan? I have pressing matters back in California. Consultations and patients and—"

"Shouldn't your aunt's last wishes take precedence here?" Nick asked, his tone cold. His voice held a raw edge she didn't recall from their high-school days together. Gone were his easy smiles and easy banter. Then again, they were different people now. After graduation, she'd gone off to UCLA, then a surgical fellowship at Harvard. Nick had graduated at the top of his class from the University of Michigan, then done medical school at Northwestern. He'd also gotten married before he'd finished his residency, the very thing he'd told Belle he'd never do.

She gave an ironic snort. He'd broken up with her in

senior year, saying they were too young and being tied down would only hold her back. Then he'd turned right around and married someone else a few years later. Of course, it didn't help she'd found out by accident either. God, what a naive fool she'd been back then. She'd shown up at his apartment complex in Evanston, Illinois, hoping to talk to him about the career choice looming on her horizon. After all, she and Nick had been friends since childhood, despite their painful breakup. No one had ever known her better or understood her more. So she'd made a rash decision and shown up at his place, only to find a celebration in full swing in the common area of his building. An engagement party for Nick and the woman he was going to marry. A woman who'd also been obviously pregnant with his baby.

Even all these years later, those memories sliced deep.

Hurt and embarrassed, she'd left without ever speaking to Nick.

Belle had still loved him then, but he'd moved on. Moved on and left her behind, shattering her hopes they might one day reconcile and get back together. Now she'd put her work and her professional life first, only dating men who weren't interested in anything long term, keeping her heart and her emotions out of the equation.

She glanced over toward the corner where an eight-year-old boy played on a tablet. No denying Connor was Nick's son. Same curly brown hair and adorable dimples as his father.

Belle hazarded another look at Nick, the man who'd once been her whole world. With dark shadows marring the skin beneath his eyes and a shadow of stubble on his jaw, he looked as weary as she felt.

Aunt Marlene had mentioned his wife had passed away two years previously. Being a single parent wasn't easy and Belle couldn't imagine how hard it must've been for Nick to deal with the loss of a spouse plus raising his son alone. And poor Connor. Belle had lost her own parents at the same age Connor was now. It had been devastating. If Aunt Marlene hadn't taken her in and given her a loving, stable home, God only knew where she might've ended up.

Nick caught Belle's gaze, his expression wary. Years earlier, his soulful brown eyes had sparkled with mirth, ready for any challenge, always up for anything…

Now they stared at her, flat and somber.

"You said there was a stipulation?" Nick asked, refocusing his attention on the attorney.

"Right. Yes," Dylan said. "Marlene wants you both to reopen the free clinic one last time before you settle the estate."

"What?" Belle sat back, shocked. She only had three days of bereavement leave. "The free clinic isn't held until Christmas Eve."

"Dad?" Connor said from the corner. "I'm hungry."

"We'll eat in a minute." Nick frowned at Dylan. "That's nine days from now."

Belle rubbed her forehead. "I'm sorry. I want to respect my aunt's wishes, but I've got obligations in Beverly Hills. I can't drop everything. There has to be a way around it. Perhaps we could hold the clinic sooner?"

"That's impossible." Nick scrubbed a hand over his face and gave an aggrieved sigh. "It'll take a week or more just to get everything ready and I'm sure there are repairs to be made. The clinic was pretty run-down the last time I was there. Besides, I have my own practice to contend with before the holidays."

"Sorry, guys," Dylan said. "But Marlene had this will drafted through an estate lawyer in Lansing last year and it's airtight. I've checked. Honestly, the fastest way to get all of this settled is to honor your aunt's final wishes and reopen the free clinic on Christmas Eve."

Frustrated, Belle finally gave in and pulled out her cell phone, to find a text from Dr. Reyes shown on-screen.

Why aren't you answering my calls?

Irritated, Belle clicked off the device and slid it back into her pocket, heat prickling her cheeks. In the operating room she was famous for her cool, calm demeanor under pressure, but spending five minutes with Nick beside her again—bringing up memories of the past—had her cage thoroughly rattled. Belle didn't like it. Not to mention the free clinic was what had brought her and Nick together in the first place, helping out Aunt Marlene, working side by side to clean exam rooms or prep patients or wrap instruments for sterilization. It was because of those days that the smell of antiseptic still made her smile...

Ugh. Belle shook off those memories and turned to Nick. "I'm trying to be practical here. I'd think you'd appreciate my efforts, considering your busy work schedule and your son. I loved my aunt. I'd do anything for her, but—"

"Except honor her final wishes."

"How dare you?" Outrage stormed through Belle like a thundercloud. She sat back and crossed her arms. "Dylan, are we finished? I'd like to get a good night's sleep and consider this all again with a clear head in the morning. Can we continue this tomorrow?"

"Not so fast," Nick answered instead, pinching the bridge of his nose between his thumb and forefinger. "I'll need to check my schedule to see if I can fit in another meeting. My clinic is slammed this time of year as it is, and I need to check with my physician's assistant to be sure she can handle the extra workload. Plus, Connor needs to be picked up from school. Then there's dinner and getting him to bed." At Belle's irritated sigh, he narrowed his gaze on her. "Or maybe you'd prefer I pull an all-nighter like I did in college?"

She hid her cringe admirably. Any reminder of college and that awful night she'd made her surprise visit to see him had the knots of tension in Belle's upper back quadrupling.

"Dad." Connor's tone grew more plaintive. "I'm starving."

"Give me one more minute." Nick gave a long-suffering sigh, his voice dull. "Look, I realize I'm the last person you want to partner with here, Belle, but Marlene made it clear in her will this is what she wanted and unless we do this together, it will never work."

Darn it, he was right. Much as she hated to admit it.

Fatigue and sadness crowded in around her once more, but duty compelled her to stand firm. "I want to help, I do. But my boss is already texting me about his unreturned calls." She shook her head. Disappointing people was her least favorite thing, even people like Nick. "Plus, I've got opportunities on the line back in California. I have to keep my priorities straight."

"What about your aunt's wishes?" Nick said. "Shouldn't *she* be your priority right now?"

The words struck her like a slap in the face and ricocheted inside her chest like shrapnel. When she'd been eighteen she would've given anything to hear him ask her to stay. Now it felt like one more complication in an already chaotic mess.

Her cell phone buzzed again, most likely with another text from Dr. Reyes.

Through the window behind Dylan's desk the sky glowed pink and gold and deepest purple as the sun set and people milled about outside after the funeral. Belle smoothed her hand down her black skirt, her head aching. She'd only returned to Bayside to close this chapter of her life for good. With Aunt Marlene gone, there was no reason for her to come back here again after this. She was alone in the world now and the thought made her weary beyond her thirty-six years.

"Don't mean to rush you, folks." Dylan cleared his throat. "But I've got a holiday dance recital for my daughter tonight, so if we could wrap this up, I'd really appreciate it."

"Right." Determined, Belle stood and grabbed her bright red cashmere coat from the back of her chair. "I guess that's it, then."

"Oh, there is one more thing." Dylan pulled something out of one of his desk drawers. "Marlene had a small amount left in her savings after the medical bills were paid. It goes to each of you." He passed two envelopes across the desk. "Ten thousand dollars each. And there's a copy of the will in there for each of you too."

Belle tucked the envelope inside her handbag without looking at it. "Nick, if you can't make a formal meeting, perhaps we can schedule a conference call tomorrow to discuss this further?"

He shook his head. "I'll make it work. Your aunt wanted us to do this and I intend to honor her final wishes."

A swirling vortex of grief opened in the pit of Belle's stomach, making her temples throb.

"Dad," Connor said, frowning. "I'm hungry-y-y..."

Nick waved his son over then walked to the door before turning back to Belle. "Do you have plans for dinner? If not, you're welcome to join us at Pat's. We can talk more there."

Honestly, she didn't have plans. In fact, her stomach was rumbling, and her new designer pumps were pinching her toes something terrible. She'd also not had a chance to pick up any groceries and nothing stayed open past eight in Bayside. "Fine. But only to discuss the clinic, not to socialize."

"Agreed." Nick pulled on his own black wool coat then ushered her and his son outside. "No socializing here. Promise."

As they headed into the chilly mid-December night, Nick eyed Belle's stiletto pumps with trepidation. Seemed she'd forgotten what winters could be like here in Michigan. Sure enough, as they trudged across the slick pavement, her feet slipped, and she clutched his arm like a lifeline.

"You need boots."

"I have boots. They're in my suitcase inside the funeral home." She stiffened beside him and released his arm, clutching her coat tighter around herself. "I'll be sure to wear them tomorrow."

He shook his head. Her coat probably cost more than his house and all its contents. When he'd been at the top of the pediatric surgery ladder in Atlanta, he'd seen plenty of women dressed to the nines in designer duds. Hell, he'd worn his share of tuxes back then too. Now, though, he dressed for comfort. He'd moved back to Bayside a year and a half ago, given up his high-pressure lifestyle and all the stress along with it, and wouldn't change his decision for the world. Connor was better off with fresh air and room to grow. Losing his wife, Vicki, had been hard on both of them, but Bayside was home.

Always had been. Always would be. At least for him.

He hunched farther down inside his wool coat and turned the collar up against the brisk wind now rolling in off Lake Michigan. Weathermen predicted snow tonight, from what he'd heard on the radio on his way over to the funeral.

Belle slipped again. He reached for her elbow, but she pulled away. "I've got it."

"Yeah. I can see that."

He stifled a grin at her peeved glare.

Connor walked along ahead of them, oblivious.

"Don't cross the street by yourself, son," Nick called. "Wait for us."

Belle gave him some serious side-eye at the same time his son gave him a perturbed stare.

"He's eight, right?" she asked.

"Yes." Nick bristled at her judgmental tone. Fine. Maybe Connor was old enough to start doing things on his own, but Nick wasn't there yet. He was trying, but his son was growing up—far faster than Nick wanted sometimes—and guilt lingered in his heart. He did his best to be both mom and dad to Connor, but there were only so many hours in a day and it was just the two of them. Besides, Belle had no right to question his parenting style. Still, in an effort to keep the peace he swallowed the words he wanted to say and instead pointed to a redbrick building across the street on the corner. "Diner's over there."

"I know where Pat's is." Belle's tone snapped with

affront. So much for not arguing. "I'm from here, remember?"

"Figured you forgot. Kind of like your boots."

She glared at him, her green eyes glittering in the dim streetlight.

The three of them crossed the street and pushed inside the restaurant. Pat Randall—the diner's proud owner for over thirty years—waved to Nick from behind the counter, oblivious to the tension pulsating around them like a force field. "Hey, Doc. Con."

A few other patrons were eating a late dinner there too, probably having wandered over after Marlene's service. Some were his patients, like little Analia Hernandez and her family. She was the same age as Connor and would've been in his class at school, but she'd been born with Crouzon syndrome, a rare genetic condition that had caused the bones of her skull to fuse prematurely. There was no mental deficiency associated with the disorder, thank goodness, but the concave shape of her midface did contribute to the little girl's breathing issues. Still, Analia was happy and confident, always quick with a grin and brimming with curiosity. Analia raised a hand at Connor as they passed their table. "Hey, Con."

"Hey, Ana." Con waved back.

They took a table near the far wall and Belle sat gingerly, like the whole place might blow up in her face. Nick sat in the chair beside Connor's, across from Belle, and raked a hand through his hair, his appetite buried under the uncomfortable feelings stirred by seeing Belle again after all these years. With her living out in California, it had been easier for him to keep her as more of an abstract notion in his head.

A woman, *the* woman, from his past. Always there,

but quarantined, like a dangerous virus that could easily hijack his system. Now, though, with her back in Bayside, even temporarily, he was forced to reconcile the promise he'd made to Vicki with reality. He'd let Belle go back in high school and obviously she'd moved on and done well for herself. She'd left Bayside and him behind eighteen years ago and hadn't looked back since. He should be happy, overjoyed, well and truly done with it all.

Why then did his heart pinch a little each time he caught sight of Belle now?

Must be stress. Had to be. He'd headed to Marlene's funeral directly after spending sixteen hours in his clinic and he had another full schedule tomorrow. Maybe Belle had been correct. Maybe they should have put this conversation off until he'd gotten some sleep, had some peace and quiet to get his life in order again.

Except deep down he knew it wouldn't change anything.

Work. Connor. Home.

Those were his driving forces now.

The only things that mattered.

Dinner with Belle, anything to do with Belle really, shouldn't be on his radar.

Other than reopening the free clinic one last time. He owed that to Marlene, even if it would be about as much fun as a root canal.

"What can I get you folks to drink?" Pat asked, setting three glasses of water on the table.

Belle perused her choices, frowning. "Do you have anything organic?"

"Uh…we've got tea."

"Is it green?"

"Brown, last time I checked." Pat chuckled. "Unless it's gone bad."

"I'll stick with water, thank you," Belle said, her expression dour.

"Sure thing." Pat jotted something on his little pad, then grinned. "So great to see you again, Belle. I'm so sorry about what happened to Marlene."

"Thank you, Mr. Randall."

"Please, call me Pat. We're like family around here."

She nodded, then went back to looking at her menu.

Nick cleared his throat. "Con and I will have sodas, Pat."

"Cherry flavor in those?"

"Of course." Nick winked at his son.

"Be right back." Pat walked away, leaving them alone again.

Even beneath the diner's fluorescent lights, Belle's auburn hair still glowed like wildfire. A trait she and her aunt had shared. Her mom too, if Nick remembered right. Of course, he'd only been eight too when her parents had died in a car accident. The whole town had turned out for their funeral, as well. He pictured little Belle back then, sitting alone on Marlene's porch, not crying, not scared, just sort of oddly stoic.

Kind of like she was now.

Belle leaned closer to him, close enough for him to catch a hint of scent—something fresh and floral with a hint of mint. "You don't let him order his own food either? How controlling of you."

"Remind me again when you became a parenting expert?" He clasped his hands on the table, all traces of tenderness toward Belle vanishing. Connor's well-being was his top priority in life. Period. Amen. He'd promised Vicki he'd take care of their son and he intended to keep that vow. He changed subjects to safer territory. "How's California?"

"Sunny." Her phone continued buzzing like an angry bee.

"Can't you just turn that thing off while we eat?" he asked her. "Don't you have an answering service to field calls when you're out of the office?"

"Yes." Her green eyes flashed again with annoyance. "My boss is trying to reach me."

"Here we are, folks." Pat returned with their drinks. "What are we having for dinner?"

"Connor and I will split a burger and fries. Cheese, no onion. Medium-well."

"Great." Pat wrote down his order. "And for you, Belle?"

"I'll have the house salad. No cheese or croutons. Dressing on the side. Fat-free Italian. Hold the bread stick too."

"Or you could just bring her a cardboard box, Pat. It'll be just as tasty," Nick said.

The two men chuckled, and she gave them an impassive stare.

"While I always appreciate your culinary opinions, Nick, I'll stick with what's healthy." She jammed her menu back into the holder and gave Pat a cool smile. "And could I have a lemon wedge for my water? Thank you."

Pat left, shaking his head.

"Are your parents still in town?" Belle asked as she unbelted her expensive coat to reveal the equally expensive tailored suit beneath, all sharp lines and jagged edges. So different from the cute, geeky girl he'd fallen in love with back in high school. Gone were her soft heart and pretty curves, her lilting giggles as they'd dreamed about taking the medical world by storm, like all those TV doctors on their favorite shows.

Nope. Not going there.

He shoved away the pang of nostalgia welling inside him for the kids they'd once been—so young, so idealistic, so naive—and took a deep breath. The air filled with the smell of grease and the sizzle of frying meat.

What had happened between them in the past didn't matter.

What mattered was the here and now.

"No. They moved to Florida right after Dad retired a few years back."

He glanced across the diner at the Hernandez family, laughing and talking, and yearned to join their relaxed group. Juan and his family had moved to Bayside about a month after Nick and Connor. Juan had transferred to the auto plant nearby from a factory near Guaymas, Mexico. After a bit of a rocky start with learning the language and resettling in a new country, they'd become a beloved part of the community, with little Analia basically having the run of Bayside. Good thing too, since the auto plant had been closed now and Juan was out of work and couldn't afford to move his family back to Mexico. The community had rallied around them, making sure they had food and clothes and enough money to survive on. Juan was also working construction to make ends meet while his wife tutored high-school kids in Spanish.

"Do you know them?" Belle asked, watching the Hernandez family, as well.

"I do. Their daughter is a patient of mine," he said. "Why?"

"No reason." She shrugged and fiddled with her napkin. "Crouzon's?"

"Yep."

"How old is she?"

"Con's age."

"She should be ready for the second phase of her surgery soon," Belle said, all animosity between them gone as they discussed medicine. Funny how that worked.

"She is, but it's expensive. Analia's father lost his job and I've been working to get their case taken on pro bono by a colleague of mine in Detroit, but so far the paperwork is still tied up." Nick sighed and sipped his cherry cola. "They're doing the best they can. Analia's happy."

"Is she?" Belle glanced at the little girl again, then looked away. "Let's get back to discussing the free clinic. It's why we're here."

"The first thing we need to do is get into there and assess the state of things," he said, forcing an ease he didn't quite feel. "I'll call my PA tonight and tell her the situation. See if she can handle the patient load tomorrow by herself until we can work out a schedule."

"If repairs need to be made, we'll have to hire someone. Might be hard to get the work done on such short notice." Belle surveyed the interior of the diner as she spoke, and he tried to see it through her eyes. Far from the pristine interiors of Rodeo Drive, Pat's looked like a thrift store had exploded—local knickknacks and memorabilia covering every square inch of wall space.

"Juan Hernandez might be able to help. He does good work." He'd helped renovate the house Nick had bought after returning to Bayside. "I'll ask him if he can stop in tomorrow and take a look." Nick glanced at the calendar on the wall, donated courtesy of the local volunteer fire department. "If we get started in the morning, that gives us eight days until Christmas Eve."

"Fine. But this is all still contingent on my boss granting me an extension on my bereavement leave." She folded her hands atop the table, prim as a church lady on Sunday.

Pat set their plates down a few minutes later. "Dinner is served. Enjoy."

Nick thanked him then divided the huge burger in two and put half on Con's plate, along with half the fries, then reached for the ketchup and mustard, noticing Belle picking through her salad. "Are you going to eat your food or sort it to death?"

"I want to make sure there's no cheese or croutons hidden in here."

"You ordered it without and I'm sure Pat fixed it that way."

She kept picking and he rolled his eyes.

Belle turned her attention to Connor instead. "What do you like to do for fun?"

His son swallowed a fry, ketchup smeared on his cheek. "I play hockey."

"Really?" She gave Nick a surprised look. "So, you won't let him cross the street or order for himself, but you let him go out on the ice and risk life and limb over a puck?"

"Hockey is a very safe sport," Nick ground out, a muscle pulsating near his tense jaw. "The coach supervises the team at all times and takes every precaution to ensure the kids' safety. Besides, I played when I was his age. It's good exercise and the team-building skills he learns are essential for later in life." He gave her arch stare, as if challenging her to contradict him. For reasons he didn't want to contemplate, he wanted to get a rise out of her. Disrupt that cool exterior of hers and get her as riled up as he felt inside. "If you're so concerned for my son's well-being, Connor's got his last game for the year the day before Christmas Eve in Manistee. Come with us and check it out."

The moment the words left his mouth he wanted to take them back. Spending more time around Belle than what he'd already be doing to get the free clinic ready wasn't a good idea.

Thankfully, she turned him down anyway. "I'm sure I'll be busy preparing to reopen the clinic, but I appreciate the invitation."

Nick exhaled slowly, feeling like he'd dodged a major bullet. He chewed his burger without tasting it, glancing over to find Connor fiddling with his tablet again. Normally he banned devices at the dinner table and was about to tell his son to stow the electronics away then hesitated.

Controlling. Belle's description rubbed him wrong in all the worst place. He wasn't controlling. He was doing the best he could here, dammit.

So, instead, he bit back the reprimand for Connor and swallowed it down with another swig of cherry soda. One night of web surfing during dinner wouldn't hurt anything, right?

Belle continued nibbling her food like she was at some fancy society luncheon and not Bayside's best greasy spoon. Nick wasn't fooled by her pretension, though. She must've forgotten he'd seen her covered with mashed potatoes and dripping with cheesy macaroni after a particularly heinous food fight in the school cafeteria. Regardless of their years apart, he knew the real Belle—even if that girl now seemed buried deeper than his beloved Vicki and the future they'd planned. After Connor had been born, he'd dreamed of having more children, more family vacations, more time to just enjoy the life he and Vicki had built together. They'd not married for love, but over their time together their friendship had grown into something better—affection, support, loyalty, trust. Rare and valuable things these days. Vicki had been his go-to person for talking out his problems and sharing his victories. He'd even told her about Belle. In the big and the small ways, he and Vicki had been there for each other. Without her, he'd done his best to manage on his own, charging forward, putting one foot in front of the other each day, doing what had to be done.

Life had gone on. Different than he'd expected, but onward just the same.

"After I talk to my boss tonight, I'll come up with a list of tasks for you to handle and a schedule so we can make sure nothing gets missed," Belle said, jarring him back to the present.

Nick snorted and shook his head, focusing on his exhaustion and the grumpiness it caused, because if he didn't, he'd be too vulnerable, too raw, and that was unacceptable. "Just like old times."

"Excuse me?" Belle paused in midbite and gave him a fractious look.

"You were always bossing everyone around," he said matter-of-factly, knowing he was pushing her buttons.

"I am not bossy." She put down her fork, her movement stiff. "I simply try to show people better ways of doing things."

"Sounds bossy to me."

"Shut up."

"Make me."

And just like that they were kids again, back in Marlene's clinic, him teasing the pretty girl who'd always seemed way out of his league. Melancholy squeezed his heart again and he looked away. Dammit. He was tired, yes, but the funeral had really thrown him. He hated funerals. They always reminded him of Vicki.

They ate the rest of their meal in silence. Once they'd finished, he waited while Pat cleared their plates then tried his best to get back to normal, even though normal seemed a thousand miles away at present. "We get started in the morning, then?"

"Yes. Pending my boss's approval." She stood and slipped her coat on then belted it up. "I'll meet you in front of the clinic in the morning at nine. If something changes, I'll call you. I have your number."

Nick swiped the check before she could, flashing what he hoped was a polite smile. "My treat, Belle. We're partners now. You need a ride to your aunt's place?"

"No. I got a rental at the airport in Lansing." Belle lifted her chin and walked toward the exit, saying over her shoulder, "Thank you for dinner. Bye, Connor."

Nick lingered after she left. "You want pie, Con?"

His son grinned. "With ice cream?"

"Of course." Nick hailed Pat and ordered dessert while Analia wandered over to take the seat vacated by Belle.

"She's pretty," the little girl said, lisping due to dental issues. "What's her name?"

"Christabelle Watson. She was Marlene's niece. And she's a doctor like me."

"Wow." Analia stared at the front door while Pat delivered dessert. "Are you friends?"

"We used to be." Nick exhaled and rubbed a hand over his face, fatigue and grief threatening to overwhelm him once more. "I'm not so sure now."

"Okay. Bye." Analia said, ending the conversation

abruptly, as eight-year-olds were prone to do, and headed back to her family's table.

Nick turned back to find half the pie and ice cream already gone. As a growing kid, Connor could put away the food. Still, his son was healthy and strong and smart, and Nick said a silent prayer every night that things would stay that way. Being a doctor had good and bad sides. People joked about self-diagnosing themselves on the internet with every disease under the sun. Nick wasn't that bad, but he did like to err on the side of caution when it came to Connor. He was only being a good parent.

Belle's words looped back through his tired brain before he could stop them.

How controlling of you...

He sighed and scrubbed a hand over his face. Yeah, maybe he had been a bit overbearing, but some days it was all he had. He just wanted to protect his child, since life could be so easily lost at any time.

After they'd finished their meal and he'd paid the bill, Nick stopped on their way out to check with Juan about working on the clinic. Luckily, the guy said he was between jobs and agreed to meet him in the morning. Then Nick and Connor walked back out into the cold night air, their breath frosting as they returned to his SUV parked behind the funeral home. He spotted Belle at the funeral home across the street, scraping the windshield of the compact car she'd rented while trying not to fall on her butt in those stilettos of hers, looking just as determined as he remembered.

He turned away and pulled out his phone to call his PA about taking over for the most part until after Christmas. Hopefully, it wouldn't be a problem. Elise was always bugging him to give her a bigger role in the clinic anyway and she and her family were Jewish. Hanukkah had fallen early that year, so he felt optimistic she might help him out. The last thing he wanted to do was close during one of their busiest times of the year when the people of Bayside needed them most. The closest hospital was in Manistee, about an hour away, so anything he could treat here in town was faster and cheaper for everyone involved.

Regardless of what happened at his office, one thing was for sure.

The next two weeks would be mighty interesting.

CHAPTER TWO

BELLE PARKED IN the driveway of her aunt Marlene's modest ranch-style home on Hancock Street and stumbled inside the foyer, her feet numb and her arm aching from toting her heavy wheeled suitcase behind her. At least the ride had given her some much-needed time to herself to recalibrate. Hard to believe after all this time that he still affected her like no other man.

It made no sense whatsoever.

She'd dated plenty of men in Beverly Hills—rich, gorgeous, successful, highly desirable men. Yet not one of them had seemed to hold a candle to Nick when it came to physical attraction. Maybe because he'd been her first.

First kiss, first boyfriend, first...*everything*.

And they said you never forgot your first...

No. She shook off those unwanted thoughts and slumped back against the closed door, listening to the lonesome sound of the wind howling as the snowstorm picked up outside and the reality of her situation crept into her bones. She was back in Bayside. She was unexpectedly partnered with Nick again. She was all alone because Aunt Marlene was gone.

Forever.

The tears she'd struggled to hold back since her

arrival spilled forth as she toed off her pumps then walked into the living room, spotting all the reminders of the life she'd left behind. There was the lopsided ceramic mug she'd made for Aunt Marlene in sixth grade. And a picture of the two of them at Belle's high-school graduation. On the wall in the hallway were photos of her aunt with her patients at various local events—the July Fourth band concert in the gazebo on the town green, the annual Christmas tree lighting ceremony.

There were pictures of Belle's parents too on their wedding day. Aunt Marlene had been her mom's maid of honor. Memories of her parents were blurry and soft in Belle's mind, like watercolors. She remembered her mother making a birthday cake, her father teaching Belle how to fish for salmon in the Manistee River, their trip to Tahquamenon Falls State Park when Belle had thought the iron-rich falls were made of root beer.

Her heart ached and more tears fell. Her parents had both been doctors too. Family medicine. They'd always talked about Belle taking over their practice someday. Perhaps that was another reason she'd been so torn about choosing plastic surgery as her specialty in college. If she'd stayed with GP, it would have been another link to them, but fate had had other ideas—especially after her ill-fated trip to see Nick in college. Finding out about his engagement and his impending fatherhood had left her feeling untethered, powerless. She'd focused on the one area where she still felt like she had control—her career.

She gave a sad little ironic snort. Seemed Nick wasn't the only one with control issues.

With the back of her hand, Belle swiped at her damp cheeks. God, she missed her family. Aunt Marlene had been so young, so vital, despite her age and heart condition. She'd always seemed immortal to Belle, even though rationally she'd known someday the end would come. She'd just never expected it to happen so fast.

If only I'd known...

She hadn't, though, because Aunt Marlene had never told Belle how sick she was. That stubborn, independent streak ran in their family and had reared its ugly head again apparently. Aunt Marlene had always been the type to do for others, yet never let anyone help her in her time of need. She'd not wanted to be a bother to anyone, she'd always said.

Belle would've loved nothing more than to be bothered by her aunt just one more time.

Maybe it was being back home again after all this time, but Belle felt at a loose end and was reconsidering everything in her life. Her career, her relationships, her future. Funerals always seemed to bring out her introspective side and this one was worst of all.

When her parents had died, Belle had been a child and Aunt Marlene had made the choices for her. Now it all fell on Belle to pick up the pieces and decide how best to move forward.

Sniffling, she returned to the living room and sank down on the sofa to stare at the Christmas tree in the corner. Her aunt must have put it up before going into the hospital after Thanksgiving. Grief flooded her anew at all the memories of holidays past. The tree glowed with twinkling lights and tinsel and she finally let herself sob for all she'd lost and for the beloved aunt she'd never see again.

Pain and doubt scraped her raw inside. Sticking to her career plans had been a way of remaining close to her parents and Aunt Marlene over the years, even if she'd left Bayside and chosen a different field of practice. Her rational brain said they'd all want her to be happy, but the scared child still lurking inside her feared maybe she'd not done enough to fulfill their dreams for her. Maybe she'd not done enough to fulfill her dreams for herself.

A buzzing sound finally pulled her out of her tears and self-recriminations and back to reality. Dabbing her eyes with a tissue, Belle rushed to grab her bag from the foyer and pull out her cell phone to see an incoming video call from Dr. Reyes.

Doing her best to restore some semblance of order to her appearance, Belle tapped the screen. Dr. Reyes's tanned, perfectly sculpted face appeared. His dark eyes narrowed as she forced a smile.

"Hello, sir," Belle said, her voice still rough from crying.

"Dr. Watson, are you all right? You didn't return any of my calls today."

Belle took a deep breath, forcing her emotions down deep and switching to professional mode. "I'm fine. Thank you. Just tired."

"My condolences again on the passing of your aunt. Were you close?"

"Yes." She blinked hard against the unwanted sting of more tears. "She raised me after my parents died."

"I'm sorry. There's nothing more important than family."

At least she had the presence of mind not to point out the oddness of Dr. Reyes's statement, since he'd been married three times.

"What's the name of the town where you're staying?" he asked. "Seaport?"

"Bayside."

"Ah. I come from in a small town myself in Brazil. Five hundred people."

Belle steeled herself to declare the bad news. "There may be an issue with my return date, sir."

"What?" Dr. Reyes frowned. "Why? The standard three days to mourn and take care of your aunt's affairs should be more than sufficient, Dr. Watson. And what of the patient I'm seeing in your absence? The breast reconstruction?"

Belle winced. In all the stress of today she'd forgotten about poor Cassie Gordon. At just twenty, her young patient had already been through five previous procedures to correct what should've been a simple case of asymmetry. But now her case had become a nightmare of complications due the earlier botched surgeries by other physicians. The procedure had taken Belle three hours for what should have been forty-minute surgery. There'd been vast amounts of scar tissue to remove and internal suturing required to close things up properly. "Is Miss Gordon doing well?"

"For now." Annoyance crept into Dr. Reyes's tone. "Explain to me why you must stay."

Belle cleared her suddenly constricted throat. "There's more to do than I expected to settle my aunt's estate and I'm the only family she had left. Plus, there was a stipulation."

"A stipulation?"

"Yes. Her final wish was for us to reopen the free clinic on Christmas Eve before we liquidate the proceeds."

"We?"

Images of Nick tonight at the diner flooded Belle's mind once more before she shoved them aside. "I inherited half of my aunt's estate, along with another person."

Dr. Reyes frowned. "Splitting assets is a complicated business, but you went home to pay respects, not revive your aunt's medical practice."

"I know, sir." Bristling under the censure in his tone, Belle raised her chin. "None of this was my intention, but things are a bit more complicated than I anticipated." Her heart pinched as she remembered her aunt soldiering on through what must have been one of the most difficult times in her life on Belle's behalf all those years ago. If her aunt could do it, then she could too. "The free clinic will reopen on Christmas Eve, then I'll fly home on the holiday. I realize this is an inconvenience, but I'll work double shifts, triple even, once I return. Whatever you need."

"What I need, Dr. Watson, is to know your priorities are straight," Dr. Reyes said, then sighed. "Fine. But I expect you to be back in California on Christmas, nine days from now. Not too much to ask, I think, after everything I've done for you in your career."

His words pulled Belle up short. Yes, he'd hired Belle fresh out of residency, advising her on the ins and outs of conquering the Everest-sized mountain of Beverly Hills plastic surgery. But she'd had other lucrative offers, as well. And she'd worked hard, made a lot of sacrifices herself to get where she was. If all she'd accomplished on her own volition didn't win her the right to take sole ownership of her success, then she didn't know what did. It also made her doubts about the partnership and what she truly wanted stir more strongly inside her. Still, she was resolved to do her duty, for now. "Thank you. I appreciate your kindness."

In truth, wrapping everything up here by Christmas was pushing it, but she'd figure it out. She worked miracles on a daily basis with her patients. She'd survived losing her parents and losing the boy she'd loved back in high school. She'd survive losing Aunt Marlene too.

"Good," Dr. Reyes said, bringing her back to the present. "I'll check in with you again tomorrow re your patient."

He ended the call and she sat there staring at the Christmas tree for a long time afterward, her mind racing. For the past eighteen years she'd worked so hard to get where she was, never once stopping to look at all the things she'd missed, all the things that had slipped away or fallen by the wayside in her pursuit of success. But she loved her life, loved her work, loved the new opportunities on her horizon.

Don't I?

To be honest, it had begun to ring a bit hollow lately. A bit lonely too.

Letting her head fall back against the cushions, Belle picked up a crocheted pillow and stared at the quote embroidered there: *Bloom where you're planted.*

Belle was trying hard to keep on blooming, even if the soil right now felt pretty rocky.

"Time for bed, Con," Nick called as he turned down the flannel sheets in his son's room. They'd picked them out a few weeks previously during a trip to the big-box store in Manistee. Goofy lime-green monsters and bright orange superheroes covered the material. Nick had been obsessed with the latest space movie characters when he'd been a kid too.

Like father, like son.

"Dad, who was the woman at dinner tonight?" Con asked as he walked into the room and climbed into bed in his pajamas, wiping toothpaste from his mouth with his sleeve. "She seemed kind of…stressed out."

"She probably was," Nick sighed as he tucked his son in. Honestly, Belle had seemed ready to shatter at any minute. The idea bothered Nick more than he cared to admit. He had no business worrying about Belle. He'd made a vow to his dying wife on the day she'd passed away—to put their son first, to keep him happy and safe. His needs came second, if at all. After everything Vicki had sacrificed to marry him, it was the least he could do. He sat on the edge of the bed. "Belle's been through a lot. Dr. Marlene was her aunt."

"Are you guys friends?" Con leaned back against the pillows resting against his headboard, looking as energetic as ever. Nick's hopes for a quick good night faded.

"We used to be. Go to sleep. You've got school in the morning." He stood and walked to the door. The past was over and bringing it up now would only lead to more questions from Connor. Questions Nick did not want to answer tonight. Maybe not ever.

Unfortunately, his son wasn't going to let the subject of Belle drop so easily. "So, why aren't you friends anymore?"

Because Belle and I have too much history. Instead, he said, "It's complicated."

His son's determination gave way to obstinacy. "Mom said talking about things made them better."

"Your mom…" Nick started, then stopped. It was true. Vicki had been a good talker. A good listener too. It was one of the reasons she and Nick had first become pals in medical school. In fact, the night Vicki had gotten pregnant, she'd been consoling Nick about his loneliness over Belle. She'd been nursing her wounds over a bad breakup herself. They'd both had too much to drink and one thing had led to another. It had been a fluke, a one-night stand, but eight weeks later Vicki had told him she was pregnant. Nick had done the noble thing, of course, and proposed. Vicki had agreed, despite the fact she'd had dreams too, had been on track for a career as a nurse practitioner in Manhattan. She'd given it all up to marry him and raise their son together.

Connor was still staring at him, waiting for his answer, so Nick did the best he could. "Your mom did like to talk things out. But she also knew when to let things rest."

"Please, Dad? I miss her. You never mention Mom anymore. I dreamed about her again last night. She was walking away and no matter how loud I screamed for her to come back, she just left me behind."

At the catch in his son's voice, Nick caved like a crumbling mine shaft. He'd thought that by not bringing Vicki up so much he'd save Connor the pain of her loss, but it seemed he'd only made things worse. Feeling like the world's worst parent ever, he toed off his shoes then climbed back onto the bed beside his son, resting against the headboard next to Connor. "Fine. You want to know about me and Belle? I'll tell you. But I'm making this quick because we both have to be up early. Got it?"

Con grinned and settled back against his favorite monster pillow. "Got it."

Nick took a deep breath. "Belle and I both volunteered after school in Marlene's clinic."

"You used to clean up blood and guts and yucky stuff? Cool!"

"No. We used to sterilize instruments and scrub down exam tables." He put an arm around Connor and tugged the boy into his side, ruffling his hair. "No gore. Well, unless you consider taking care of the parakeet cages in the lobby yucky."

"Super-yucky." His son wrinkled his nose. "Go on."

"We spent a lot of time together at the clinic, since we both wanted to be doctors. Later, Belle and I dated in high school. We were even prom king and queen."

"Wow. I'm never going to date anyone. Especially a girl."

"Never say never." Nick laughed. "Trust me."

"So, why don't you like her anymore?" Connor asked.

An uncomfortable twinge of regret pinched his chest before he tamped it down. "Nothing happened. Belle moved away from Bayside, and I did too. Our paths diverged."

"Diverged?" Con looked up at him, frowning. "What's that mean?"

"It means we ended up in different places." He rested his head back against the headboard and closed his eyes. Truth was, he'd loved Belle enough to let her go. The fact she'd shared with him all her hopes and dreams and her parents' aspirations for her had sealed the deal. He couldn't hold her back. Wouldn't hold her back.

Then he'd gone down a different path with Vicki and their destinies hadn't crossed again, until now. Belle was his past. Connor was his future. The sooner Nick got that straight, the better off he'd be. "Belle and I parted ways a long time ago, son. We're different people now."

His son seemed to consider that a moment. "And then you met Mom."

"And then I met your mother."

Connor yawned and Nick took his cue to leave. He slipped out of the bed and walked to the door again, picking up his shoes along the way. "Good night, son."

"'Night." Con snuggled down under the covers. "Hey, Dad?"

"Yeah?"

"If Belle decides to stay, would she be able to help Analia?"

Nick exhaled slowly and hung his head. "She won't stay, son. She needs to get back to California. Her life is there."

"Miracles happen all the time." Connor peered at Nick, the covers tucked beneath his chin as icy snow tapped against the window panes. "Mom used to say that too."

The chances of Belle choosing Bayside over Beverly Hills were slim to none, but it was late and Nick was tired. "We'll see. Now, get some sleep. We've got a busy day tomorrow."

"Hey, Dad?" Connor's yawn obscured the words.

Nick stopped halfway out of the room. "Yes, son?"

"When are you going to let me walk to school like Eric does?"

He sighed. The question struck far close to home after Belle's judgmental remarks earlier. He didn't want to smother Connor, but he'd do anything to keep him safe. "We'll talk about it tomorrow, okay? Now go to sleep."

"Okay," Connor said, his tone resigned. "Love you."

"Love you too, son." Nick closed the door, feeling like he'd gone ten rounds with an MMA fighter instead of put his kid to bed. When Vicki had been alive, they'd used to talk about stuff they wanted to do with Connor. Take him across the country and visit all the national parks. Let him have free rein in what he wanted to learn and do and be, within reason. Raise him to be an independent, free-thinking, fearless boy.

Now Nick watched his kid like a hawk. He didn't let Connor cross the street alone because another child had been hit last year on Main Street on his way home from school. Granted, it had been the beginning of summer and with the tourists beginning to flock to the area the number of distracted drivers on the road had increased, but it didn't reassure Nick at all. He trusted Connor. It was everyone else who made him wary. In the rational part of his mind, he knew he couldn't keep Con under his wing forever, but he wasn't sure how he'd cope if anything happened to his son.

Bone-weary, he checked the locks then shut off the lights before heading to bed himself, Belle's words still echoing through his head. He didn't want to be controlling. Back in the day, he'd gone with the flow and dealt with the punches as they came.

But as he brushed his teeth then finally climbed between the sheets, he realized life had changed him. Much as he hated to admit it, maybe he should allow Connor a little more freedom. After all, that was why he'd moved back to Bayside. The safety, the security.

Except with Belle back in town, the well-ordered life he'd tried to rebuild and protect suddenly felt threatened. He turned onto his back and stared up at the ceiling. He closed his eyes, but all he could see was Belle sitting in the diner, shiny as a new penny under the harsh fluorescent lights, and his chest squeezed with an odd mix of apprehension and anticipation.

Grumbling, he turned over and punched his pillow before burying his face in it. Hell, he wasn't sure why he was getting all riled up over her return anyway. Wasn't like he was interested in getting involved with her again. Just the opposite. For all he knew, she was seeing someone out in California. The thought nipped at him despite his wish to the contrary.

No. In a few hours he'd face her again, clear-headed

and logical this time because if he was honest, having Belle back in Bayside was far more dangerous to him than any hit-and-run driver would ever be.

CHAPTER THREE

BELLE ARRIVED AT the clinic at nine sharp the next morning, only to find Nick already there. She went inside and took off her coat, hanging it on a peg behind the receptionist's desk. The short drive from her aunt's house had done little to improve her outlook, though wearing her sturdy boots this morning had helped on the slick pavement outside. She'd slept poorly the night before, a mixture of replaying in her head the phone call with Dr. Reyes and the dinner with Nick. It had all created a swirl of insomnia she'd been unable to conquer.

Nick leaned out of one of the exam rooms down the short hallway in front of her and flashed a polite smile. "Good morning."

"What's good about it?" she mumbled. "Is there coffee?"

He strolled out, looking far better than any man had a right to in faded jeans and T-shirt hugging his muscular torso in all the right places. Belle wasn't sure why she'd expected him to show up in his lab coat again, but that would have been far preferable, and safer, than what he was wearing now. Her pulse sped as he slouched a shoulder against the wall, his ankles crossed. "I thought you liked tea."

"I do," she snapped, feeling even more out of sorts

thanks to the man across from her. "But since there isn't a decent cup in this town, I'll settle for coffee."

He disappeared back into the exam room again, emerging moments later with a cardboard tray bearing two covered cups from a shop she'd never heard of and the stout man from the diner the night before following close at his heels. Nick held out the tray to her. "I ran up to Manistee after I dropped Connor off at school this morning. Consider it my peace offering. And let me introduce you to Mr. Juan Hernandez. He's agreed to help us fix up the clinic."

Belle shook the man's hand. "Hello. You were at Pat's last night with your family."

"Yes. My wife and daughter." Juan smiled. "Analia is my little princess."

"Juan's a great carpenter. Did all the renovations on my house here in Bayside. He'll be a big help getting the clinic reopened." Nick glanced over at Belle. "If you're staying."

"I'm staying." She took one of the cups, lifting the lid to sniff the steaming liquid inside.

"It's green tea," Nick said. "You tried to order it last night, right?"

"Right." She took a sip and couldn't suppress a tiny sigh of pleasure.

"Good, huh?" The amusement twinkling in his warm brown eyes had her turning away fast. His continued effect on her was crazy. Stupid. Beyond inconvenient, considering they had exactly eight days until they reopened the clinic on Christmas Eve. After that, she'd be on the first plane back to California. She took another swallow of tea for fortitude. "This is very good. Thank you. Dr. Reyes gave me an extension on my bereavement leave through Christmas Eve. We have a little over a week to get the clinic ready to reopen. Thus, we need a plan."

"'Thus, we need a plan,'" Nick parroted back to her. "Since when do you say 'thus'?"

"People change." She walked around the reception- ist desk, trailing her finger though a thick coating of dust. The paint on the walls was faded and the carpets were worn. The ceiling tiles above sported a few water stains, as well. One of the fluorescent lights popped and hissed ominously and a strange wheezing noise echoed from the heating vent above the desk. All in all, the place was a mess. "You weren't kidding about the clinic being run-down."

"When Marlene's health took a turn for the worse, she had a hard time keeping up. I offered to help her, but she refused," Nick said. "You know how she was. Always doing for other people, never accepting assis- tance herself."

"Yes." Belle headed down to check out the three exam rooms. The equipment had to be as old as she was. It was going to take a massive effort to get this all up to snuff. Good thing her can-do attitude was what had gotten her where she was today.

"Juan will oversee the repairs and any issues with the heating and electrical. What he can't fix himself, he knows the people who can. My PA's agreed to take on extra patients, which allows me to split my time be- tween this place and my office." Nick stepped into the small exam room behind her, his warmth surrounding her. "And my office manager, Jeanette, volunteered to handle the front-desk duties at the free clinic, so we can check that off the list. Between all of us, we should have all the boxes checked."

Juan excused himself to inspect the rest of the clinic

and Belle blinked at the anatomy poster on the wall, the paper yellowing around the edges. It had hung there for as long as she could remember.

"I just have one remaining question," Nick said.

Belle looked back at him over her shoulder. "What?"

"Yesterday, you were all about leaving. What changed your mind?"

When she hadn't been able to sleep the night before, she'd gone through more of her aunt's things. Photos, letters, mementos. All of it had reminded Belle how much Aunt Marlene had loved this place. How much she'd loved Belle too. It had been enough to make Belle determined to see her aunt's last wishes fulfilled, no matter how difficult it might be to have Nick hovering around her for the next two weeks. "You were right. My aunt deserves better. If reopening the free clinic one last time was important to her, I'll make it happen."

"Hmm." Nick stepped closer and her pulse kicked up a notch. "Say that again."

Belle frowned. "If reopening the clinic is impor-tant—"

"No. The other part."

"What other part?"

"Where you said I was right. I don't hear it often enough. Especially from you."

"Too bad." Belle walked out of the exam room and headed for the lobby once more, doing her best to focus on the job ahead and not the irritating man behind her. "We need to make a list of supplies to order, both clean-ing and medical."

"I can take care of the medical part." Nick shrugged. "I have a shipment coming in for my practice next Monday. We can take what we need from that then I'll restock again after Christmas. It's only for one day, so we should have plenty to cover both clinics."

"Okay. Then I'll stop by the store in Manistee and pick up cleaning supplies when I go to the hospital later to spread the word about the clinic. Maybe I'll stop by the office supply place too and have some flyers made up so we can post them around town to help us spread the word."

"Sounds good." Nick grinned. "Maybe we could see about doing a little promo at the Chamber of Commerce Holiday Ball next week, as well. I can talk to the mayor's office."

"Great. I need to be there anyway to accept Aunt Marlene's award."

"Right. We could go together, schmooze the locals, build some buzz for the clinic."

It almost felt like old times, back when they'd both worked here after school, but she stopped herself. This was all only temporary. Things were different now. The sooner she remembered that, the better. She looked at Nick again for a moment before grabbing her coat. "Maybe. I should probably get going up to Manistee."

"But you just got here," he started, only to be interrupted by the front door opening.

A beautiful woman about Belle's age, with long dark hair and sparkling onyx eyes walked in holding the hand of the little girl with Crouzon syndrome from the night before.

"I know you," the little girl said, her words slightly lisped. She pulled free from her mother and headed for Belle. "You were at Pat's last night. You're pretty."

"Thank you." Belle crouched in front of the child. "What's your name?"

"Analia," the little girl said, reaching out to touch Belle's red coat. "Red's my favorite color."

"Mine too." Up close, she studied the little girl's features—wide-set and bulging eyes, beaked nose, and an underdeveloped upper jaw. Classic Crouzon's. The premature fusion of certain skull bones had resulted in the abnormal shape of the girl's head and face. Nick had mentioned breathing problems too. Not uncommon. Belle had worked with two children with similar cases back in California, performing the complicated surgery and follow-ups to correct problems like Analia's. Too bad she wouldn't be here long enough this time.

Her heart tugged as she straightened. Part of her wanted to throw caution to the wind and take the case anyway. It would be simple enough to do a consult and examination, obtain the necessary releases, then book an OR in Manistee. But she already had more than enough on her plate to keep her busy during her short stay in Bayside and Nick had mentioned working the little girl in with his colleague in Detroit. The most prudent course of action was to let him handle it.

Instead, she introduced herself to Analia's mother. "Dr. Watson. Please call me Belle."

"Rosa Hernandez." The woman's grip was firm and sure. "We came to take my husband to breakfast, if you can spare him for an hour or so."

"I think we can," Nick said, calling over his shoulder. "Juan, your family's here."

The guy came out and picked up Analia, hugging her tight before kissing his wife. "I'll be back. After we eat, I'll swing by the hardware store and pick up what I need to get started."

Belle watched them leave, then turned back to Nick. "She needs the surgery done."

"She does. Too bad you won't be sticking around." Nick flinched. "Sorry. I shouldn't have said anything. I know you've got other commitments."

Hurt pinched her chest. He made the word *commitments* sound more like *excuses*. "The procedure required to correct her abnormalities is major. Wires on her jaw for at least a month to spur new bone growth. She'd have to wear a halo device for at least four months to stabilize everything. It wouldn't be fair of me to take a case, Nick, knowing I wouldn't be around to see it through. My time in Bayside is limited. I need to be honest about what I can and can't do here."

"You're right." He sighed and turned away, wandering back down the hall. "Drive safely to Manistee. I'll see you when you get back."

Belle grabbed her bag then left the clinic, feeling like she was caught in a trap with no safe way out.

Nick spent the rest of his day dealing with what felt like one emergency after another. Turned out all those water stains on the ceiling tiles were due to a pipe with a slow leak in the ceiling. Juan had no more than gotten a plumber there to correct the problem than his PA called.

"Sorry to bother you, but I'm afraid I've got a suspected case of bacterial meningitis."

"Damn." Nick's heart sped. Meningitis was highly contagious and would require reporting to the local Board of Health. He prayed it wasn't someone from Connor's school. "Who's the patient?"

"Lisa Merkel, age twelve. Homeschooled," the PA said. The knot of tension between Nick's shoulder blades eased slightly. "Patient has a high fever, stiff neck, headache, and nausea."

He scrubbed a hand over his face. "I'm on my way."

After letting Juan know he was leaving, Nick raced over to his offices. The white limestone exterior of the building gleamed in the sunshine as he pulled into his reserved spot. He walked in, still dressed in jeans and a sweatshirt but slipped on a lab coat to look more professional before going in to see the Merkels.

The parents were understandably upset, and poor Lisa looked horrible, her face pale and clammy and her body racked with shivers from the fever. Nick went over the chart and immediately called an ambulance to transport the girl to the hospital in Manistee. After talking with the ER doc on duty about the case, he went back into the exam room to console the parents until the EMTs arrived.

"We'll do everything we can to help her. The ER at Manistee General is prepared for her arrival. The doc there will do a lumbar puncture to confirm the meningitis then begin antibiotics prophylactically while we wait for the results. She's in good hands."

By the time he made it home that night it was well past ten and Connor was already asleep. He sent the sitter home then slumped down on the sofa in his living room, the TV droning in the background. Medicine wasn't a nine-to-five job and he was grateful to have found Mollie to watch his son. She was an older woman whose husband had passed away a few years before Nick had moved back to Bayside. She loved Connor almost as much as Nick did and treated the little boy like one of her grandsons.

After a yawn and a stretch, Nick got up and wandered upstairs to Con's room, sneaking over to give the kid a kiss, narrowly avoiding tripping over the toys and hockey equipment strewn across the floor, before he headed back down to the kitchen to fix himself some dinner.

Bless Mollie's heart, she'd left him a plate of home-made chicken and dumplings in the fridge. The dish was Connor's favorite. Nick popped it into the microwave then got a glass of water to drink. As he waited for his food to heat, he felt a weird pang in his chest.

Not sadness. Not grief over Marlene either.

Loneliness. That's what it was. Except he didn't have any business feeling lonely.

He'd chosen his path and he was at peace with it.

Aren't I?

The microwave beeped and he took out his food, then grabbed a fork and a napkin before carrying it all back into the living room to eat in front of the TV. He should be used to it by now. Vicki had been gone nearly two years. He'd made the right choice.

Then an image of Belle from earlier popped into his head.

He'd been glad to see she'd dressed more sensibly in jeans and a sweater and boots. A vast improvement from the day before. In fact, she'd almost reminded him of the old Belle—same killer curves, same killer smile, same sweet, clean scent…

No. No, no, no.

Nick squeezed his eyes shut as new images flashed into his brain. Vicki's last days in the oncology unit, her once strong, healthy body ravaged by ovarian cancer, her once bright eyes dimmed by pain and medication. She'd given up so much for him. He couldn't forget his vow.

Not now.

He shoveled more food into his mouth and scowled at the TV.

Never mind Belle all but had a flashing neon sign above her head warning him to stay away. He was done with relationships. He was happy alone. He had his work, his patients, his son. And if sometimes it felt like something—someone—was missing, then that was his penance.

It was all good.

Is it, though?

Yes. Yes, it was. Because it had to be.

He devoured more food, staring at the news without really listening. His cell phone buzzed on the coffee table and the number for the lab at the Manistee hospital flashed on the caller ID. Nick hit redial then listened as the tech rattled off the results of Lisa's bloodwork and lumbar puncture. Positive for bacterial meningitis. Manistee General would handle filing the necessary reports with the local Board of Health. He finished up with the tech then called Lisa's parents.

"The ER doctor told us they've got Lisa on the highest does of antibiotics possible for her age." Mrs. Merkel sniffled into the phone. "We homeschooled her because we thought she'd be safer. We just wanted to keep her secure and happy."

Nick's heart went out to them, the situation hitting far too close to home. "Don't blame yourself. Lisa's in the best possible hands. They'll keep her well hydrated to bring down her fever and watch her closely. Lisa's young and strong and otherwise healthy. There's no reason she shouldn't pull through this. Try and get some rest. She'll need your support as she recovers."

He went over what to expect for the next few days and answered all of their questions then ended the call.

Nick sat there a moment afterward. By then, the rest of his dinner was cold. Just as well, since he'd lost his appetite anyway. He took his dishes to the kitchen and cleaned up before going to bed and attempting to read a new medical journal he'd had sitting around for weeks, but his concentration was shot.

After half an hour he turned off the lights. Sleep eluded him, despite his fatigue. He closed his eyes, running through Lisa's case and the work to be done at the clinic. Belle kept resurfacing in his head too, regardless of his wishes to the contrary.

Guilt gurgled inside him before he tamped it down fast.

This wasn't about attraction. Belle was a challenge. That was all. The same as working on the clinic during the holiday season, which was still hard for Nick. The strange wave of excitement he felt around Belle was nothing more than relief at being knocked out of the rut his life had fallen into lately.

Isn't it?

CHAPTER FOUR

THE NEXT MORNING Belle walked into the clinic at seven thirty sharp, happy to see she was the first one there this time. She set the travel cups of hot tea on the counter and put the bags slung over her arms on the floor. She'd brewed the tea herself at Aunt Marlene's house on the new tea-maker she'd bought in Manistee. She'd also picked up some Christmas decorations for the clinic.

Belle flipped on the lights then stared at a large hole cut into the ceiling tiles and the "Wet Floor" hazard signs placed around a ladder extending into said hole. Yikes. Nick hadn't mentioned anything wrong when she'd texted him yesterday, but something was obviously awry.

She'd just taken off her coat when a portly man in a navy blue hoodie and knit skullcap walked in.

"I'm sorry, sir, but we're not open for business yet," Belle said, startled.

"I ain't sick, lady. I'm here to fix your pipes." The guy hiked up his pants as he walked past her, then climbed the ladder to the ceiling, his top half disappearing into the hole.

Before she could ask him to explain exactly what the problem was, the front door opened again and Nick entered, looking as gorgeous as ever in clean jeans and

T-shirt, despite the dark circles beneath his eyes. Juan Hernandez came in too, giving Belle a quick wave of greeting before talking with the plumber.

"Good morning." Belle shoved a travel mug into Nick's hand. "You look like hell."

"Thanks," he said, his tone dry. "You always did know how to make a guy feel better. Must be why you're a doctor, huh?"

She ignored his sarcasm and unpacked the decorations instead. There were garlands and ornaments and red bows and sprigs of holly. She stacked them all neatly on the counter before reaching for the last bag and pulling out a box containing a small prelit Christmas tree. Minutes later she had it set up in the corner of the lobby. Belle plugged it in and fluffed the artificial branches before standing back to observe her work. Not exactly the North Pole, but the place looked a bit more festive already. She glanced at Nick, who was looking more Grinch-like by the second as he stared at the tree.

"What?" she asked.

"Nothing. I just prefer real ones."

"Well, when you buy the decorations, you can get what you like." She walked around him to pull a clipboard and pen out of her tote bag. "I'm going to take inventory. What are you doing?"

"Well, besides checking in on my patient with meningitis and helping Juan where I can, I'll be cleaning the carpets and prepping the walls for a fresh coat of paint."

"Right." Belle tucked her hair behind her ear. A patient with meningitis took a lot of time and attention. No wonder he looked tired today. Unwanted sympathy swelled inside her. Feeling sorry for Nick could lead to other feelings and that was a road best not traveled. "I'm sorry about your patient with meningitis."

"Thank you. She's doing better this morning. The antibiotics seem to be working, and her fever's down. Hopefully, she's out of the woods. And thanks for the tea." He took a sip. "This is good. Not green, though."

"Peppermint. Bought the leaves in town yesterday."

"How very Santa of you." Nick took off his coat and hung it up beside hers. "Sorry. Didn't mean to be a grouch earlier. You know how it is with an involved case."

"I do." Belle smiled, glad to have found some common ground again. "I've been getting updates on one of my patients back in California. A twenty-year-old woman I'd performed a breast augmentation on right before coming here. The case was complicated, to say the least."

"Because of her age?" Nick leaned a hip against the reception desk and watched her over the rim of his cup. "Twenty's awfully young for plastic surgery, isn't it?"

"Yes, but this patient was born with severe breast asymmetry. Unfortunately, the condition only worsened following several botched procedures by previous, underqualified surgeons." Anger fizzed in her bloodstream before she tamped it down. "Nothing makes me more furious than physicians taking a case simply because of greed. It's unforgivable."

"Wow." Nick's eyes widened. "I hope she sued."

"She might. And I'd back her up all the way." Belle exhaled, forcing her tense shoulders to relax. "Sorry. It's a pet peeve of mine."

"You were always a champion for the underdog." Nick winked at her. "Glad to see that hasn't changed."

"Thanks." At his unexpected compliment, heat prickled her cheeks. Dr. Reyes took her talents for granted. Then again, she didn't need constant praise. Doing good work was its own reward. But it was still nice to be appreciated. She took a long swig of her own tea, the peppermint sparkling on her tongue and clearing her sinuses. "Normally a breast augmentation takes me forty minutes. This poor patient's surgery took three hours because of all the scar tissue. One hundred and fifty stiches to close up the internal damage. She's doing well now, though, thank goodness. Dr. Reyes says she's very happy with the results."

"This Dr. Reyes is the head of your practice?" Nick's dark hair was still damp from a recent shower and there was a tiny red spot on his jaw where he'd cut himself shaving. The comfortable, relaxed picture he presented was far too endearing for Belle's comfort.

"Yes. Hired me straight out of residency." Already off-kilter because of her unwanted attraction to the man before her, the mention of residency only discombobulated Belle further. Memories of her ill-fated trip to see Nick caused the words to catch in her throat. From his lack of reaction, he had no idea she'd gone to visit him. It was probably for the best. It didn't matter now anyway. They were partners in this clinic venture. Nothing more. Never mind her racing pulse and wobbling knees whenever he was close. Belle headed down the hall, away from temptation. "Time to get to work."

Ugh. Whatever hormones were causing her emotional awareness of him had better clear up fast. She bustled from exam room to exam room, checking drawers and opening cabinets, making notes on her clipboard, falling into an old routine. Organization had always been one of her strong suits. She remembered keeping things in line for Aunt Marlene when she'd worked here as a teenager.

From out in the hallway the sounds of the plumber working mixed with the lilt of Juan's Spanish as he spoke to someone on the phone, presumably his wife based on the endearments he was using. Being bilingual in California was almost a given in her profession and though she did her best not to eavesdrop, Belle couldn't help picking up Analia's name and the words *too expensive*.

Her chest tightened. Given the little girl's age and breathing impairments, it would be the optimal time to do the operation. Perhaps a diagnosis of OSP—obstructive sleep apnea—would help speed the insurance company's approval. The condition was common enough in children with Crouzon's and could be life-threatening if left untreated.

"Excuse me," Nick said, scooting past her in the exam room, measuring tape in hand. "Trying to calculate out how much paint we'll need to cover the walls."

"Sure." She met his gaze before he looked away.

"So, are you dating anyone?" he asked a moment later out of the blue.

"No," she said, a bit taken aback. "I have my reasons for being single. And you?"

"Ditto."

Conversation lagged and Belle had no intention of delving deeper into their personal lives. She had enough trouble keeping her thoughts from straying to Nick whenever he was around. She changed subjects instead. "Does Analia suffer from sleep apnea?"

"Yes. She uses a CPAP machine at night because of it." Nick made a few measurements and jotted the numbers down before facing her once more. "Why?"

"If you diagnosed her with OSP, it might be enough to get her surgery approved by the insurance company." Belle leaned back against the counter, her analytical mind working overtime. "Unless you've already tried that."

"I haven't, because Juan's insurance disappeared along with his job. The Medicaid paperwork is a nightmare and with the holidays everything's on hold." He sighed. "She hasn't even been evaluated by a plastic surgeon yet. I'd like to speed things along, but it is what it is."

In her mind, Belle could already picture doing the LeFort III operation to fix little Analia's deformities—and that wasn't good. Dr. Reyes's words echoed in her head again.

You went home to pay respects to your aunt, not revive her medical practice...

Belle needed to remind herself of her duties, no matter how much she wanted to help one small girl.

"Analia's one of the bravest people I know," Nick said, a spark of admiration flaring in his gaze. Belle had forgotten how expressive his eyes were. He could say more with a look than most people could say in three days. "There are days I wish I had a quarter of her chutzpah."

Belle chuckled. She didn't know Analia well, but even she'd seen the girl's confidence and joy. "Agreed."

A moment passed between them as they watched each other over the span of a few feet. Nick's gaze flicked from Belle's eyes to her lips and she felt his look like a physical caress. Then there was a loud thud in the hallway, followed by an equally loud curse from the plumber, and the spell was broken.

Nick tensed and turned away. "Don't worry about Analia. We'll get by fine on our own."

Belle got the feeling he was talking about more than his patient. In fact, one of the first things she'd picked

up on with new Nick was his isolation. Sure, he was polite enough around her, for the most part, but she sensed
he kept a part of himself locked away these days. She
wondered if it was because of his wife's death but didn't
feel comfortable enough to ask.

Nick continued to take his measurements and she
couldn't help glancing his way before forcing her attention back to her clipboard. Being so close to him again
was messing with her head. She should get things done
here and move on before he noticed her staring.

"Maybe you'd like to stop by Aunt Marlene's place
and see if there's anything you'd like to keep. I'm trying to clear the house out for the realtor, and whatever's
left over I'll have to sell. It would make things easier if
there was less to deal with. I could make dinner."

Nick stopped and gave her a long look.

"What? It's dinner. We get together, eat."

"I know how dinner works, Belle," he said, reaching past her to grab a paper towel from the dispenser.
His arm brushed hers and a sudden urge to put her
arms around him and hold him close and bury her face
in his chest like she used to threatened to take Belle
under. If she rose on tiptoe, she could kiss his mouth,
his neck, nuzzle the spot below his ear that used to
drive him wild…

Oh, God.

"Let me ask you something," Nick said. "Why are
you being so nice to me today?"

"Because we'll be working together and we might
as well make the best of it," she said, her mind racing
to come up with a plausible non-X-rated excuse. "And
because it's the holidays and because it's rather lonely
sitting in my aunt's house alone."

She hadn't meant to confess the last part, but there it was. Her face flushed hotter.

A shadow crossed his handsome face before he sighed. "I'm not sure it's good idea."

Belle bristled under his rejection. "Whatever. I was only trying to be friendly. Forget it. Should've known better."

"What's that supposed to mean?" His posture stiffened.

"Exactly what I said. Nice doesn't work with you, does it? I've been nice to you all my life and where did it get me? Nowhere."

"Hey. Wait a minute." Nick raked a hand through his dark hair and shook his head. "Look, I'm sorry things didn't work out between us back in high school, but going our separate ways was best for both of us."

Belle snorted. "Well, it certainly worked out for you, didn't it? You couldn't wait to get rid of me so you could move on."

A small muscle pulsed in his cheek and his gaze burned into her. "You want to do this now? Fine. All I ever heard from you growing up was how important a career in medicine was to you, how it made you feel connected with your parents, how it helped you stay close to them. Being with me would've destroyed the future you were meant to have. You went off to California and never looked back. Tell me it's not true, Belle."

She wanted to tell him about her impromptu visit all those years ago but couldn't bring herself to do it. The old knot of betrayal inside her tightened and once again she bit back her confession. Now wasn't the time or the place. Belle walked out instead. "I need to finish decorating the lobby."

* * *

Considering his focus was split between his work and the woman busy turning Marlene's old clinic into a Christmas wonderland, Nick got a lot more accomplished than he'd expected. He'd calculated their paint needs and paid the plumber, even lent Juan a hand and drove to the local hardware store to pick up enough new ceiling tiles to replace the stained ones. Then he'd checked in with his PA and with the hospital in Manistee on Lisa's case. Finally, he'd moved on to patching holes in the drywall, taping off the trim, and getting everything ready for the next day's painting. The manual labor helped work out the tightness in his muscles, though none of it kept his earlier conversation with Belle from replaying in his head on an endless loop.

He should've just let it go, but then she'd reacted so strangely to his question and now his interest was piqued. He hadn't been lying when he'd said she'd talked constantly about her parents and making them proud when she was a kid. Nick got it. He did. Unexpected separations made people cling to what had been lost.

An annoying whisper started in his head.

Dammit. His situation with Vicki was different. Belle's parents had died when she was a kid. She'd had no control over what had happened to them. He and Vicki had been adults. She'd given up a promising future to be with him and raise Connor together. And, while she'd never once mentioned regretting her choice, he felt guilty just the same. Maybe if she hadn't married him, hadn't had Connor and moved to Atlanta, she might still be alive.

Pressure built at the back of his skull and he slammed a lid on those ideas fast.

The physician in him knew it was baseless. Ovarian cancer was one of the most difficult to detect, often spreading to the abdomen and pelvis before it was ever detected. It was also often symptomless, so the victim didn't know they had it until it was too late. Chances were high Vicki would've succumbed to the disease whether she'd married him or not.

But at least she could have achieved her goals in her career.

Dammit. His heart clenched. This wasn't doing him any good at all. He glanced at the clock on the wall. Almost time to pick Connor up from hockey practice at school. The kid had been bouncing off the walls this morning. Today was Con's last day before holiday break and he hadn't stopped chattering about the Christmas tree lighting celebration on the town green later that night. It was a Bayside tradition.

As Nick put away the ladder, he couldn't help remembering going to the tree lighting ceremony himself as a kid. Back in the day, he and Belle had helped Marlene host the event and had even flipped the switch one year, transforming their little town into a sparkling fairy tale. Since he'd returned to Bayside, Nick hadn't really done much beyond the usual stuff at home for the holidays, other than driving by so Con could see the tree lit. This year, though, he felt an unaccountable urge to experience it all again. The community band, the huge Douglas fir decorated in lights and tinsel.

If he wanted to make it on time he'd better get a move on, especially since they needed to eat beforehand. After shutting down the rooms in the back, he headed up to the lobby. The light outside was fading already as the shortest day of the year quickly approached. It lent a sense of urgency to the already near-impossible timeline for reopening the clinic.

At the end of the hall, he caught sight of Belle teetering on one of the vinyl chairs in the lobby, doing her best to hang garland and tinsel from the ceiling. For most of the afternoon, she'd carried the clipboard around in front of her like a shield, but there was nothing preventing her from toppling off the arms of a wobbly chair and breaking her neck.

Without thinking, Nick rushed over and grabbed her hips to steady her as she rose on tiptoe to tuck a length of garland through the bars securing the new tiles to the ceiling. At his touch she froze, staring down at him with wide green eyes. "What are you—"

Sure enough, the old vinyl chair gave an ominous creak and tilted sideways, sending Belle careening against Nick and knocking him back a step. He held her tight against him and moved toward the reception desk, her floral shampoo teasing his nose.

"Put me down, please," she said, her voice muffled by his shoulder.

He did as she asked, setting her on her feet then releasing her, his pulse thudding and his mouth as dry as sandpaper. Nick shoved his hands into the back pockets of his jeans so she wouldn't see them shake as adrenaline pumped hot and fierce through his bloodstream.

She'd slipped. He'd caught her before she fell. That was all.

Why then did he feel sweaty and stunned and swirling with energy?

"Thanks." She dusted the white powder from the ceiling tiles off her hands. "Guess using the chair wasn't such a good idea."

"No, it wasn't." His words emerged harsher than he'd intended, but she could've been hurt or worse…

Vicki's face flashed into his mind. The slow beep, beep, beep of the heart monitor until it flatlined. Nick scrubbed his hands over his face, making the connection. Belle could've died.

And it would've been his fault. Again. Just like Vicki.

"Hey," she said, moving closer to him. The touch of her hand felt cool on the heated skin. "It's okay. I'm fine. You saved the day."

He shook his head and turned away. "Except I didn't."

Nick paced for a minute as he gathered the tattered shreds of his composure. God, he was a complete wreck. He walked behind the reception desk and grabbed a bottle of water from the stash beneath the counter, drinking half a bottle before focusing on Belle again. She was still standing there, watching him, her expression concerned. The last thing he wanted right now was her pity. "Tell me about Beverly Hills."

She seemed surprised. "What do you want to know?"

"What's your practice like? Is it what you expected? How's your patient load?" He set the water aside and leaned his palms on the desktop, feeling a modicum of his control returning. "I don't remember you ever expressing an interest in making people more beautiful."

She walked over to right the toppled chair. "That's not why I chose my specialty."

"Why, then?" Nick tilted his head to the side, far more interested in her answer than was wise. He wanted to know what had changed her, what had made her into the person who stood before him today.

She fiddled with one of the numerous decals of elves and ornaments and stars and gifts she'd stuck all over the front windows and he couldn't stop recalling the Christmas Eve they'd spent together eighteen years before. He'd held Belle in his arms beneath the stars at the top of the sand dunes, listening to the waves on Lake Michigan in the distance. That was the night she'd told him about her scholarship offer from UCLA and how she wasn't going to accept it because it would be too far away from home and from him. The night that had changed Nick's life forever and put him on the path he followed now.

Belle glanced back at him. "I thought we weren't discussing the past."

Damn. She had him there. Nick hung his head. "What else are we going to talk about?"

"We could just not talk at all."

"Sure. Because silence is so much less awkward."

Her gaze held his for a long moment then she smiled. It transformed her from beautiful to stunning, and for a second Nick's guilt evaporated, replaced instead by a yearning that had never entirely disappeared, even after all these years. Want danced through him like sparks from a fire. He still remembered what it felt like holding her, stroking her, nuzzling her neck, her breasts, her...

"Hello?" Belle said, breaking him out of his thoughts. "Earth to Nick."

Reality crashed back onto him like a ton of iron bricks.

He wondered how he could forget his promise so easily. He was a loner now. A father. A doctor. Belle had her own life, her own career back in California. She'd be gone after Christmas and he'd still be here in Bayside, with a thriving practice to run and a growing son to raise.

"Sorry. Thinking about my meningitis case," he lied.

She gave him a skeptical look, as if she knew it, then began neatly stacking her inventory lists on the counter and stapling the corner. "Any new updates?"

"My patient's still stable. It's a good sign, but I don't want to be too optimistic too soon." Nick crossed his arms, determined to keep things strictly platonic between him and Belle.

Because that's what he wanted.

Wasn't it?

"I'm taking off for the night," Juan said, coming out of the utility room in the back, raising a hand toward them as he exited.

"Say hello to Analia for me," Belle called, smiling.

"Will do." Juan waved. "See you both in the morning. Going to the tree lighting tonight. See you there, Nick?"

"Yep." He glanced at the clock then grabbed his coat off the rack Nick turned to face Belle again as he shrugged into his jacket. "I need to get to the school to pick up Con."

"Sure." Belle continued stapling more papers. "Have fun."

Her tone held a hint of wistful sadness and his tired heart ached. He didn't like being so conflicted, especially with everything else they were dealing with. Maybe it was time they called a truce. "Why don't you come with us?"

"Huh?" Her brows lifted in surprise. "You mean to the tree lighting ceremony?"

"Yeah." They'd go as friends. Two lonely people keeping each other company. Nothing more. He took her coat off the rack and held it for her to slip into. As she did, his fingertips grazed the soft skin at the nape of her neck. Frissons of electric awareness zinged up his arm before he could stop them. He forced an ease he didn't quite feel, turning on the charm. "I guarantee you'll have fun."

"I can't." She grabbed her bag and papers off the desk. "I really need to get these over to your office to make sure we have our supplies on time for the free clinic."

"Not a problem." He snatched the list from her and tucked the papers in his coat pocket. "I'll deliver them to Jeanette myself. C'mon. It'll make me happy."

With a shock, he realized it was true.

She tilted her head, clearly overthinking it, the same as him. "I don't want to be out late."

"We'll be back early, I promise. Con has a nine o'clock curfew anyway. He's got to be up early tomorrow for hockey." Nick held the front door for her then shut off the lights before joining Belle on the sidewalk and locking up the clinic. He hoped to keep her talking so he didn't have to think about the pounding of blood in his head and the poignant yearning in his heart. "Good. It's settled, then."

CHAPTER FIVE

BELLE CLICKED HER seat belt into place as Nick finished scraping the frost off his windshield then climbed back in behind the wheel of his SUV. The vehicle was like him—steadfast, reliable, well maintained. A no-nonsense vehicle for a no-nonsense man. So different from the ritzy sports cars and convertibles people drove around in Beverly Hills. Inside, it was warm and cozy and felt like their own private universe.

"So," he said as he started the engine and shifted into gear, "you didn't answer my question. Why plastic surgery?"

Belle shrugged and stared out the window, reliving her visit to Northwestern for the umpteenth time in her head. The sight of Nick and his bride-to-be from across the room. They'd looked so happy. She told him half the story, keeping the most painful parts to herself. "I observed a facial reconstruction on a child with a cleft palate during one of my rotations and I was hooked. The ability to create normalcy for someone who's never had it felt like a true calling. I was accepted to the fellowship program at Harvard and the rest is history." She squinted out the window at the passing scenery as they pulled onto Main Street. "Dr. Reyes was a visiting surgeon at Mass General and he approached me about joining his practice after observing my work. It was an opportunity I couldn't pass up."

Nick frowned slightly. "Isn't Beverly Hills super competitive, though?"

"Very." She smiled. "I remember telling my professors at Harvard about my decision to accept the offer and they thought I was crazy. But I chose my practice because I wanted to climb to the top of the mountain. I wanted to conquer it."

"And have you?"

"In some ways. I've built a reputation. Dr. Reyes has even offered me a partnership." Her smile faded slightly, and she looked away. "As long as I'm back in California by Christmas."

She did her best to keep the uncertainty from her tone and failed, if the look Nick gave her was any indication. "You're happy, then? It's everything you ever wanted?"

"Hmm." She tucked her hair behind her ear. "What about you? I'm sorry about your wife passing away. I don't think I ever expressed my condolences."

"Thank you." His sounded strained and Belle could've kicked herself for bringing it up. He squinted out the windshield, his face taut. "Losing Vicki was a big wake-up call."

With the door to the past wide open now, Belle couldn't help her curiosity. "Was her death the reason you gave up your practice in Atlanta moved back to Bayside?"

"Partly. I wanted Connor to grow up in the kind of place I did as a kid. Where you can go outside at night and leave your door unlocked and not worry about getting shot or robbed. Plus, I missed the community here.

And since he's my top priority now, I wanted to do what was best for him."

"And was it the best thing for you too?" He'd said he had his reasons for being single, but perhaps his went beyond the norm. One of the doctors in her practice had lost his wife a few years back and he was already remarried. She sensed there was more behind Nick's statement than he was letting on, but she had to tread lightly to avoid him shutting her down completely. "Must be hard, raising a child on your own. I know Aunt Marlene struggled sometimes with me, growing up."

"It can be hard." He slowed for a red light. "But I do my best."

"Connor seems like a great kid. You've done well with him."

"He's awesome."

She rested her head back against the seat and stared out at the snowy landscape. The sky above was overcast and gray. "What about you? Why did you choose pediatrics?"

Nick accelerated once the light turned green. "After seven years of residency in Chicago." At her questioning look, he added, "Three in GP and four in pediatric surgery, I was ready for warmer weather. The head of my practice in Atlanta was consulting on a patient in Chicago and I assisted him with a surgery. He remembered me. When he called to offer me a spot at the end of my residency, it was a godsend. By then Vicki was pregnant with Connor and we needed financial stability. Atlanta gave me those things."

Belle turned away so he wouldn't see her wince, but it was too late.

"What?" he asked, frowning. "What's wrong?"

She sighed and decided to come out with it. "I never

told you this, but I came to see you at Northwestern, right before I entered my fellowship at Harvard."

"What?" Nick scowled. "Why?"

"I wanted to get your opinion on what I should choose as my specialty." She shrugged, her heart threatening to beat out of her ribcage. "You were always my best sounding board. Anyway, when I got to the common area of your apartment complex, there was a celebration going on, an engagement party. I saw the happy couple was you and your soon-to-be wife. Her baby bump was evident. I left." She shook her head and stared down at her hands in her lap, blinking away tears. "I never should've come. You'd moved on. I realized I needed to do the same."

Nick looked flummoxed. "I don't know what to say, Belle. I figured you'd forgotten all about me by then."

"I should have, but I couldn't." She exhaled slowly, allowing herself to feel the pain of that long-ago night in the hope she could clear it away for good. "Part of the reason you broke up with me was because you didn't want to think about marriage or children before you were out of residency and working in private practice."

"True." The word emerged low and gruff. "But I didn't plan what happened with Vicki. We'd both had too much to drink and one thing led to another and…" He shook his head. "I'm not proud of it. But once she found out she was pregnant I couldn't abandon my responsibilities. The baby gave me a new perspective, a new future. One I'd never expected, but Vicki was a good wife and an excellent mother. She gave up everything to be with me. When she died, I promised to put Connor first, make sure he was happy and safe, so her sacrifice wasn't in vain. I came home to Bayside and set up practice. It's good, though. I make a real difference here. Money can't buy everything."

Belle mulled over his answer. "Are you happy?"

"My happiness doesn't matter. It's all about my son now."

She stared at his profile a moment, tension stinging inside her like a thousand wasps. She had so many emotions, so many more questions. With the truth out there, where did they stand? Could they have a future together after all they'd been through? Did she even want to try? Would they still fit like two pieces of the same puzzle?

The possibilities left her reeling.

They drove past a picturesque row of old Victorian-style homes decorated for the holidays. Nick made a left on Hancock Street, past her aunt's place and down two more blocks to the newly constructed Bayside Elementary, where kids swarmed across the parking lot, heading for yellow buses parked near the doors or the line of cars with parents waiting at the curb.

As their vehicle inched toward the front entrance where Connor waited with a backpack slung over one shoulder and a bag of gear over the other, Belle did her best to compose herself. Kids picked up on things much more acutely than adults and the last thing she wanted was for Connor to get weird vibes from her when she was still figuring this all out herself.

Nick waved to his son and he started for the front door of the vehicle, then saw Belle and clambered into the back seat instead, tossing his stuff on the floor.

"Hey, buddy. How was school?" Nick asked, glancing in the rearview mirror. "You remember Belle, right?"

"Yeah. Hey." The boy busied himself buckling up and rummaging around in his backpack. "Guess what, Dad? I got an A on my science project."

"Awesome!" Nick grinned, glancing over at Belle. "He made a volcano."

"Cool." She turned slightly to peer at Connor. He looked just like a mini version of his dad at the same age. She swallowed the tiny bubble of nervous energy fizzing inside her and forced a smile. "I loved science when I was your age. So did your father."

Connor looked at her speculatively. "He told me you guys used to be friends in school."

"Really?" Belle gave Nick some serious side-eye, her heart beating faster. He'd talked to his son about her? The thought was unexpected and unsettling and a tad bit thrilling. "Yes. We grew up together in Bayside."

"He said you work in some fancy clinic."

"I live in California, near the ocean."

"The movie stars are out there," Nick added, staring straight ahead as he drove back toward downtown. "Belle's a famous plastic surgeon."

"Well, I don't know about the famous part..." she said, watching the scenery again.

Con scrunched his nose. "Are you going to help Analia?"

"Unfortunately, there's not enough time." Belle glanced at Nick again, hoping for some guidance. "But your dad's working on getting her the help she needs."

"Crap." Connor frowned and shifted his weight in his seat.

"Con," Nick said, his tone full of warning. "We don't use that word."

"Sorry." The little boy sat back in his seat again, his expression contemplative. "So, people come to you if they want to look different?"

"Yes, in a nutshell."

"Con's the king of questions," Nick whispered, chuckling low. "He's curious about everything and he's not afraid to ask."

"He seemed so quiet the other day at the funeral," Belle frowned.

"We were both tired and hungry." Nick stopped for another red light and looked over at Belle, his handsome face relaxed as he talked about his son. "Exhausting him is my daily goal."

While Connor continued to chatter away in the back seat and Nick drove on, Belle allowed herself to enjoy the moment and take it all in. Considering this would probably be her last time in Bayside, she wanted to savor it all.

A few minutes later, they pulled up to the curb outside a small restaurant at the far end of Main Street called Piper Cove. She'd not been there since high school, but remembered they had the best chili and hot chocolate in the area. Nick cut the engine then said to Belle, "Hungry?"

Her stomach rumbled and she smiled. "I am."

"Good. Con, time to eat."

"Yum!" The kid scurried out of the back seat to wait with Nick on the sidewalk. A thin coating of fresh snow covered everything, highlighting the impending holidays.

When Belle had been little, Aunt Marlene had gone out of her way to ensure each Christmas was special. They'd bake cookies and watch old movies, even make homemade ornaments for the tree. Now that she was alone, this time of year had lost some of its magic.

Most times she purposely stayed too busy to celebrate. Took extra shifts at the clinic to let the doctors with families have the time off so she didn't sit home alone and feel sad. And, sure, it had been her decision not to turn any of her dates into relationships. Relationships were a luxury she couldn't afford on her pathway to success.

Weren't they?

She got out of the truck and went around to where the guys waited.

As they walked inside the busy restaurant, her conversation with Nick continued to swirl through her head. All this time she'd thought Nick had lied to her, but it turned out he'd been trying to do the right thing.

Belle should've known better. Nick had always had a strong moral compass, even when things were difficult or painful. He'd probably had been right about her too. She wouldn't have been able to live with herself if she'd not kept her promise to her parents back then. Even now, her career still made her feel tied her to them. If she'd stayed with Nick after high school, she probably wouldn't have achieved all she had. That didn't stop her heart breaking for the lovesick kids they'd once been and the lonely people they were now.

"Welcome to Piper Cove," the middle-aged hostess said. "Three tonight? Hey, Connor."

"Hey," Con said, hiking his thumb toward Belle. "This is Dr. Watson. She used to be my dad's friend."

The hostess smiled. "I remember you, Belle, though I doubt you remember me. I'm Mrs. Sweeten. I lived next door to your aunt for a few years. So sad to hear about Marlene."

"Thank you." Belle smiled. "And of course I remember you, Mrs. Sweeten. You used to grow the most beautiful roses."

"Still do," the hostess said, leading them to a table in the corner. "Can I get you all something to drink?"

"Two hot chocolates for us," Nick said, gesturing between himself and Connor.

"Make it three." Belle took off her coat and draped it over the back of the extra chair before sitting across from Nick and Connor. At Nick's raised brow she laughed. "What? I can drink things other than tea."

"Uh-huh. What happened to gluten-free and organic?"

"Hey, I'm entitled to be bad sometimes, right?"

"I do believe we're becoming a bad influence on you, Dr. Watson," Nick said, his little wink sending inappropriate flutters through her insides.

"Perhaps you are, Dr. Marlowe." She picked up her menu, studying it far more closely than was necessary, hoping to avoid doing something silly, like swooning in front of the whole restaurant. She wasn't some teenager anymore. She had an image to uphold. Plus, she'd be gone soon. Best to keep things light and easy, no matter how she might yearn for a real connection. Nick was not the man to help her with that. Not when he was obviously dealing with stuff of his own. She perused the selections, already knowing what she was going to have.

Mrs. Sweeten returned a few moments later with their drinks and took their orders. Three chili and an order of onion rings to split between them all. Not exactly on her list of healthy, low-carb options, but she'd missed the town's home-cooked delights and it was nearly Christmas. If you couldn't splurge at the holidays, when could you?

She took a sip of her hot chocolate, closing her eyes in delight as the warm sweetness hit her taste buds, followed by the rich cream of the whipped topping and the burst of the crushed peppermint topping. The flavors reminded her of all the good times she and Nick had spent here together after school. In fact, the first time she'd kissed him in freshman year had been outside this restaurant, in the little garden to the left of the gift shop. He'd tasted of cherries from his cola and sweet desire.

Belle found herself staring at Nick's mouth now, so firm and full and...

"How'd practice go today, Con?" Nick asked, jarring Belle out of her reverie.

She fiddled with her silverware, doing her best to ignore the heat flowing inside her like honey.

"Okay." Con leaned to the side and waved to someone behind Belle. "My friend Eric's over there by the gift shop. Can I say hi to him? Please?"

"Yes. But be back before the food comes," Nick said, moving his chair forward to let his son get past him. "And no running."

Con hurried away, leaving Belle and Nick alone once more, the confessions they'd made hanging heavily between them like Santa's full sleigh.

"Thank you for telling me about Vicki," Belle said. "It means a lot."

Nick sighed and nodded. "I tend to keep things bottled up these days. It's been hard since she died, with me working so much and trying to do my best for Con."

He looked so forlorn she couldn't help reaching across the table to place her hand over his. His skin felt warm and soft beneath her touch. "I'm sorry."

"It's okay." Nick stared down at her hand covering his before pulling away. "I just... She gave up so much to marry me and I feel like I owe her, you know?"

The guilt in his voice was heartrending. "She wouldn't want you to be miserable, though, would she?"

"I'm not miserable. I'm happy." Nick looked up at

her, his flat tone suggesting the exact opposite. "What's not to be happy about?"

She took another sip of her hot chocolate. She understood his feelings maybe better than most. "Do you remember after my parents died? How I walked around like a robot for weeks?"

"Yeah." His shoulders slumped a bit. "I remember."

"I didn't eat, wouldn't sleep. I was desperate to find a way to bring them back. I thought if I was just good enough, smart enough, I could make them see me from heaven and love me enough to return." She gave a sad snort. "Silly, right?"

"No. Not silly. You were only a kid, Belle. You didn't know any better."

"True." She tapped her fingers against the side of her mug, choosing her words carefully. "But you're thirty-eight, Nick. I doubt Vicki wanted you to live like a monk for the rest of your life."

He blinked at her and she held her breath, hoping she hadn't made things worse. Years had passed, and perhaps she shouldn't say what was on her mind with him like she had back in high school.

"She told me she wanted me to move on, to find someone else. After an appropriate mourning time, of course. She thought it was so funny to tack that on at the end. Vicki had a great sense of humor." He sobered. "But she also had a brilliant career lined up after college. She had her whole life ahead of her. She gave it all up because of one stupid mistake with me." He lowered his head. "I've carried the guilt for a long time, Belle. No matter what I do, I never feel like it's enough. It's a vicious cycle I don't know how to break."

Her heart ached for all he'd been through, for the way he was still torturing himself.

"Hey." She squeezed his hand and ducked to catch his gaze. "Listen to me. I never met your wife, but if she's even half as wonderful as you make her sound then she was a great lady. Smart too. Smart, wonderful women make their own choices. Was your wife a pushover?"

"No." Nick shook his head. "Far from it."

"Then I doubt you forced her to do anything. She chose to be with you and raise Connor. Single women raise children by themselves all the time these days. If she'd really wanted to go off and pursue her career, she could have." Belle sat back. "But she chose to marry you instead."

He watched her closely for a second. "When did you get so wise?"

"I've just learned my lessons over the years. Please stop beating yourself up over something you can't change." She glanced over to where Connor and his friend were playing arcade games. "You've got a wonderful son and a wonderful life here in Bayside. And if the right person comes along, don't be afraid to include them in it."

Nick toyed with his mug, then met her gaze once more. "Physician, heal thyself."

"Exactly."

He narrowed his gaze. "Goes both ways, you know."

"What?" She frowned. "I'm fine."

"Are you?" Nick's too-perceptive stare made her want to fidget. "I know you miss your parents and Marlene, but I hope you still don't think you need to chase after a career you don't love because of some misguided idea you need it to stay close to them."

Her heart lurched. Yes, she'd had her doubts about

the partnership position up for grabs in California, but that was just the usual jitters about the future.

Wasn't it?

Belle sighed and slumped back in her seat. The tiny hollow niggle of discontent in her stomach gnawed harder. She'd worked so hard to get where she was professionally that she'd never taken the time to step back and decide if it's really the place she wanted to be. Honestly, something had felt off inside her from the moment Dr. Reyes had dangled the partnership in front of her like a carrot, but she'd been too busy to contemplate if she wanted to accept. Now, getting out of it could prove more troublesome than it was worth. Especially since she had no idea what she'd do if she didn't take the promotion.

Don't you?

Sweet little Analia's face flashed in her mind again before she shook it off.

No. Giving up a certain partnership for an uncertain future would be ludicrous.

Right?

"Don't be absurd," she scoffed, as much for Nick as for herself. "I'm a grown woman. I've made my decisions based on facts."

"Sure. Uh-huh. Like the fact you made up about me and Vicki during your residency visit?" He took her hand this time and turned it over, rubbing soft circles on her palm with his thumb. "We're friends, Belle. But just in case there were any lingering doubts, your parents loved you and would've been proud of you no matter what. The same with your aunt Marlene. All any of them ever wanted was for you to be happy."

"I am happy," she said, her words emerging about

as convincingly as his had earlier. "I have my patients, my work, a lovely apartment."

"What about friends? Fun?"

"I go out to the movies and walk along the beach and—"

"And here we are, folks," Mrs. Sweeten said, delivering their food.

Belle snatched her hand back, holding it close to her chest as if she'd been burned. She was happy. She had everything she could possibly want.

Except love.

The voice in her head delivering those words was Aunt Marlene's and didn't help in the slightest. She sat back as Mrs. Sweeten placed a steaming bowl of homemade chili in front of her and Nick called Connor back to the table. A platter mounded with onion rings sat in the center of the table. It looked like enough food for six people, let alone the three of them. Then Connor dug into their feast and she realized it might not be enough after all. Nick served up a small plate of onion rings for her and himself then let Con have the rest on the platter.

They ate in silence for a while, Belle savoring her first taste of the delightful chili in almost two decades. So, so good. Thick and hearty, with ground beef and spices and chunks of tomato. And the crispy sweet and salty onion rings were the perfect compliment.

Pure, sinful heaven.

Nick finished first then sipped his cocoa. "The tree lighting ceremony hasn't changed much since you were last here, Belle. There are still vendor booths and crafts plus the community band plays in the bandstand."

"Last year one of the booths had elephant ears as big as your head," Connor said. "Can we get one of those too, Dad? Please?"

"We'll see, son," Nick said. "Finish your dinner first."

She took another bite of chili, her heart squeezing with nostalgia. "Sounds like a lovely evening. Thanks for inviting me along."

"My pleasure," Nick's gaze met hers. "Thanks for accepting."

She'd given him a lot to think about and he'd helped the seeds of doubt within in her germinate too, darn him. The connection they'd always shared flared brighter than ever. It felt as if the years had fallen away. Time seemed to slow, the noise of the restaurant fading until it was just Belle and Nick and the ache in her heart for the way things were, even though she knew it was impossible to go back.

Your parents loved you and would've been proud of you no matter what...

For years, Belle had clung to her one last tie to her parents. It was what had gotten her through med school, residency, finding out Nick had become engaged to someone else. She couldn't abandon it now, could she? No. It wasn't that simple. Couldn't be that simple.

Then Mrs. Sweeten returned to clear their plates and Nick winked at her again, and the world continued on as normal, even as the feeling she'd be losing something precious here in Bayside when she left for good lingered inside Belle.

Half an hour later they walked down the sidewalk on Main Street through the lightly falling snow, Connor and his friend Eric between them. It was night already—darkness fell quickly in the Michigan winter. The streetlights cast a bright orange glow across the glittering ground.

"Wow. The town looks gorgeous all decorated for

Christmas," Belle said, admiring the twinkling lights in a store's window display as they passed. "Beautiful."

"Yeah, it is." Nick drew in a breath and shuffled his feet.

After their unexpected conversation back in the restaurant, he was still trying to wrap his head around the fact he'd bared his soul to her about Vicki. And while the ache of guilt in his chest still lingered, getting things out in the open seemed to have lessened the burden somehow. If he'd taken the time to think about it beforehand, overanalyzing like he usually did, he'd never have brought it up with Belle. Maybe he'd felt comfortable because of her confession in the car about seeing him with Vicki. Man, those words had knocked him for another loop. He'd had no idea she'd visited, or her mistaken assumptions.

A warning claxon clanged in his head, the common-sense portion of his brain warning him that to take this evening as anything more than casual fun between friends would be beyond stupid. And Nick wasn't dumb. Not normally. But having Belle back here again, especially at holiday time, when memories crowded every corner, must have made him sentimental. That's the excuse he was going with anyway.

"Can Eric and I go check out the bandstand, Dad?" Connor asked, nearly bursting at the seams with excitement. "Please?"

"Fine," Nick said, releasing a little bit of his precious control. "But be careful. And look both ways before you cross the street."

Connor and Eric raced on ahead, leaving Nick and Belle to stroll on alone. They each carried a refill cup of hot cocoa from Piper Cove and the sweet strains of "Silent Night" drifted from the concert in the park. As they neared the festivities, things got busier and crowds jostled, all heading to the same destination.

Belle stopped a few times to avoid getting bumped and Nick placed his free hand in the small of her back to guide her safely into Bayside Community Park.

"Wow. This looks the same as I remember." The hint of awe in her voice made him smile. The normally quiet town green was bustling tonight, packed with people awaiting the tree lighting. A huge pine stood in the middle of the square, decorated and waiting for someone to flip the switch. The mayor stood on a small stage in front of the bandstand, trying to entertain the gathered crowds and preparing for her emcee duties.

"Thanks again for inviting me," Belle said, leaning closer so he could hear. Her heat penetrated the wool of his coat and the sweet scent of flowers and soap tickled his nose.

Nick watched her while she looked at the tree, remembering the last time they'd been here together. Their last Christmas before high-school graduation, the night of their trip up to the dunes. That night had been the first time they'd slept together. They'd both been virgins. He wondered if Belle was remembering the evening too.

"Lots of families in the area now, huh?" She glanced up at him before dodging out of the path of a little girl with long blonde hair running straight for them. He slipped his arm around her waist to steady her, then let Belle go when it started to feel too good.

"Yeah. This event always brings the whole community together." He didn't miss the twinge of sadness in her eyes and his own heart tugged in sympathy. Losing Marlene had to be tougher on her than she was letting on, especially at this time of year. A sudden urge to ease that pain welled up inside him, and he shifted his attention to safer territory, the vendor stalls near the side of the park. "They've got cinnamon-sugar roasted almonds. Want some?"

"Yum! Sounds good," she said.

Nick bought a bag for them to share.

"I wonder what color the lights will be this year," he said as they leaned against the brick wall of Gustaffson's World Emporium to watch the ceremonies, the building helping to block the biting wind stirring off Lake Michigan.

Belle smiled. "I think they were purple the first time Aunt Marlene brought me here."

"Then silver." Nick squinted through the crowds, keeping an eye on Connor and Eric near the bandstand. "And red the following year."

"Right. They change them a lot. Who knows what it'll be this year? Maybe all three?"

"Maybe." Nick moved closer to her as more people gathered around them, his heart squeezing with their shared memories.

"Last year they were blue," he said after clearing his throat. A lump of emotion seemed to have gathered there, making his words emerge gruffer than he'd intended. "Connor called it a Smurf tree."

"Nice." Belle laughed and returned her attention to the crowds. The band started a rousing rendition of "Jingle Bells" and people pressed closer as they sang along. Belle linked arms with him so they wouldn't get separated.

Connor and Eric returned, and his son tapped Nick on the elbow. "Dad?"

The countdown to the tree lighting began.

Ten, nine…

Nick was looking at the tree and not his son. "Turn around, Con. They're getting ready to flip the switch."

"Dad!" His son yelled, tapping his arm hard. "Look!"

Nick frowned down at his son. "What?"

"Mistletoe." Connor pointed up above Nick's head.

A quick look skyward had Nick's heart plummeting. Damn. He should've paid more attention when choosing a spot to stand. Belle too glanced upward then met Nick's gaze, a hint of shock and mirth in her emerald eyes.

Eight, seven, six…

"Forget it, Con," Nick said, shaking his head. "Doesn't count when you're just friends."

"Yeah?" his son grumbled. "Then why did you make me kiss old Mrs. Wooten on the cheek at the grocery store? She's not even my friend. She's my teacher. It was yucky."

Belle snorted. "He makes a good point."

"That was different," Nick said, ignoring the heat rising from beneath the collar of his coat. Of all the times and places to have Connor notice the mistletoe, it would have to be now. And Belle wasn't helping at all, standing there chuckling.

Five, four, three…

"C'mon, Dad. It's tradition."

Ugh. The kid wouldn't let it go. Persistence. Another trait he'd inherited from his mom. At the reminder of his wife, Nick waited for the familiar slash of guilt, but for some reason it didn't come. Instead, there was a bittersweet sting of longing.

Longing for connection, for peace, for companionship.

On stage, the mayor's hand hovered over the red button to light the tree. Belle bumped into his side, smiling up at him, as radiant as the sun. The same way she'd done their senior year of high school. The same night they'd consummated their relationship. The same night they'd confessed their love…

Two, one…

The crowd gasped as the tree lights flickered on, casting a bright fuchsia glow over the park, but Nick only had eyes for Belle.

"Does kind of seem a shame to waste it, huh?" he said, blood pounding loudly in his ears and adrenaline singing in his veins, drowning out the carolers around them. All his attention was focused on her pink lips, wondering if she tasted as sweet as he remembered.

People swayed around them, pushing him and Belle closer still. Her face was so close, her eyes darkening as their bodies brushed. Their breath mingled, frosting on the chilly air. Time seemed to halt as they seemed to really see each of for the first time after all these years.

Need drove him to take charge. Need and want and years of pent-up denial.

Nick gave up the fight and bent to brush his lips over Belle's.

One quick peck then he'd be done.

People cheered and the band played another Christmas tune, but instead of pulling away, as he'd intended, Nick snuggled Belle closer. She tasted of sugar and cinnamon and chocolate, her body tense against him before she relaxed. Then her free hand was clutching his shoulder and he shivered despite the heat thundering through his bloodstream.

It was as good as he remembered. It was just as right. It was…

Over.

"Hey, Dad?" Connor tugged on his sleeve, forcing

Nick and Belle apart. "Can Eric and I go back up to the bandstand now?"

"Uh…" Dumbfounded, Nick just nodded. His breath was jagged, and he couldn't seem to stop staring at Belle. At her lips, which were still parted. At her eyes, which were wide and looked as shocked as he felt. At her flushed cheeks, which showed he hadn't been the only one affected by their impulsive kiss.

"Yeah," he managed to say finally, turning away to toss the remains of his now-cold hot chocolate in a nearby bin. He took a deep breath and collected himself before facing Belle again. "Sorry. Guess I got carried away."

"Me too," she said, her husky tone sending ripples of awareness through him.

She threw her cup in the trash as well, then crossed her arms, rubbing them against the chill. "We should, um, probably get going. I need to be up early in the morning."

"Right. Sure." Nick called for Connor then started back for his truck, not daring to put his hand on Belle's back again to herd her through the people for fear he might not let her go. His pulse still pounded loudly in his ears and his lips tingled from their kiss. He wasn't sure exactly what had happened between them tonight, only that things had definitely changed.

For better or worse remained to be seen.

CHAPTER SIX

SATURDAY MORNING BELLE was due back at the clinic with Nick bright and early, but she was still feeling slightly off-kilter from their kiss the night before. She wasn't sure exactly what had possessed him to do it, or her to respond, but respond she had. In fact, her insides continued to flutter from the memory of his lips against hers—warm and soft and perfect.

Maybe it had been their conversation in the restaurant. She knew what it was like, carrying around survivor's guilt. She'd done it for years after her parents had died, and it was exhausting. Perhaps Nick had kissed her out of relief after she'd told him it wasn't his fault Vicki had died. Then there was also the fact that last night had been an anniversary of sorts, the night they'd made love for the first time all those years ago, though she doubted he remembered.

No. Last night had been a fluke. A dare started by the stupid mistletoe placed strategically above their heads. No sense getting all nostalgic and sentimental and lovesick about it because she couldn't go there. She had enough on her plate as it was. Belle liked things to be neat and tidy, no messy emotions, no scars. And this resurgence of her connection with Nick was most definitely *not* tidy.

Kissing him last night had been irrational and irresponsible and totally intoxicating and...

Ugh.

Belle pushed through the front door of the clinic, her arms loaded down with donuts and coffee from the bakery down the block and a white plastic bag filled with extra brushes and rollers for their painting job today.

"Hey," Nick greeted her as she walked into the lobby, rushing over to take the box of pastries from her. "You look tired this morning."

"I am. I didn't sleep well last night." She'd tossed and turned, unable to get Nick and his kisses out of her head.

He frowned, his expression concerned. "I hope you're not coming down with something. There's a nasty flu bug going around. My PA said new cases of it are nonstop in my office."

"I'm fine," she said, grateful he'd not brought up the previous evening. Whether he was choosing to ignore it or giving her an easy out, she was good with it. Or she would be, once she got her head on straight. No more stewing about this thing between them. It would all be over soon enough anyway. She only had five more days after this one left in Bayside. A tiny pang of regret pinched her chest before she shoved it aside. It was good. It was all good. And if she just told herself that enough times, maybe she'd begin to believe it. To distract herself, she set the tray of drinks on the counter then took off her coat. "I had my flu vaccination months ago and I'm healthy. Where's Connor?"

"In one of the exam rooms with Eric. I showed them how to use the painter's tape and put them to work blocking off the electrical outlets. Hey, guys?" Nick called down the hallway. "Breakfast is here. Come and get your bear claws before I eat them all."

He turned back to Belle and gave her a guarded smile as Connor and his friend came running, their hair sticking up at odd angles and their matching superhero T-shirts on crooked.

"Good morning," she said, handing each boy a donut wrapped in a napkin. "How are you today, Connor? Eric?"

"Better now that these are here. Thanks." Connor took a huge bite of donut and grabbed a bottled water before tearing back down the hallway.

Eric followed suit, shouting behind him, "Thanks for the bear claw."

"You're welcome," she called after them, laughing. "Looks like the donuts were a success."

"Food's always a big hit with boys. Even big ones like me." Nick took a glazed donut and cup of tea then rested a hip against the receptionist desk while he ate. Her heart flip-flopped. Belle swallowed hard and nibbled on an éclair to hide her flushed cheeks. Nick took a large swig of his tea then held up his cup. "You know, before you came, I was a coffee guy through and through. But you've converted me to your crazy California ways."

She gave a nervous chuckle, looking anywhere but at him. Standing this close to him again, remembering the feel of his lips on hers, the warmth of his breath on her face, his scent surrounding her as he'd held her so close, threatened the careful stability she'd worked so hard to achieve this morning. She needed to stay focused on her goals—get the clinic ready, get the clinic open, get home. Then Nick shifted slightly, his arm brushing her shoulder, and fresh tingles zipped through her nerve endings.

Aw, man. She was in serious trouble.

Not to mention the fact Dr. Reyes had called her

again last night after she'd gotten back to her aunt's house, which was the other reason why she'd not slept well. In addition to the partnership, he'd also offered to let her head up the practice's charity activities. Meaning she'd have free rein and ample resources to put toward the neediest cases. She could travel the world and make a real difference. It was almost too good to pass up, and yet she'd hesitated. Why? She wasn't sure. Perhaps because of the past. Or because of the man in front of her. Whatever the reason, she'd thanked Dr. Reyes and assured him she still planned on being back in California the day after Christmas.

To reinforce the idea to herself, she'd even booked her flight out of Lansing for 5 p.m. on Christmas Day. That should give her plenty of time to run the free clinic with Nick on Christmas Eve, then pack up what was left of her aunt's things before saying goodbye to Bayside for good.

Her heart ached at the thought, but it had to be done.

Amazing as last night had been, it wasn't reality. Reality was that she and Nick had separate lives, separate responsibilities, and Belle wasn't one for flings. So, with her mind firmly made up, she took her tea and her éclair and headed toward the exam rooms they were going to paint. "Best get to work."

"Hey." Nick caught up with her. He lowered his voice and rubbed his hand over the back of his neck, obviously uncomfortable. "About last night…"

"Don't worry," she said, doing her best to sound flippant. "It was just a kiss."

"Right." He narrowed his gaze as he leaned his hand against the wall beside her head. Her breath hitched at his nearness. "Wouldn't happen to have anything to do with your insomnia, would it?"

"No. Don't be ridiculous. We made a mistake standing under the mistletoe and your son called us out on it. It didn't mean anything." She tossed her hair over her shoulder and raised her chin, feigning a confidence she didn't quite feel. "Did it?"

He opened his mouth. Closed it. Looked away, his frown deepening. "No. I suppose not."

"Good." She sidled around him and headed for the exam-room door, her heart thudding and her throat dry. "I'm going to start painting now. Lots to do and little time."

Thankfully, he didn't follow her this time.

She finished her éclair without really tasting it, hoping the sugar rush would help clear her head and keep her alert. After finishing her tea, she got busy setting up to paint the tiny room. Connor and Eric had already taped over all the outlets and Nick had covered the floors, exam table, and cabinets with tarps. A gallon of beige paint sat on the counter along with a pan, a roller, and a brush. She'd never really used any of this stuff before, but it couldn't be hard. After prying the lid off a paint can and pouring some into a pan, she picked up the roller and moved the stepladder into position. Starting from the top down would be the most prudent form of attack.

With her paint pan balanced on the top of the small ladder, she climbed up and began. The repetitive movements helped soothe away some of her stress and centered her. She could see why people enjoyed interior decorating.

"Belle, I think—" Nick walked into the exam room, startling her.

She turned too quickly and the stepladder wobbled precariously. Belle squeaked.

Cursing, Nick rushed forward, pulling her close to his chest, his hands on her hips, his muscles rippling beneath the soft cotton of his gray sweatshirt. Molten heat surged through her bloodstream once more, the same kind she'd tried so hard to deny since last night.

"Be careful," he said, voice shaky. "I don't want anything to happen to you too."

Belle saw his face was as white as a sheet, his dark eyes troubled and anxious.

"It's okay." She kept her tone deliberately quiet. "I'm fine. Everything's okay."

Nick let her go and turned away, running a shaky hand through his hair. "Sorry. I'm used to being overly cautious now, since..." Cursing, he rubbed his eyes and forced a stiff smile. "I overreacted. Bad habit these days. After Vicki, I..."

His voice trailed off as he walked back toward the door and her gut wrenched. His normally affable, superman façade faltered. Yep. She'd definitely opened a bubbling cauldron of pain for him last night and now she wasn't sure how to contain it, or if she even should. Aunt Marlene had taught her usually the easiest path to a solution was through the problem. If so, she needed to reassure Nick nothing was going to happen. She rushed forward and placed her hand on his arm. "Hey. Seriously. I'm fine. See?"

"Are you?" Nick looked back at her over his shoulder. "This is all so nuts. I thought I'd dealt with all this stuff already. I'm sorry to bring you into it."

Pretending it's not there won't make it go away. Aunt Marlene's words echoed through Belle's head and she bit her tongue to keep from saying them. Nick was dealing with enough already. Instead, she looked around at the paint now splattering the tarps, ladder and wall.

"Ack! What a mess." *In more ways than one.* Inappropriate laughter bubbled up inside her and before she could stop it, giggles erupted.

"This is not funny, Belle." Nick gave her a stern look before his own lips twitched. Soon he shook his head and started chuckling right along with her. "Okay, yeah, maybe it is a little funny. And definitely a mess."

"I don't even know why it's so hilarious," she wheezed, tears streaming from her eyes. She couldn't remember the last time she'd laughed hard like this and it felt too good to stop.

"Dad, what's going on?" Connor came in with Eric, the two boys looking totally perplexed. When Nick didn't answer right away because he was laughing too hard, Connor rolled his eyes at his friend. "Adults are so weird. Can we have another donut?"

Nick finally collected himself enough to nod then wiped his eyes. "Yes. In fact, bring the box in here. I think we're all going to need extra sugar today. What time are Eric's parents picking you guys up for practice again?"

"Coach said we need to be there by two."

Connor and his friend left, and Belle straightened, attempting to salvage what she could from her pan of paint.

"Listen," Nick said, moving in closer behind her. "I'm sorry about what happened last night at the tree lighting. I don't want things to be weird between us and I had no right to kiss you, okay? It was a mistake and I take full responsibility."

His eager expression was at direct odds with the sharp sting of sadness inside her. She should be happy he regretted their kiss. She didn't want to start anything with him again. She was leaving in less than a week for a glorious new future. So why did it feel like their prom night breakup all over again?

"Apology accepted," Belle said, not looking at him for fear he'd see the hurt in her eyes. Hurt that had no business being there but existed all the same. Darn it. She'd vowed to put Nick and all her feelings for him squarely in her past and now she found herself right back drowning in the emotional deep end with him again. He was right. This was all a huge mistake, but it was too late to get out now. The only way forward for them was through.

She nodded and kept working. "Let's get this cleaned up before the paint dries."

Nick worked for the next few hours, painting alongside Belle, while Connor and Eric played video games in the lobby. Eric's mom picked the boys up around one thirty and he helped Con transfer his gear from their SUV to Eric's mom's station wagon then wished the boys luck before walking back into the clinic. He snorted as he stood in the doorway of the last exam room, pretty sure Belle had almost as much paint on herself as she'd put on the walls, but she was a trouper. Besides, she looked adorable covered in beige.

He stopped short.

Don't go there. You told her the kiss was a mistake. Leave it be.

He should. Nick knew he should. He closed his eyes and pictured Vicki in the hospital. Pictured those last awful days in Atlanta. Pictured Connor waking up crying for his mother in those first terrible nights after his mother had died. Anything to keep him from imagining what it might be like to try again with Belle.

The whole idea was insane. She was only here for a

few more days. Short-term affairs had never been his style. It's why he'd remained alone for two years. Well, that and respect for Vicki. Nick retreated back into the hall and leaned against the wall, taking a deep breath, his final conversation with his deceased wife running through his mind again, as it had so many times the last two years.

I want you to move on, Nick. I don't want you to be alone. Find love again. Be happy. Promise me...

If he concentrated hard enough, he could still smell the sharp astringent odor of disinfectant, could still feel Vicki's frail hand in his as her life had slipped away. He'd promised her he'd be happy, but in his heart he'd vowed to put Connor before all else. Two years later he wondered if Vicki was looking down on him and shaking her head over his lies.

Find love again. Be happy.

It seemed nearly impossible now. It wasn't like love fell from the sky. Not the true kind anyway. Relationships took time and work. Then Belle's off-key humming drifted past his ears and he smiled. They'd loved each other once, but it wouldn't happen this time. She was only here temporarily. Still, the chemistry between them was burning brightly, if the kiss they'd shared was any indication.

Maybe they could enjoy each other while they had a chance. A fling. A brief holiday affair. Maybe he could split his focus between Belle and Connor, if only until after Christmas.

Belle had tried to hide it, but he'd not missed the flash of hurt in her eyes when he'd called last night a mistake.

Perhaps he wasn't the only one who was lonely...

Deep in thought, Nick walked back into the exam

room and picked up his roller to start the final wall. Physically, the work helped ease the tension in his muscles. Mentally, he was a ball of uncertainty, wondering exactly how to bring up pursuing this wildfire attraction between them. It had been so long since he'd dated anyone he wasn't even sure how to start. He turned it over and over in his head so many times, but nothing was certain anymore.

Analyzing every detail made for a great doctor, but not necessarily a great life partner. Vicki had taken a more laid-back approach to things, but Nick and Belle were much more similar personality-wise. Sometimes that was good. Others, not so much. Like now, for instance.

He sighed and ran his roller through the paint again. It was nearly three and they'd worked hard all day. The place looked much better already. Once they finished here and took the tarps down, he'd call the flooring professionals in to do what they could.

Belle's phone buzzed on the counter and she walked over to answer it, wiping her hands on a paint-stained rag. There were splashes of beige on her jeans and in her hair and one streak on her left cheek. He didn't think he'd ever seen a more beautiful sight in his life.

"It's a text from Jeanette. Our supplies will be ready for pick up tomorrow afternoon." She walked over to show him. "I'm done painting my section. Looks pretty good."

"Looks great," he said, straightening to survey the room, then feeling self-conscious as she peered up at him. "I, uh, just need to clean up in here, then you want to grab some dinner? Con's going to spend the night at Eric's after their practice so..."

Smooth, dude. Real smooth.

"Oh." She fiddled with the rag in her hands, twining the cloth between her long, graceful fingers. He couldn't help remembering the feel of those hands on his body, stroking his hair, his neck, his chest, lower still… "Are you sure? I mean, I've got plenty to do at my aunt's house and I wouldn't want you to make another mistake and…"

He took her hand. "I'm sorry, Belle. I shouldn't have said anything. Kissing you wasn't a mistake. In fact, it was pretty great."

"It was?" She blinked up at him and his pulse stumbled. His gaze dropped to her pink lips, reminding him of how she'd felt against him, how she'd tasted. He met her eyes again and saw the same want there that lurked inside him. She recovered quicker than he did, though, her smile brighter than the sun as she bent to help him clean up the supplies. "Sure. Okay. Sounds great. Give me an hour, please. I need to call my office in California and check in on things. Will that work for you?"

Even the reminder of her other life, her other responsibilities didn't dim the joy welling inside him. *Find love again. Be happy.* Just because this was temporary it didn't mean it couldn't be real. He was still mindful of his promise to keep his son a top priority, but surely it wouldn't hurt to take a bit of time for himself this once. "An hour works perfectly. I'll wash my hands and grab our coats and we can head out."

CHAPTER SEVEN

BY THE TIME Nick rang her doorbell at around five thirty Belle had showered and changed and was finishing up her phone call with Dr. Reyes. Not exactly a great way to prepare for a date, but then this wasn't a typical date either. In fact, she really shouldn't think of tonight as a date at all. It was dinner and a movie between friends, colleagues. Nothing more. The fact she and Nick had kissed the night before wasn't relevant.

Now, if only she could get her fluttering insides to calm down, things would be fantastic.

She answered the front door and waved Nick inside while still talking to Dr. Reyes on the phone.

"Listen, Belle," her boss said in his usual crisp tone. "I'd like you to give a short speech during the partnership ceremony, perhaps discuss your plans for our new charity work."

"Yes, sir. I can come up with something. Time's a bit tight, though, at the moment. I'll do my best." She motioned for Nick to have a seat on the sofa, trying not to stare at how handsome he looked. He was dressed in a clean pair of jeans, the faded ones that cupped his tight butt and taut thighs to perfection. He'd changed out of his gray sweatshirt from earlier too and now wore a soft-looking black turtleneck sweater topped by his long wool coat and black boots. His hair was slightly damp again from a recent shower and a shadow of stubble darkened his jaw, making him look a bit rough and dangerous. Fresh waves of warmth flooded her core. "Uh, I'm sorry, Dr. Reyes, but I need to go. I'll call again tomorrow to check in, sir."

"Is everything all right, Dr. Watson? You seem a bit distracted," he said.

"Fine. Everything's fine." Her voice sounded strained to her own ears. Distracted was right. And dazed, as Nick grinned, all smooth confidence and lethal male perfection. "Talk to you tomorrow, sir."

She ended the call without waiting for Dr. Reyes's response.

"Patients doing well?" Nick asked as she stood there staring at him. "Are you sure you're not too tired tonight? If so, say the word."

"No, no. I'm good. Sorry." Belle shook off her errant desire to snuggle up on his lap, maybe slide her hands beneath his sweater to feel his warm skin. She took a step back, hoping some extra distance might clear her steamy thoughts. "We should, um, probably get going."

"Yep." His gaze narrowed on her a moment before he pushed to his feet. "Italian food okay with you? I know this great little place just outside Manistee that serves the best baked ziti in the area. Gluten-free, of course. I called and checked."

"Perfect." She smiled and forced herself to move across the room to get her coat from the hook beside the door. Nick stepped in to help her, his warmth surrounding her along with his scent of soap and clean male.

"At first I wasn't sure about this red coat, Belle, but it really suits you." He rested his hands on her shoulders while she buttoned up then turned her to face him. "Are you sure everything's all right?"

"Of course." She pulled on her gloves. "Why wouldn't it be? Let's go."

Forty minutes later, they walked into Casa Antoine's and were seated in a nice banquette for two. After removing their coats, she and Nick perused the menus a maître d' handed them. Belle did her best to concentrate on the food selections and not the man beside her, his thigh pressing against hers, his arm brushing hers occasionally.

"I don't remember this place being here when we were growing up." She took a swallow of water and gazed around at the old-world-style décor. Soft music drifted down from speakers in the ceiling and candles were lit on each table, casting a glow over the room. The place felt romantic and intimate. It only made Belle more aware of the circumstances between her and Nick, the history, the scorching kiss they'd shared. Her hand trembled as she set her water goblet back on the table. Hopefully, Nick was too busy studying the wine list to notice. "You said the baked ziti is good here?"

"The best." He grinned and her knees tingled. "It's fantastic. The house salads are excellent, as well. Do you know what you'd like?"

"I'll try the ziti and a side salad, please."

"Perfect." Nick summoned a waiter over and ordered the same thing for both of them, along with a bottle of cabernet sauvignon. Once they were alone again, Nick fiddled with his silverware, seemingly as nervous as she was despite their kiss, or maybe because of it. "So."

"So." Belle smiled at the sommelier pouring her wine, then waited until the man had finished with

Nick's and left before speaking. "Looks like everything's going to plan with the free clinic renovations."

"It does." Nick glanced around at the other patrons. "How's your patient recovering?"

"Good. Good." Belle traced her fingers over the stem of her wine glass, imagining she was trailing them up Nick's chest instead. She swallowed hard against the sudden tightness in her throat. "She's been back for a dressing change and Dr. Reyes says her healing is progressing well. And she's happy, which is the most important thing. How about your meningitis patient?" Belle asked, watching Nick over the rim of her glass as she sipped her wine. "Still improving?"

"Yes. In fact, if she keeps doing well, the hospital plans to discharge her the day after tomorrow."

"Wonderful. She'll get to spend Christmas with her family." Belle sat back as the waiter delivered their salads—finely chopped lettuce and cheese with a light vinaigrette dressing. She took a bite and the tang of fresh greens, garlic and anchovies danced on her tongue. "You were right. This is fantastic."

"Glad you like it," Nick said around a bite of his own salad. "Bread?"

Normally, Belle would've said no, but tonight she couldn't resist the freshly baked yumminess. Her dietary restrictions weren't because of any health reasons, just that appearances were everything in Beverly Hills. But here with Nick, tonight, she was all about living her life to the fullest. Tonight she'd choose bread and love it too.

After smearing on a healthy dose of the honey butter provided, Belle bit into the still warm crusty bread. It tasted so unbelievable that she couldn't contain her groan of pleasure.

Nick paused to watch her, a small smile playing around his lips. "Good?"

"You have no idea."

They ate for a few minutes in silence.

"Is Connor's team any good?" she asked, making small talk.

"Not bad. I mean, they're only eight, so it's not like they're Wayne Gretzky out there or anything." The waiter cleared away their empty salad plates and replaced them with steaming crocks of baked ziti and a fresh basket of bread. Nick thanked the guy then waited for him to leave before continuing. "But, yeah, Connor does pretty well. And he loves the sport, even though I worry about him." At Belle's look, he smiled. "Okay, fine. You were right about that. Those games can get rough sometimes, even in the junior league. But the coach is great, like I said, and takes all the precautions. I'm trying to be better about letting Con have more freedom, like you said. Cut me some slack. I'm working on it."

Warmth spread through Belle over the fact he'd taken her advice, at least a little. "That's great. Connor's a really good kid." She took a bite of the cheesy pasta. "Wow. This is marvelous too."

"See?" Nick grinned. "I wish you'd learn to trust me again."

"I'm working on it," she said, mimicking his words back to him with a grin. And she was too. Belle wanted to rid herself of all her Nick-related hang-ups, but with so little time left she wasn't sure she could open up and let him into her heart once more like she had way back when, no matter how much she might wish she could.

They ate until Belle couldn't force down another bite. She sat back in the booth, feeling full and happy for the first time in recent memory. "Thank you for bringing me here tonight."

"Thanks for accepting." He finished his pasta and wine, then exhaled slowly. "I won't lie. I did have another agenda in asking you here."

"Uh-oh," Belle said, eyeing him warily. "Are you going to seduce me, Dr. Marlowe?"

Belle couldn't quite believe those teasing words had come out of her mouth. Perhaps it was the wine. Or the easy company. Or the fact that for the first time in a really long time she felt at peace and comfortable, without the stress of her job or her future looming over her. Perhaps coming home again hadn't been such a huge mistake after all.

Nick's low chuckle sent a rush of molten heat all the way to her toes. He shook his head, a slight flush staining his tanned cheeks. "Actually, I wanted to talk about our breakup."

Yikes. Talk about a mood-killer.

"Oh." She straightened and fiddled with her napkin again. "It was a long time ago, Nick. I don't really think there's anything left to talk about."

"I feel like I owe you an explanation. Especially after what you told me in the car the other day about coming to see me at Northwestern." He reached over and placed his hand over hers, stilling it. His warm touch was gentle as he rubbed her knuckles with his thumb. "You seem to be under the impression I got over you and moved on a lot quicker than I did."

Belle nodded, staring down at the table. "Okay."

"I didn't." Nick sighed and sat back, pulling her toward him, so their entwined fingers rested in the middle of the table. "I loved you, Belle. You were my first true love. One of the hardest things I've ever done was letting you go back then, even if it was for the best. Afterward, I kept wanting to talk to you, to see if you were doing all right, but you avoided me like the plague. I guess I deserved it after the way I broke your heart, but at least you had your friends and your aunt to talk to. I didn't have anyone."

She frowned at him. "You were the most popular guy in school. What about your friends? Your parents?"

"My parents were both too busy working all the time to have much energy to deal with my teenaged woes. And you'd be surprised how lonely being Mr. Popular can be. Besides, guys don't usually rally around to wallow in feelings the way women do. So I dealt with it like I deal with most things that trouble me. I forged ahead, thinking I'd get over you at some point. By the time I'd gotten to the University of Michigan, I almost believed I'd moved on."

"But you hadn't?" Belle asked, the words scraping a little in her throat on the way out.

"No." Nick shook his head and stared at their joined hands on the table. "I was a mess. I tried dating other people, but it never worked out. I just wasn't into them the way I'd been into you."

"Oh, Nick. What about Vicki?"

"We didn't meet until Northwestern. I was in medical school and she was doing her graduate nursing degree. Nope. U of M was a pretty lonely time for me. I can't tell you how many times I longed to pick up the phone and call you, just to talk and find out about your day."

Her heart ached at the depth of loneliness in his words. "You should have."

"No. I shouldn't." He exhaled slow. "I'd set you free. To call you would have meant my sacrifice was all in vain. You needed to explore your future on your own and I needed to make my own way too. I figured we'd reconnect again if it was right."

Wow. All this time she'd imagined him with a new life without her, happy and content, but it seemed she'd been wrong about that too. So much wasted time.

"Once I met Vicki, we became friends. She was a great listener and gave the best advice. It helped she'd been through a similar breakup. I'm sure she probably got sick of me talking her ear off about you, but she never complained."

"You talked to her about me?" Belle blinked at him, surprised.

"Sure. You're the most important person in my life, and the source of my greatest heartache. Why wouldn't I talk about you? I needed to talk to someone." He shrugged. "Vicki let me get it all out. We bonded. Then one night she asked me to go with her to a party and pretend to be her boyfriend so she could show her ex she was over him. We had a bit too much to drink and one thing led to another…and, well, I've already told you the rest."

His voice trailed off and Belle let her fingers slip free of his. A jumble of emotions wrestled inside her—gratefulness he'd finally shared his side of things, melancholy for what might have been if they'd only reconnected all those years ago, and an odd buzz of adrenaline for the possibilities now during her brief stay in Bayside.

"Wow. I don't know what to say…"

"It's okay. I wanted you to know the truth. Finally." Nick pulled his wallet from his pocket, handing his credit card to the waiter. "Ready to head out?"

She nodded, not trusting her voice at the moment.

"Great." He signed off on the check, then stood and tugged on his coat before helping Belle with hers. "Let's go home."

* * *

The ride back to Bayside was quiet, both of them apparently deep in thought. Or, in Nick's case, feeling a bit hollow after getting all his emotions off his chest at the restaurant. In their wake was a restless energy, pinballing around inside him, making him unsure what to say now. As they took the exit to Business Highway 31 leading into Bayside, Nick glanced over at Belle, trying to gauge her mood. "I enjoyed tonight. Thanks for listening to my rambling."

"Thanks for telling me." Belle looked over at him.

He flipped on the turn signal to make a right onto Hancock Street. "I'm glad we got it all out there. Cleared the air. It was very therapeutic."

Belle snorted. "Gah! Therapeutic? There's a word most people never want to hear on a date."

"Date?" He pulled up at the curb in front of Belle's house and parked his SUV, cutting the engine but keeping the heater running as he grinned over at her through the shadows. Not that he needed any help. Nick was feeling pretty warm already. He unwrapped and shoved one of the mints from the restaurant in his mouth before handing one to Belle too. "Is this a date?"

Belle didn't answer, just ate her mint and stared out the window beside her, making no move to leave. "Dinner was delicious. Back in Beverly Hills I'm usually eating on the run, racing from one procedure to the next. I try to make the healthiest choices."

"Another reason I'm glad I left Atlanta behind." Nick frowned. "Not the healthy choices. The eating on the run."

"Right." She sighed and her smile turned bittersweet. "Well, I guess this is good night."

Belle put her hand on the door handle and Nick

turned slightly to face her, resting one arm atop the steering wheel.

"Wait, Belle," he said, stopping her, his pulse jack-hammering in his ears. It was now or never, and he couldn't remember ever wanting another woman more than he wanted Belle at that moment. Even if it was all temporary. Maybe *because* it was all temporary. "I'd like to keep doing this, with you, for as long as you're here." At her confused look, he said, "Seeing each other, I mean. I'm out of practice with the whole dating thing, but I'm afraid if I don't take the chance now, you'll go running back to California on Christmas Day and I'll regret it."

"I'm not running anywhere, Nick. California is my home." Belle slumped back in her seat and stared straight ahead. "Please don't think I'm not tempted, but we're both dealing with a lot right now. I don't want us to be just another complication. Last night you were mired in guilt over your wife's death and the promise you made to her. What changed?"

"I'm not sure." *Liar.* He knew exactly what had changed. That kiss. He exhaled slowly and stared out the windshield, trying to articulate all the feelings roiling around inside him—apprehension, anticipation, need, nervousness. "I've been living alone for nearly two years now, slogging through my days, thinking it was enough. Then you came back to Bayside and it's like the sun came out again. You made me realize maybe I could do both, be a good father and have a life, at least while you're here. The short duration doesn't make it any less real."

He looked over at her again, hoping his sincerity showed in his eyes. "That's why I think we should have a fling. Explore the sparks we ignited with our kiss.

Take a risk, knowing if it doesn't work out it will all be over soon anyway."

Snow fell softly and Christmas lights twinkled on the neighboring homes. Belle didn't respond and Nick beat himself up internally for making a mess of it all. Vicki was probably shaking her head at him up in heaven.

Tension filled the interior of the SUV like a thick fog. *Way to go, idiot.*

Finally, Belle took a deep breath and squinted down at her hands in her lap. "I found this old embroidered pillow on Aunt Marlene's sofa the other night. It said, 'Bloom where you're planted.' She always used to tell me that growing up. It got me through a lot of hard times."

The pain in her voice stabbed him. Nick scrubbed a hand over his face then faced her again. "I hurt you in the past and I'm sorry. That was never what I wanted. Never. I only ever wanted what was best for you, Belle. I still do."

She gave a little snort. "And you think a fling is what's best?"

"I think we're both lonely and could use a dose of good, old-fashioned intimacy."

His gaze flickered from her eyes to her lips and he leaned in, kissing her slowly and tenderly. She tasted of wine and mint and endless possibilities.

Belle pulled away to look at him, her pupils dilated. "Do you want to come in?"

Nick nodded slowly, his heart feeling too big for his chest. "I do."

CHAPTER EIGHT

BELLE FUMBLED HER keys in the lock, her hands shaking—not from cold but from nerves and anticipation. She was doing it. She was taking Nick Marlowe, her old flame, to bed.

Yes, it would be temporary because she was leaving soon, and quite possibly she was doing it for the wrong reasons—loneliness, grief, desperation—but she couldn't seem to make herself care. Neither could she shake the feeling deep down inside that there was a good chance this wasn't all wrong. She still cared for him, far more than was wise. But first they had to get inside.

She dropped the keys in the snow on the porch.

"Dammit." Belle bent to grab them. "Sorry. This isn't my usual MO."

"Mine neither." Nick grabbed the keys first and unlocked the front door. "I've got it."

The moment they crossed the threshold he turned and cupped her face in his hands to kiss her again, more deeply this time, as if he too needed confirmation this was really happening. Between the feel of his mouth on hers, coupled with the memories of how it used to be, the way they fit—it all seemed a bit like a fantasy.

Then Nick took off his coat and pressed more firmly

against her and she felt his body—hot, hard, ready—and it became all too real.

This. Was. Happening.

Nick pulled her into the foyer, closed the door then pushed Belle up against it, his hands sinking into her hair, tugging gently so her throat was exposed for his kisses, shoving her scarf aside so his teeth scraped the sweet spot where her neck met her collarbone. Belle shuddered with sensation, sliding her hands under his sweater, to feel the hot skin of his abdomen against her palms. Her breath caught, tiny, shallow gasps escaping as she kissed him back hard, urgency driving her onward.

They shed the rest of their clothing on the way down the hall to the bedroom, not caring where it landed, only caring about this night, this moment, together. So good, so right, so real.

But by the time they stood beside the mattress, Belle was nervous again. It had been eighteen years since they'd been together. They'd both changed. What if he was disappointed?

Nick sat on the edge of the bed and looked at her, his brown eyes warm and dark with desire. He took her hand and kissed the inside of her wrist, meeting her gaze. Unexpected tears prickled her eyes. This was Nick, the first man she'd ever loved. The only man she'd ever loved. Finally, she stopped fighting the craving that had burned inside her since she'd returned to Bayside. "I missed you."

He pulled her down and kissed her gently, wiping away her tears. "I missed you too."

Then his warm hands skimmed her skin, making her shiver. She leaned into him, nuzzling his neck, her fingers digging into his strong shoulders. Heat sizzled through her blood like an uncontrolled wildfire.

Belle clung to Nick as he lowered her down beneath him. His solid weight atop her felt like home, at last. She'd never forgotten this. She'd only blocked it out, only tried to pretend she didn't need this. But she did need it, needed him. So much she ached.

He watched her, waiting. "Okay?"

"More than okay," Belle said with a small smile.

His answering grin had joy blossoming in her heart. All those constant worries and warning bells quieted, and she surrendered to this man, this moment. Yes, she'd dated after Nick, but no one else had measured up to this, to him.

She pulled him down for another kiss, their bodies flush.

They couldn't have forever, but they could have tonight.

He licked the pulse point at the base of her neck and chuckled. "Your heart's racing."

"Yours too," she said, pressing her palm to his chest.

His eyes glimmered in the moonlight streaming in through the curtains and he rocked his hips against hers. He was ready. So was she. Belle slid her hand down to caress the length of him. His breath hitched and he cupped her bottom, his face buried in her throat. Her skin tingled from his touch and she arched against him, wanting to be closer, wanting all the space between them to disappear.

Nick got up and quickly put on a condom then rejoined her on the bed. She parted her thighs, letting his weight settle between them. His talented hands seemed to caress her everywhere at once and he took one of her nipples into his warm, wet mouth, suckling her sensitive flesh. Tightness coiled inside her and heat built between her legs. She couldn't wait any longer. She needed him now. Belle reached between them to palm him again, but this time he grabbed her wrist and pinned her hands over her head.

"Sorry," he panted. "It's been too long, and I want you too badly. If you touch me now, it'll all be over. And I don't want this to end."

In response, Belle wrapped her legs around his waist and rocked against him, allowing him to feel how ready she was for him too.

Hanging his head, Nick kissed her and stroked her once more, sliding his fingers down to gently tease her most sensitive flesh. She gasped and pressed harder into his hand. "Yes. Please, Nick. Please."

"Belle," he whispered, his gaze locked with hers as he entered her, stretching and filling her completely. "My Belle."

White-hot desire scorched through her. All that mattered now was this man, this moment, this night. She gave a low, feral groan of satisfaction.

His thrusts began slow and steady, growing stronger and harder as Belle moved with him. Soon passion took over and had them both teetering on the brink of completion. He reached between them once more to stroke her and Belle cried out as she climaxed hard.

After a few more hard, fast thrusts Nick joined her in bliss, his body tight as waves of pleasure washed over him. He buried his face in her hair, whispering words she didn't catch.

Finally, they settled back to earth, his breath warm on her skin, his head resting in the valley between her breasts. She felt weightless and heavy all at the same time, her usual quicksilver thoughts sluggish in the wake of endorphins. Tonight had been as good as she remembered. Maybe even better.

As his breath evened out into the patterns of sleep and her eyes drifted closed, Belle knew tomorrow would bring a return of all the issues between them— their separate careers, his unresolved guilt over his deceased wife, his son and her responsibilities back in Beverly Hills. But tonight it felt like they had their own private bubble, their own private escape from reality.

It was enough. It had to be enough.

Nick awoke before sunrise. Through a gap in the gauzy curtains he saw the snow had finally stopped falling. In the predawn haze he glanced over to find Belle sound asleep on her stomach, her dark auburn lashes fanned on her cheeks and her glorious hair tangled and mussed from his lovemaking. She looked breathtakingly, achingly beautiful.

He waited for the familiar guilt to slam into him hard, but it never came.

Instead, all he felt was tenderness. Tenderness and a tug of nostalgia.

Hard to believe nearly two decades had passed since he'd been with this woman, since he'd let her go and moved on with his life. Yet the connection between them still blazed brightly.

He gently brushed the hair back from her temple. Belle gave a small groan and swatted his hand away, still asleep, rolling over to reveal the creamy stretch of her spine. Unable to resist, Nick kissed the nape of her neck then trailed his lips down her back and inhaled deeply. Flowers and mint and warm, sweet woman. Resting his forehead against her shoulder blade, he did his best to remember every second of their night together, wanting to hold onto it forever.

Belle sighed and he put his arm around her waist, snuggling in behind her again, her soft, plump breast cupped in the palm of his hand. She turned to face him, kissing him before wrapping herself around him. Nick rolled her onto her back and made love to her again.

After they'd floated back from paradise, he kissed her one last time then climbed out of bed, heading for the bathroom and a quick shower before tugging on his jeans. "I don't know about you, but I'm starving."

She leaned up on her elbows, frowning. "Sorry, I don't have much food in the house."

"That's fine." He leaned over to kiss her again, then handed Belle her clothes. "Get up. I've got an idea."

Following a yawn and a stretch, she rushed into the bathroom and closed the door, emerging ten minutes later freshly showered and dressed. She'd braided her damp hair and her green eyes sparkled in the gloom. She looked so happy and beautiful he nearly tumbled her right back into bed again but he stopped himself.

This wasn't real. This would all be over soon. *What about Connor?*

A small twinge of remorse stung his chest before he pushed it away.

His son was fine, tucked away safe and sound at Eric's house.

It was just that it had been so long since Nick had had time to himself he wasn't sure how to handle it. Must be it. He glanced over at Belle and saw her grin. He grinned back. "C'mon."

After bundling up and grabbing his wallet and keys, they headed out to his truck.

Holding her hand, Nick steered with the other

through the deserted streets of Bayside, heading for the bakery downtown, pretty much the only thing open this early. He left the truck running while he ran inside and picked up fresh donuts and tea, then drove to the state park down by the beach. The temperatures were near freezing and their breath crystalized in the air as they climbed the trail to the top of the huge sand dune there, aptly named Old Baldy because of the clearing at the top.

At the summit, he spread out one of the blankets he'd carried up and Belle set out their small feast atop it. Then they huddled beneath a second blanket to await the coming sunrise, just like old times.

The silence between them now felt comfortable as they ate and snuggled while the world around them woke up. From somewhere nearby, an owl hooted. The icy trees crackled in the slight breeze. Everything was quiet and peaceful and pristine in the crisp winter cold.

Nick finished his donut then took a long swig of hot tea and checked his watch. Soon enough, it would be time to pick up Connor. As Christmas Eve approached, things seemed to speed up and the days slipped by so fast. There was still some work to be done on Marlene's old clinic and things to get ready, but all he could think about was spending more time with Belle that didn't involve paint or inventory or work.

His chest squeezed with a sharp pang of warning.

Somewhere inside, a small part of him knew there was a good chance he was using her as a temporary fix for his long-term loneliness, as a way to avoid dealing with his guilt over Vicki once and for all. But he didn't want to think about that now. It had been a long time since he'd been this happy and content and he just wanted it to last a bit longer before reality returned.

He sighed and stared out over the dark, churning waters of Lake Michigan. Being up here again reminded him of their last summer before senior year. Swimming, playing volleyball on the beach, cooking out over a campfire. The first time Nick had realized she was The One had been right here in this spot.

She shifted slightly in his arms and smiled up at him, brushing away a bit of sugar glaze from the corner of his mouth. He kissed her cheek then rested his chin atop her head, her knit hat soft against his skin.

"There's Orion's Belt." Belle pointed at the crooked line of three stars above. "It's the only constellation I know, other than the Big Dipper."

"Me too." He snuggled her closer as she sipped her tea. A thin line of orange brightened the horizon, signaling the impending sunrise.

Belle sighed and leaned away, meeting his gaze as an adorable blush colored her cheeks. "Thanks."

"For what?" The rush of waves against the shore below helped eased the sudden anxiety knotting his gut. It rarely got cold enough for the lake to completely freeze over. Belle shrugged then stared off into the distance. His heart seemed swollen, aching and tender. He tipped her chin up and kissed her again as the sun crested the horizon and the snow shimmered around them. Longing and loneliness pierced him before he pulled back and rested his forehead against hers. "I haven't stayed out all night with a girl for a long time."

Belle chuckled, the sound warming him. "Remember the time we went out on the lake in your dad's boat and fell asleep? We drifted miles up the coast."

"How could I forget?" He smiled and waggled his brows. "You wore a black bikini, the one with the pink flower in the front."

"We stayed up all night then too. It was July Fourth. They shot fireworks out over the water and lit up the sky."

Nick hugged her close once more. "I remember holding you all night."

"Me too." She tucked her head back under his chin for a moment before pulling away. "We should get going before we get frostbite. What time is Connor due home?"

The reminder of his son brought Nick back to earth. "He'll call me when he's ready to be picked up from Eric's."

"Right." She kissed him one last time then pushed to her feet, holding her gloved hand down to help him up. "C'mon. Let's clean up then I'll race you down to the truck. Last one there has to pick up the medical supplies this afternoon."

Belle grabbed their trash while he shook out the blankets then took off after her down the dune. He didn't even try to catch her, knowing he'd be the one heading back to his office that afternoon anyway—to check on his cases and handle some paperwork.

Back to reality, whether he was ready or not.

CHAPTER NINE

BELLE HUMMED TO herself later that day as she restocked gloves and swabs and gauze in each exam room at the clinic. Connor was there helping her, telling her all about his hockey practice earlier and the new video game he and his friend Eric had played the previous evening.

She nodded and smiled when appropriate, though she had no clue about hockey or video games. But it was just as well since her thoughts were still wrapped up in memories of her and Nick together the night before.

In the years she and Nick had been apart she'd been far too focused on her career to consider putting a relationship before her work. Part of it had been ambition, but part of it had been the promise she'd made to her parents, the need to stay close to them. And perhaps another part of it was a tiny secret hope that maybe one day fate would bring her and Nick back together again.

Oh, boy. Don't go there.

"What's this thing?" Connor asked, nose scrunched as he held up a speculum.

"Oh, Um…that's for female exams," she said, shoving the thing back into a drawer below the exam table. "Why don't you fill up the jars on the counter with cotton balls?"

"Sure." Connor grabbed the plastic bag full of white puffs and started stuffing them by the handful into the glass canisters while giving her some serious side-eye. "Do you like my dad?"

Belle froze. Kids were far more perceptive than people gave them credit for, and she shouldn't have been surprised he'd picked up on the connection between her and Nick. Still, knowing what he'd been through with his mother, she certainly wasn't comfortable telling him the truth yet. "Your father and I are friends."

Connor narrowed his gaze. "Like Eric and me?"

"Sort of." Belle fumbled the roll of paper she was putting on the exam table, heat prickling her cheeks.

Connor looked away, shoving more cotton balls into the jar. "My mom died."

Her heart went into freefall and her breath hitched. "I know, honey. I'm so sorry."

"Dad doesn't talk about her anymore." Connor jammed down the cotton balls with more force than necessary. "He thinks if he doesn't talk about Mom, I won't be sad, but it makes me miss her more."

She'd wondered if this conversation might occur and led little boy over to the two chairs along the wall. The fact Nick didn't discuss his wife anymore didn't surprise her. Considering his guilt and his desire to protect his son, it was understandable, if misguided. Still, it wouldn't have helped Connor deal with his loss. Those kinds of wounds didn't heal overnight. She should know. "Tell me about her."

Connor stared down at his toes, his expression bereft. "Like what?"

"I don't know." Belle recalled the things she still remembered most about her own parents, what brought her comfort, things only someone who'd lost a loved one would understand. "What did your mom's favorite perfume smell like? What made her laugh? What was her nickname for you? My mother always smelled like lilacs. And she laughed at cows. Don't ask me why. She's the one who first called me Belle. My dad always called me Chris, but it never stuck the way Belle did."

The little boy sighed, the shoulders of his Blackhawks jersey rising and falling. He looked up at her finally, the sorrow in his eyes squeezing her chest with compassion. "My mom didn't wear perfume. She was allergic. But I always thought she smelled like snow, even in the summer. Crisp and clean. She called me Con, same as Dad. She used to laugh at silly cat videos on the internet. There was one called 'Surprised Kitty' she loved. Want to see it?"

Belle nodded and he pulled out his phone, pulling up an adorable video for her to watch. She couldn't help laughing herself. "Amazing."

"Yeah." Connor gave a sad little smile. "I watch this a lot. Makes me feel better."

"It's good to have things that remind you of her." She put her arm around him, rubbing his arm. "I've found some things at my aunt's house to take back with me to California. Mementos of my parents." She sighed. "I didn't realize how much I missed them until I saw those things again."

Connor blinked up at her. "Must've been hard to lose both your parents. Even though Dad bugs me sometimes, I can't imagine not having him." He stared down at his phone screen. "It's hard, missing people."

"Yes, it is." She pulled the little boy into her side. "But we're lucky, we had people who love us and who took care of us as we healed."

"Dad tries really hard make up for Mom being gone, but sometimes I still talk to her. Weird, huh?"

"No." Belle frowned. "I still talk to my parents too on occasion." She ruffled Connor's hair. "And you should tell your dad this stuff too. Let him know what you're thinking about. You know he's only protective of you because he loves you, right?"

"I guess." He shrugged. "But I'm eight. I can take care of myself." Connor narrowed his gaze on her once more. "If you and my dad are friends, I bet he's bummed you're leaving."

Me too, she wanted to say, but swallowed the words down deep. "He'll be fine."

"My dad's lonely." Connor crossed his arms. "He doesn't think I know, but I do."

She placed her hand on his small shoulder, feeling a warm tug of tenderness. "Your dad's one of the best guys I know. Be patient with him. He's trying." Warm affection swelled inside her for Nick and his son. "Someday you'll both be happy again."

"Really?" Connor scrunched his nose, clearly skeptical.

"Really." Belle laughed. "Thanks for telling me about your mom."

"Thanks for letting me talk about her. I see why my dad likes you so much. Maybe we can be friends too?"

"We can." Her heart felt full to bursting and she blinked back unexpected tears before she stifled them. "We should get back to work before your dad comes in here and sees us slacking. He mentioned something about going for ice cream tomorrow."

"Seriously?" Connor's face lit up.

"Seriously. What's your favorite flavor?"

"Blue moon!" Connor hopped down from his chair

and went back over to the counter to fill a second jar with cotton balls. Belle went back to the exam table, cherishing the fragile bond she'd just forged with Nick's son. Considering she was in her midthirties now, the chances of her having a family of her own were growing slimmer by the year. She'd always thought she'd have children of her own one day. She would've loved to have a little boy like Connor.

"I wish House of Flavors was open in the winter," he said. "I'd kill for a Super Pig."

"Really?" she said, hoping to distract herself from the throb of yearning in her heart. The sundaes he was talking about were huge. Nine scoops of ice cream plus toppings. Nick had eaten a whole one himself once in high school and gotten a badge for his efforts. Belle grinned and finished installing a roll of paper on the table, then grabbed a box of paper gowns to fill the drawer below. "My favorite was the Almond Joy, but your dad always loved—"

"Loved what?" Nick asked, poking his head around the door. "Sounds like you guys are having way too much fun without me."

"We are," Connor said, glancing at Belle. "She and I are friends now too, Dad."

"Great. Belle's an awesome friend." Nick gave Belle an inquiring look as he shrugged out of his coat and slung it over his arm. He winked at her when Connor wasn't looking, and molten warmth spread through her once more. "Don't forget we've got the Chamber of Commerce Holiday Ball later."

"Right." She tucked her hair behind her ear. She'd kind of been hoping to get out of it actually after last night with Nick. It was an annual event in Bayside, lots of townsfolk, lots of dancing and revelry. Lots of gos-

sip over who was doing what and whom. They'd originally planned on attending to promote the free clinic,
but now Belle would just as soon skip it. Word had already spread about the Christmas Eve reopening and
with what had happened between them last night, everything felt too new and confusing and a bit much, to
be honest. But she had promised the mayor she'd be
there, and she hated to let people down. No. It was too
late to back out now.

She forced a smile and said, "Yep."

As father and son bantered back and forth about Connor's night at Eric's house and the upcoming big hockey
game in Manistee, Belle continued to work and ignored
the sudden sadness welling inside her. She had helped
Aunt Marlene restock these rooms when she was Connor's age. They'd have long talks about life and love and
whatever issues Belle was dealing with. Kind of like the
conversation she'd had with Connor. Up until now, Belle
had done her best to compartmentalize things, keeping her emotions about Bayside away from the situation with Dr. Reyes and her patients back in California.

Now, though, as the last few days in her hometown
drew near and reality sank in, the weight threatened to
crush her like a runaway train. Her crazy schedule had
never bothered Belle before but being back home again
had made her long for a simpler life, for what she'd had
once upon a time here in Bayside.

Thoughts like those were dangerous, though. What
if last night with Nick had been so magical and special and unforgettable because it was fleeting? Rare
things were often the most prized. Long-distance relationships never worked, and Nick hadn't mentioned
wanting one anyway.

He was happy here and she had her place in California.

For eighteen years she'd managed not to get her heart broken again, by Nick or anyone else. And not being heartbroken, not having your life shattered into a million tiny pieces, was way better than the alternative.

Nick pulled up to Belle's house promptly at seven and walked to the front door, adjusting the jacket of his tux with one hand while holding a bouquet of pink roses in the other. He'd remembered they were Belle's favorites, or at least he thought they were. If last night had felt like a date, this evening felt like a test. A test of what life could have been like if they'd both stayed in Bayside and not gone on separate paths. After making love with Belle, they were...

Well, he wasn't quite sure what exactly they were, but the thought of her happy and smiling made wearing a tux again bearable. Con had snorted when he'd taken a look at Nick tonight and shaken his head, telling his dad to say hi to Belle for him. Mollie had looked him up and down and given him a thumbs-up, as well. The residents of Bayside didn't get glammed up often—it was a summer beach town, after all—so the holiday ball was a big occasion. Plus, it would give him another chance to hold Belle in his arms, so Nick couldn't really complain.

He rang the bell then waited, his blood zinging with anticipation.

Belle opened the door, looking amazing. Her auburn hair was twisted atop her head and tiny crystals sparkled from her earlobes. Her long red dress was cut high in the front and low in the back, the fabric falling in a silky rush to her toes. He was pretty sure Vicki had called those necklines halter-style once, but whatever it was

named, he was all for it. Eyeing the closure at the back
of her neck, it appeared he could give it one tug later
when they were alone and remove said gown in a hurry.

Or not. Maybe he'd take his time instead. Nice and
slow. Trace his tongue down her creamy flesh, inch by
inch, tasting her smooth skin, nipping the spot at the
base of her neck that drove her wild, feel her fingers
catch in his hair, hear her gasp his name, all breathy
and wanton, as his fingers crept up her thigh, taking
the dress with them, leaving her fantastic legs bare...

Good Lord. One night with his old flame had turned
him into a randy teen again.

"Do I look all right?" she asked, breaking him out
of his erotic haze.

"Perfect." He handed her the roses then leaned in for
a quick kiss. "Gorgeous."

"You don't think it's too much for Bayside?" she
asked, waving him into the foyer while she carried the
flowers to the kitchen, putting them into a vase on the
table, before she returned to grab her coat and bag. She
was wearing the same pumps she'd had on at Marlene's
funeral. The slippery, spiky ones that had made her
cling to him for support. He was beginning to love those
shoes more each day. "I found it in my old closet. I must
have bought it to wear to something, but never did."

"No. I would've remembered you in that, Belle. And
it's not too much. You look amazing. Every man there
tonight will wish he was me." Nick slipped her coat over
her shoulders then kissed the nape of her neck, enjoying her slight shiver. "Ready?"

"Yep." She checked her appearance in the mirror
once more, then linked arms with him and followed
him out to his truck.

* * *

Half an hour later, they were inside the ballroom at the chamber of commerce building on Main Street, a nineteen-twenties architectural gem, filled with intricate parquet floors and art deco décor. The place looked beautiful, filled with poinsettias and white roses and clear twinkling lights. Candles flickered on the tables and wall sconces glowed. They were sharing a table with Jeanette and her husband and Juan and Rosa Hernandez. Nick and Belle took seats across from Jeanette and beside Juan and his wife.

"Hey, Doc." Juan raised his hand. "I'm glad you two are here. I got a call from the plastic surgery office in Detroit today. They want to see Analia after the first of the year to evaluate her for their pro bono program."

"Fantastic!" Nick reached across Belle to shake the man's hand. "Congratulations, my friend. I'm glad all the paperwork we filled out finally paid off."

"We're pretty excited," Juan said. "Haven't told Analia yet. Figured we'd wait until Christmas. She's been praying for this surgery, so it'll be the best present ever."

"Wonderful," Belle said, smiling. "Really great."

Nick squeezed her shoulder, not missing the flicker of disappointment across her lovely face. He frowned slightly and leaned in to whisper, "Everything okay?"

"Fine. Thanks." She waited until the Juan and his wife left the table to dance before continuing. "I just couldn't help picturing myself doing the surgery, even though that's totally impossible. I'm not here long enough to get involved and I'm sure your colleague in Detroit will do an awesome job. Silly, right?"

"No. Not silly at all." He kissed her cheek and pulled her closer into his side for a moment before noticing the scrutiny of his receptionist, Jeanette, from across the table. She watched them closely over the rim of her punch glass, her gaze darting between the two of them before she murmured, "Good for you, boss."

Nick resisted the urge to deny everything, because frankly it was true. Being with Belle these past few days had shown him perhaps there was another way to live, another way to be happy, without his constant burden of guilt. Connor seemed to be adjusting and thriving too, even without Nick's constant hovering. Perhaps his promise to Vicki had been fulfilled. His son was safe and secure. Maybe it was time to stop worrying so much.

"I want you to move on, Nick. I don't want you to be alone."

Vicki's words looped through his head again. A week ago he would've scoffed, unable to picture allowing himself ever falling in love again. But now maybe…

The song ended and Juan and his wife returned just as the salads were being served. Nick sat back, removing his arm from around Belle's shoulders and missing her warmth immediately.

She scooted a bit closer to the table and flicked her napkin open across her lap, picking up her fork and chatting with Juan and Rosa as they ate. "If either of you have any questions about what to expect with Analia's surgery, please feel free to ask. I obviously won't know the specifics but can speak to general things about such cases."

"Perfect," Rosa said. "I actually do have so many questions. What can we expect for our daughter post-operatively?"

"Analia's a lovely girl," Belle said. "But I've not done a full examination so, again, I can only speak in generalities. Be sure to verify all of this with your surgeon in Detroit." She dabbed her mouth with a napkin and took a swallow of chardonnay. "But based on my brief observations of your daughter and my past experience with Crouzon's, I'd say most likely the surgeon with choose to go with what's called a Lefort III procedure. Given Analia's age and the fact she's having issues with sleep apnea, it's the most efficient surgery at this point, though not without complications. It's a long recovery. About eighteen months from start to finish. And it can be challenging."

"What about her eating?" Juan said. "I've done some looking online and belong to a couple of social media support groups."

"Your daughter will need to be on a liquid diet until she graduates to soft foods, so make sure you have straws." Belle sat back as the waiter removed her salad plate and replaced it with the main entrée—roasted chicken breast with veggies. Nick couldn't help thinking how relaxed she seemed, talking shop, and how she'd fit right back into life here in Bayside. For once the idea didn't bother him at all. "Also, be sure she has plenty of clothes she can get in and out of through the front or back, since she won't be able to slip things over her head."

Juan nodded and pulled out his phone to type in notes. "Anything else?"

"You might want to consider counseling, as well."

"Counseling?" Nick stiffened. "Why? Analia's the most well-adjusted child I've ever met. She's always happy. Is a therapist really necessary?"

"Sometimes it helps," Belle said, cutting up her food into small, neat bites. "All of this will be a lot for little Analia to deal with, no matter how excited she is about the surgery. The healing process can be painful. Even the happiest of patients will reach a point of despair before it's all over." She reached over and covered Rosa's hand with hers. "I just want you to be prepared for what you're getting into. It's not easy, but it is worth it, in my experience."

Rosa nodded and Juan put his arm around his wife, tugging her into his side. "We just want our daughter to have a good life. If this surgery makes that possible, then we'll help her through it. That's what families do."

"She's lucky to have you both," Belle said, a hint of sadness in her tone. Nick longed to pull her closer again, but wasn't sure how she'd feel about that, since they'd not really discussed taking this thing between them public. Sure, Jeanette had guessed, but then she spent a lot of time around him. Didn't mean the rest of the town knew. They'd been careful, right?

A string quartet from the local community band began to play again and Nick seized his opportunity. He stood and extended a hand to Belle, bowing slightly. "May I have this dance?"

He didn't miss her slight blush at his request or the sizzle of want inside him it conjured. She took his hand and he led her out onto the dancefloor.

"I'm so happy for Analia," she said. "The surgery will change her life."

"But you wish you could be the one doing it," he murmured against her temple.

"Yes, but as long as you trust this surgeon in Detroit to do a good job, I'm okay with it." She leaned into him, resting her head on his shoulder. "I can't believe I'm saying this, but I'm going to miss this place when I'm gone."

His heart tugged. She hadn't mentioned missing him or Connor, but deep inside he hoped they'd been included in that statement. Swaying gently to the music, he could have stayed there, holding Belle, for an eternity, but unfortunately the song and the moment ended all too soon.

"Ladies and gentlemen, it's time for our annual town service award," the mayor said, taking the stage. Nick and Belle returned to their seats just as dessert was being delivered—a scrumptious gingerbread brandy trifle. "This year we're honoring a very special woman who touched the lives of everyone here in Bayside, Dr. Marlene Watson. And though she's no longer with us, Marlene's spirit lives on in the free clinic which her niece and our own Dr. Nicholas Marlowe will be reopening for one final time this Christmas Eve. Let's give them both a round of applause for all their hard work during this difficult time."

The mayor waved Nick and Belle up onto the stage to accept a plaque on Marlene's behalf. Once the applause subsided, Nick shook the mayor's hand while Belle stepped up to the mic.

"Thank you all for this. I'm sure my aunt Marlene would've been honored," Belle said, her smile tight with grief. "She loved this town and everyone who lived here. We're honored to grant her final wishes and reopen the clinic for one final hurrah. Please be sure to stop by on Christmas Eve Day starting at eight in the morning until the last patient is seen. No one will be turned away. It's my honor to be back in Bayside and continue to provide the town with the excellent medical care it deserves. Thank you!"

Belle bowed to the crowd then she and Nick headed back to the table. He kept glancing over at her, wondering if she'd realized her parting words made it sound like she might be back in town for good, but she gave no outward sign of it. He shook off the spark of hope inside him. Probably just his wishful thinking.

The quartet started up again and it seemed like the entire town of Bayside was on the dance floor. Everyone was laughing and having a great time and Marlene would've loved it. Afterward Nick placed his hand on Belle's lower back and whispered in her ear, "Want to get out of here?"

"I thought you'd never ask," she said, her voice velvety and low.

They said their goodbyes and Belle gave Juan and Rosa her business card, telling them to call her anytime about Analia. After claiming their coats, he and Belle went out into the crisp December night once more. Thick clouds blocked the moonlight this evening, hinting at more snowy weather moving in.

"Marlene would've loved the ball," Nick said, as he helped Belle across the icy parking lot, his arm around her waist to keep her steady and safe. "You were right. She loved everything about this place."

"Just like you," Belle said, giving him a sidelong glance.

"True." He clicked the button on his key fob to unlock the doors and the SUV's lights flickered. "You too, once upon a time."

"I still do," she said, her head lowered. "More than I should."

"Your speech was nice," he said, wavering about whether to mention it or not, then thinking what the hell. "You should be careful, though. At the end there you almost made it sound like you were staying."

"What?" She gave him a sharp look. "No. I didn't. I just wanted everyone to know we'd give them the best medical care possible, regardless of cost."

"Sure. Okay." Nick didn't miss the way her posture had stiffened or the defensiveness in her tone. He'd obviously touched on a sore spot and didn't want to prod further for fear he'd ruin the amazing thing they had going, no matter how he might want to know what she was thinking.

The drive back to Hancock Street was quiet, with Belle looking out the passenger side window or straight ahead, basically anywhere but at him. Nick knew he'd stepped in it with her and he wanted to apologize, but then they were back at the curb in front of her aunt's house and there was no more time. There never seemed to be enough time for them. He got out and walked around to open her door, escorting Belle up to the house.

"Thank you for answering all the Hernandezes' questions tonight," Nick said while she unlocked the door, debating whether or not to say what was in his heart. Finally, he decided it was better to ask than to regret it forever. "You know, if you did decide to stay—"

Belle sighed. "Please, Nick. Let's not do this right now, okay?" She opened the door and flipped on the lights inside the house. "Want to come in again?"

What he wanted was to continue their discussion, but he didn't want to push her too hard. Not when he could tell she was so close to breaking. So he followed her into the foyer then closed and locked the door behind them before taking Belle into his arms and kissing her gently. This thing they'd started might be messy and complicated and downright impossible, but holding her, kissing her, being with her…felt truer than anything else in his universe.

At last Nick took her hand to lead her down the hall to the bedroom. As he pulled her to him and kissed her once more, undressing her then himself before picking her up and placing her on the bed and stretching out beside her, he reminded himself for the umpteenth time that this was all temporary. Even if it was getting harder and harder to convince himself of that.

CHAPTER TEN

THE NEXT MORNING Belle rolled over in bed, alone, and stared at the ceiling of her bedroom. In the distance she heard the sounds of Nick bumping around in the kitchen.

Despite having him beside her through the night, she'd slept badly. Again. Thanks to thoughts about California and her boss and the new slew of patients waiting for consultations when she got home. A month ago it would've made her happy. Now it just increased the already burgeoning pressure she felt inside. Pressure to do the right thing. Pressure to succeed. Pressure to not let her parents down.

Pressure to make the best decisions for her future.

Being back in her hometown had rekindled her love for this place and its people. It had reopened her eyes to the possibilities of this area and the needs she could fill here. Made her doubt her career trajectory and what she'd thought she'd wanted for herself in the years to come. That might not have been her aunt's intention, but it was true all the same.

She sighed and closed her eyes, whispering a prayer to heaven to please help point her in the right direction. Reality was smacking her hard. Soon this would all be over, and she and Nick would go their separate ways once more.

Pulling away from him at this point would make it less painful.

Now, if she could just get her foolish heart to stop its yearning, she'd be all set.

Belle rubbed her tired eyes and yawned, then forced herself out of bed and into the shower. After scrubbing down and drying off then brushing her teeth, she pulled on clean jeans and an ugly green holiday sweater with a huge reindeer face she'd found in the back of her aunt's closet. It didn't really matter what she wore, since they'd be back in the clinic, making sure all the final touches were in place for the reopening in two days.

Nick was fixing a pot of her favorite tea when she padded down the hall in her stockinged feet.

"Good morning," she grumbled, rubbing her eyes.

"Don't you sound chipper today," he drawled, his tone thick with sarcasm.

"Sorry. Lack of sleep."

"Nothing wrong, I hope."

"No…" She sighed and leaned back against the edge of the kitchen counter. The sound of his voice did things to her—made her think of cozy nights by the fire and sweet kisses and naughty confessions whispered after midnight. Before she could think better of it, she said, "Just thinking about work."

"Uh-oh." He chuckled, making her insides clench and tremble with want. "None of that. Not yet, anyway."

"Are we heading into the clinic again?" she asked, taking a large swallow from the mug of tea he handed her. "I'm ready when you are."

"Stop," Nick said.

"Stop what?" she paused in midsip. "I will fight you for my tea."

"No." He laughed. "I mean let's not go into the clinic today."

"What?" She frowned. "Why? Don't tell me something happened again. We've just replaced all those ceiling tiles and painted and had the floors redone and—"

"No. The clinic's fine. There are only a few minor things left to do and we can take care of them tomorrow. I've got something more fun planned."

The excitement in Nick's tone was contagious and she perked up. "Like what?"

"Come with me and Connor to meet Santa."

"Santa?" She wrinkled her nose. "I think I'm a little old to sit on some man's knee."

"Funny. No, seriously. Con and I went last year, and I think you'll love it. It's on a farm outside town and there'll be shops and live animals and everything. Lots of homemade crafts and food. Come on, Belle. I promise you'll enjoy yourself."

She tried to suppress her smile and failed. It did sound like fun and she didn't have much time left in the area. Might as well enjoy it while she could. "Okay."

"Great. Go put on your boots. No spiky heels," he said. "Even though those shoes of yours give me all sorts of wicked ideas."

"They do, huh?" she grinned widely, the speeding up of her pulse having nothing to do with the caffeine in her tea.

"Oh, yeah. I'll meet you at the door. We'll stop and pick up Con on the way."

Belle went back to the bathroom to put on a bit of lip gloss and smooth her hair back into a ponytail at the nape of her neck, then tugged on her boots. She thought about changing her sweater then decided against it. A festive reindeer with jingle bells on its antlers sounded like perfect Santa-meeting gear. On her way to the front door she pulled on her coat and grabbed her bag before rushing outside. Nick locked the door for her then led her down to his SUV. Hard to believe she'd only been back in Bayside five days. Being with Nick and Connor felt comfortable now, almost like a real family.

Her thoughts snagged on that. No. Not a real family. Only pretend.

She'd be gone the day after tomorrow.

She took a deep breath and climbed into the passenger seat of the vehicle. Twenty minutes later they'd stopped at Nick's and he'd sent the sitter on her way then gotten Connor loaded into the back seat. She flashed the little boy a smile over her shoulder while he buckled his seat belt. "Morning, Con. How are you today?"

He shrugged and looked at his tablet. "Good, I guess. I'm trying to figure out what to ask Santa for this Christmas."

"A very important question." She nodded, glancing over at Nick. "When I was your age, I used to start planning my list in October."

"Oh, I've got stuff," Connor said, frowning down at his screen. "But it feels like I'm missing something."

"I know the feeling," Nick said under his breath, giving Belle a look that had her toes curling inside her hiking boots. "In case I forgot to mention it, you look nice today."

"Thanks. I wore my best Christmas sweater." Belle grinned. "Actually, it's my only Christmas sweater. Another item I found in my aunt's closet." They pulled out of Nick's driveway and she flipped down the sun visor to adjust her hat, settling in for the ride. Snowy hills dotted with cows and horses stretched on as far as the eye could see as they headed out of town. "Doesn't seem as cold today."

"No." Nick glanced in the rearview mirror as a semi passed them, then reached over and took Belle's hand. "It doesn't."

As they drove north, they passed through several small towns. The sun peeked through the overcast sky above, streaming light down on the barren fields. Nick signaled, turning onto a long gravel road. A large sign depicted Santa and his reindeer and read Holiday Farm Ahead. Five Miles. Slow-moving cars rolled along in front of them.

"Ten more minutes and we'll be there," Nick said, glancing at his son in the rearview mirror. "You hungry, Con?"

"Always." the boy said, not looking up from his device.

Nick squeezed Belle's hand, and all felt right with her world, at least for a now. Finally, they reached the large frozen field where attendants were directing people to park. Nick pulled into a slot between two compact cars. "Here we are."

Connor tucked his tablet into the backpack at his feet, his voice excited as he pointed out the window. "Look, Dad. They've got the sleigh again and everything!"

They exited the vehicle and Nick and Belle started toward the ticket booth at the entrance to the farm. Connor raced on ahead of them and Nick slipped his arm around her waist.

"I'm glad you're here today," he said.

"Me too." She nodded, spotting Connor in line for tickets already, nearing the cashier. "We should hurry so I can pay for the admission. My treat this time."

"Belle, I—" Nick started.

"No." She held up her hand, cutting off his protests. "You've paid for all my meals so far. Time for a little reciprocation on my part."

She hurried toward the ticket booth, leaving Nick behind to stare after her.

After buying their admission tickets, they walked through the holiday-themed farm, past brightly lit and decorated trees lining a maze of pathways and vendor booths, displays of fake snowmen and pens with baby animals. The air smelled of hay and livestock mixed with fried food, hot apple cider, and cinnamon.

Inside a large white pole barn was Santa's Workshop, where volunteer elves worked with groups of kids on craft projects—making their own ornaments or wreaths or even small wooden toys. Belle remembered doing something similar with Aunt Marlene one year, shortly after her parents had died. She remembered those hand-made ornaments on her aunt's tree at home.

No. Wait. Not home. Her aunt's house.

Belle's home was in California.

Isn't it?

Crowds jostled past them toward where Santa and Mrs. Claus were stationed near the back of the barn, along with the real reindeer.

"C'mon, Dad!" Connor grabbed Nick's hand and tugged him forward, then did the same with her. "You too, Belle."

She laughed as the boy dragged them inside the pole barn. It was gorgeous and elaborate. Tons more trees, all sparkling in a rainbow of hues. Display after display of animatronic figurines. Ornaments and brightly colored gifts, even a live nativity scene. Above the roar of the crowds, holiday tunes were streaming from speakers overhead, adding to the jolliness. Children and families clustered together, squealing with delight or posing for pictures with the displays.

"The line for Santa's over here," Connor said, pulling on her hand again.

She looked down into the boy's excited gaze and her heart melted. "Did you decide what you're going to ask him for?"

Connor's grin widened, his gaze darting between her and his dad. "Yeah, I think I have."

"Good." She swiveled to look at Nick. "And what about you?"

"I already have everything I need." He leaned in to kiss her sweetly.

"Dad!" Connor scrunched his nose. "There's not even any mistletoe."

Nick pulled away and grinned, his stare amused as Belle's cheeks heated. "Really? I would've sworn I saw some around here somewhere." Then he frowned down at their tickets. "There are specific Santa-visiting times listed on here. We're early for ours. How about we eat first?"

Connor snatched a ticket to verify that then nodded. "Okay. If you're sure."

They walked over to the corner of the barn where tables had been set up near the food stalls. "You two have a seat," Nick said. "I'll get the food. Con, you want a hot dog and fries?"

"Yep," Connor said. "Hey, Dad? Can I run over to the vendor shops really quick? There's something I need to buy. I won't be gone long, I promise."

"I can go with you, if you want," Belle offered.

"No," Connor said fast. "I need to go myself. Please, Dad?"

At first Nick looked like he would say no, but then

he took a deep breath and nodded. "Okay. But only to the vendors, then right back here. I want you at the table by the time the food's ready, yeah?"

"Yeah!" Connor took off. "Thanks, Dad!"

"A hot dog and fries for me too, please," Belle said, taking some money out of her bag to hand to him.

"No, Belle. Keep it. My treat this time." He turned to head for the food line.

Belle sat by herself watching the crowds and thinking how far Nick had come in the past week. She knew what an effort it had taken him to let Connor go off on his own to the vendor booths just now and she was proud of him. Chances were slim anything would happen here in Santa's workshop, but just in case she kept an eye on the shops across the way, spotting the red pom-pom on the top of Connor's hat as he made his way around inside one of the handmade ornament shops, though she couldn't see what he was buying. Probably something for Nick.

A few minutes later, both Marlowe guys were back at the table, safe and sound.

"Here we are." Nick set everything out, including condiments and napkins, then took a seat beside Connor at the table, across from Belle. "Did you get what you needed, son?"

"Yep," the kid said, keeping a protective hand on the small bag he'd carried back.

"Time to see Santa yet?" Connor asked once they had finished their food.

Nick checked his watch. "Still got a half-hour. How about we visit the reindeer now and take some pictures?"

"Cool!" Connor took off down the path ahead of

Nick and Belle. Once they were alone, Nick slipped his fingers through Belle's, warming her chilled skin. An older couple passed them, laughing and snuggling.

"Hello, Dr. Marlowe," the older man said, greeting Nick as they walked by. "Great to see you and Belle back together again."

"Oh, we're not—" Belle started, stiffening, but it was too late. The older couple was already lost in the crowd again.

He did his best to hide the prick of disappointment her denial had caused, even knowing it was silly. He'd known this was all temporary when he'd started this crazy whirlwind affair. This thing between them would end soon. No matter how perfect it might feel to him now.

He squeezed Belle's hand and pulled her into his side as they neared the pens where the reindeer were held. The smell of wet fur and animals was stronger here. Connor's voice echoed from nearby as he talked to one of the reindeer, but all Nick could focus on at the moment was the woman beside him.

They stopped near the corner of one of the enclosures and Nick slid his arms around Belle's waist, turning her to face him. She kept her head lowered and her gaze averted. "Hey, don't worry about what people think. Today's just for fun." He used the same tone he did to soothe his patients through a crisis. "Let's enjoy the time we have left."

He rubbed her back as people wandered past them. Connor was still making his way through the reindeer, petting each snout as he watched Nick and Belle through the fencing.

Gradually, Belle relaxed and Nick pulled back

slightly to brush a few loose strands of hair from her face. "Okay?"

"Okay." She nodded, her cheeks flushing pink. "Sorry. I guess the stress got to me."

"You don't have to carry the weight of the world alone, Belle." He took her chin between his thumb and forefinger. "You helped relieve my burden of guilt over Vicki. Let me repay you now by helping you relax. Ready to see some reindeer?"

Belle gave him a tremulous smile. "Yes. I'd love to."

They joined Connor near a wide pen with the name "Vixen" painted on the wall behind it. The reindeer inside sported a fancy leather collar bedecked with silver bells. Two volunteers stood nearby as the animal nuzzled Connor's hand through the slats, the reindeer's pink tongue reaching for the carrot on his son's palm.

"Dad, take my picture!" Connor called.

Nick pulled out his cell phone and snapped a few photos. When he'd finished, Belle gave him a nudge. "Go over there with him and I'll take a few of the two of you."

Once those were done, Connor piped up again. "I want pics with Belle too."

Nick motioned for her to switch places with him. All of it felt so easy and right. He hated to think about Christmas arriving and this all being over, but he also had to be strong. If not for himself, then for Connor. He'd sworn to keep things in perspective, no strings, no heartbreak. But the more time he spent with Belle the harder his vow was to keep.

"Is it time yet, Dad?" Connor bounced up and down on the heels of his sneakers.

Nick checked the time once more. "Yep. Almost time. Let's get in line."

"Yes!" Connor led them down the fake-frost-covered path. In the distance, Santa's cottage was visible. The sound of a train whistle echoed and through the front entrance to the barn Nick saw a small tractor-pulled locomotive chugging to a stop. He'd read they had one set up around the perimeter of the farm.

Connor noticed it too. "Can we go on the train when we're done?"

"We can," Nick said.

Once they were in line, things moved along fairly quickly. An elf escorted Connor over to a large book on a pedestal and checked whether his name was on the naughty or nice list, then led him toward Santa's cottage. He kept the bag with whatever he'd bought with him the whole time, not allowing anyone else to hold it. While he talked to Santa, Nick and Belle wandered through the vendor booths until Connor emerged from the red and white striped cottage, looking quite pleased with himself.

"Did you tell him everything you wanted?" Belle asked, as they headed back toward the front entrance once more.

"I did," Connor said, walking backward ahead of Nick. "I think it's going to be a great Christmas."

Outside, they took the train around the farm, the snow-covered landscape beautiful, then they stopped for hot cocoa before walking back to the SUV.

"Thanks for today," Belle said, looking over at Nick, her green gaze warm.

"You're welcome," he replied, his words emerging gruffer than he'd intended.

She frowned. "I hope you're not coming down with a cold."

"No, no. I'm good."

"You sure?" Belle tilted her head, watching him closely, her expression concerned.

The fact she was worried about him touched Nick more than he could say. He was used to taking care of everyone else. Having the roles reversed for a change was nice, even if it was only for a short while.

"I'm sure." He leaned over and kissed Belle again. "Let's go back to Bayside."

CHAPTER ELEVEN

THE DAY BEFORE Christmas Eve, Belle was back in the clinic early to scrub down the exam rooms one final time. They were already spotless, but after the supplies had been put away and the front desk readied for patient check-ins, Belle had needed something to keep her from obsessing over the situation with Nick. It seemed like the more she tried not to think about him, the more she did. Their time together was rapidly coming to a close.

Yesterday at the farm had been magical and afterward they'd gone for a nice dinner in town, then Nick had dropped Connor off at home with his sitter so he could rest up for his big game today. Nick and Belle had spent the night together at her house again, but it had been different. The intensity of their lovemaking, the meaning, the poignancy was almost too much, too overwhelming. Especially since they'd say goodbye again in less than forty-eight hours.

She'd been honest with Nick when she'd told him Bayside wasn't her home anymore, no matter how she'd loved revisiting and how much she'd miss the place after she'd gone. She'd built a new life for herself in Beverly Hills, with new opportunities and new responsibilities.

And he had a thriving practice here in town. He

loved Bayside. Neither of them should give up what they'd worked so hard to achieve.

And trying to do the long-distance thing seemed doomed to failure.

Right?

Right. Rock, meet hard place.

After finishing up, she shut off the lights in the exam rooms then wandered down the hall to the reception area. It was quiet here all by herself, but Nick would arrive soon to pick her up. He was handling things in his clinic this morning before taking her to Connor's hockey game in Manistee. She had no idea what she'd be watching, but it would give her more time with her Marlowe guys, so she was happy.

She took a seat behind the reception desk and closed her eyes for what felt like a second. Her lack of sleep was catching up with her, what with the work here to get the clinic reopened, on top of cleaning out all of her aunt's things. Add in the late nights with Nick and her phone calls with Dr. Reyes and she was well and truly exhausted.

"Sleeping on the job?" Nick's deep voice jolted her awake and Belle snapped upright, blinking under the bright fluorescent lights.

"What time is it?" she asked, yawning and squinting at the clock on the wall. "I was resting my eyes and…"

"It's nearly noon. We need to get a move on if we're going to make Con's game on time."

"Oh." She ran a hand over her hair then down the sweatshirt and jeans she'd worn. "Do I look all right?"

"You look perfect, as always." Nick kissed her quick before straightening and handing Belle her coat. "C'mon. Let's get moving."

Thankfully, traffic was lighter today and they made

it to the arena in Manistee with time to spare. They walked inside the cavernous concrete and granite structure and past the ticket booths, up a ramp and into the ice arena. The air was chilly and the shushing sound of skates on ice filled the space. From what Belle could see, both teams were practicing out on the rink on their respective sides before the game. She and Nick took seats near the front row, behind the protective shield of plexiglass, and he helped her off with her coat.

"Where's Connor?" she asked, scanning the names on the backs of the kids' jerseys.

"Over there," Nick said, pointing toward the far side of the rink. "He's playing right defense today."

"Okay." She did her best to get comfortable on the hard, plastic seat and rubbed her icy hands together to generate heat. Connor seemed good at his position from what she'd been able to see in practice, stopping the puck and keeping it from reaching the goaltender behind him. A vendor came by, selling hot chocolates, and she bought one for herself and Nick as the seats around them filled with other parents, including Eric's.

Nick put his arm around Belle again and snuggled her into his side. She was grateful for his heat, though she was still wary of them being seen as a couple. With her returning to California the day after tomorrow, she didn't want to leave him behind to deal with a lot of uncomfortable questions about what had happened. He had too much on his plate as it was. It would be hellish enough to leave. Best to rip the bandage off cleanly, as the old adage went.

She gave him a small smile then pulled away, not missing his frown at her action.

The game began as a referee sailed onto the ice and the national anthem played. They all stood, hand over hearts, to sing the "Star-Spangled Banner." When it was over, she hazarded another glance at Nick and saw those faint lines of tension had returned around his mouth and eyes and her heart sank. She didn't want to hurt him, but this was for the best.

A whistle sounded and the ref dropped the puck and the action increased.

Soon her distress over things with Nick was lost in the cheers of the crowd and rooting for Connor and his team. The kid was good. Even a casual observer like her could tell. Belle vaguely remembered going to Nick's games with Aunt Marlene when they'd been kids, but she'd never really been into sports and hadn't followed that part of his life as much.

"Boo!" Nick stood, shouting as the ref called a penalty against Connor's team. He sat back down, his expression disgusted. "Totally uncalled for. The ref called a body foul on Eric because he bumped into that other kid and tripped him, but it wasn't his fault." Nick cupped his hands around his mouth again. "Bad call!"

Okay. She'd not really seen this side of Nick before, growling and aggressive and alpha, and she had to admit it was kind of a turn-on. Belle grinned and focused on the game once more, doing her best to get into the spirit of things. After Connor's team scored a goal, she jumped to her feet and cheered alongside Nick. "Yay, Connor! Go, Mighty Pucks!"

Nick gave her a side glance, his crooked grin warming her from the inside out.

"You sure you don't want to stick around Bayside?" he asked, laughing. "You make a heck of a cheerleader." He leaned in to kiss her again just as a warning buzzer sounded and everyone on the ice from both teams swarmed to the middle of the rink.

A murmur spread fast through the crowd and Belle looked at Nick. "What's wrong?"

"I'm not sure," he said, scowling. "I wasn't paying attention. Looks like someone's hurt."

Eric's parents were on their feet and heading down onto the ice and it felt like a pit opened up in Belle's stomach as she searched the names on the jerseys, none of them Marlowe. "Where's Con?"

A glance at Nick showed all the color had drained from his face as he stood and raced down onto the ice as well, leaving Belle to follow on his heels. As they pushed closer to the center of the circle of onlookers, the coppery scent of blood filled the air and dread constricted her lungs. Scarlet splotches colored the ice beneath their feet and Belle's pulse kicked into overdrive.

"I'm a doctor, let me through," Nick yelled, shoving parents and coaches aside to reveal Connor flat on his back on the ice, blood gushing from his left wrist as he held it close to his chest and screamed. Nick dropped to his knees beside his son, his voice brittle with shock. "I'm sorry, son. I'm so sorry. What happened?"

Belle pulled out her cell phone to call 911 while one of the coaches fashioned a tourniquet out of gauze.

Nick gently tied it around the gash on Connor's wrist, applying pressure while yelling, "Will someone please tell me what the hell happened to my son?"

"I don't know," Eric said, crying in his mother's arms. "Con covered it right away."

"It was an accident," the coach said, clearly shaken by the amount of blood everywhere. "Con slipped and fell and another kid was right there. The skate blade caught him across the wrist."

After relaying the information and location to the

dispatcher over the phone, Belle moved in beside Nick. "EMS is on the way. What can I do?"

Nick didn't answer, just stared down at his son.

Within minutes, sirens wailed through the arena and two EMTs barreled onto the ice with a gurney, rushing over to where Connor was, in the center of the rink. While one first responder took over the tourniquet from Nick and made an initial assessment, the other talked into the radio mic attached to his collar, sending stats directly to the ER at Manistee General. Once they had Connor stabilized and loaded onto the gurney, one of the EMTs patted Nick on the shoulder. "Don't worry, Doc. We'll take good care of him."

They rushed Connor off the ice and back toward the entrance while Nick ran alongside them, stopping only long enough to toss Belle the keys to his SUV. "I'm riding with my son in the ambulance."

Belle nodded then watched as the group disappeared down the ramp. She quickly ran back to their seats in the arena and grabbed their coats and her bag then hurried to Nick's vehicle, her blood pounding and her heart beating triple time. It was one thing to be the doctor in control, to have emotional distance from the events taking place. It was quite another to have the son of the man she loved in peril.

The ambulance ride to the hospital passed in a blur for Nick.

Dammit. He should've been watching Connor, should've been paying attention. Maybe then he could've warned his son about the impending danger about to strike.

But instead he'd been focused on kissing Belle.

He'd allowed himself to be distracted and everything had gone straight to hell.

I'm sorry, Connor. I'm so sorry.

He'd failed. The final promise he'd made to his dying wife, the woman who'd given up so much for him, and he'd failed her. All for a fling that would be over in days anyway.

No. Belle was more than a fling. Always had been. And damn if that didn't mean he'd let her down too. She'd been up front that what they had was only temporary and Nick had gone ahead and fallen off the deep end for her all over again, heart and soul.

While his world crashed down around him, the EMTs continued to assess Connor's injuries. His son, at least, had stopped crying in agony and now seemed comfortable, an IV of pain meds hooked up to his right arm.

"Can you tell me what you remember happening?" the EMT asked Connor, as he checked his vitals. "Did the blood squirt out or did it ooze?"

Never one to shy away from gore, Connor looked at Nick before answering. "Squirt, I guess. The left winger from the other team was right behind me when I slipped. I hit the ice and his blade went right down my wrist. I covered it as soon as it happened, like my dad taught me."

"Good job, son," Nick said, his words thick, picturing his precious little boy hurt out on the rink. He cleared his throat and blinked hard against the sting in his eyes. This was ridiculous. He was a trained physician. He handled emergency situations with his patients every day. He was supposed to be the calm, rational one. One more area he was screwing up, apparently. He was a horrible father. Familiar guilt descended once more, stealing his breath. This was his fault. He closed his eyes and said a silent prayer. If Connor was okay, he'd do better. He'd not shirk his responsibilities again.

Just please let my son be okay.

They pulled into a bay at Manistee General and Nick waited while the EMTs unloaded the gurney from the back of the ambulance then followed them inside. An ER doc—the same woman who'd handled Nick's meningitis patient days earlier—met them at the entrance in a gown and mask, fully gloved and ready to go. She gave Nick a quick nod of recognition before getting the rundown from the EMTs. Several nurses and techs joined their group as they made their way toward an open trauma bay.

"Sounds like a possible arterial bleed," the ER said as they transferred Connor from the gurney to the hospital bed while Nick stood off to the side. No way was he letting his son out of his sight again, good care or not. "He'll lose blood fast, if that's the case."

"Blood pressure's high," a nurse said, ripping the Velcro of the cuff off Connor's injured arm. "One twenty-six over eighty-four."

Nick's own pulse skyrocketed.

"All right," the ER doc said, smiling down at Connor. "I know it hurts, but I need to take a look at your wrist, okay?"

Connor looked at Nick and he moved in beside the bed, taking his son's right hand. "It's okay, Con. I'm right here with you. I promise."

"Okay." He nodded and tightened his grip on his dad's hand as the ER doc peeled away the bloody gauze from Connor's left wrist. "Ow, ow, ow!"

If Nick could've taken the agony on himself, he would have. Proper punishment for his failures. Instead, all he could do was stand by helplessly and watch as the ER team worked.

"Good, Connor. You're doing great," the doctor encouraged, peering down at the wound. "Can you open up your fingers the whole way?"

His son did as the doctor asked and a bit of the tension constricting Nick's chest unfurled.

"Nice, Connor. Okay." The ER doc looked up at Nick. "He's got good motor function. Good pulses, as well. I'd say we're lucky and it looks like a venous bleed through the muscle only, not arterial. And the tendons look intact, as well."

Nick exhaled his pent-up breath and gave his son what he hoped was a confident smile. "That's good, son. Real good. You're going to be all right."

Connor nodded, the fear in his eyes shifting to relief. "Okay."

"Right." The ER doc straightened as the nurses and techs buzzed around her, checking the monitors hooked up to his son. "What team do you play for?"

"Mighty Pucks."

"I play on the staff soccer team here at the hospital every Sunday. Accidents happen. You try not to get hurt or break anything but, yeah." She glanced at Nick again. "Don't worry, Dr. Marlowe. Once this is healed, your son will be back on his skates and playing as soon as he can hold a hockey stick again."

Nick nodded then allowed one of the nurses to escort him down the hall to the waiting area while they got Connor stitched up. She offered him something to drink, but he declined. The nurse left and he slumped in his seat, wondering how such a great day could go south so fast.

All my fault.

The words continued to loop through his head even though his rational brain knew better. Still, between the guilt and the anxiety and the overall exhaustion of the past two weeks, it was more than he could fight.

He was done. He'd tried opening up with Belle and look where it had gotten him.

She was leaving anyway. Best to end it now so he could focus on his son again.

"There you are," Belle said, running through the automatic doors at the ER entrance and over to his side. "I got here as soon as I could. How's Connor?"

Nick filled her in on the ER doc's findings, his voice robotic, even to his own ears. "They're fixing him up right now."

"I'm so glad. When I saw all the blood on the ice, I suspected an arterial laceration." She took the seat beside his and stared up at the ceiling. "All things considered, you couldn't have asked for a better outcome."

"I can't do this anymore, Belle," he said quietly.

"I'm sorry?" She looked over at him.

"I can't do this anymore." He gestured between them. "Us. I thought I could. I thought I could open up and let myself be with you temporarily, and it would be okay, but it's not. Look what happened to Connor. I let myself get distracted and everything went to hell. I can't allow that to happen again. I'm sorry. This is all my fault. Connor has to be my top priority, now and always."

"Hey." She reached over to take his hand, but he pulled away. "This isn't your fault, Nick. You've been through a shock. Take some time to rest, get Connor home and we can talk later. I'll pick up dinner for you guys and drop it off. Tomorrow we've got the free clinic and—"

"No. I'm sorry, but I'm done." He stood and looked

down at her, his heart breaking even as he knew this was the right thing to do. She had her life and he had his. Trying to mix the two had only led to disaster. "I'll be there for clinic tomorrow, but otherwise it's best if we don't see one another again outside work."

She blinked up at him, as the warmth in her was replaced by sadness. "Um...okay. Sure. Fine. I understand." Belle pushed to her feet as well, avoiding his gaze as she pulled out her cell phone. "I'll just...uh... call a cab to pick me up."

Shit. He'd forgotten she'd driven his SUV here in all the craziness. "No. I'll take you home."

"No, no. You're right. We should be done." Her voice broke a little and part of him died inside. He didn't want to hurt her. Had never meant to hurt her. But it seemed that was their destiny. She sniffled then tapped on her screen. "There. Done. My ride's on its way."

Belle slid the phone back into her bag then glanced up at him, her eyes sparkling with unshed tears. "I'll wait over here. See you in the morning."

He wanted to respond, to tell her to come back, to beg her to stay, but it was all over now. Their fling was done and soon she'd be gone. His life would go back to normal. Just him and Connor and lots of long, lonely nights ahead. He'd get through it because that's what he did.

He wouldn't fail Vicki's memory, or their son, again.

CHAPTER TWELVE

AFTER A SILENT car ride back to Bayside, Belle paid her driver then climbed out to stand on the snowy sidewalk in front of Aunt Marlene's place, watching the glow of the vehicle's taillights disappear around the corner. It was near dusk now and she felt weary to her bones. She slogged inside and flipped on the lights to pull off her soggy boots.

The house was quiet, too quiet, after the hustle and bustle of the hockey game and then the ER. She shouldn't feel so sad, but she did. Nick ending it all this afternoon had been tough, no matter that she should've expected it. With his son getting injured, on top of the guilt still lurking beneath the surface, all of his buttons had definitely been pushed. As a physician well trained in the psychology of her patients, it was a no-brainer. Nick might be a doctor, but when it came to his son's health he'd reverted back to his comfort zone of guilt and Belle had been left out in the cold. Literally.

With a sigh, she padded to the kitchen in her stock-inged feet and made a nice cup of tea, hoping it would ease the ache in her chest and soothe the thoughts racing through her mind. At least Connor was okay. Her heart—which should never have been involved in this mess to begin with—was broken, but she'd survive.

She'd suck it up and hide the anguish deep inside, just like she'd done the last time Nick had let her go. Just like she'd done when her parents had died. Just like she was doing with Aunt Marlene passing and the end of her time here in Bayside.

She refused to sit around and feel sorry for herself. She'd keep busy. Lord knew, there was still plenty to get done in her aunt's house before she put it on the market and moved on after Christmas.

Carrying her mug with her, she picked up an empty box in the living room then shuffled to the den to begin packing away the rest of Aunt Marlene's knickknacks. She'd gotten most of the other rooms cleared over the past eight days but had left this one for last. It was the most personal of her aunt's spaces, the one she'd used as her home office and a storehouse for her most treasured mementos.

As she removed each of the framed degrees off the wall with great care, all the repressed sadness and nostalgia inside Belle welled to the surface, despite her wishes, causing her nose to itch and her eyes to sting. She wrapped each frame in tissue paper before tucking the certificate safely in the storage box. Once those were done, next came the local awards for community service, then finally the photos.

Belle couldn't help but smile as she traced her fingers over the pictures. Here was one of her and Aunt Marlene at the county fair shortly after Belle had come to live with her. Another showed her and her aunt at Belle's eighth-grade graduation, a lanky, goofy Nick in the background making bunny ears above Belle's head. Yet another showed a smiling and affectionate Belle and Nick before prom. He'd worn a scarlet bowtie and suspenders with his black tux to match the color of her strapless chiffon dress. Both of them had on their rhine-stone king and queen crowns and lovesick, silly grins.

Later that night he'd told Belle he was breaking up with her.

Things between them had been so fun and so magical… until they hadn't been anymore.

Kind of like today.

Dammit.

Her vision blurred and she blinked hard. She wouldn't cry over this. She wouldn't.

She'd gone into this whole affair with her eyes open. It was temporary.

It was over. End of story. Get over it. Move on.

Cursing herself inwardly, she swiped the back of her hand across her damp cheeks and shoved more me-mentos into the box. She had the clinic to think about in Beverly Hills. She had her successful practice and a promotion waiting for her in California. She was not the same pathetic loser she'd been back in high school the last time Nick had walked away from her, no mat-ter how it might feel now.

Belle pulled their prom picture off the wall and wrapped it tightly in paper before shoving it in the box with the rest of the stuff. Done. She moved on to her aunt's desk. Inside the top drawer were the usual of-fice supplies—pens, paper clips, a stapler, a few rub-ber bands and a letter opener. She boxed those up too then proceeded to drawer number two.

This one contained duplicate copies of her aunt's ledgers for the clinic. Belle took those out and set them on the desktop. She'd get those to the attorney's office before she left Bayside. They'd fixed up the clinic but given the current real estate market the property would still be a tough sell. Perhaps showing prospective buyers the need for affordable health care in this area would entice their interest.

A glance at the clock showed it was only 8 p.m., but with the lack of sunlight and her exhaustion it felt more like midnight to Belle.

Her heart pinched as she crouched to clear out the final drawer at the bottom. Inside were a few legal pads and an empty scrapbook. Belle pulled them out to put them in the box with the rest of the stuff, then noticed an envelope clipped to the outside of the scrapbook along with another photo of Belle, Nick, and Marlene— this one taken at the clinic. Belle's name was scrawled across the front of the envelope in her aunt's cursive handwriting.

Belle swallowed hard and traced her fingers over the letters, her tears flowing again. Grief over losing her aunt and hurt over ending things with Nick melded with the deeper loss of her parents and her old life here in Bayside. Belle sobbed as she held the envelope to her face and inhaled her aunt's scent—lavender soap and antiseptic. If she closed her eyes, it was almost like Aunt Marlene was in the room with her. She rested her back against the wall and slid down to the floor behind the desk, her fingers trembling as she opened the envelope and pulled out the letter inside. It was dated late October, about a month before her aunt had passed.

Dearest Belle,
Bayside has always been my home and I love it
with all my heart, just as I love you. But if you're
reading this note it means I'm gone. Please don't
mourn for me too long. I had a full and wonder-
ful life with lots of friends and you to keep me
company.

*I'm so proud of all you've accomplished in your
life, just as your parents would have been. You
are my daughter, if not by birth, then by love. You
have more courage and strength and heart than
anyone I know, and you are a true blessing to
your patients and to all of us who love you.*

*But I hope being back in Bayside has reminded
you there's more to life than success and money.
This town is a good place, and there's a real need
for your talents here, Belle. You could make a
good life and a real difference right here in your
hometown.*

*I'm not trying to force you into anything or
make your choices for you, just making sure you
see all your options. Regardless of what you decide for your future, Bayside will always be your
true home.*

Think about it. That's all I ask.
Love always,
Aunt Marlene

After fetching some tissues, Belle sat behind her
aunt's desk for a long time, thinking about everything.
The truth of her aunt's words resonated in her heart.
There was a need here. She'd seen it herself with Analia. She could make a difference, even if she and Nick
weren't together, and honestly that's all she'd ever
wanted. She sighed and lowered her head.

Being here, living in Bayside again would be difficult without Nick, seeing him every day and not being
with him, but she'd cope. The same way she'd coped
with being the new kid on the block in Beverly Hills.
The same way she'd coped with clawing her way to the

top of her profession. The same way she'd coped the first time Nick had said goodbye.

If she stayed in Bayside, she could work out of the old clinic, live here in this house, start a new life from the ashes of her old one. It wasn't perfect, but it felt right.

Still, she wanted to sleep on such a major decision. Considering the day she'd had, waiting until morning made sense.

After a yawn and a stretch, Belle headed for bed.

Nick awoke before dawn on Christmas Eve morning and automatically reached for Belle, before he realized there was only cold mattress beside him. Damn. He covered his eyes with his arm and groaned. All he could picture in his mind was Belle's stricken expression from the day before when he'd told her they were done.

Chances were high he might have overreacted a bit. He sighed and rubbed his eyes.

Okay, a lot.

Idiot.

Opening himself up again to love after years of living in self-imposed denial had been difficult, to say the least. He felt vulnerable and raw and irrational in a way that both thrilled and terrified him. Then yesterday, when he'd seen Connor lying there on the ice, surrounded by blood and crying in agony, every one of his old demons had raced right back to sucker punch him in the gut. He'd immediately closed up, battened down the hatches, circled the wagons. He withdrew, he conquered, he persevered. It's what he'd done after he'd broken up with Belle back in high school. It's what he'd done after Vicki died. And it's what he'd done yesterday.

Such an idiot. A pathetic, gutless idiot.

He lay in the dark and listened to the wind whistle

past the frosty windows. Never mind Belle had been there to support him, that she'd tried to comfort him and point out what had happened to Connor wasn't his fault. Hell, he of all people should've known accidents happened in hockey. He'd played enough of the sport himself and had the scars to prove it. No amount of watching over his son could have prevented what had happened yesterday.

Loneliness threatened to pull him under, but he forced it aside and got up, pulled on a pair of jeans from the day before then padded down the hall to check on Connor. Nick had been up every two hours or so to look in on his son and make sure he was comfortable and not in pain. When he peeked into Con's bedroom, the kid was still snoring away, the white bandages encasing his left wrist glowing in the early morning gloom.

With a sigh, Nick shut the door then went downstairs to start some coffee.

If he was honest, he'd been using his promise to Vicki to push Belle away because he'd been hurting. He didn't want to let her go. Which made no sense, but there it was—he'd pushed her away before she could leave him behind.

Genius. Not.

Yeah, he felt like a real Einstein at the moment. God, he was a doctor. He'd spent more time in school than he'd spent out of it. He was an intelligent guy, a respected part of his small community, yet when it came to his personal life, he was a mess. He tried to put on a brave front, tried to project confidence and control, but in reality he didn't control anything.

Especially the last two weeks.

Belle's image flashed into his mind again—how prim and proper she'd been the night of her aunt's funeral, how she'd gradually loosened up the longer she'd been around him and Connor, how she'd really begun to open up around them. Those thoughts quickly shifted to their kiss at the tree lighting ceremony, the first night they'd made love, the day at Santa's Workshop.

In truth, looking back, the past two weeks hadn't been a mess at all. In fact, they'd been pretty wonderful, because of Belle. She'd made him laugh again, live again, love again, despite his wishes to the contrary.

Find love again. Be happy. Promise me...

Vicki's words returned to his head, making him wince.

Another failure on his part.

Belle had never said the words, but she'd cared about him. Maybe not love, not yet, not on her part anyway, but certainly on his. Then he'd shut her down. Just like last time.

With a groan, he leaned his hips back against the counter as the coffeemaker gurgled away and the rich aroma of fresh brew filled the air. Today was the big day. The free clinic they'd worked so tirelessly to re-open. He should've felt happier about that than he did. Instead he just felt tired. Tired of making the same stupid mistakes over and over. Tired of living like a monk under his self-imposed burden of his guilt. Tired of failing those he loved. How he'd fix things and change his actions in the future, he wasn't sure yet, but, dammit, he was determined to try. He just prayed it wasn't too late. With Connor or with Belle.

She was leaving tomorrow, but there were planes, phones, computers.

Long-distance wasn't ideal, but if she could find a way to forgive him, he'd give her everything he had. He closed his eyes and said a silent prayer.

I'm trying to move on. If I'm doing this right, Vicki, give me a sign. Any sign.

The coffeemaker beeped.

Okay, maybe not the divine choir Nick had been hoping for, but he'd take it.

He poured himself a cup of caffeine then headed back upstairs to shower and change before Connor got up. The clock on his nightstand read six thirty. The clinic was set to open at eight. Mollie would be here soon to stay with his son for the day.

Now he just needed to figure out how to apologize to Belle.

Nick got cleaned up and shaved before dressing in his standard work uniform of black pants, white buttondown shirt, blue tie and lab coat. His mind churned and he felt on edge, despite the hot shower. The right words wouldn't come, no matter how he tried to force them. It was frustrating. Today, of all days, he needed to be on his game, needed to be productive and in the flow, needed to have the right thing to say at the right time so Belle would forgive him. There was too much riding on this to mess it up.

After combing his still-damp hair into place, Nick went downstairs to find Connor at the kitchen table, toying with the bandages around his left wrist. Guilt constricted Nick's chest before he shoved it aside. Belle had been right. His son's injury wasn't his fault.

Mollie was in the kitchen, cooking up what smelled like eggs and bacon. She gave Nick a smile as he descended the stairs into the great room. From the open kitchen the sitter waved to him, a spatula in her hand. "Morning, Doc. Looks like you had some excitement yesterday."

"Yeah. Con got a nasty gash on his wrist during his hockey game."

"He told me," Mollie said, unfazed. "Same thing happened to my oldest boy years ago. Live and learn. And watch out for those skate blades."

Nick gave his son a kiss on the top of his tousled head then ruffled his hair. "How are you feeling this morning, kiddo?"

Connor mumbled, giving his dad a sleepy scowl.

"I'm getting ready to go into the clinic," Nick said, walking across the hardwood floor to the fridge. "I wanted to tell you both good morning and I love you, Con."

He swallowed the glass of orange juice he'd poured in one long swallow then set the glass in the sink. After showing Mollie where his son's pain meds were and the instructions from the hospital for changing the bandages, Nick grabbed his coat from the hook beside the door. "Be good, Con."

"Where's Belle?" his son asked.

"At home, probably getting ready for the clinic like I am."

"I don't want her to leave Bayside," Con said, and Nick's heart went into freefall.

Nick sighed and walked back over to the table to take a seat beside his son. "I don't want her to go either, but she's got things waiting for her at home."

"Why can't this be her home?" He jutted out his chin. "Were you mean to her yesterday?"

"No." *Yes.* Nick's chest squeezed, his words sounding hollow even as he said them. "Belle's got a life back in California, son. Don't worry. We'll be fine, no matter what happens."

Connor scowled and crossed his arms. "It's not fine. What about Analia? You're ruining my wish to—" His son covered his mouth before saying any more, his eyes wide.

"Analia's got an appointment with a doctor in Detroit after the holidays." Nick's thoughts ran back over the last few days and his gaze narrowed with suspicion. "Wait. Is that what you asked Santa for? To have Belle stay and operate on your friend?"

"No." His son picked at the pine tabletop. "And fine isn't fine at all. Nobody's happy."

Nick sighed and glanced at the clock then stood. This conversation was going nowhere fast. "Look, I'm sorry, Con. Sometimes there are no easy answers, but I really have to go or I'll be late."

"Whatever." Con waved him off and put his head down on the table.

Talk about feeling like the world's worst father.

As Nick drove to the clinic, he did his best not to dwell on the argument with his son and instead focused on finding the right words to say to Belle.

I'm sorry. I'm an idiot. I'm in love with you and I don't want to lose you again.

As he sat at a red light, Nick's stomach knotted. Today really wasn't the day to blurt out his feelings to Belle, but if not now, then when? She was leaving Bayside tomorrow, most likely never to return. The light turned green and he drove on slowly through the slick streets, still snow covered from the night before.

Uncertainty twisted tight knots in the muscles of his upper back between his shoulder blades. He'd been playing it safe for two years since Vicki's death, not causing any waves that might bring up painful memories for Connor and trying to control the world. But now Nick wanted more. He wanted Belle by his side, through good times and bad. To see her face first thing in the morning and last thing at night. He wanted to plan for a future for the three of them together, as a family. He was not prepared to say goodbye again.

But the only way to get to the future he wanted was to deal with the present. To talk to Belle today and find out what she wanted.

He pulled onto Main Street and spotted a line already forming in front of the clinic. Old people, young people, kids, infants. Nick parked his truck in the employee lot behind the building and huddled in his coat as he headed toward the back entrance. All the lights were on inside, meaning Belle was already there. Anticipation and apprehension tingled in his gut.

He walked inside and took a deep breath, catching the scent of antiseptic and fresh paint. The low hum from the heating vents in the ceiling and the buzz of the fluorescent lights filled his ears. Beyond them were the sounds of Belle tinkering around in the lobby. He took off his wool coat and straightened his lab jacket then headed up front, spotting Belle behind the registration desk. According to his watch, they had about half an hour before the doors opened.

"Hey," he said quietly, when she glanced over at him. "Can we talk?"

Before Belle could respond, Jeanette arrived to take over the front desk. Disappointment bit deep. He didn't want to have a difficult conversation with Belle in front of his office manager. Dammit. Heat prickled up from beneath the collar of his starched white shirt as faces pressed to the glass doors at the entrance and patients jostled to get inside out of the cold. Normally, before a long day in the office, he liked to take a few moments to center himself, get his head in the right space, but today he felt completely discombobulated.

Maybe it was better to dive right in and deal with work first.

Then he and Belle could talk later, after they closed.

That would give him more time to consider his actions too. The rational part of him was still insistent that ending things with Belle had been the right thing, even if his timing had been questionable. Perhaps instead of apologizing and begging her to stay, he should instead make sure she understood this was all for the best. After all, his guilt and need for control were his issues to deal with, not hers. Until he made things right within himself, he shouldn't bring her into it. She had a whole life waiting for her in California. He'd never ask her to leave her career and her dreams behind. He'd been through the same with Vicki and had learned his lesson. He didn't want to live with regrets anymore. Even if his heart felt shattered into a million pieces.

CHAPTER THIRTEEN

BELLE'S DAY HAD started two hours earlier with a phone call to Beverly Hills. It had been the middle of the night there, but Dr. Reyes had still been in the office. A cautionary tale of workaholism she was grateful she wouldn't be repeating. He'd picked up on the second ring, and Belle had squared her shoulders, preparing for the difficult conversation.

"On your way home already?" Dr. Reyes had said by way of greeting. "I knew you'd be anxious to get home to civilization."

"I am home, Dr. Reyes."

"Back in California? Perfect. I'll send a driver to pick you up and bring you down to the office. There are a few things we need to go over on the new cases you'll be taking on after the partnership is finalized."

"No, sir." Belle had taken a deep breath. "I've decided I'm staying in Bayside."

"Excuse me?" His surprised tone had quickly turned to anger. "Don't be ridiculous, Belle. You're tired. Get on a plane and get back to Beverly Hills. I need you here."

"Perhaps, but there are people in this area who need me more." She'd sighed and rubbed her eyes. "I'm sorry, Dr. Reyes, but I can make a real difference in Bayside."

Analia's face had flashed into her mind and the more she'd talked, the more confident she'd felt about her decision. "You know my ultimate goal was always to help people. I feel the best place for me to do that is right here in this area. There's a great need for medical resources and I believe I can do more to help others here in Bayside. Therefore, I'm resigning from the practice effective immediately. I'll continue to follow up with my current patients remotely until their cases are concluded, as per my original contract, but once those are closed, I'm done. Thank you for the opportunity, but I'm just not happy there anymore."

He'd continued to sputter but she'd ended the call and put the phone down.

One difficult situation concluded. Today was the second. They had the free clinic to run, which meant working side by side with Nick. But deep inside her sense of inner peace had returned. She'd made the right choice, no matter how things with Nick turned out.

When she'd gotten in to the clinic this morning, the first thing she'd done had been to call Juan Hernandez. He'd been surprised too, thinking something else had gone wrong at the clinic. But when she'd asked him to come in today, along with his wife and daughter, Belle had felt an excitement bubble up inside her she hadn't felt since med school.

Signal two she was on the right track.

The minute Nick walked into the clinic, Belle's skin prickled with awareness and her chest pinched with yearning. She longed to tell him about her conversation with Dr. Reyes and her decision to stay in Bayside, but then she remembered his words from the day before.

It's best if we don't see each other again outside work...

Work. Right. That's what she was here to do. That was why she was staying.

She hazarded a quick glance at him over her shoulder as she went through the appointment book again with Jeanette and her heart skipped a beat at his handsomeness. Even in his work clothes he was still the most gorgeous man she'd ever seen. Nick would find out soon enough about her change in plans anyway. She'd need to buy out his half of the clinic in order to use it for her new plastic surgery practice.

"How's Connor this morning?" she asked, looking away again.

"Good. Slept through the night," Nick said, his tone gruffer than usual. "He's on the mend. Look, Belle, I—"

An older lady with a cane outside rapped on the glass, pointing at her watch.

"We should probably get started," Belle said, ignoring the rush of nerves inside her. Not nerves over seeing patients but over what Nick had been about to say. She didn't need any more drama right now, good or bad. "I'll go unlock the doors. Everyone ready?"

Jeanette nodded. So did Nick, though his expression looked as conflicted as she felt.

The minute she had the doors unlocked, the older lady with the cane limped in and headed straight for Jeanette. "Twyla Phillips. I need a refill on my diabetes meds pronto. With the weather, I haven't been able to get in to see my doctor in Lansing and now they're closed for the holidays."

"Sure, Mrs. Phillips," Jeanette said, handing the older lady a clipboard. "Just have a seat over there and fill out these forms and we'll be happy to help you."

Twyla toddled off to the chairs against the windows

and Jeanette began slowing working her way through the line of people coming in.

Belle went back into one of the exam rooms to wait for the first patient to complete their paperwork and make their way down the hall. As she was fiddling with the instruments laid out on the counter—tongue depressors, cotton swabs, an otoscope, a reflex hammer—she heard the sound of a wet, hacking cough echo from the hall, followed by Nick's calm, professional tone.

"I'm glad you came in to see us today, Mr. Banks," Nick said, leading the patient into the exam room across the hall from hers. "Regular checks of your CHF are important. Can you tell me what meds you're currently on?"

Nick glanced up and caught Belle's gaze as he started to close the door. The warmth in his brown eyes hit her first, followed by the instant sizzle of connection that was always there between them, whether they wanted it or not. Her lips parted and her breath caught and she nearly ran across the hall to beg him to let her back inside his life again, but then the moment passed as Nick shut his door and Belle's first patient appeared.

"Doctor?" Twyla Phillips said, limping into the room and handing Belle the papers in her hand. "I need help with my diabetes meds."

"Sure thing." Belle's professional persona slipped firmly back into place. "Have a seat on the exam table for me and we'll see how we can help you today."

After going over Mrs. Phillips's vitals and medical history, Belle wrote her out a two-week prescription for her insulin to get her through the holidays then sent her on her way. Next came Mrs. Welkins and her grandson, who was also her caretaker. Her dementia had progressed far enough that she didn't verbalize much and she was quite thin, but really the only problem she had was a need for more of her medication.

The patients became a bit of a blur after that. There was John d'Andre, who suffered from morbid obesity and diabetes and had also developed a small ulcer as a result of poor circulation. He got a certificate for some free antacid, courtesy of Bayside's local drug store, and a referral to a gastroenterologist in Manistee. Then there was Mr. Whitlaw, the father of one Belle's elementary school classmates, who'd sliced his finger open making breakfast. Belle gave him three neat stitches and sent him on his way.

Between visits, she ran into Nick in the hallway as she took her files back up to Jeanette, but other than a murmured "Excuse me" as they passed each other, they didn't have a chance to talk at all. Even lunch was rushed, consisting of a quickly consumed half of a sandwich in the back storeroom between cases. It was hectic and crazy, and Belle loved every minute of it.

It only reinforced to her she'd made the right choice to stay in Bayside.

Even if Nick didn't want to see her anymore.

Finally, around five that afternoon the crowd of patients began to ebb. Belle was finishing up with a little boy with food allergies who'd developed a rash after eating some Chinese food. She'd been explaining to the mother how her son should take the medications she'd prescribed him when there was a knock on the exam-room door followed by Jeanette poking her head inside.

"The Hernandez family are here to see you, Dr. Watson."

"Great." Belle walked her patients up to the reception desk and greeted Juan and his wife before crouching before Analia. "Hello, pretty girl."

"Hi." Analia grinned, her dark eyes sparkling with energy.

"You wanted to talk to us, Doc?" Rosa asked.

"Yep. C'mon back to the exam room and I'll fill you in." Belle led them down the hall and gestured for the trio to enter before her then followed them inside. She was just about to close the door when Nick opened his door across the hall. Their gazes met, his eyes flickering to the Hernandezes behind her before returning to Belle.

"Is there a problem with Analia?" he asked, his expression concerned. "She's my patient. Perhaps I should take her case."

"Hey, Doc," Juan called out, raising his hand in greeting to Nick.

"There's nothing wrong with Analia," Belle said, swallowing hard. He'd find out soon enough anyway and though this wasn't the ideal situation to tell him about her plans, it worked as well as any considering how busy their day had been. She took a deep breath and raised her chin. "Nothing I can't fix anyway. I've decided to stay in Bayside and open my own plastic surgery practice here. I wanted to speak to Analia and her parents about the possibility of me taking over the surgery for her Crouzon's."

For a moment all Nick could do was stare down at her.

Belle was staying.

Part of him wanted to whoop and holler. The other part of him, the analytical part, wanted to ask her why, wanted to know what had brought her decision about, wanted to know if she planned to live in her aunt's house and work out of this very clinic.

"If you'd like to sit in on my consultation with them, as Analia's pediatrician, that would be most helpful," Belle said. "You obviously know them better than I do and might put their minds at ease."

He opened his mouth to respond. He'd love nothing more than to work on a case with Belle, to work on building a life together too, but before he could say a word, Jeanette hurried down the hall toward them.

"Sorry to interrupt, but Bayside PD just pulled up out front. Seems one of their officers was injured in the line of duty."

Nick snapped his attention from Belle to Jeanette. "How bad?"

"Not sure, but they brought him here first since it was the only clinic open in town today." Jeanette headed back up front as the bell over the front entrance jangled.

Damn. "Sorry." Nick winced. "I should see what's up."

He started to back away as Belle nodded. "No problem. I'll fill you in later."

She walked into the exam room and closed the door behind her and for the first time since before Connor's accident, hope flooded Nick's system. Belle was staying. She was staying and he'd have another chance with her. One he did not intend to miss.

But first he had another patient to treat.

The once crowded lobby was empty now as closing time rapidly approached. Blue lights from the squad car parked at the curb flashed intermittently through the frosted front windows of the clinic. Nick walked over to help the female officer get her injured comrade inside.

"What happened?" he asked, as they maneuvered the hurt cop into an empty exam room. The man was middle-aged and doubled over, holding his right side.

Nick didn't see any blood or signs of trauma, but he couldn't rule out anything serious just yet. Bayside was hardly a hotbed of violent crime, but there was the occasional gunshot wound from a hunting accident.

"We stopped to help a motorist with a flat tire out on Highway 31 and my partner slipped on the ice and fell on his shoulder," the female cop said. "He only had surgery on it last year."

"Okay." Relief spread through Nick. A possible torn rotator cuff was much easier to handle. He and the other cop got the guy into the exam room and up on the table. The injured officer scooted around awkwardly, apparently unable to use his right arm. "You're going to be all right, Officer…?"

"Mowbray," the injured cop said, his voice strained, his face pale. "Stupid of me. My wife told me to wear my good boots today, but did I listen? Nope."

Nick scribbled down the man's account of what had happened in the file. "Don't worry, Officer Mowbray, I'm going to take good care of you." He set the file aside and moved in to examine the man's shoulder and arm more closely. "Can you slide out of your jacket and shirt for me so I can see the extent of bruising?"

The officer did as he asked and Nick palpated the man's shoulder joint, noting the white scars crisscrossing the area from the aforementioned surgery. Gently he tested for range of motion and extension of the patient's arm then checked the officer's blood pressure on his uninjured arm before allowing him to put his shirt back on.

"Okay. Well, the good news is I don't think it's broken or another tear. The bad news is you should have an X-ray to be sure and we don't have a machine here.

You'll need to go up to Manistee General to have it done. Sorry."

He stepped over to the counter and pulled out his cell phone, making a quick call to the hospital to see if they could fit the officer in. After getting the okay from the tech, Nick returned to his patient. "Right. The hospital says if you can get there within an hour, they'll fit you right in. Otherwise it could be awhile, with the holiday rush and all."

"I'll make sure he gets there," the female officer said. "Safely this time."

"I'm fine, Ethel. Stop fussing," Officer Mowbray said, waving off his partner. "You're worse than my wife."

Nick grinned, pulling out a sling from the cabinet and fitting it over the officer's right arm before turning back to the counter to write out two scripts, one for an NSAID pain reliever and the other to put the man off work pending the results of his X-ray and a consult with his orthopedic surgeon. He turned back to Officer Mowbray and handed him the papers. "The tech has instructions to call me with the results when they're done. Even if everything's okay, you'll most likely still end up with a nasty bruise. Take it easy until you hear back from me. Got it?"

"Got it," Officer Mowbray said, letting his partner help him down from the exam table. "Thanks for this. Merry Christmas to me, huh?"

"Yeah," Nick snorted, opening the exam-room door for them. "Merry Christmas indeed."

He glanced over to find the exam room Belle had been working in with the Hernandez family dark and empty. Damn. He checked his watch and realized he'd been in with the cops longer than he'd anticipated. Following them up to the reception desk, he glanced at the clock on the wall. Five forty-five.

"Drive carefully," he said to the officers as they exited. "Happy Holidays."

"Same to you, Doc," Officer Mowbray said, raising his good hand at Nick. "And Happy New Year too."

Once they'd gone, Nick turned to his office manager. "Where's Belle?"

"She left about five minutes before you finished," Jeanette said, walking over to lock up the clinic door and flip off the lights. They were officially done. "Said she had some things she needed to take care of before Christmas."

Nick's first instinct was to go after her, track her down and beg her forgiveness.

But first he needed to get Connor. Mollie had family coming to stay with her for Christmas and she needed to get home. He tossed Officer Mowbray's paperwork on the desk, then took off for the back of the clinic. "Thanks for your help today, Jeanette. I'll come back and clean this place up later. Right now I need to get going. Can you lock up behind you?"

"Sure thing, boss," Jeanette called from behind him. "Merry Christmas!"

"Merry Christmas," he yelled back, as he grabbed his coat and headed for his SUV. If he could get to Belle and convince her to give him another chance, it would be a very happy holiday indeed.

CHAPTER FOURTEEN

THE BAYSIDE TOWN green looked even more magical to Belle than it had the night of the tree lighting ceremony. The huge tree glowed from the center of the space, shades of pink and silver and white glimmering off the newly fallen snow on the ground. Carols were piped in from speakers attached to the nearby buildings and the area was nearly deserted as people spent the day with family and friends. Belle strolled through the winter wonderland, enjoying the peace and quiet after the controlled chaos of the clinic all day.

Home. She was finally home. It had taken her eighteen years and reuniting with one complicated, compassionate, completely wonderful doc and his son to make her realize this was where she belonged, and now she was here, she wasn't leaving again for a long, long time.

Well, if you didn't count the drive up to Manistee for little Analia's surgery.

She couldn't help smiling when she recalled the conversation with the Hernandez family back at the clinic. They'd barely let her finish explaining her plans to stay in Bayside before they'd accepted her offer to take on Analia's case free of charge to them for the chance to do the difficult but necessary surgery. There'd still be bills from the hospital, of course, but the donation of her services would help immensely. And perhaps Manistee General and the other doctors and technicians involved would get on the bandwagon, as well. Analia was such a special case and she seemed to charm everyone around her.

Belle walked around the tree then took a seat on one of the ornate wrought-iron benches toward the back of the area. Hopefully, Nick's last case with the police officer went well. After she'd finished with the Hernandez family, he'd still been in the exam room with his patient, so she'd gotten the rundown from Jeanette. No blood, so perhaps a fight or a fall. Whatever the injury, she prayed it wasn't life-threatening and the officer would be home with his family for Christmas.

Then she'd come out here to collect her thoughts before talking with Nick again.

She blinked up at the dark sky, icy flakes melting on her cheeks. "Thank you, Aunt Marlene. Thank you for bringing me back to Bayside. Thank you for giving me another chance with Nick."

Even if he doesn't want to be more than colleagues.

Belle sighed and stared down at her red-mitten-covered hands in her lap. Soon she'd have to head back to the clinic and face the man she loved, explain her reasons for staying here in Bayside. She wanted nothing more than for him to sweep her off her feet and proclaim his undying love and whisk her off to happily-ever-after. Except this wasn't some fairy tale, and she was hardly a princess in an ivory tower. She was a world-class plastic surgeon and a force to be reckoned with, both in and out of the operating room. She'd be fine, with or without Nick.

Her heart squeezed.

But things would be so much better with him. Him and Connor.

The sound of a car door slamming resonated through the small park, followed by a voice.

A very familiar voice.

"Belle?" Nick called. "Dr. Christabelle Watson, where are you? I saw your rental car at the curb. I know you're here somewhere. You can't hide from me forever."

You could make a good life and a real difference right here in your hometown...

"Thanks again, Aunt Marlene," Belle whispered, then stood. Her breath hitched and her legs shook as she moved around the enormous tree to see her Marlowe guys waiting for her on the other side. Hope shimmered between them like tinsel. "Hey."

"Hey." Nick moved closer. "Jeanette said you left for the night."

"I did." She smiled down at Connor. "How's your wrist today?"

"Better, thanks." The little boy squinted up at her. "My dad says you're not leaving."

"True." Belle crouched to be closer to his eye level. She noticed he had the bag from Santa's Workshop in his hand. "I'm going to stay in Bayside and work here from now on."

"Will you operate on my friend Analia?" Excitement flared brightly in the little boy's eyes, so like his father's. "Help make her normal?"

"I will. And Analia is already normal. I'm just going to make her outside better reflect the beautiful girl she is inside. I spoke to her family about it an hour ago." She grinned at Connor then looked up at Nick. "As long as it's acceptable to her pediatrician, of course."

"Of course." Nick held out his hand to her as she straightened. "Thank you."

"No." She squeezed his gloved fingers with hers, tears stinging her eyes. "Thank you. Thanks for letting me be a part of your family and your life these past two weeks. Thanks for reminding me of what I loved about Bayside and why this place still feels like home even after all these years away. Thanks for showing me I can make a real difference here." She sniffled and shook her head, lowering her gaze. "I know you've got things you're dealing with and you don't want another relationship, and I respect that. But I hope we can at least be good friends and colleagues."

He tipped her chin up, forcing her to meet his gaze. The lights from the tree cast them in a rosy pink glow and the tune on the speakers switched to Aunt Marlene's favorite carol. It all seemed too good to be true, and yet the heat of Nick's leather-covered thumb stroking her jaw told her it was real. It was also better than a fairy tale because they'd both weathered the storms of life and survived. They'd survive the future too. Together.

"I want to apologize for the things I said yesterday at the ice rink. I overreacted and I'm sorry. I saw Con hurt and in pain and let my emotions take over." He looked away, shaking his head. "I'm a doctor. I should have known better, done better. I've been trained to be cool, calm, rational in trauma situations, but I lost it yesterday and that's all on me. Can you forgive me?"

She pulled his hand from her jaw closer to her chest, over her heart. "There's nothing to forgive. Your son was in pain and injured. You acted like a father, not a physician, which is exactly what you should've done. We're good."

"We are?"

"Yes." Belle nodded, doing her best to keep the flare of apprehension welling inside her from bubbling over and failing miserably. "And you're sure you're okay with me working on Analia's case? I know you put a lot of time into setting things up in Detroit and—"

He stopped her with a finger over her lips. "I'm good with it. In fact, I'm thrilled. It will make things a lot easier for Analia and her parents to be close to home during the whole process. Plus, it will save them money in the long run." He smiled, his warm gaze igniting a wildfire inside her. "I'd love to observe and consult as needed, if you'll let me."

"I wouldn't have it any other way, Dr. Marlowe." She turned her face slightly to smile. "We're still partners, remember?"

Heat sparked in his eyes as he leaned in to kiss her. "Always."

Nick's lips brushed hers, softly, gently, before capturing her mouth and deepening the kiss. The hesitation inside her vanished and the tiny ball of tension in her core unfurled. This was right. This was good. This was perfect. This was...

The clearing of a throat broke them apart.

"Dad," Connor said, staring up at them. "No mistletoe again."

"I'm sure we can find some around here," Nick said, grinning, his arms still around Belle's waist, holding her close, his heat warming her from the inside out. "And you'd better get used to it, son. I'll be kissing her a lot in the future, if she'll let me."

"She will," Belle said, laughing. "Are you finally going to show us what's in the bag, Connor?"

"Well, it is Christmas Eve, so..." He pulled out a small wrapped gift and handed it to Belle. "Here."

Pulling free from Nick, she sat on the bench to open it. "For me?"

"Yep." Connor bounced on the toes of his snow boots. "Picked it out the day we went to the Santa Farm."

She carefully unwrapped the tiny box to find a pink crystal heart inside. Engraved on the front were all three of their names.

Belle looked from Connor to Nick then back again. Nick took a seat beside her on the bench and wrapped an arm around her shoulders, pulling her into his side. Her voice shook as she said to Nick, "Did you know about this?"

"Nope." He put his arm around his son and pulled the little boy into his other side, hugging him tight. "But considering the weird trajectory of our relationship so far, why should our proposal be any different, eh?"

"Our proposal?" Belle asked, glancing back and forth between father and son.

"Yep." Connor grinned at his dad. "We talked about it on the way over here. We want you to come live with us forever, Belle. We promise to love you always, even when my dad acts like kind of a doofus."

"Con," Nick warned.

The little boy just shrugged. "So, Belle. Will you marry us?"

Her vision blurred with tears as she lifted the delicate object from its tissue paper nest and nodded. "It's beautiful."

"You're beautiful." Nick leaned his forehead against hers. "Is that a yes?"

She kissed Nick sweetly then reached over to carefully hug Connor as well, mindful of his injured wrist. She couldn't have wished for anything more. A true home. A new family, not just for Christmas but forever. A second chance to build the life she'd always wanted. "Definitely a yes. Merry Christmas, Nick. Merry Christmas, Connor."

"Merry Christmas, Belle," Nick kissed her sweetly on one cheek while Connor did the same on the other. "I love you. Always have, always will."

"Me too," she said, cupping Nick's cheek then kissing the top of Connor's head. "I love you both too."

* * * * *

COMING SOON!

We really hope you enjoyed reading this book. If you're looking for more romance, be sure to head to the shops when new books are available on

Thursday 31st October

To see which titles are coming soon, please visit

millsandboon.co.uk/nextmonth

MILLS & BOON

MILLS & BOON

Coming next month

HIGHLAND DOC'S CHRISTMAS RESCUE
Susan Carlisle

Cass picked up her other shoes and placed them in the box while Lyle held it. She met his gaze. "By the way, what's your favorite color?"

"Green." His eyes didn't waver. "I'm particularly fond of the shade of green of your eyes."

Her breath caught. "Are you flirting with me?"

"What if I am?" He took the box and set it on the bench. "I've been thinking about that kiss."

A tingle ran through her. "You shouldn't."

"What? Think about it or think about doing it again?"

"Both," she squeaked.

"Why?" His voice turned gravelly, went soft. Lyle stepped toward her.

Because she was damaged. Because she was scared. Because she couldn't handle caring about anything or anyone again. "Because I'm leaving soon."

"Cass, we can share an interest in each other without it becoming a lifelong commitment. I'd like to get to know you better. Couldn't we be friends? Enjoy each other's company while you're here?"

Put that way, it sounded reasonable. Lyle moved so close that his heat warmed her. Why was it so hard to breathe? She simmered with anticipation. His hands came to rest at her waist as his mouth lowered to hers.

She didn't want his kiss. That wasn't true. Until that

moment she'd had no idea how desperately she did want Lyle's lips on hers. Her breath caught as his mouth made a light brush over hers. He pulled away. Cass ran her tongue over her bottom lip, tasting him.

Lyle groaned and pulled her tight against his chest. His lips firmly settled over hers. Cass grabbed his shoulders to steady herself. Slowly she went up on her toes, her desire drawing her nearer to him. Sweet heat curled and twisted through her center and seeped into her every cell. She'd found her cozy fire in a winter storm.

The sound of the door opening brought both their heads up. Their gazes locked with each other's.

Continue reading
HIGHLAND DOC'S CHRISTMAS RESCUE
Susan Carlisle

Available next month
www.millsandboon.co.uk

MILLS & BOON

THE HEART OF ROMANCE

A ROMANCE FOR EVERY KIND OF READER

MODERN

Prepare to be swept off your feet by sophisticated, sexy and seductive heroes, in some of the world's most glamourous an romantic locations, where power and passion collide.
8 stories per month.

HISTORICAL

Escape with historical heroes from time gone by. Whether yo passion is for wicked Regency Rakes, muscled Vikings or rug Highlanders, awaken the romance of the past.
6 stories per month.

MEDICAL

Set your pulse racing with dedicated, delectable doctors in t high-pressure world of medicine, where emotions run high a passion, comfort and love are the best medicine.
6 stories per month.

True Love

Celebrate true love with tender stories of heartfelt romance, the rush of falling in love to the joy a new baby can bring, ar focus on the emotional heart of a relationship.
8 stories per month.

Desire

Indulge in secrets and scandal, intense drama and plenty of hot action with powerful and passionate heroes who have it a wealth, status, good looks…everything but the right woman.
6 stories per month.

HEROES

Experience all the excitement of a gripping thriller, with an romance at its heart. Resourceful, true-to-life women and str fearless men face danger and desire - a killer combination!
8 stories per month.

DARE

Sensual love stories featuring smart, sassy heroines you'd war best friend, and compelling intense heroes who are worthy c
4 stories per month.

To see which titles are coming soon, please visit

millsandboon.co.uk/nextmonth